A D

The sorceress's eyes were fixed on me. I met her gaze for a few moments, trying to guess a reason for this interest. Her eyes glittered like the faceted stones on her spell-chains; their darkness made me think of night on the steppe and the dangers that lurked beyond the Elpisia walls.

She leaned forward in her chair. "If you were a slave, Lauria, how would you reach the bandits?"

"I wouldn't run," I said.

"No, of course not." Her lips curved into a smile. "But suppose you did. How would you go about finding the bandits?"

"Why?" I demanded.

"Things are changing," the sorceress said. "The Arch-Magia has reason to believe that the bandits are planning a larger offensive against us. And she's sent word that the officers on the border"—she nodded toward Kyros—"should find out more." The sorceress sat back and waited.

Kyros sighed. "Lauria, you are my most trusted aide," he said. "And you are half Danibeki. I want you to infiltrate the bandits . . ."

Also by Naomi Kritzer

Fires of the Faithful

Turning the Storm

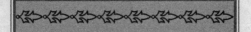

FREEDOM'S GATE

Naomi Kritzer

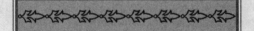

BANTAM BOOKS

FREEDOM'S GATE
A Bantam Spectra Book / July 2004

Published by
Bantam Dell
A Division of Random House, Inc.
New York, New York

Bantam Books, the rooster colophon, Spectra, and the portrayal of a
boxed "s" are registered trademarks of Random House, Inc.

ISBN 0-553-58673-4

Manufactured in the United States of America
Published simultaneously in Canada

OPM 10 9 8 7 6 5 4 3 2 1

To my very first fans,
Abigail and Nathaniel Kritzer

FREEDOM'S GATE

CHAPTER ONE

It was before sunrise when the shamefaced man-at-arms knocked on my door to tell me that there had been an escape—Alibek, one of the boys from Kyros's harem. I sent him to the stable to fetch my horse while I dressed, and met him in the courtyard, where I quickly checked over my gear. "What time was he found missing?" I asked, buckling an extra waterskin to Zhade's saddle.

"Nearly two hours ago, Lauria," he said, avoiding my eyes.

"Why didn't you—"

"We thought he must be somewhere within the walls."

So they'd wasted time searching, and they probably wouldn't wake Kyros until after I had set out. Well, that was fine with me. "Did he take anything with him?"

"One waterskin turned up missing."

"He'd better hope I find him, then," I said, and gave the guardsman a quick smile as I mounted

Zhade. It had been foolish to search before waking Kyros, but it was an understandable impulse. He had an unpredictable temperament.

Even in the twilight of early dawn, the streets of Elpisia were alive with movement. Just outside Kyros's gate, a man pushed a wheelbarrow piled high with apples, a little musty from their winter storage. I flipped him a coin and leaned down to pluck two from the pile: one for me and one for Zhade. Across the street, I could see two women, the wives of Greek officers, with jars of honey tucked under their arms to offer to Athena. Farther down, a slave—Danibeki, like my mother—hauled water from one of the public wells. I spared only a cursory glance at the street as I closed the gate behind me. If Alibek had left any signs of his flight, they would be long gone by now.

Besides, I had a hunch that I knew where he'd jumped the Elpisia wall. There was a spot on the northern edge where the wall was a bit crumbled, and the weathering had created footholds. Once out of the city, I planned to head straight for that spot and look for any traces he might have left. If I was lucky, I might pick up his track from there; if not, I'd at least know for certain that he'd made it out of the city.

First, though, I had to make it out of the city myself.

Kyros's household was close to the military garrison, which was close to the city gate, so it wasn't a terribly long way. It was early enough that the streets weren't yet crowded, and Zhade and I could move quickly. A slave carrying water back to his master's household stepped quickly out of my way; in turn, I moved aside for some of the soldiers from the garrison, who rode through the street. In the distance, I could hear a fruiter selling his wares: *Apples, fine apples; oranges from Persia; grapes from the south, fresh from the aeriko caravan. Apples, fine apples . . .* Elpisia was almost on the frontier of Greek territory, and no one wanted to live outside the protective walls, where they would be vulnerable to a bandit raid, so the houses were packed in tightly, leaning against each other like a crowd of friends gathered in too small a space.

The gate was guarded by bored, surly soldiers from the Greek garrison. They stopped me, of course, and asked to see my credentials. I always carried a scroll with Kyros's seal on it, plus I wore his ring—a heavy piece of gold set with a garnet as dark as a pomegranate seed—on a chain around my neck. The guards on duty this morning were Alex and Thales; neither could read, but they squinted suspiciously at my scroll anyway. I offered the ring as evidence that I was on official business, but they waved it off; I could have stolen it, after all. Along with the horse. And my sword. And my clothes, which were more like a man's clothes than a woman's, but which had been tailored to fit me perfectly. "You'll have to wait while we get our captain to look at this," Thales said.

"Ask him to hurry, please, Thales. Kyros won't be happy if his slave escapes because you held me up." I passed through these gates, on average, six times in a week. I recognized nearly every guard. I even knew Thales's home province and the name of Alex's sister. Yet I was stopped every time, and asked to prove that I was truly a free woman and Kyros's most trusted lieutenant, and not an escaping slave myself. *Every* time.

"Lauria!"

I turned, reluctantly. "Myron," I said. Myron was one of Kyros's other lieutenants. One of his *Greek* lieutenants.

"She's with me," he said airily to Thales, who quickly handed back my scroll and waved us both through.

"Kyros thought I could probably catch up with you," Myron said. "I almost didn't! I'm glad the guards held you up."

"I'm sure you could have guessed where I'd go," I said, forcing myself to be friendly.

"Well, I guessed you'd head straight out of the city."

I nodded. "There's a spot along the city wall, toward the north, where a lot of slaves come over. I was planning to ride around the outside of the wall and see if Alibek left any trace behind."

"Great idea."

I mounted Zhade, gritting my teeth. Myron was never rude to me; that wasn't the problem. He unfailingly treated me with a certain patronizing kindness—the compliments of a superior to a trusted servant. I didn't mind being treated this way by Kyros; though some of his other subordinates complained about him, I always found his judgment to be fair and his praise of my work effusive. But Myron was not my boss. He was not, in my opinion, even my equal. I smiled stiffly and let our horses break into a canter as we rode out of the gate.

I miss Nikon, I thought. Distant kin to Kyros, he had served Kyros in a job much like mine for several years. Like Myron, he was Greek; unlike Myron, he'd been a worthy friend, occasionally even a confidante. But a year ago he'd been assigned as a young officer to one of the border garrisons; he was killed in a bandit raid a few months later. Myron was distant kin to Kyros as well. *He must come from the other side of the family.* I gritted my teeth as Myron gave me a cheerful grin over his shoulder.

Beyond the city wall, the hills and sky opened up around us as if we'd climbed out of a closed box. The sky was blue with a faint veil of haze, and I could smell a little moisture in the air. It was early spring, and it had rained a bit the previous night. Perhaps that was why Alibek thought he might make it to the bandits—the Alashi—with only one waterskin. Or perhaps he just saw the opportunity to break and didn't think about it at all. Maybe he preferred death to slavery. I turned the possibilities over in my mind as we cantered, riding along the edge of the wall to circle around to the north side of the city. The wall rose up well over our heads; it was built from hewed blocks of purple-gray stone, and was covered with a fine layer of reddish dust. Green plants sprouted here and there from the mortar, thanks to the spring rains.

Last night's rain had already soaked down into the ground, feeding the brief burst of spring growth that carpeted the land around Elpisia. On the hills to the north I could see a jumble of wildflowers: brilliant red poppies, star-shaped yellow flowers, cream-colored snowdrops, something purple that wound its way close to the ground. They would fade fast enough once the rains stopped, but for now they served as a reminder that before the great rivers were dammed, Elpisia had been part of a large, fertile oasis, the confluence of the Arys River and the Jaxartes. Under the hot sun, though, the Arys quickly petered out into a muddy trickle, then dried up completely, even in the spring. I wondered if Alibek knew that.

The desert hills rose up around us. Below our feet, under the spring growth, the brittle soil was golden-red in the sunrise, darkening to blue-black in the shadows. Far off, goats dotted the hillsides, tearing away at the mossy grass. I wondered idly who it was that herded the goats. A trusted slave? A half-caste Danibeki, like me? Or a Greek?

The sun was well and truly up by the time we reached the northern edge of the city. I dismounted, leading Zhade to the spot where Alibek might have climbed over, then hoisted myself up to get a good look at the edge. Sure enough, caught in the rough stone was a fragment of sheer white cloth. It was very clean; left recently by someone who normally lived indoors. If Alibek hadn't left this behind, there had been another escape last night.

I held the fragment briefly to my nose and smelled the perfume used by the slaves in Kyros's harem. The smell seemed to catch in the back of my throat; it was too sweet, like the cloying smell of a bruised, slightly rotten apple. I tucked the cloth into my pouch and jumped down from the wall. "He came over here," I said.

"Can I see?"

I took the cloth back out of my pouch and passed it to Myron. "How can you be so sure Alibek left this?" he asked, squinting at the cloth in the bright morning sun.

"It has the scent of Kyros's harem."

Myron sniffed it. "All harems smell like this, and some free women use the same perfume."

I plucked it out of his fingers. "It was freshly torn.

And it's clean, still even a little damp. This was really recent. Who climbs over the wall *other* than slaves trying to get away? If you're not running away, it's easier to use the gate."

"Well, there are other reasons you might climb the wall. You might be a criminal, fleeing from the law."

"Criminals don't dress in sheer white cotton," I said, and tucked the cloth away again.

We checked the ground near that part of the wall, but Alibek had left no more traces behind. "Well, it's probably safe to assume he headed over the hills," Myron said after a quick look. "That's where the bandits are, so where else would he have gone?"

"If he has any sense, he's found a hole somewhere to curl up in for the day," I said. "He has to know Kyros will send searchers. Besides, he didn't take much water."

Myron shrugged. "There are plenty of holes in the hills just north of here. Let's start looking."

We spent the next few hours riding north into the desert, dismounting whenever we reached a hill or a cluster of bracken where Alibek might have found somewhere to hide and searching carefully on foot. A curious goat wandered up to lip my sleeve; I shook it off impatiently. The goatherd was sleeping in the sun; I nudged him awake to ask if he'd seen anyone pass, but he mumbled something unhelpful and went back to sleep. He was Greek, as it turned out; a young boy.

As the sun rose high overhead, I grew hot and increasingly frustrated. "Do they know what time he escaped?" I asked Myron.

"Kyros said it was sometime after midnight."

"I can't imagine that he got this far last night."

"Where else would he have gone? Penelopeia?" Myron laughed lightly.

"But we haven't found even a trace of him."

"That's not that surprising. It's not as if he's trying to leave a trail."

A hawk wheeled overhead; I tipped my head back to watch it dive for a smaller bird and then glanced back toward Elpisia, gauging how far we'd come. North was the logical path for an escaping slave— north, into the desert, over the mountains, toward the bandit tribes. "Alibek would have known this was where we'd look for him."

"Well, yeah. But that's because he'd be an idiot to go any other way. If we haven't found him yet, maybe it's because he's been moving this whole time."

"He didn't have enough water . . ."

"We only *know* about one waterskin. He might have had a friend in another household who stole another for him."

I shook my head. If Alibek had an ally able to give him waterskins to carry, that person probably could have hidden him for a few days, until Kyros stopped sending out searchers and gave him up for lost. And then I wouldn't have found that fragment of cloth. But Myron didn't think the cloth had been left by Alibek.

"I'll tell you what," Myron said, smiling blandly at my frown. "I think it's possible he kept moving. That would be foolish, running around in the sun, but slaves aren't always as sensible as Greeks. I'll ride north and keep looking there; you go look for him wherever it is *you* think he might have hidden."

"Fine," I said, with my first real smile since Myron had caught up with me. "Great idea, Myron."

Myron rode northwest; I watched him go for a moment, then wheeled Zhade back toward the city.

My Danibeki great-grandparents had lived between two great rivers—the Jaxartes and the Oxus, or as the Danibeki had called them, the Syr Darya and the Amu Darya. Though Alexander had conquered and subdued the entire region during his long lifetime, after his ascent to Olympus, Greek control had gradually eroded until there was just a fragment left of Alexander's empire, closer to my homeland than to his.

After Penelope, the founder of the Sisterhood of Weavers, had discovered how to summon and bind aerika, the Greek empire had begun its slow rise back to power. When they'd gone west, back into Greece, the stories claimed that they were met with enthusiasm. The rest of Persia accepted their renewed yoke with at least reasonable grace. But the Danibeki had resisted fiercely, and so the Sisterhood had summoned vast numbers of aerika to bind the waters of the two rivers. They'd bottled up the northern Jaxartes in a vast reservoir, drowning the once-fertile valley near its source under a deep lake. Occasionally they allowed out a trickle of water to supply the Peneleopeian garrisons along the old river, but access to the water was strictly controlled. Meanwhile, the waters of the southern Oxus flowed through a tunnel to Persia, where the people had been more easily subdued. *Cooperate, and you will be rewarded. Defy us, and our wrath will be worse than you could ever have imagined.*

Most of the Danibeki had been enslaved; a few had fled north into the steppe, scraping out a living with herds and what water they could find. They called themselves the Alashi, and the rumors about them were both hair-raising and conflicting. Some stories said that they would accept any escaped slave who managed to reach them. Other stories said that there were tests first: escaped slaves were made to walk through fire or endure the bite of a poisonous spider to prove their worthiness. Still more stories said that outsiders who approached them were thrown onto pyres as a human sacrifice to Prometheus—and that Greek soldiers who made the mistake of surrendering were sacrificed as well. The more terrifying stories failed to deter a few determined and optimistic escapees, like Alibek.

Before it was dammed, the Jaxartes had flowed very close to Elpisia. Even with the Arys flowing into it, the ancient riverbed was mostly a dry, rocky canyon now, with baked mud and sharp rocks at the bottom and plenty of odd crevices in the walls. That, I thought, was where Alibek had hidden himself. The Danibeki had revered the great rivers. Some still did. Maybe Alibek, in his superstition, believed that the river would hide him. Striking out across the desert was the most direct route, but required a modicum of navigational ability; perhaps he lacked it and planned to follow the dry riverbed instead. Or perhaps he hoped to find water that way. In any case, the old riverbed provided plenty of places to hide; maybe he planned to hide until we stopped looking. Whatever his intent, it was not an entirely foolish choice.

The riverbank was rough and steep; I left Zhade tied at the top and half scrambled, half slid to the bottom. I checked to make sure I hadn't lost anything, but my sword, knife, and manacles were all where they belonged. Good. This was the spot closest to where Alibek had jumped the wall.

The waters from the Arys flowed in a muddy trickle at the very bottom of the canyon, winding their way through rocks and silt. The ground was muddy from the spring rains, and I picked my way carefully, leaping from rock to rock to avoid sinking into the mud. I saw a footprint almost immediately and squatted to examine it. The foot was a little larger than mine, so certainly a boy's or man's foot had left it—probably Alibek's, but I couldn't be sure just yet. After a quarter hour of walking, my hunch was rewarded: a fragment of cloth, caught on a thornbush. I compared it quickly to the piece in my pouch. It was the same cloth and had the same smell. I slowed my step, moving as quietly as I could, and listening.

There—another piece. A larger one. It was caught quite securely, and I unwound it carefully from the thorns that had grabbed it, imagining Alibek ripping himself free in the moonlight. The moon was only in its first quarter; there would have been little enough light last night. Alibek must not have planned this very well; he must have seen an opportunity and grabbed it. If he'd planned, he'd have had more water. And he'd have left on a night with more moon.

If he'd been caught so firmly by the bush, he might have panicked. Would he have run, or looked for the first hiding place? I looked at the ground again and saw a footprint, then another one; both had deep imprints from the heels. He had run. I picked up my pace, certain I was getting close.

If he's watching me, I thought, *he'll know that I'm going to find him. It's just a matter of time. Will he hide, trying to disappear into the rock, or leap out and try to attack me?* I rested my hand on my sword, just in case.

But Alibek didn't make a desperate charge from hiding. After a few minutes of walking, I saw a rock-fall at the edge of the bank. That would have been quite visible at night; it probably would have looked like a good place to hide. I couldn't see any evidence of Alibek—it probably *would* have been a good place to hide if Myron had been the only one searching for him. Stepping quietly, I walked over to it, reached behind, and laid hands on something soft. I heard a sharp breath of fear, and then I had dragged Alibek out, blinking and struggling, into the sun.

It was just noon, I noted with satisfaction.

"Let me go," Alibek whispered hoarsely. "Please."

I locked his wrists with the manacles before he could do something foolish. Kyros wanted him back in one piece. Alibek's delicate cheeks were flushed from the heat; the waterskin he'd stolen hung limp and empty from his belt. He'd been unable to fill it since morning—possibly even since he'd taken shelter behind the rockfall in the night. Even though he was chained, I thought for a moment that he might try to attack me, but instead he put his bound hands to his face and wept. He was my age, I thought; there was a faint stubble on his cheeks. He was older than most of the boys in the harem.

"Why are you doing this?" he asked, speaking the Danibeki tongue. "You are one of us."

"I am nothing like you," I said, speaking Greek. I took his arm and began to lead him back to where I'd left Zhade.

"I am a slave, and you are free—free to do as

Kyros tells you, but free to quit his service, too. You don't have to do this. Come with me to the steppe. We'll tell the Alashi that you were a slave, too."

I didn't respond.

"You are a child of the river, the steppe, and the djinni," Alibek insisted. "We both are."

"The river's dead," I said. "The steppe is a desert, and the aerika" —I used the Greek word, not the Danibeki— "are the slaves of the Penelopeians. Even the bandits worship Prometheus and Arachne now instead of the spirits. *I* am a child of Athena."

Alibek turned. He might be chained, he might be cooperating, but his eyes were definitely not those of someone who felt himself beaten. "You have never seen Prometheus," he said. "And you have certainly never seen Athena. I've seen a djinn, and so have you."

"I've seen djinni, all right," I muttered. "I've seen them do Kyros's bidding."

Getting back up to the top of the riverbank with Alibek was difficult. When Alibek realized that our position gave him a modicum of power, he went limp, meaning I'd have to drag him up the steep, rocky bank. Instead, I left him at the bottom—he could run, but he wouldn't get far—and scrambled up to get the length of rope I'd left on Zhade's saddle. I tied it to a dead tree at the top of the bank, testing to make sure it was still securely rooted, and tossed it down to the bottom. Then I scrambled back down to talk to Alibek, who was sitting in the mud watching me.

"I'm not going to drag you to the top," I said. "Either I can take your manacles off and you can climb up yourself, with the rope, or we can sit here and wait for Myron to come back looking for us and he can help me haul you up. If you climb up willingly, I'll let you finish off the water I've got with me—there's a full waterskin tied to Zhade's saddle—and you can ride back with me. If we have to wait, I'll let you drink some of the water from the Arys, but it's pretty muddy and brackish where it flows through here; the water I brought is well water. And Myron will want to make you stumble behind the horses back into the city." I met his eyes and shrugged. "You're going back either way. How we do it is up to you."

Alibek considered for a moment. Then he held out his hands and I unlocked the manacles. I climbed up first, so that he couldn't mount Zhade and flee. He climbed quickly to the top of the embankment, holding on to the rope, then took the waterskin I gave him and drained it. He mounted Zhade smoothly; I swung up behind him and urged Zhade to a fast walk.

"Don't take me back there," he whispered as the city walls rose up before us, black against the golden hills. "Don't give me back to Kyros."

"Your life can't be that hard. I saw your hands; they're as soft as a baby's. You spend most of the day lying around on cushions."

"Have you ever *visited* a harem, Lauria?"

I laughed a little. "I am Kyros's servant, not one of his guests. He's never offered me the pleasure. And even if he did, I wouldn't be interested."

Alibek breathed out a sharp, quick laugh and twisted around in the saddle to look at me. "Take me into the desert and I'll *show* you why Kyros wants me back so badly."

Now I laughed for real. Alibek was a pretty boy, undoubtedly a half-caste Danibeki with Greek blood, like me. His eyes were green, and his glossy black hair had a little bit of a curl, but I had no interest in having sex with a slave. "Sorry, Alibek, I'm not tempted."

"You don't know Kyros," Alibek said, turning away from me again. "You don't know what he's like."

"I think I know Kyros pretty well," I said.

"You see what he wants you to see." Alibek's hands clenched against his thighs. "He made me a slave in his harem to punish my sister for running away. She's with the Alashi now, free, but he took me to rape and sent one of his djinn slaves to tell my sister what he'd done. Is that the act of an honorable man?"

"She shouldn't have run," I said.

"You're Kyros's slave, as much as I am," Alibek said, carefully unclenching his hands and smoothing out the frayed and dirty edges of his tunic. "Even if you don't realize it."

We were approaching the city gates. "You should be glad I found you," I said. "The water from the Arys gives out well before the desert. You'd have died of thirst before you ever reached the bandits."

"Next time I'll bring more water," he said. "Thank you for your advice. I'll remember it."

"If you listen to my advice, you won't run again. The Alashi welcome slaves with open arms because they sacrifice humans to their gods—burning them alive on Prometheus's fire. Of course they'd rather sacrifice strangers than their own people."

"Now you're repeating Greek lies. But I'm sure you mean your concern kindly, so I thank you for it."

I helped Alibek down from the horse as we returned to Kyros's compound. Relieved guardsmen took him off my hands; he shot me a look over his shoulder as they led him away. I met his eyes but felt a queer tremor go through me, as if I'd been shot with an arrow. I tried to shrug it off as I led Zhade to the stables. I had brought slaves back for Kyros before; I had no doubt that I would do so again. I told myself that I felt no kinship with Alibek. Perhaps I looked Danibeki, but I had far more in common with my unknown Greek father. I was free, I chose who I served, and Kyros had proved himself worthy of my loyalty time and time again. I left Zhade for the stable boys to groom and headed for Kyros's office.

Kyros's wife maintained a small garden in the courtyard just outside his office, and as I came around the trellis, I saw something I had not been expecting: an aeriko-borne palanquin, the green silk that enclosed it flapping out the open door in the desert wind. It was a sorceress's conveyance—no one else dared use aerika for transportation so casually. I had planned to head straight into Kyros's office, but I hesitated when I realized he already had a visitor—an important visitor, at that. But out of the corner of my eye I saw the sparkle of an aeriko, and a moment later I heard Kyros call for me to come in.

"I hear you've returned with my little straying bird already," Kyros said as I came in. "And not a mark on him! You never fail to amaze me, Lauria. Make yourself comfortable while I send a message to Myron." He gestured for me to pull out a chair and sit down.

The sorceress sat in the corner of the room—facing the door, not in a spot that a visitor would normally sit. I had met a few members of the Sisterhood of Weavers while working for Kyros; I'd carried a message to a sorceress in Daphnia just a few weeks earlier. But I'd never met this woman before. She was clearly senior to the woman I'd carried a message to, though she was still quite young. Over her green silk dress, she wore scores of spell-chains, looped around her neck, around her wrists, even a few fastened around her slim waist like a glittering belt. It was a dizzying display of casual power, and for a moment I could do nothing but try to count just how many aerika she carried at her command.

"What about her?" the sorceress asked.

Kyros gave her a guarded glance and shook his head slightly. "Sit," he said to me again, and I pulled out a chair and sat down.

The sorceress's eyes were very dark and were fixed on me. I met her gaze for a few moments, trying to guess a reason for this interest. Her eyes glittered like the faceted stones on her spell-chains; their darkness made me think of night on the steppe, and the dangers that lurked beyond the Elpisia walls. I murmured some courteous phrase and looked away.

Kyros carried two spell-chains, on loan from the Sisterhood; most military officers of his rank had only one, or none at all. He wore one around his neck and the other looped around his right wrist. The aeriko he used as a messenger most often was prisoned in a necklace of blue stones and red glass, linked with gold wire. Kyros held the largest stone in the palm of his hand, muttering something under his breath, and with a sound like the echo of a large bell, the aeriko was in the room. I could see it, barely, like drifting smoke—a shimmer in the air.

"Find Myron and tell him this: Return; Alibek has been found. If he has a message for me, bring it back. Otherwise simply return. Now go."

I blinked, and the aeriko was gone, off to find Myron. It might take awhile. Prisoned aerika obeyed their orders, but they didn't always look in the most obvious places first unless you told them to, and Kyros hadn't bothered. I smothered my smile as Kyros poured me a glass of tea.

"It's an honor to serve you, Kyros," I said.

Kyros added a dollop of honey to the tea, and passed it to me across his desk. "So where was Alibek hiding?"

"Along the dead river." Kyros was ignoring the sorceress, so I did as well. I recounted the steps I'd taken to track Alibek; Kyros poured me more tea and offered me a small honey cake. "He didn't resist, once I found him. I told him he was lucky he didn't get away; he'd have died of thirst before ever reaching the bandits."

Kyros laughed and took another cake. I thought he was getting ready to dismiss me, to finish his meeting with the sorceress, when the sorceress leaned forward in her chair. "If you were a slave, Lauria, how would you reach the bandits?"

"I wouldn't run," I said.

"No, of course not." Her lips curved into a smile. "But suppose you did. How would you go about finding the bandits?"

I glanced at Kyros. His eyes were fixed on his desk, but he looked up and gave me a slight nod.

I sat back in my chair, thinking it over. "Well, I wouldn't take the riverbed—that's much too long if you can navigate. The key would be to bring as much water as I could carry, I think, and to know how to find more, since I couldn't possibly carry enough to get me all the way to the Alashi." I sipped my tea. "At minimum, a person needs to drink two waterskins of water a day, and even then they'll be pretty thirsty. If

I carried nothing but waterskins, I could probably carry eight of them. Four days wouldn't get me to the bandits, but I'd probably be able to find water before I ran out. So I'd carry water, I guess, and no food. I won't starve in a week or two, and if I can't find the bandits in two weeks I'm probably going to die anyway." I set down my glass. "Alibek did do one thing right—he didn't take the most obvious route. If I were going to run, I'd leave the city and then head in the wrong direction. I'd hide in the hills for two days; by then, if the searchers hadn't found me, I'd expect them to give up. Then I'd strike out into the desert; travel at night when it's cool and hide during the day, both from the sun and any searchers. Watch for signs of water and pray to Athena I'd find the bandits fast. Although I suppose if I were an escaping slave, I'd be praying to the aerika, or maybe to Prometheus and Arachne."

"An admirable plan," the sorceress said.

"Why do you ask?"

The sorceress fingered one of the spell-chains around her wrist. "You haven't ever seen a raid from one of the bandit tribes, have you?"

"No."

"I have," Kyros said. At a nod from the sorceress, he went on: "It was years ago, when I was a young officer at one of the garrisons right on the edge of our territory. It was terrifying, to realize how defenseless we were. The bandits have no mercy. They don't accept surrender; they just keep shooting arrows at you until everyone they can see is dead or running. I'll freely admit that they are more skilled on horseback than we are, but also, they fight dishonorably: they poison their arrows, so that even a scratch can kill a strong man. After watching twenty of my men cut down in a matter of minutes, I ordered the rest to run. The bandits looted and fired the garrison, cut the throats of the wounded, then rode back out to wherever it is they come from."

I laced my fingers around my teacup, thinking bitterly of Nikon. I had never seen a bandit raid with my own eyes, but it wasn't hard to imagine—Nikon on horseback, the bandits appearing on the horizon like a swarm of scorpions, the rain of arrows. The man who'd brought the news of Nikon's death had said that he died from an arrow in the side. He might well have died from that regardless, but with poisoned arrows, he'd had no chance at all.

"When you take the larger view, for years the bandits have been mostly just an annoyance," Kyros said. He glanced at the sorceress. "We've really had more headaches recently from the bands of our own deserters. There are a few groups that settled just north of Helladia, and they come down to steal supplies."

"Things are changing," the sorceress said.

"So you said," Kyros muttered.

"The Arch-Magia has reason to believe that the bandits are planning a larger offensive against us. And she's sent word that the officers on the border—" she nodded toward Kyros "—should find out more." The sorceress sat back and waited.

Kyros sighed. "Lauria, you are my most trusted aide," he said. "And, you are half Danibeki. I want you to infiltrate the bandits."

I sat back, stunned. "Infiltrate the bandits?" I repeated, just to be certain he was serious.

"That's right."

My first question was why one of the sorceresses

couldn't just send an aeriko. But there were things an aeriko was useless for. Aerika could not be ordered to kill a human being; for reasons that were not well understood, the act of murder broke the binding spell. Sometimes even just an accidental death allowed the aeriko to escape its bonds, so having an aeriko seize and move an unwilling person was very risky. No one knew why this was, because escaped aerika always returned to kill the person who'd summoned and imprisoned them, and often the holder of the spell-chain as well, before vanishing to wherever it was that aerika came from. This tended to discourage experimental research.

Even on lesser matters, aerika were not reliable for anything as complicated as surveillance. They were not willing servants and couldn't be trusted.

I could be trusted, but I had never done anything like this. "You're thinking I'd just walk up there and pretend to be an escaped slave?"

There was a rustle from the sorceress. "We had discussed a slightly more elaborate plan," she said.

Her eyes still made me uncomfortable. Contact with the aerika was known to sometimes make people mercurial; even mad. Kyros's wife had once apprenticed in the Sisterhood of Weavers, and I'd heard servants mutter that her bouts of melancholy were the result of that. This sorceress didn't look at all melancholy, though. Quite the opposite; her eyes shone as if fevered.

Kyros cleared his throat. "One of the other officers, Sophos, lives up in Helladia, at the last garrison before you reach the steppe. Well, there are a few small military outposts, but Helladia is a town, and I think it would be easier to arrange your escape from a town. I was thinking that you could enter Sophos's household, posing as a new slave. After a week or two, at a prearranged time, you will escape and head northwest from there."

"Why have me pose as a slave?" I asked. "I could claim to have escaped from him, whether I had or not. Or I could claim to have escaped from you."

"A short stay with Sophos will lend your story credibility. You won't have to make up details that might get confused later."

"I suppose." I fingered the fringe of the cushion on my chair. I felt uneasy about this whole idea. "Just how far would this pretense go? Sophos wouldn't beat me if I got caught escaping, would he?"

"No, of course not. You're a free woman, Lauria, and you work for me. This would just be to establish your story."

"And who . . ." I glanced Kyros, then the sorceress. "Would I be reporting back to you, or to someone else?"

"Me, of course," Kyros said. "Once you're in the desert, I'll give you some time before I contact you. You'll need some time to win their trust, to become one of them. Then I'll send an aeriko messenger. We'll communicate through the aeriko and decide what to do next. It may be best just to have you monitor their movements, but if you're really trusted, maybe you could lead them into a trap. But we'll take that step when we reach it." The sorceress nodded agreement.

"I haven't spied before," I said. "Sir, I'm not sure I will succeed in this."

"You should have more confidence in yourself, Lauria." Kyros smiled broadly and offered me another cake. "You spend most of your time 'spying'—

visiting garrisons on my behalf and reporting back on what you find. You've never failed me yet."

"That's different." When I visited a garrison, I came in with borrowed authority; the soldiers might not be happy that I was there, but I didn't really have to worry about winning their trust. My scroll and my ring from Kyros bought me whatever access I needed. If they refused, there would be hell to pay, and they knew it. On one occasion, someone had tried to poison me, so obviously there were dangers, but . . .

"You will be an excellent spy, Lauria," Kyros said. He glanced at the sorceress. "Ligeia will send for Sophos, but it will take him a few days to get here. Take four days off to do as you like, then report back here and we'll get you ready." He leaned across his desk and took my glass, setting it down and shooting me a look, a slight smile on his face. "Go visit your mother."

I clenched my teeth and forced myself to smile. "Of course, Kyros. Thank you."

I glanced at the sorceress one more time before I left. Her eyes were still fixed on me; this time, I was reminded of a cat, patiently stalking its prey. I bowed to her slightly—*Ligeia*, I thought, that must be her name—and left.

I caught a glimpse of Kyros's wife in the inner courtyard as I passed. She seldom went out beyond its walls, and almost never left Kyros's compound. She had never liked me, and I generally tried to avoid her. She looked up as I passed, and quickly turned away. As usual, my very presence seemed to irritate her, and I quickly headed for my room.

I had a comfortable room in one of the towers in Kyros's compound, with two windows, a soft chair, a softer bed, and a writing desk. I fetched down my journal—a leather-bound book of expensive blank paper—and my pen and ink. I jotted down the day's events quickly, noting that Myron had come along, but that I'd found Alibek by myself. Then I started to write about my next assignment and paused, realizing that I wouldn't be able to take my journal with me. Normally I carried it along on trips. I spent little enough time in this room; as Kyros's assistant, or his "spy," I spent most of my time visiting garrisons. The usual justification was that I was carrying a message too sensitive to be trusted to an aeriko. An aeriko couldn't give you its opinion of a garrison's morale, the commander's relationship with his officers, and so on. An aeriko also couldn't audit the books, privately question the second-in-command, smell the commander's breath for alcohol, or peek into the shrine to Athena to make sure it hadn't become a shrine to Arachne (as had happened in one particularly bizarre instance at one very isolated garrison).

That had been a strange trip, and a good example of the limits of aerika as messengers. Kyros sent me to check in on the garrison because the commander had stopped sending messages, though he had a spell-chain for precisely that purpose. The first strange thing I noticed was that the commander wasn't wearing his spell-chain around his neck or wrist. I also noticed that he found an excuse to get a look at my wrists shortly after I arrived, and that he became slightly less guarded once he confirmed that I wasn't carrying a spell-chain, either. He took me to his office, offered me wine, and gave me a fairly leisurely update on their last few months.

But he left something out: *he* was not in fact the garrison commander. He was the second-in-command. The commander himself was in bed and under guard. Contact with aerika had made him mercurial—exceptionally so. It wasn't clear to me whether he had simply dropped the burden of command like a bag that had become too heavy, or whether his subordinates had wrested it from his grasp because his behavior had become so unpredictable. The second-in-command had taken over and then, like a superstitious child, had locked the spell-chain inside a strongbox and locked the strongbox in a closet, which he placed under guard.

I wouldn't normally have even entered the shrine to Athena and Alexander while visiting a garrison, but it was also under guard, and that was what made me curious. After shedding my own escort I managed a peek inside, and saw the vast web of spiders, with Prometheus's fire burning where Alexander's helmet should have been. I thought that no one had seen me, but later that night I found a deadly spider in my own room. And while it might have simply wandered in of its own accord, I decided that the situation was quickly getting out of control.

Kyros sent his aeriko to speak with me that evening, and I instructed it to simply remove me, and the rightful commander, and carry us back to Kyros. It had been a stomach-turning and terrifying trip, but the aeriko had set us down gently on our feet just within Kyros's walls. Kyros had dealt with the garrison. I had worried that something bad would happen to Zhade; in particular, I'd feared that they'd use her as a sacrifice to Prometheus and Arachne. But when Kyros's soldiers rode into the garrison a day later, they found her safe in the stable. The renegade soldiers were gone.

Off into the desert to become their own group of bandit deserters, apparently. Despite their fear of it, they took the spell-chain with them.

The aeriko Kyros had sent had interpreted its orders to speak to the commander of the garrison to mean that it should speak to the person it found in command, rather than the real commander, under guard. And it neglected to mention this change of command, along with the other changes of note. Aerika would obey your commands but not your intent anytime they could; Kyros's aeriko must have been delighted with all the information it could fail to pass along.

With a sigh, I dragged my thoughts back to the matter at hand, and tried to order them enough to set it all down on paper. *Kyros is sending me first to the home of a man called Sophos. Will escape from there, using Sophos as a cover story.* I sat back, stroking my lips with the edge of the quill. *Dislike the idea of posing as a slave. Also, uncertain of what kind of slave I could credibly pose as.* I had the horse skills to work in a stable; I supposed I could work in Sophos's stables for a few weeks. I had a bad feeling that there would be some chore I couldn't do right—something that any slave would have done a hundred times. And that would be just as true in any other part of Sophos's household. *The Alashi pose their own dangers. I just warned Alibek about their practice of human sacrifice; I have no desire to be tossed onto the flames myself.* I paused and read that over, then added, *The Alashi also poison their arrows when raiding Greek garrisons. What if I have to go on a raid, to maintain my disguise?*

At least the stories about the Alashi couldn't *all* be true. In addition to the stories about people being burned alive, I'd heard that the Alashi sacrificed captives with the bite of a poisonous spider. I'd also heard that runaways who asked to join the Alashi were subjected to the bite of a poisonous spider to prove their worthiness, if they survived. That seemed a little more likely, as young, strong people often survived spider bites; it wouldn't be a terribly reliable form of human sacrifice.

They were also said to eat horses and the flesh of scavenger birds. I was fairly certain that the stories claiming they ate human flesh were poetic exaggeration. *I think I could eat horse meat, if necessary,* I wrote in my journal. *Using poison against Greeks like Nikon—I suppose I could always shoot over their heads.*

I stood up to look out my window. It was midafternoon, and quite hot; slow-moving servants passed below me outside. I disliked time off from work; I hated visiting my mother. I stared for a while at a loose goat, wandering at large through the compound, then sighed and pushed back my chair. It crossed my mind, as I walked down to the gate, to visit Alibek in the harem, but I pushed the thought firmly away.

I didn't like to think about this fact, but my mother had herself once been a harem slave, like Alibek. Set free by her generous master, she was now the mistress of one of the Greek officers from the garrison. I did not actually know who, as I'd never met him. When I was a young child, my mother would send me away well in advance of his arrival; as I grew older, I deliberately avoided crossing his path. There are things no one really wants to know about her mother.

She lived above a gem-cutter's shop in a neighborhood of Elpisia inhabited mostly by free Danibeki and foreigners; there were also some Greek tradespeople here, like the gem cutter, who'd come out to the edges of the Empire for one reason or another. I'd grown up in this neighborhood, playing games with the other children in the narrow streets. My mother had no trade for me to learn, and sent me away whenever her officer was coming to visit. I grew up an outcast; until I started working for Kyros I had never quite fit in anywhere. Not with the Danibeki, and certainly not with the Greeks.

There was a flower vendor in the street, selling flowers from one of the tended gardens within the city walls. I stopped to buy some flowers for my mother—white roses, I decided, after looking over the options. An offering of sorts. I tucked the roses under one arm, wished that I'd combed my hair a bit more carefully, then went up the steps to her apartment.

Even when I was a child, I had compared my mother to the Greek women in Elpisia—the merchants and wives of Greek officers. In particular, there was a lady who lived across the street from the gem-cutter's shop who I would watch out the window, the wife of a Greek goldsmith. When I was very young, she seemed to me to be Athena personified, and even when I was older, she seemed to be everything my mother was not: crisp and immaculate, as calm as a still pool. When it was time for her children to come home at night she had a bell she would ring; she didn't stand in the doorway and bellow their names at the top of her lungs, like my mother and the other free Danibeki. My mother might be able to present the impression of being a still pool, for a few moments, until you got close enough to see the whirl of sand and fish, broken branches and wave-pounded rocks. She was a still pool like the Arys River at the height of the spring rains.

When she was expecting me, or anyone else, she wore a white Greek-style gown of pressed linen. She was expecting no visitors today, however, and when she answered the door she was wearing a loose robe of faded red silk, a long-ago gift from her officer. Her face went from sleepy to animated in a moment: "Lauria! Oh, it's delightful to see you, my darling. Come upstairs and sit down." I proffered the roses in silence as we reached her sitting room. "Are those for me? Oh, you shouldn't have. Let me find some water for them . . ." I could hear her humming as she dipped some water out of a bucket into a vase, and set the flowers in the window. "Come, darling, let me look at you."

I gave my mother a hug and a kiss on the cheek; she pulled me down beside her to stroke my hair. "Tsk," she murmured. "When are you going to grow out your hair, little one? You have such beautiful hair when it's long."

"It's not *that* short." I pulled a black curl loose and held it out. "It's down to my shoulders."

"When you were little it went all the way down to your waist . . ."

"And tangled horribly."

"You have beautiful hair." She stroked it again. "But it *is* tangled. Go get my brush, darling."

I fetched the brush with a sigh and sat at her feet.

She unbound my hair, which I kept braided so that it didn't fall into my eyes, and began to brush it slowly.

"So what have you been up to since I saw you last?"

I'd visited last a month ago—no, two months ago. "I went down to Daphnia," I said. "Kyros had me carry a message to lady there in the Sisterhood of Weavers."

My mother stood up abruptly and strode over to look out her window. "I don't understand why Kyros can't send an aeriko with messages," she said.

"All you can trust an aeriko to do is carry words back and forth," I said. "I could tell Kyros that the sorceress was pregnant, that she seemed pleased by his message, that her husband was there as well. I can tell him what I *see*. What I hear, smell, taste. If something makes me suspicious I can even take more of a look around, not that I really wanted to piss off a sorceress."

My mother's mouth was tight and unhappy. "I wish you stayed closer to home."

"What would I do here?"

"Constanta's daughter has been married for a year and a half now. When are you going to get married?"

I snorted in disgust, louder than I'd meant to. "I don't know. Sometime."

Her pale hand was clenched in a fist. "Daphnia. My daughter goes to Daphnia. *I've* never been there."

Maybe you should look for a job other than "mistress" if you want to travel. I didn't say that out loud, of course, but my mother glared at me so fiercely for a moment I thought she'd heard my thoughts. There are Danibeki slaves who believe that some people can read the thoughts of their blood kin, if they try. Or even control their thoughts, up to a point—but if my mother could do *that,* she'd have the daughter she wanted instead of being stuck with me. "You're a beautiful girl, Lauria," she said after a moment. "You're as beautiful as I was at your age, or you would be if you took better care of your hair and your hands. If I was beautiful enough to win my own freedom, you're certainly beautiful enough to have a husband by now." She paused, then said, "Cybela has a son, Brasidas . . ."

"No! Thank you, Mother, but no."

"You haven't even met the boy. How do you know—"

"I happen to *like* working for Kyros. Brasidas is the son of a carpet weaver. I'm sure a carpet weaver would not be happy to have a wife who goes off for months at a time carrying messages . . ."

"He's Greek—"

"He is three years younger than I am. He used to pick his nose and try to wipe his hands off on the other kids."

"That was *years* ago! He's grown up into a perfectly nice young man—"

"Mother—"

"—and *you* had some nasty enough habits as a child!"

"I'm leaving in four days," I said.

"For how long?"

"I don't know, exactly. A long time."

Something in my tone of voice made her sink back down in her chair. "Where is Kyros sending you now?" Her voice was shaking.

I sat down quietly beside her. "I'm going to infiltrate the bandits," I said. "Kyros is going to have me pose as a slave of one of his friends and pretend to escape."

"But—you're half Greek!"

"So are a good quarter of the slaves in the cities. Apparently the Alashi don't care."

"Lauria, this sounds dangerous!"

"My job is always dangerous," I said, exasperated.

"This was all Kyros's idea?"

"No," I said. "I think the idea might have been suggested by a sorceress." At my mother's look of alarm, I hastily added, "Kyros wouldn't send me off to certain doom! The Alashi are going to have no idea that I'm anything but an escaped slave."

"But to *pose* as a slave . . ." My mother looked oddly distant for a moment, then examined me with a critical eye. "You carry yourself as a free woman, not someone who fears being beaten. You don't have the reserve, the shyness, the *slyness*. Anyone looking at you would know you weren't a slave."

I laughed. "Mother, the guards at the Elpisia gate stop me every time I leave the city! Clearly not *everyone* knows I'm a free woman. They look at me and see my Danibeki mother, not my Greek father."

"The *Greeks* see that. A slave would know. Any slave would know."

"It's not really Sophos's slaves I have to fool, is it? It's the Alashi. Staying with Sophos is just to give me a cover story, somewhere to escape from."

My mother shook her head, still horrified. "You're really set on doing this?"

I rolled my eyes. "Yes, I'm really 'set' on doing this."

"Well, a slave wouldn't stand like you're standing."

"How am I standing?"

My mother stood up, then sighed as she looked me

over. "Imagine a point at the center of your body, and try to disappear into it." She nudged my back, my shoulders, my hips. Then she demonstrated: "Like this." Her arms were pressed to her sides, her head slightly bent. "You don't want to be noticed. Being noticed means that you'll probably just get into trouble."

"Did getting noticed get *you* in trouble? I thought you were freed because your master's wife 'noticed' you."

My mother's eyes narrowed. "Fine," she said. "If you don't want my advice, you don't have to listen to it." She sat back down and picked up some mending from a basket by her chair.

I bit my lip, wishing I'd just kept my mouth shut. My mother's advice would almost certainly be useful, but I hated to ask her for it. Finally I bit down on my pride and asked, "Is this better?"

My mother looked up from her mending. "Oh perfect," she said. "I'm sure whatever you do is just right. Why don't you ask Kyros anyway? He's the one who thought this would be a good idea."

I clenched my teeth, trying not to spit out any of the dozen bitter rejoinders that had occurred to me. My mother bit off the thread and tucked her needle into a leather case. "Would you like a cup of tea, darling?"

"No. Thank you."

"Oh well. I'll have one myself, I think." She had a little brazier in the corner of her room, and poked at it to perk the fire up a bit, setting on her kettle. "So. Other than rides to Daphnia and impersonating a slave, what have you been up to?"

"Not much," I muttered.

"Kyros keeps you so busy? You never have time to have fun?"

"I ride Zhade."

"Ah." My mother poked at the fire again. "Now, Cybela's daughter Daphnis, she's taken up the three-stringed lute. Cybela has invited me over to hear her play sometimes."

"How lovely." I had meant to sound sincere, but I knew as soon as the words were out that I sounded anything but.

"Well." She slammed the poker down. "Maybe spending some time pretending to be a slave will teach you some manners. Will your 'master' beat you if he thinks you're being insolent?"

"He'd better not."

"And *that* is precisely the attitude that will tell the slaves that you are *not* really one of them."

I had a bad feeling that she was right, but I didn't want to admit it. "I'd better go."

"So soon?" In an instant, my mother had gone from cold outrage to placating clinginess. "But you aren't leaving for four days!"

"I have preparations to make." I stooped to kiss her cheek.

My mother returned my kiss and then grabbed the collar of my shirt, holding me close to her for a moment. "Come back tomorrow. I'll show you how to move and speak like a slave. This is not the sort of thing that you can learn from Kyros. And I—" Her voice faltered. "I am afraid of the consequences if you fail."

"Don't worry," I said, and she released me. "Good-bye."

* * *

I first met Kyros when I was eleven. I had gone out furious after a fight with my mother; as I grew into a woman, her frantic desire to shape me into the beautiful, graceful daughter she wanted had become an ongoing feud between us. I had decided to go for a walk outside the city and had jumped the wall. I'd done this hundreds, maybe thousands of times by then, but that day a guard was passing by and grabbed me, mistaking me for an escaping slave.

He dragged me before his commander, who demanded that I identify my master. I told him I was no one's slave, and bit the guard holding me. Attacking a guard was a terribly stupid thing to do; it could have gotten me killed. But Kyros stopped by the guard post just as the commander was deciding how to deal with me, and when I named my mother and told him where I lived, he told the guards that I was telling the truth and ordered them to let me go. Then he walked me back to my mother's house: "To keep you from getting into any *more* trouble," he said.

He asked me how old I was, and some other questions about myself. I told him about my mother, my friends, how I didn't want to grow up if it meant sitting inside all the time embroidering and trying to look pretty, like my mother. He listened sympathetically, and when we reached my mother's house, he made her a proposition. I was clearly unsuited to the demure future my mother wanted for me; I was the terror of the neighborhood, regularly jumped the city wall to explore the desert hills beyond, and bit guards. But I would be suited quite well, he said, for a job working for him.

"Doing *what*?" My mother's hands had clenched her gown, listening to him. "She's only eleven."

"She's only eleven *now*. But she could begin to learn the skills she'll need: riding, tracking, observing. In addition to the soldiers and officers in the garrison, I employ a number of people as assistants. They keep my books, or records of my meetings. They carry messages and return with observations. They find and return lost property."

"Why do you need *assistants*?" my mother asked. "How many officers report to you?"

"Well, I prefer not to send out soldiers or officers on personal errands, first of all," Kyros said. "And when I need to know what's going on at a distant garrison, it's nice to get this information from someone who works only for me."

"This sounds dangerous," my mother muttered.

It sounded *exciting* to me. I'm not sure if my mother would have refused Kyros anyway, but when she saw the look on my face, she gave in. I knocked on Kyros's door the next morning and began my training.

I didn't knock on the door anymore when I reached Kyros's compound; I strode in wearily, nodding absently at the elderly slave who watched the door. "Kyros was looking for you," he said.

"I was visiting my mother."

"He said he'd like you to come see him when you returned."

I nodded and headed to Kyros's office. One of his other assistants, the one who kept his books and his schedule, leapt to his feet to tell Kyros that I had arrived. When I reached his office, Kyros stood behind his desk, waiting for me.

"I heard you had another run-in with the gate guards," he said. My eyes widened, and he added, "Myron told me, of course." He shook his head. "I wish you'd bring problems like this to me; when the gate guards hassle one of my adjutants, it's a problem for *me* as well as you. Really, Lauria, you can trust me."

"I do trust you," I said.

"I wish you'd trust me to know that this is a *problem,* and not tale-bearing." There was another rustle from the secretary in the hall, and Alex and Thales, the two soldiers who'd hassled me on my way out to find Alibek, strode in, looking a little confused.

"Names?" Kyros demanded.

The two men mumbled their names. Kyros pointed at me and said, "Right. I want you to *remember this woman's face* from now on. Lauria works for *me.* She carries my ring, she carries my scroll, and she carries a sword I gave her. If I hear again that you delayed her on an errand, I'll have you reassigned somewhere even colder." It was hard to imagine cold weather on a brilliant spring day like this one, but the winters were bitter, and by far the worst complaint among the soldiers who'd come up from Persia or Greece.

"Am I very, very clear?" Kyros said.

"Yes, sir." The men spoke together.

"Good. You can go." We waited until they'd gone back out, then Kyros gestured for me to sit and offered me a honey cake. "I hope they won't trouble you again."

I shook my head, my mouth full. When I could talk again, I said, "It'll be some other set of soldiers who can't tell me from a runaway slave."

"Well, if we have to haul the garrison in here two at a time, I'll do it. But *tell* me next time!"

"I will," I said, and left with a light heart.

I didn't visit my mother again before I left. But I did take some time during my days of leisure to watch the slaves. I wanted to spend some time in the stables with Zhade anyway. I wouldn't be able to take her with me, and that rankled; she was a beautiful bay mare with a flowing black mane and tail. Kyros had given her to me to train, and while she was a gentle horse that would let almost anyone ride her, she made it clear that she liked me best. The stable hands would take good care of her in my absence, but I wanted her coat to shine like polished brass before I left.

I had concluded that it made the most sense to have me pose as a stable hand. I knew horses and had done all the skilled work at one time or another. The unskilled work, I thought, would be easy enough to do. But my mother's words ate at me, and so I hid behind the currycomb and brushes and watched the stable hands at their work.

Kyros kept a good-sized stable. He needed horses for himself and for his family; he had a white mare that his wife rode, and lovely little ponies for his younger children. Zhade was my horse; Myron also had a horse, as did Kyros's other retainers, and there were spare mounts for use in need.

There were ten stable hands altogether. The stables were overseen by an older male slave, a grizzled old man who was stooped and bad tempered. Of the remaining nine, most were boys or men, but there was one girl, about eleven years old, with short hair and a fleeting, nervous smile. The slaves moved quickly and very quietly; the girl, in particular, had a way of almost sliding right out of my sight. Most avoided my eyes, and after a while I thought I knew what my mother meant, about trying to disappear, though I wasn't sure I could actually imitate it. Besides, even if I knew how slaves acted around *me,* that didn't mean I knew how slaves acted around *each other.*

Even if I go back to my mother, I thought, watching the stable girl carrying in buckets of water for the horses to drink, *there's too much to learn, and too little time. And I'm not as strong as the slaves, physically, at least not in the same ways. I don't have the right muscles, I don't have calluses in the right places, I wouldn't be able to shovel horse shit like I'd shoveled it all my life. I'm going to have to tell Kyros I really can't do this.*

I should have felt relief at that decision, but instead I felt foreboding. Kyros, I thought, would not accept *I can't do this* as an answer. And neither would the sorceress.

On the morning of the fourth day, I went early to see Kyros, and found Sophos already there. The sorceress, I was relieved to see, had not returned. Sophos was laughing at some joke when I entered, his hands splayed out against his knees. He had rings on all of his fingers except for his thumbs, and a heavy gold chain around his neck. Though technically he and Kyros were equals, he had only one spell-chain. His robes were crisp white cotton and he wore a small, colorful hat on the crown of his head. "Ah! This must be Lauria," he said, quite enthusiastically, and looked me up and down as if I really were a slave girl he was purchasing.

"Good morning, Kyros. Sophos." I hesitated, then added, "Kyros, I was hoping to speak with you alone for a moment."

"That's fine, Lauria," he said, gesturing for me to pull up a chair. "Let's just go over some logistics first."

"That's just it." I lowered my voice. "I really, *really* don't think I can do this."

"I see." Kyros shot Sophos a quick look, and Sophos nodded, stood up, and stepped out, his smile never wavering. "What's wrong?" he asked when Sophos was gone.

"I visited my mother, as you suggested. She . . . used to be a slave herself." I felt terribly uncomfortable talking about this, though of course Kyros *did* know; I'd mentioned it before. And any freeborn Danibeki was descended from *someone* who'd been a slave—a grandparent, if not a parent. "She didn't think I could pass; she said any slave looking at me would know that I wasn't one of them. And so I've spent the last few days observing slaves, and I think my mother is right. I don't think I can pull it off."

"Which slaves were you watching?" Kyros asked.

"The stable hands," I said. "I'd figured it would make the most sense to have me pose as a stable hand."

He broke into a smile and he leaned back in his chair, pouring a glass of tea and handing it to me. "Oh, Lauria. I truly don't deserve a servant like you. You are so—here, take a honey cake." He offered me a plate. "Take two. You, among all the people who offer me their service, never miss a thing. So many people would have spent the last four days sleeping, or drinking tea with their friends, or riding. You spent it *observing,* so that you could be the best, most believable slave you could possibly be. And now, of course, you're convinced that you won't measure up.

"Well, first of all, you need to remember that the slaves at Sophos's household will not be watching you in the way that you were watching *my* slaves these past few days. They will have other things to do, tasks and jobs, and while you will be a novelty, you won't be their focus. And none are the trained observer that you are. They may know that something's *off* about you, but it will never occur to them that you're a free Danibeki who's posing as a slave to run off and join the Alashi. And remember, it's the Alashi that we need to fool, ultimately. Really, part of the point of having you pose as a slave is just what your mother pointed out—you don't act like a slave, look like a slave. A few weeks pretending to be a slave in Sophos's house will give you the chance to practice precisely those skills on people who don't matter.

"But in any case—well, here we get to the logistics. Why don't I bring Sophos back in?" He got up to open the door; Sophos must have been standing about just outside, because he came right back, still wearing his ingratiating smile. Kyros poured more tea for Sophos and offered each of us another honey cake. "You're quite right, Lauria, that you know far more about horses than you'd know about working in, say, a kitchen. The story will be that you were *my* stable hand, but you caught Sophos's eye and he bought you for his harem."

"For his *harem*?"

"No one would believe that I'd buy such a lovely

young woman to work in my stables." Sophos lifted his glass of tea in a brief toast; his eyes sparkled.

"This will explain many of the apparent inconsistencies about you," Kyros said. "You won't be expected to know how to act as a harem slave, because you used to work in a stable. If he actually put you to work in his stable, you would be spotted fast as a fake of some kind—you simply don't have the raw physical strength you'd get from hauling water and horse feed all day. But the harem slaves won't know that. They'll see that you're strong, callused, and sunburned; you won't be shoveling horse manure, so they won't see that it's not natural for you. Any strange behavior can *probably* be passed off as the result of having come from another city and another position."

My stomach hurt. "Just how far would this pretense go? I won't have to sleep with Sophos or any of his guests, right?"

Sophos laughed, though I'd addressed Kyros. "No one will lay a hand on you," he said. "If anyone does, I'll cut it off myself." I found myself curiously unreassured. "It will be a little unusual for a harem slave to be totally off-limits. The story that will be circulated is that you're a virgin, and that I've reserved the privilege of your blood for an honored guest who's not expected for a few weeks."

I gripped my tea in one hand and knew that my cheeks were flaming. Sophos turned to Kyros. "I think she'll do fine."

Kyros caught my eye and gave me a sympathetic look; I almost thought he understood, really understood, how very uncomfortable I was with all of this.

"How long will I need to stay there?" I asked.

"I think two weeks will be enough time," Kyros said.

"Plus the three days to ride back, of course," Sophos said.

I nodded. My mouth had gone very dry.

"Go make sure Zhade is settled, take care of any other last-minute errands, and return to my office after dark," Kyros said. "We'll transfer you to Sophos's entourage then."

Before visiting Zhade, I decided to visit the Temple of Athena. I wasn't particularly devout, but I made occasional visits anyway, mostly out of a vague feeling that it couldn't hurt and might even help. The temple was near the center of town, a newer building, very pretty. The street outside was crammed full of vendors selling honey and other items to offer up. Alexander's Temple was around the corner, so I could hear the din of animals being sold for sacrifice quite close by. I bought a jar of honey and carried it in, laying it down in front of the altar.

It was a busy afternoon, with other supplicants and worshippers going in and out. Most were female—men tended to worship Alexander. I paused to meditate for a few minutes and articulate my request. *Let my mission be successful.* No, best to be specific: *Let me accomplish my mission and return in triumph.* And then, my vague, nagging worry: *Let me accomplish my mission and return alive and unhurt.*

As I gazed absently at the altar, I saw a sudden movement out of the corner of my eye and swung around to see an acolyte stomping on something. "Sorry," she whispered apologetically when she saw that she'd disturbed me. "Spider."

I nodded. I could see why she was so disturbed.

The Alashi worshipped Arachne, the spider-goddess, who had been cursed by Athena herself for her false pride in her weaving. They also worshipped Prometheus, the fire-bringer, but at least he didn't send his avatars to creep into Alexander's Temple . . . I tried to focus on the altar again, but my prayer was done; I went back out into the street.

I spent the rest of the day with Zhade, first taking her out to the hills for a gallop, then bringing her back to the stable to feed and groom her. The stable girl was there, quietly grooming one of the ponies. She was even dirtier than usual, and she shrank even farther into the shadows when she realized that I was looking at her. I turned self-consciously back to Zhade.

"Lauria!" It was Myron, coming in to get his own horse. "I heard a rumor you'd be leaving for a while."

"Yeah." I looked up, resting my brush on Zhade, trying to make it clear that he'd interrupted me in the middle of something.

But Myron just leaned back against a stable box, oblivious to my irritation. "So! Where's the old man sending you?"

"You'd better ask Kyros if you really want to know." I wasn't sure how much Myron knew about my mission, but I couldn't imagine the details were public.

"Oh, Lauria. You're the best of all of us, you know?" He capped that with a patronizing laugh and went to get his horse. "I'm off to Daphnia with another message for that sorceress."

I forced a smile, trying to suppress the jealousy that rose in my throat. I'd enjoyed that last trip.

"I'll be glad to be back and done with that. Just between you and me, the Sisterhood makes me nervous. They always give you that look, like they're toying with the idea of having their pet aeriko pick you up and dangle you upside down over a high balcony. It's just to see us squirm, but still."

That wasn't quite how I'd have described the sorceress's dark-eyed stare, but I still knew what he meant. I bit my lip and turned my eyes back to Zhade. "Have a lovely trip, Myron."

"Bye, then! I'll see you when I get back, or when you get back, or . . . sometime." He laughed some more and led his horse out of the stable. As the door swung shut behind him, the stable girl appeared from the shadows again and silently continued grooming the pony.

I returned to Kyros's study just after sundown. Sophos had clothes for me to change into: a thin robe of sheer cotton, with a light cloak of gray wool to drape over it. Sandals for my feet. I sat down to pull my boots off, and the two men stepped out while I changed my clothes. Nights are cold in the desert, and the temperature was falling fast; I shivered in the sheer cotton and hugged the wool cloak close around me. When they returned, by lantern-light, Sophos and Kyros examined the effect.

"I'll have her cleaned up and prettied up back home," Sophos said to Kyros. "If we're claiming she used to work in the stables, there's no reason she needs to look like a concubine now."

"True enough," Kyros said. "As long as you think people will believe she might have caught your eye."

"Oh, that's a given." Sophos bowed slightly toward me before addressing Kyros again: "Your assistant really is quite attractive."

Kyros glanced at me and smiled a little ruefully at my expression. "Two weeks," he said. "That's all. Then you'll be off to see the bandits."

"What if they won't take me in?"

"Then leave and come back here."

"Across the desert?"

"You are the most resourceful person I've ever met, Lauria. If you can't do it, no one can. Besides, I'll send an aeriko to look in on you."

"But I'll still be alone most of the time."

"Lauria." Kyros's voice was serious. "This isn't like you. Normally you're so pleased to go out on assignment."

Normally I didn't have to pretend that I'd just been sold as a slave.

"I have a lot of confidence that you can do this, Lauria," Kyros added. "So does Ligeia, the sorceress you met the other day. But if you think we're wrong, if you want to stay here, I won't force you. Say the word, and I'll send someone else."

I bit my lip, thinking of Myron. Myron couldn't do this; he was Greek. I was the best one for the job. I might even be the *only* one for the job. "I'll go," I said, forcing resolve into my voice.

Kyros smiled, his whole face warming with his trust in me. "Thank you," he said, and clasped my elbow.

Kyros rose, and Sophos did, too. Then Sophos snapped something cold around my left wrist, and I jerked away in horror before I could catch myself. "*What are you doing?*"

Sophos held out the length of chain, almost apologetically. "A new slave would ride in chains, of course. I'm sorry, should I have brought this up earlier?" He was addressing Kyros again. "The rest of my household will not be privy to these arrangements. She'll need to start posing as a slave right away."

Kyros bit his lip and jerked his head, as if to say, *Talk to her—not me.* Sophos turned and held up the other end of the chain, reluctantly meeting my eyes. "May I?"

"I am not a slave, Sophos. I am Kyros's freeborn assistant—his *willing* servant. You may not forget that fact."

Sophos bowed slightly. "Please understand that I will have to speak to you as if you are a slave when we are near other people. But I will not forget again, my lady."

Two weeks, I told myself. Trembling, I held out my right hand, and he snapped the manacle around it. Hugging my thin cloak around myself, I followed Sophos out to the wagon that waited by the door of the compound.

CHAPTER TWO

I had traveled by wagon before, but everything seemed different when I was traveling as a slave. In part, this was simply because it was so much more uncomfortable. The wagon bounced and jolted over the ruts in the road. The manacles bruised my wrists and, after particularly hard jolts, the chains would sometimes slap down and bruise my legs. As the purported owner of a newly acquired concubine, Sophos was able to take at least a small concern for my flesh; he had tossed a pillow down for me to sit on. But it did little to make me more comfortable.

Sophos's entourage was not large. He was accompanied by a few guardsmen and one other household slave, a trusted servant who traveled untethered. Conversation was minimal. At midmorning on the first day, when we stopped to rest, the other slave took my chains in hand like a leash and escorted me a short distance from the wagon to allow me to relieve myself. The slave was an older man; Sophos had brought no women with him on the trip, I realized, and I would have to be escorted to relieve myself, every time, for the rest of the trip. I clutched my cotton shift as closely around myself as I could without soiling it. I glanced at my escort, expecting that he'd at least be pretending to look off into the distance, but instead he was looking me over with a faint leer. I finished my business as quickly as I could and straightened up. "Did you get a good look?" I hissed as he started back to the wagon.

He jerked on my chains to make me fall to my knees, and slapped my face hard enough to make my ears ring for a moment. "Keep your tongue behind your teeth, lamb, or you'll regret it."

"Elubai!" Sophos snapped from the wagon. "I didn't give you leave to discipline her. Hands off."

Muttering to himself, Elubai jerked the chains again, but I was expecting it this time and managed not to fall. I climbed back up to the wagon, rubbing my cheek with my fist and trying to hold back tears. *This wasn't what I agreed to.* Sophos didn't look back at me, merely signaled for the wagon to start up again. Still, my mother in a temper had slapped me harder than this, on occasion. I tried to straighten my shoulders—then, remembering, tried to sink into myself.

Helladia was on the other side of the hills, one of the last outposts before the open steppe; there were mines and military garrisons dotted throughout the hills, and Helladia existed to provide a supply point and communication center for those garrisons. The road to Helladia couldn't go straight up and over the hills; they were much too high and steep for that. Instead, the road cut across the hill at an angle, climbing much more slowly, then reversed its course. It was the only way that horses could possibly pull a wagon up, but it made our progress seem terribly slow.

The hills were a dusky green from the spring rain, with the red-gold of the soil showing through the leaves. As we crested the first hill and looked beyond, they darkened to gray and brown, but I couldn't tell if it was dryness or distance that made them look that way. I saw animals, occasionally—sheep, goats, cattle, and horses—with their keepers. I could sometimes hear their lowing a long way off. Elubai was not one for talking; neither was Sophos, nor the guards.

Undistracted by conversation, I spent most of the trip worrying about all the many things that could go wrong. I could die of thirst on my way across the desert; I could be caught and murdered by one of the gangs of non-Alashi bandits that preyed on Greek and Danibek alike; the Alashi could refuse to trust me. I tried to focus my thoughts on contingency plans instead of mere worry. If the Alashi leaders said, "We are *certain* you are not a slave—you must be a spy," what would I say to that? How would I know I was close to a camp of deserter bandits, and how would I avoid them? If I encountered them, what would I say to buy time while I watched for the opportunity to escape? As irrational as I knew it was, though, my greatest fear was that Sophos would betray me and Kyros, and I would somehow find myself a slave forever, subject to nasty old men like Elubai. *If that happens, I'll run,* I told myself firmly. Back to Kyros, who would never betray me. I had tracked six slaves through the hills outside of Elpisia. Certainly I could evade a tracker myself.

Partway across the hills, we stopped at a mine.

From what I could catch from listening, Sophos was a part-owner. These hills at the edge of Greek territory were full of valuable minerals; this mine was extracting iron. I could feel it before I could see or hear it: outside the digging pits, there was a furnace to purify the iron before it was sent on down to the Greek cities to be forged into weapons. I felt its pulsing heat as we approached. The mine shafts went into the side of one of the hills, and then down. There was a system of wheels and pulleys to draw up the heavy ore that had been dug out of the ground, and slaves used wheelbarrows to carry it from the mouths of the shafts over to the furnace.

"Sophos!" The overseer strode over to our wagon and clapped my escort on the shoulder. "What a wonderful surprise. Give me an hour and I'll have an excellent lunch for you. Are you staying long?"

Very enthusiastic, I thought. *But he's forcing it.* I glanced away. Kyros would hardly care whether the overseer of Sophos's mine was genuinely happy to see him, and I didn't work for Sophos. Besides, if Sophos couldn't guess that the man was feigning his welcome, he was an idiot.

Sophos climbed down from the wagon, returning the man's enthusiastic greeting with a reserve of his own, and they walked off together, presumably to find the promised lunch. My stomach growled. Elubai had the horses pull the wagon over to a shady spot, a good distance away from the heat of the furnace. He folded a blanket, lay down with his head against it, and took a nap.

I watched the slaves. The mine was not heavily guarded, and the area where they worked was not surrounded by a wall. Yet few looked like they'd have the energy to run away, even if they had the opportunity. All were coated with a layer of dust and soot; it was hard to tell whether a particular slave was male or female, young or old. They all moved like old men, but I suspected that none were over thirty.

The slaves here didn't try to disappear the way some of Kyros's slaves had. They simply put one foot in front of the other, dragging loads of ore back and forth from the top of the mine shaft over to the furnace. One team of slaves seemed to be in charge of cranking a giant wheel that brought up loads of ore. They would crank up a barrel, and then other slaves caught it and emptied it into a series of wheelbarrows; then they swung it back over the mine shaft and the slaves working the wheel let it slide back down. A few minutes of rest, presumably while the barrel was loaded, and then they began to crank it up again.

It occurred to me that there must be slaves down at the bottom of the shaft—quite a few, in fact. Working by torchlight, even though it was broad day, to dig iron out of the hillside and load it into that barrel.

I wondered how extensive the workings were.

When the sun was directly overhead, one of the guards blew a small horn, and the slaves put down their loads and went over to stand in the shade. From one of the little stone buildings in the shade of the hill, a handful of much older slaves brought out bread, cheese, and waterskins, using some of the same wheelbarrows that were used to move the iron around. The slaves lined up to receive their lunch, then sat down to eat it. I wondered if the deep mine slaves would come up for lunch, but no, others loaded the food into the barrel and sent it down to the bottom of the shaft. Elubai had woken when the horn blew; he took bread and cheese out from the bottom of the wagon and passed it around to me and Sophos's slaves.

I should try to think of them as Sophos's other slaves, I thought. *If I'm supposed to try to pass myself off as one of them.* I glanced over at the mine slaves again. They'd finished their food and were slowly getting up. It took me a few minutes of watching to realize that they'd switched tasks; the slaves who'd previously been turning the wheel were now pushing wheelbarrows, and the slaves who'd been pushing wheelbarrows were on the wheel.

Elubai was drinking from the waterskin, and he followed my gaze. Turning back, he gave me a slow wink. "Behave yourself well for Sophos," he said. "I don't know what Kyros does with sulky, lazy slaves, but Sophos sends them to work in his mine." He paused to let this sink in, and took another swallow of water. "See that one?" he said, and pointed to one of the slaves pushing the wheelbarrow. "She was in the harem. I'm not sure what she did, but it must've been bad. So now she'll dig iron until she dies."

I shivered, even though I knew this could *not* happen to me. But something of that thought must have showed on my face, because Elubai chuckled a little and said, "Don't count on your pretty face to save you, either. She was beautiful, too, once." I lowered my eyes at that point, and Elubai lay down again for another nap.

I watched the former harem slave for a while. Now that I knew she was female, I could see the faint curve of a breast under her filthy shirt. And she was not that old. I wondered what she'd done. Disobeyed Sophos? Mistreated one of his guests? It must have been bad, for him to send her here. At least, it had probably been bad. Kyros had sold a slave to a mine owner once. It had been one of the men who'd run away. I'd tracked him down and brought him back. He'd made it even less far than Alibek.

It was midafternoon by the time Sophos came back out, flushed and a little drunk and roaring with companionable laughter as the overseer said something I couldn't hear. He climbed back into the wagon and settled himself in. I watched to see if he looked at his old slave, but he gave her no special regard. She also made no attempt to attract his attention; either she'd given up hope that he'd take her back to his harem, or she preferred the mine. Elubai chirruped to the horses, and we continued on.

We reached Helladia late the following morning. It was a desolate outpost, far enough from any river that it had to depend on wells. Water had to be conserved much more carefully here than in Elpisia. The town consisted of a military garrison and the sort of businesses that provided supplies and services to mines and the outlying garrisons: wheelwrights, blacksmiths, weaponsmiths, boot makers. It was small and miserable looking; we could see nothing until we were almost upon it. The soldiers at the gate greeted Sophos without interest or alarm, and we proceeded on to his house. It was by far the largest house I saw in Helladia.

Someone must have been watching for us, because the courtyard of Sophos's house was swarming with activity as we came in. Stable boys came to unhitch the wagon and take the horses to the stables; a pretty boy slave brought Sophos a cup of wine to refresh himself. Sophos's wife and children came out to greet him with a kiss. His wife was calm and matronly in crisp cloud-white linen; his children lined up in an orderly row to greet their father. An older Danibeki woman with a pockmarked face waited a few steps behind them, and at Sophos's signal, she brought over a set of keys to unlock my chains. I rubbed my wrists and stretched my hands; I noticed Sophos give his wife an almost apologetic look and a tiny shrug, and he said to the pockmarked woman, "Boradai, this is Lauria. Have her bathed and dressed and sent to the harem. Make sure no one touches her; she's a virgin, and I'm going to save her as a present for Alcaeus when he visits in a month's time. Oh, and—" He gave Boradai a wink. "Be kind to the child, or I'll have your head. Would you believe that Kyros had her working in the stables? Don't expect her to know the social graces of a concubine yet, though I think she'll be a quick study."

Boradai gave me a nudge, and I followed her into the house, up a staircase, down a hallway, and up another staircase. Sophos's house looked much like Kyros's, but with better furniture and nicer rugs. The door at the very top was shut. Boradai rested her hand briefly on the latch and turned to me. "Sophos paid for a virgin. Stay away from the boys, and do as you're told. If you aren't pure when your time comes, not only will I flay the skin from your body, but every other slave in the harem will be flogged and the boy you slept with will be castrated." With that, she swung open the door, and I stepped into Sophos's harem.

Sophos kept his concubines, male and female together, in a single large room on the third floor of his house. There were large windows at each end, to admit light and air. The concubines lived comfortable lives, for slaves; the floor was covered in soft Danibeki rugs and cushions, and everyone appeared to be well fed. There were twelve harem slaves, not counting Boradai or myself; six male and six female. When I came in, one of the young men was playing a dombra, a stringed Danibeki instrument; a few others were reclined on cushions to listen. Two of the young women were working on a tapestry, and one was taking a nap.

The room had fallen to a slight hush as we'd come in, but Boradai clapped her hands anyway, as if she needed their attention. "Tamar," she said. The napping girl sat up. "This is Lauria. She's new here and hasn't served as a concubine before. The servants will get a bath for her; take her down to bathe in a few minutes. I want you to help her." Boradai swept a slow, beady eye over everyone there. "She is a virgin. If anyone despoils her before her time, there will be *hell* to pay."

My cheeks flamed as every eye in the room turned toward me. Boradai left, banging the door shut behind her. Tamar stood up slowly. She was much younger than me, and short; her glossy black hair hung unbound all the way to her compact hips. Her face was quite ordinary, her lips a little too thin and her eyelashes a little too short, though she had nice white teeth. She wore a light cotton shift, like mine, and her feet were bare. She squared her shoulders and narrowed her eyes as if she hoped to intimidate me, despite coming up only to my shoulder. "A virgin," she said with a little bit of a sneer, and pinched the muscles of my arm. "However did you manage that?"

"I wasn't a concubine before."

"What were you?"

"A stable hand." My voice quavered a little. I had thought my story through in my head a hundred times in the last three days, but there was something different about speaking the lies out loud.

The young man who'd been playing the dombra laughed. He set his instrument down and stood up. He was the oldest of the boy concubines; though adolescent and lanky, his face was still smooth and unblemished. Fine black hair curled like feathers around his ears; one lock fell forward to brush his cheekbone. "She'll clean up well enough," he said.

Tamar closed her hand around my wrist. "That's Jaran," she said.

Jaran bowed with a flourish; I couldn't tell if he was mocking me or not. I nodded back to him and everyone laughed; apparently he had been mocking me.

"Come on, we'll go give you your bath," Tamar muttered, and I followed her back out and down the stairs.

The bathhouse was a small stone shack in the courtyard. There was no tub as such; that would have wasted too much water. One of the other slaves had brought a few buckets of water from their cistern. Tamar started by having me take off my now-filthy cotton shift, and gave me a wet cloth to wipe down my body. I washed my face first, then my arms and legs, body and feet. Tamar washed my back. "Where does Kyros live?" she asked.

"Elpisia," I said.

"Did you ever get to see the city?"

"Sometimes. Have you lived anywhere other than Helladia?"

"No. I used to belong to Sophos's friend Androcles. My mother worked in his kitchen." She wrung out the cloth. "Sit down. We'll need to soak your hands and feet."

She filled two small basins with water, one for my hands, one for my feet, and began to work tangles out of my hair with a metal comb. On the journey, the wind had whipped it into knots, and my sweat had mixed with sand to form a sticky, gritty mat. Fortunately, it was only shoulder length. I couldn't imagine trying to comb tangles like this out of truly long hair, like Tamar's. Tamar dipped the comb into olive oil to work out the tangles. "How many times did you see Elpisia?" she asked.

"I don't know. I used to get sent out on errands occasionally."

Tamar jerked the comb, ripping a tangle out. I clenched my teeth and said nothing. "I've never been sent on an 'errand,' " she said.

Probably because they know they can't trust you, I thought. In Elpisia, there were guards at the gate and people in the streets; running away would be impractical, if not entirely impossible, though impracticality hadn't stopped Alibek. "Elpisia has a lot of people," I said. "And a wall, and guards. It's not an easy city to get out of."

Tamar sighed. "Tip your head back."

She poured a sharp-smelling oil over my hair and wrapped a cloth around my head. "Ugh," I said. "That's not perfume, is it?"

"It's to kill the lice in your hair. Boradai has a terror of lice. I'll wash it out in a minute. Perfume comes last."

Tamar checked my feet and hands; some of the ground-in dirt was beginning to come away. "You're cleaner than I'd have expected for a stable girl," she said. "Didn't Kyros's horses shit?"

"Sophos paid Kyros extra to have me bathe before we left. He said he didn't want to have that smell with him all the way back to Helladia."

Tamar smiled a little, reluctantly. I was relieved to see that. As short as my stay was going to be, I thought it would be easier if I had someone on my side. She took one of my hands out of the basin and scrubbed my skin and nails with a brush. My fingertips had wrinkled like raisins. I looked at my clean hand as Tamar scrubbed the other; the hand of a stranger. I lived a working life. My hands had never been this clean. Even my skin was a full shade lighter. I thought of Alibek's soft, unmarked hands and pushed the image away.

Tamar washed my feet, scrubbing them with a brush, too. Now it was time for my hair again. I tipped my head back, and she poured a small stream of water over my hair to wet it. She had a bar of harsh soap, and she scrubbed it into my hair, washing away dirt, oil, sand, sweat, and dead lice. It was a mass of tangles again when she was done. She rinsed away the soap with a little more water. "Dry off," she said, handing me a towel. "We'll go sit in the sun while I comb your hair and pick nits."

Tamar led me to an out-of-the-way spot in the courtyard, and pulled up a low stool to sit on. I sat on the ground. It was clear from her slow, patient work that she was in no particular hurry to get back up to the harem. "So you're a virgin."

Of all the things I'd claimed that day, this was actually the truth. I'd had offers occasionally, usually obscene ones from drunken, rude men—some Greek, some Danibeki. Offers that wouldn't have interested me even if the men had been attractive, which generally they were not. Everyone else in Kyros's household was either my superior, like Kyros, or my inferior, like his Danibeki slaves. Myron was the closest to an equal that I saw regularly, and I certainly wasn't interested in sleeping with him. If Nikon had lived, maybe . . . but he hadn't. I shrugged and then nodded. "Yes," I said.

"Then I'm sure Boradai told you to stay clear of Jaran and the younger boys."

"She said if I wasn't pure when my time came, she'd flay me, flog the rest of the concubines, and castrate the boy."

"Yeah." Tamar raised an eyebrow. "She'll flay me, too, since I'm supposed to be keeping an eye on you. So don't."

"Has this happened before?"

"No. But I've seen what happens when Sophos gets angry. Sooner or later you'll see it, too. Believe me, you don't want to be the target."

"He looks so . . ." I hesitated. How did slaves talk about their masters?

"He smiles all the time," Tamar said. "He smiles when he's angry, too."

"I really hope I don't do something wrong," I said. "I don't know anything about being a concubine."

Tamar shrugged. "There isn't much to know. Spread your legs and close your eyes. Or open your mouth. Though usually if that's what they want, they send for one of the boys." Her voice was flat. I couldn't tell if she intended any humor at all in what she was saying.

"There must be other things I need to know. Maybe not about . . . but about other things."

Tamar laughed out loud at my hesitant speech. "You're so sweet," she said, and her tone was unquestionably mocking now. "Well. You've probably guessed that you'd better do as Boradai says. There's a certain pecking order in the harem, just as there was in the stables, but who goes where depends on who you ask, just as in the stables. You're at the bottom, of course, because you're new." She flicked a nit into a small cup of water. "I don't know how the stable hands viewed the harem in Kyros's household, but here most of the other servants think that we've got the easiest job, and that we make their jobs harder by adding to their work. And we certainly do that. The water for your bath didn't walk itself to the bathhouse. How did *you* view Kyros's harem, when you were a stable hand?"

"I guess I felt kind of like you're describing," I said, faintly.

Tamar laughed maliciously. "Well, lucky you. Now you have the *easiest* job in the household. No more shoveling horse shit for *you.*"

"So what do we do? Other than—the obvious?"

"Sophos has us do the mending, since we can do that without getting dirty. Also, sometimes Sophos has us dance for his guests, so we practice our singing and dancing. Jaran plays the dombra, and so do some of the women. Other than that, we amuse ourselves until called on. We nap during the day, since we're usually called on in the evenings. Boradai will probably want us to teach you some dancing. I'd just wait and see, if I were you." She paused. "How old *are* you anyway?"

"Twenty," I said. "How old are you?"

"Fourteen," she said. She paused for a moment, the comb resting lightly in my hair. "I haven't been a virgin since I was ten."

I wasn't sure what to say to that. Although—as my mother never failed to point out—the vast majority of women my age were married, I didn't know any who'd married before they started their menses, at fourteen or fifteen. Although obviously Tamar hadn't been married. After a short silence, Tamar began combing my hair again.

"How careful do we have to be with water here?" I asked. "We had a small river that flowed past Elpisia . . ."

Tamar laughed a little—a dry chuckle, not a friendly laugh. "That's the biggest reason Sophos doesn't have his concubines do any real work. He wants us clean for his pleasure, and that of his guests, and water is expensive. It's cheaper to have a few slaves who stay inside all the time than to have to bathe them regularly." She pointed to a small shelter near the bathhouse. "There's the cistern; we fill it during the rainy season. Once that runs out, there are wells in town, but Sophos has to pay for that water."

Tamar's voice dropped. "Of course, our great-grandparents drew water from the Great Rivers."

"Of course," I said.

"As they flowed once, they shall return," Tamar whispered.

I didn't know what to say to that, so I said nothing. That turned out to be the wrong thing; Tamar jerked the comb hard enough to hurt and said, "We worship the djinni here, even if, for now, they are slaves like us. Not Prometheus and Arachne. And *not* Athena and Alexander."

I knew I needed to bridge that chasm, and fast. I let my throat thicken a little from my worry and the pain of my pulled hair and said, "My mother worshipped Arachne. All my mother's people did."

"*Greek* gods," Tamar muttered. I didn't say anything; the worshippers of Arachne and Prometheus whispered that, like the ancestors of the Alashi and the Danibeki who escaped to the steppe, their gods had *escaped* the Greeks and were now the protectors of any who sought freedom. But I wasn't going to point that out, not when I was trying not to make Tamar even angrier.

"I've never seen Arachne or Prometheus," Tamar said after a moment. "I've never seen Alexander or Athena."

"Neither have I," I whispered, though of course I'd seen Alexander on his throne in the sky.

"And who hasn't seen a djinn, shimmering in the air, at least once?"

"No one," I whispered.

"So you see? *We* worship the true ones. Arachne and Prometheus are a fantasy. Athena and Alexander are old stories. We are the friends of the djinni, the only gods that all know to be real."

I nodded, and that seemed to satisfy Tamar; her hands became gentle again.

A shadow fell over us. "Just how many nits did Lauria pick up in the stables?" Boradai asked.

Tamar looked up, her voice becoming flat and slightly frightened. "I wanted to be absolutely sure I wasn't missing any," she said.

Boradai sighed and took the comb; Tamar relinquished

the low stool and Boradai took a moment to examine my scalp. "She's clean," she said. "Take the perfumes and go on back upstairs."

Tamar fetched some bottles of oil from the bath-house, her steps as slow as she could get away with; I followed her back upstairs. In the harem, we with-drew to a corner and she combed a little sweet-smelling oil through my hair. I had never worn perfume, not once, and I found the smell cloying. "If Boradai gives us a little warning before you're sum-moned, be sure to wake me if I'm sleeping. I'll do your hair and put on more perfume."

I nodded, feeling a little sick to my stomach, as if this was something I really *did* have to dread. I tried to shake it off and saw Tamar looking at me a little curiously.

"So what do you think of her?"

One of the other women had padded over to our corner. She was beautiful: long lashes, full breasts, and perfect, white teeth. She was addressing Tamar, not me.

"What do *you* think of her, Aislan?" Tamar asked, standing up. She was much shorter than Aislan, and much younger.

"I think she's ugly." Aislan's gaze swept over me briefly, then returned to Tamar. "Even uglier than you."

Her irritation made me wonder if I should apolo-gize—and if so, what I should apologize for. I felt my cheeks go red, and lowered my eyes. I might not have anything to fear from Sophos, but the other slaves scared me. I wasn't sure what Aislan could do to me if I gave her cause to be angry—slap me, presumably, and possibly beat me more seriously. Even if she wasn't allowed to hit me, I had no doubt that there was plenty she could do to make my life difficult. I bit my lip, wishing I could disappear. I felt much like I had when I was nine years old and an older girl who lived nearby had refused to talk to me, on the grounds that I was half-caste and had no father.

"Lauria." Aislan's tone was mocking. "Don't you have anything to say for yourself?"

I looked up and met her eyes. "What do you expect me to say? I can't help it if you think I'm ugly."

"What kind of name is 'Lauria' anyway?"

It was a Greek name. "I don't know," I said.

"And a *stable hand*." She sniffed the air. "Tamar, I think you needed to give her a more thorough bath."

"Sorry," Tamar mumbled. "I did the best I could. Maybe you'd like to take her back out and tell Boradai that you want to redo the job."

Aislan sniffed. "Just keep her well away from me; I don't want to have to smell her stink." She swept away. I noticed that she wore a gold bracelet with a stone set in it.

Tamar followed my gaze. "Yes, she's the favorite of Sophos's best friend. He visits often, mostly to see her, and he gave that to her."

"He must be very wealthy," I said.

"Or the gem is paste. I haven't ever gotten a close enough look to know." Tamar's voice was barely audible, but Aislan shot her a venomous glance anyway, as if she'd overheard.

Dinner was rice and lentils, simple fare with few spices. I had eaten similar meals often enough at Kyros's house, but this was bland, and there wasn't quite enough of it. Aislan served the food; Tamar got less than Aislan, and I got less than Tamar. We ate early, and afterward the other concubines dressed and prepared to go downstairs. On Tamar's instructions, I brushed her hair. There was paint on her face already, but some had smeared or worn off, and when it became clear I hadn't the faintest idea what to do with the pots, she took them back with an irritated huff and did it herself, telling me to watch carefully so I could help her next time. A fine white powder lightened her face; she rubbed a red stain into her cheeks, and painted a darker red onto her lips. With a stick that looked like greasy charred wood, she lined her eyes with black. There was a mirror that Aislan and some of the others used as they prepared to go downstairs; Tamar did not so much as glance at it. As Aislan was adding a touch more of the black to her eyes, Boradai opened the door and everyone else went downstairs.

A short time later, a few of them returned: Aislan was missing, and Tamar, but Jaran had returned, along with two women whose names I didn't know. The other two women wiped the excess paint off their faces so they wouldn't get it all over the linens, then curled up on some of the pillows and went to sleep. Jaran sat down on a cushion and began to strum his dombra, the same sequence of strings, over and over again.

I carried a pillow to the corner where I'd sat with Tamar earlier and lay down, but it was still very early, and I was too keyed up really to even close my eyes. I stared at the ceiling and thought, *Fourteen days. Fourteen days.* The repetition fell in time with the tuneless strumming.

Jaran's dombra went suddenly silent, and after a moment I rolled over to look at him. His eyes were closed; then they opened and he looked directly at me. "You," he said. His voice was harsh and strained; his speech was thick, as if he were very drunk.

I sat up, unnerved. One of the concubines who'd come back and gone to sleep turned over and opened her eyes. "Are you with us again, Fair One?" she asked.

"*You,*" Jaran said. He was still speaking to me.

The hair on the back of my neck stood up as I suddenly realized that he was possessed by a rogue aeriko. Even among the Greeks, possession was not unheard of—but slaves would occasionally seek it out, inviting the presence of any rogue aeriko that might be nearby. Was Jaran possessed against his will, or had he invited it in? Of course, he probably worshipped them anyway; Tamar had said they all worshipped aerika—djinni—and not any of the gods.

The concubine who had woken up rose to her knees, then bowed three times and sat back on her heels. "Fair One, will the rivers return?"

"As they flowed once, they shall return."

"Have you brought us a message?"

Jaran pointed at me, his eyes wild and cold. "I have brought her a message."

"Why her?"

"I know who you are," the aeriko inside of Jaran said.

I went very cold. Maybe the aeriko *did* know. What if it knew?

"Are you afraid I'll tell your secret?" it said. "That would be funny. Whatever would your old master say?"

I bit my lip, aware that the concubine was looking at me with sudden interest. But the aeriko had said my "master"—it was bluffing, I thought. But then it said, "I see what the slaver in green did not." With a final short bark of a laugh, Jaran's eyes rolled back in his head, and he sagged to the floor against his dombra.

"Wait," the other concubine wailed. "I didn't get to ask you whether I bear a son this time, or a daughter! Oh," she muttered, cast a slightly nasty look in my direction, and went to aid Jaran.

The slaver in green? I thought of the sorceress, of the glinting eyes that had searched my face. Was that what the aeriko was talking about? *It's another bluff. "Slaver" could be any slaveholder; surely any slave could think of a Greek who wore green clothes.* But I didn't want anyone to start demanding to know what secret I was hiding. While the others were distracted with Jaran, I went back to Tamar's corner and feigned sleep as quickly as I thought I could get away with it.

I must have slept for a while, because I woke when Tamar came in. "This is my corner," she whispered harshly in the darkness. "You need to move." Her face was damp and her breath was thick and rank with wine.

I groped my way to another pillow and heard Tamar settle herself down where I'd been. Her breath was a little ragged, with a small catch in it. As I listened, it evened out, and finally, I thought, she fell asleep. I could hear someone snoring very loudly on the other side of the room. As uncomfortable as my trip had been, I wished that I were back chained to the wagon, under the night sky. Around the time I started seeing people's outlines in the gray twilight of dawn, I fell back to sleep.

T amar had managed to wipe her face almost clean of paint by the time I woke up in the morning. Boradai had brought up a basket of mending, and all the concubines had threaded needles and were squinting through sleep-bleared eyes at socks and vests and robes that needed repairs.

Tamar dropped a darned sock onto her pile of finished items, and pulled out a robe with a badly worn edge. She tucked the edge under and began to hem.

"I heard the Fair One came to chat with you last night," Tamar said.

I felt my hands grow damp and surreptitiously wiped them on the vest I was mending. "I haven't ever seen a djinn-possession before. Does that happen to Jaran often?"

"He's a shaman," Tamar said. "The Fair One visits him often."

I hoped that next time the Fair One would talk to someone else. "When I've heard of djinn possession before, there usually seemed to be an exorcism involved."

"There was no shaman at Kyros's?" Tamar seemed genuinely shocked by this. Across the circle, I noticed that other women were listening to our conversation, and looking at me. Two whispered to each other, shooting looks at me as they conferred. I bit my lip, certain now that *someone* in Kyros's household was a shaman who talked to the aerika, just as Jaran did.

"I didn't know about one, but my mother worshipped Arachne and so did I," I said. "Maybe he . . . wasn't in the stables."

"Or she. There are women who are shamans. Jaran thinks I could become one." Tamar adjusted the robe she was working on and continued hemming. "Not all the free djinni are friendly. Some are angry and quite dangerous. The Fair One isn't like that. She visits Jaran often, and tells us things."

"Like what?"

"Well, she always knows when we're pregnant, and she can tell us early on whether the baby will be a boy or a girl. A few years ago, one of the boys got very sick and died; the Fair One knew that it was hopeless, he wasn't going to recover. Sometimes the Fair One carries messages from other households. She also visits the shaman at the household where Jaran grew up, and carries messages from his mother and brother."

"And she says the rivers will return."

"Well, of course. Everyone knows the rivers will be free again someday, just like we will."

I nodded silently, hoping that this would close the subject. It didn't.

"Meruert said that the Fair One spoke to you."

"I really didn't understand what she said. She said she knew my secret, but I don't know what she meant."

"Are you not really a virgin?" Tamar asked. She dropped her voice to a whisper and glanced to see if Aislan was listening. "There are ways to fake the blood, if you have to. I would have expected Sophos to check, though, before paying a virgin's price."

"I really am a virgin," I said, and stabbed at the vest I was mending, jabbing myself in the finger. "I think she was just harassing me. I swear before Prom— I swear before the djinn, Tamar, I don't know what she was talking about."

Tamar shot me a dubious look, then glanced at the

circle of silent women with their eyes on their sewing, and shrugged. I thought she'd probably want to discuss this later. Aislan strolled over and picked up Tamar's finished mending to inspect it; she flashed another bracelet, this one a slender thread of silver around her wrist. "How was your night, Tamar?" Her voice was falsely sweet.

Tamar looked up at Aislan with undisguised loathing and said nothing.

"You know, if you'd *pretend* to like it, he'd find someone else. One of the young boys, maybe."

"Thank you for the advice, Aislan." Tamar's voice was thick.

Aislan shrugged and looked down to smile at me. "Let this be a lesson to you, Lauria," she said, flashing her bracelet again. "If you act like you're enjoying yourself, you'll get to spend your nights with men who want to treat you well. If you act like you're hating every minute of it, you'll get to spend your nights with men who take pleasure in your pain." She patted me on the cheek and ambled back to drop the mended socks into the basket.

I glanced at Tamar. Her face was scarlet and her jaw was tight. The stitches of her seam had gone from tiny and careful to huge and ugly; after a moment she looked down, bit her lip, and picked out those stitches. I felt my own anger flare at Aislan. As prickly and inexplicable as she might be, I found myself liking Tamar much more.

During our evening meal that day, Aislan's face went suddenly gray and she dropped her plate of food. Her limbs tremored like she was going to have a seizure, but her eyes didn't roll back in her head; they stayed wide, though unfocused and glazed, as if she were staring at something just five inches from her nose. *Aeriko possession.* This sort of visitation from an aeriko—a *djinn,* I reminded myself—I recognized.

"It's back," someone murmured. I looked at Tamar; she was trying to suppress a smile, without much success. When she saw that I was looking at her, she quickly pushed a bite of food into her mouth and composed her features.

Everyone else was looking at Jaran. He put down his plate of food and rose from his cushion in a quick, fluid gesture; he crossed the room slowly, his eyes fixed on Aislan's. "Why are you bothering her?" he asked in a conversational tone.

If the djinn had a reply, I couldn't hear it. Jaran shook his head and slowly lowered himself to a crouch, cupping Aislan's shoulders gently with his slender hands. "You know I'll throw you out eventually. Why don't you just leave her alone?"

Aislan began to drool. Meruert whisked Aislan's plate of unfinished food out of the way and, after a minute or two, finished it. Jaran shrugged and went back to his own abandoned plate. When Boradai came up a little while later to escort the concubines downstairs, she saw Aislan and turned furiously to glare at Jaran. He inclined his head respectfully. "I'm going to take care of it," he said. "I needed to finish my meal first. Exorcisms require a great deal of strength."

"And you'll need assistants, no doubt," Boradai said, her tone acid.

"I'm so glad you understand that." Jaran glanced around the room and his eyes lit on me. "I don't need the new one, of course."

"She can't go down today," Boradai said through

clenched teeth. "Since she'll be staying here, she can take someone else's place. Tamar can go down."

"Oh no, Tamar is my apprentice," Jaran said. "She needs to stay here. But . . ." He looked around and shrugged. "With Lauria here, I suppose we could spare Meruert."

Meruert stood up quickly to put on cosmetics and perfume, then followed Boradai out the door.

Once they were gone, one of the other women led the unresponsive Aislan to a seat in the corner of the room. Jaran finished eating, then stood up and stretched. He sat down across from Aislan and began to strum his dombra, the same two notes over and over, just as he had last night before the visitation from the aeriko.

There were cabinets along one of the walls, and Tamar began to fetch things from them. She brought him a drawstring bag made of polished leather, and a copper incense burner shaped like a stylized sun. A dozen quill feathers bundled together and tied with thread. A vest covered in twisting vines worked with bright thread. Jaran shrugged on the vest and resumed strumming. One of the boys lit incense and placed it in the holder, and one of the women untied the feathers and laid them out in front of Jaran. Tamar brought a small, covered clay pot down from the cabinet, and then all the concubines sat, arraying themselves loosely around Jaran and Aislan. Tamar gestured to me and I sat down beside her.

Jaran played for what seemed like a very long time, though it may have only seemed like a long time because of the tedium. Smoke coiled up from the incense burner like a dark snake in the air, then broke and dissipated as a cold night breeze wafted through the room. It smelled musky, like spices mixed with wet sand. Finally, Jaran set down his dombra. He uncovered the pot; then he picked up a large black feather and lowered it briefly inside. I saw moisture glistening on the tip of the feather; the pot held something liquid. Very delicately, Jaran took Aislan's hand, and brushed her palm with the moistened feather.

"Aislan is a child of the river, the steppe, and the djinni," he said. "Tamar, do you claim her?"

"I do," Tamar said.

"Lauria, do you claim her?"

I was hardly qualified, but the expected response was pretty clear. "I do," I said.

He went around the circle; each woman and boy gave the expected response. When everyone had spoken, he dipped the feather into the pot again, and brushed her forehead, cheeks, and lips. "Aislan belongs to us. Be gone." He pressed the heel of his hand to her forehead, and for a brief moment, I saw the shimmer of a djinn in the air, like an aura around Aislan. A look of strain crossed Jaran's face and he sank back on his heels. Aislan was still drooling.

He picked up his dombra and began to strum again. Two notes, faster and faster. This time, he dipped his fingers into the water and flicked the water over Aislan's hair before pressing his hand against her head. "Aislan belongs to us. Be gone!" This time, there wasn't even the sparkle of the djinn starting to leave.

Jaran glanced at Tamar; she jumped up and ran to the cabinet, and came back with a small drum. She sat down and began to beat a slow, steady rhythm. Jaran stood up and began to dance to the drumbeat. Jaran's dance made me think of a bird in flight. He started out with a slow, measured step but began to whirl as Tamar sped up the beat, his arms outstretched. He grew breathless from exertion; I could see the sweat beading on his face. Finally he clasped Aislan's hands and jerked her to her feet, grasping her face in both hands, his palms on her cheeks. "Aislan belongs to *me*!" he shouted. "Return to the Silent Lands, lost one of your kind, and trouble us no more!"

The harem went silent—a breathless, expectant hush as everyone watched Aislan. For a moment, we all saw it: the djinn, like a golden shimmer in the air, lighting the face of both Aislan and Jaran. Then, like water draining from a funnel, we saw the djinn slip into Jaran's chest; I could see Jaran's face, and for a heartbeat, I could see the djinn in his eyes, wild and staring and angry. Then it was gone.

Aislan slipped out of Jaran's hands and fell to the floor. Jaran collapsed beside her, exhausted.

After a few more hushed moments, Tamar tenderly covered Jaran with a blanket where he lay, and slipped a pillow under his head. She did the same for Aislan, in a more cursory way, and then began to pick up the ritual implements. The other concubines started to chat in whispers that slowly became normal speech. Aislan's eyes were closed; someone checked to make sure she was breathing, then covered her with a blanket to let her sleep where she'd fallen. I wasn't sure if I should help pick up the ritual items, but I trailed Tamar as she put them away. "What's in the pot?" I asked her.

"River water, from the wet season when there's water in the old riverbed. One of the yard slaves gets it for us."

"I'm not sure I understand why Jaran needed so many people here."

Tamar gave me a slightly exasperated look. "Well, he *doesn't*, exactly. But Aislan is a favorite and Sophos wants to be sure this gets fixed right away, and no one's going to argue with Jaran. This way, none of us had to go downstairs."

"Except for Meruert."

Tamar shrugged. "She likes going down. One of Sophos's friends likes to give her things, like Aislan. Aislan likes going down, too. But she was possessed by the djinn, so too bad for her."

"It's still pretty early," I said, as Tamar closed the cabinet where the water pot and feathers were stored.

"If Boradai comes up to bother us, Jaran will tell her that we're guarding Aislan to make sure the djinn doesn't come back." Tamar shrugged and flopped down on her pillow. "Don't you go telling this to Boradai or Sophos or anything."

"You think I would?" I gave my voice a slight edge.

Tamar shrugged. "No offense, Lauria, but you seem pretty witless in some ways. I figured I'd better tell you to keep your mouth shut."

Witless? Well, that was better than "suspicious." I shrugged and lay down near Tamar, though not in "her" corner. "I won't tell anyone," I said, truthfully enough. I supposed that I shouldn't feel any sort of allegiance to Tamar and the other concubines, but in truth I was beginning to feel a real sympathy for Tamar. She hated going downstairs, and if I were really stuck here, I thought I might hate it, too. Besides, if someone ratted Jaran out, suspicion would naturally focus on me. That would definitely not be helpful to my real goal here.

As the other women blew out the lamps and we all settled down to sleep, I found myself thinking about Tamar's angry, slightly drunken face when she'd woken me, and her relief tonight at being able to stay safely upstairs. Against my will, my thoughts turned to Alibek. *Do you know what they do to me?* I clenched my teeth together and rolled to my side, pulling my covers over my head. Kyros was a good man. He was nothing like Sophos. And Alibek . . . Alibek was nothing like Tamar.

*T*en days passed. I did my best to maintain a cautious distance between myself and the slaves in the harem, knowing that every time I spoke I gave myself away: I was too bold, too loud, too ready to meet Aislan's eyes. I was insufficiently frightened and definitely not as hungry as I should be—there was *never* quite enough food. And I was too old—absurdly old for a fairly attractive woman to still be a virgin. I knew this had attracted some discussion, because I overheard Tamar and Meruert discussing it one afternoon. "I think perhaps her old owner was her father," Meruert said. "Some men have special scruples when it's their own daughter."

There was dancing practice each afternoon, supervised by Boradai. After giving me a few days to settle into the harem, Boradai had put me through my paces in front of everyone. She'd had me stand and mimic Meruert's fluid movements as well as I could, sweeping my arms through the air, stretching out one leg and bowing at the waist over it, turning my wrists in a graceful gesture. When we'd finished—Meruert with unruffled grace and me stumbling along behind—Boradai had Meruert sit down and turned on me with disgust. "You are worthless as a dancer, with neither grace nor flexibility," she said.

I wasn't exactly raised for this, I thought, but managed to keep the words behind my teeth.

"You'll need a great deal of work before you'll be able to take your place with the others. Tamar, teach her the limbering exercises, to begin with. Meruert, we'll need to excuse you from dancing soon enough"—her gaze swept disdainfully over Meruert's still-flat belly—"and you can work with her on moving gracefully."

She allowed me to sit down, finally, and I watched the women of the harem dance. They moved in slow, choreographed unison. Each move seemed designed to show off a part of their body; they wore shifts without sleeves, leaving their arms bare, and the skirts had a slit to expose the line of their leg. Tamar's face was always carefully neutral when Boradai was looking at her, even as Boradai tapped her leg with a stick, urging her to show a bit more of it. I found myself thinking of Aislan's comment about how Tamar attracted men who enjoyed her pain, and my mother's advice about standing as if you wanted to disappear into yourself. Her advice, I thought, was a double-edged sword. Before Boradai and Aislan, it was best if I tried to disappear. But were I sent down to dance with the others, to be chosen by one of Sophos's guests for a night of my company . . . well, for a harem slave to make it clear that she only wanted to disappear was to invite attention from precisely the wrong men. *My mother knew that once,* I thought, looking at Aislan—the "favorite"—and thinking of her, alone with her tea, watching the neighbors from her window. *But it's been a long time*.

Boradai looked me over carefully after the dance lesson, and then took herself out. There was a burst of stifled giggles from Meruert and one of the other women. I knew that I was the subject of a fair amount of cynical amusement, even from Tamar, and that everyone was watching me for signs of dread and fear when contemplating my appointment with Sophos or the friend he was supposedly giving me to. Unfortunately, I wasn't sure how much dread I should be trying to show. I certainly had no desire to sleep with Sophos or any of his friends. On the other hand, Tamar's open revulsion and dread each evening were more the exception than the rule among the concubines; while few were pleased to go downstairs, as Aislan was, most seemed to see it as a chore to be completed, the way stable hands might shovel manure. I figured that someone in my position—in the position I was pretending to be in—would probably be resigned to her fate.

It wasn't as if sex itself could be *that* bad. The sorceress I'd visited with the message from Kyros had been heavily pregnant when I arrived, and I'd met two older children. No one in his right mind would force a woman who could summon and bind aerika to do *anything* she didn't want to do. If all women found sex as awful as Tamar found it, no sorceresses would have children. Of course, a sorceress was likely to have chosen her own husband. Tamar certainly hadn't chosen Sophos as her master. But still . . .

In the early afternoon of my twelfth day in the harem, Boradai came upstairs; I didn't pay a lot of attention until I realized that her gaze was focused on *me*. "Lauria," she said. "Sophos would like you to attend on him after dinner tonight. Tamar, make Lauria ready."

Tamar and I went back down to the bathhouse. I had seen the way Tamar had looked at me during my twelve days in the harem, and I looked to see if she was smirking now, but she wasn't. In fact, she avoided my eyes entirely as much as she could, her face distracted. "No lice," she said when she'd finished checking my hair in the sunshine. "I did a good job on you last time, didn't I?"

"You did a very good job."

"Now for the perfume," Tamar said. She dipped the comb in oil that turned out to be heavily scented. I recognized the smell from Alibek. It was heavy and cloying and gave me the sense of an overpowering sweetness in the back of my throat. I felt vaguely sick to my stomach. I hoped that Tamar would take my pale face and queasy disinterest in dinner as nervousness; they might be more convincing than my acting.

Tamar dressed me in a clean shift of very sheer white linen. I felt exposed, especially as every concubine in the harem watched me during dinner. I pushed my plate away. "I'm not very hungry," I muttered.

"Let me get you some wine." Tamar jumped up and brought back a large metal goblet, filled almost to the lip of the cup. I took a sip and gagged; the wine had a strange taste, as if it had started to sour. "Drink it," Tamar urged. I took another sip, then another, and pushed the cup away. She pushed it back to my lips. Slowly, I downed most of the cup. I was unsteady when I stood back up—far more unsteady than wine alone would have made me, and I realized that the strange taste had been from something else in the wine. Tamar supported my arm, and I cursed myself for not being firmer about pushing it away. The purpose of this conference would be to get information: to find out when and how, exactly, I was to escape. I hoped I wasn't too drunk and drugged to remember my instructions.

We arrived at a closed door of heavy wood. Boradai stood outside. "He wants you to go in first," she said to Tamar.

"I'm not prepared—"

"Go on."

Tamar shrugged with false nonchalance and went in, closing the door behind her. She came out only a few minutes later, looking none the worse for wear. "Go on in," she said to me. "He said he's ready for you now."

My hands were shaking. I stepped inside and closed the door.

"Drop the bar in place," Sophos called from the bed. "To make sure we're not interrupted."

It fell into place with a thud.

We were in Sophos's bedchamber. His bed was built on a platform, piled high with cushions; gauze drapes to deter insects were pushed casually to the side. Sophos had been lounging on the bed, but swung himself off and stood up, offering me a chair at the small table off to the side. "Sorry for my casual dress," he said, gesturing at his dressing gown. "Best to keep up the charade for Tamar and Boradai, though, don't you think?"

"Oh yes," I said, relieved.

"So. How have things been going?"

"Well—first of all, I'm sorry, but I'm a little drunk.

Tamar insisted." He nodded with a smile. "It's been a bit tedious. I'll be glad to be on my way to the bandits. I assume that's what this meeting is to discuss?"

"Of course." Sophos poured himself a little wine. "You won't mind if I don't offer you any, will you? I think you've had enough. Yes. Not tonight, not tomorrow night, but the night after is the night you can be on your way. I will ensure that the night guard is elsewhere. Wait until the concubines are all asleep. I'm not having any guests that night; someone will be with me, but I'll keep whoever it is occupied, so you won't have to worry about anyone returning to the harem in the middle of the night. Just get up and slip out the door. I'll have sturdy clothes and water hidden right by my front gate, along with your own boots—I brought them along from Kyros's. Pick up the bundle and head out."

"And to get out of the city?"

"Just to the east of the gate is a spot that's pretty easy to climb over. Again, I've arranged for the guards to be away from there. Hopefully there won't be any *other* slaves that try to escape that night, because they'll have an easy time of it." He laughed. I laughed with him.

"Not tonight, not tomorrow night, but the next night," I said. "Just walk out, pick up supplies, and leave. I think I can remember that."

"Good." Sophos drained his cup of wine. "There is one other small matter we need to discuss."

"Yes?"

"Your virginity. *Are* you in fact a virgin?"

I felt a flush rise to my cheeks. "What does that have to do with anything?"

"The other concubines will expect that when you

return tonight, you will be a virgin no longer. And an escaped slave—your age, with your looks—who's a virgin, that would be highly suspicious to the bandits."

He was looking at my body, not my face; at the places where the sheer fabric clung to my skin. I knew that my eyes had gone wide, but when I opened my mouth, my voice was quite steady. "No," I said. "I'm not actually a virgin. I had an affair a year ago with another one of Kyros's aides." Something in me balked at naming Nikon as my lover, so I added, "A man named Myron."

"Myron. Oh yes. Kyros said you didn't get along very well with him."

"Yes, well, that affair would be part of why we don't get along. And I was drunk that night. I probably would have had the sense not to sleep with him if I'd been sober."

Sophos nodded. "I'm going to have to check, of course."

Check? "Keep your hands off of me," I said sharply, dropping my voice so that we wouldn't be overheard. "I am a free woman, not one of your slaves." Sophos was standing up and moving toward me; I backed toward the door, cursing the drugged wine for making me so unsteady. "Anyway, you told everyone you were saving me—for some guest."

"Yes. But no one in the harem will believe that I called you here tonight and then sent you back untouched. They believe that you're mine. And they know I'm a man who doesn't like to wait."

"You said that no one would lay a hand on me. That if anyone did, you'd cut it off."

"So I did." Sophos took my hand. "But things

don't always go as planned. Go lie down on the bed, Lauria."

My blood turned cold. "No!" I shouted, and jerked my hand away. "Don't you touch me, you dirty bastard. I'll tell Kyros!"

"I'm sure you will, when you get back from the bandits. Or sooner, if you want an aeriko to carry the message. But I don't think you'll run back there right away, and you may realize later how necessary this was." Sophos wrapped his hands around my wrists and jerked me toward him.

Even barefoot, drugged, and dressed in see-through gauze, I was not a helpless ten-year-old kitchen maid like Tamar. I slammed my forehead into Sophos's nose, which promptly started streaming blood. When he let go of my wrists, I punched him in the stomach. Swearing in Greek, Sophos made another grab for me; I dodged aside, but stumbled clumsily, and Sophos punched me in the stomach, twice. The first punch knocked me back against the wall; the second knocked the breath out of me. In the moment when I was struggling to gasp, he picked me up and threw me onto the bed.

"I'm going to kill you," I screamed as soon as I had air, no longer caring who heard. "*This is not what I agreed to,* you bastard! You *pig*!" I brought my knee up, aiming for his testicles, but he had seen it coming, and caught my knee in his hand, slamming it down against the bed. He yanked a knife out of his sleeve and held it to my throat.

"Hold still," he hissed. "It'll be over a lot sooner."

"You're going to *cut my throat*? How are you going to explain *that* to Kyros?" I had frozen momentarily under the cold blade; I was starting to sob—*like*

Alibek, I thought—even as I couldn't really believe this wasn't all some sort of joke. *This is a Greek officer. Kyros's friend. Kyros sent me here.*

"I'll just tell him you escaped and must have died in the desert. That's where I'll dump your body, if I have to kill you," Sophos said. Keeping the knife at my throat, he ripped open my shift with his free hand. "Now spread your legs."

I had clenched my knees together when he'd grabbed his knife. When I hesitated, he cut me with the knife—not my throat, not enough to make me bleed to death, but a small, deep slice over my collarbone. *"Spread your legs,"* he said again.

I wanted to stare dry-eyed at the ceiling, unflinching and unmoving, but I wept, and when Sophos thrust his clammy fingers inside me, my stomach twisted and I vomited. He pushed my face to the side and let me dirty the bedclothes. "Slept with Myron. Heh. You're as pure a virgin as I've ever seen, for all that you're older than most I've met." His voice was calm and conversational. "It's actually a little surprising, given all the time you've spent on horseback."

I had no idea what he meant. "Please," I whispered. "Don't do this."

He had slipped the knife back into his sleeve while I retched; now he untied his dressing gown and pushed it back out of his way. Then he lowered himself down and thrust inside me with a grunt.

"Stop!" I screamed. "It hurts. Stop, it hurts." It felt like the whole inside of my body would rip like my shift.

Another grunt. Another. He was distracted, and for an instant, I realized that his knife was within my reach; I could pull it out of his sleeve and plunge it into his neck. But part of my mind was still insisting, *This is a friend of Kyros; this can't be really happening, this is a friend of Kyros;* and then he had grabbed my wrists and pressed them against the bed, leaning on them heavily as he thrust again. Another grunt. Another, this one louder. *Like a camel,* I thought; *He sounds like a grunting camel.* I counted fifteen grunts before he pulled out, spilling himself on my stomach. "There," he said with clear satisfaction. "You shouldn't get pregnant. Pregnancy could be a real problem on this sort of mission." He stood up, wiped himself clean, and retied his dressing gown.

I was shaking as if I'd been immersed in freezing water. There seemed to be blood everywhere—some from my collarbone, some from . . . elsewhere. "Kyros is going to kill you," I said, between sobs. "He will have you staked out naked in the desert so the vultures can tear you to pieces. Like they do with military commanders who misuse aerika."

"Indeed." Sophos poured himself more wine. "I'll look forward to it, then."

I desperately wanted my voice to be cold and steady, but it caught like fabric on thorns. "I think I'll tell him I want you castrated first. But I want the wound cauterized so that you can't bleed to death before the vultures find you."

"Good thought." He unbarred the door. "If you're back from the field then, you can do the honors." He sat down in his chair. "You can go back to the harem whenever you want. Our business is concluded."

I stood up. My legs would barely hold me, but I wanted to get away as fast as I could. My ripped shift hung open; I gathered it around me as well as I could, with my shaking hands, and shuffled toward the door.

"Don't forget," Sophos said, behind me. "Not tonight, not tomorrow night, but the night after." I glanced back as I opened the door, and he raised his wine cup in a mocking toast. "Good luck with the Alashi."

CHAPTER THREE

I stumbled out into the open air of the courtyard, shaking so hard that my teeth rattled. The dry air had turned cold. I had no lamp; the moon was bright enough for me to see my way back to the harem, but I had no intention of going there. I wanted to go scrub my body raw in the Arys River, but there was water closer at hand than that, and I was going to use it.

The well house was close to the bathhouse, a little shack, gray in the moonlight. I pulled up a bucket of water, then set it on the ground at my feet and ripped a piece of cloth loose from my shift. I wet the cloth and scrubbed blood, sweat, and semen from my body. When I thought the cloth was probably filthy, I threw it down and ripped off another piece to scrub at my face, washing away paint and vomit and the flecks of Sophos's spittle that had dripped onto me.

A gust of wind whipped suddenly into the well house and I shuddered. If I ripped any more cloth from my shift, I'd be naked, so I heaved the bucket up and turned it over my head, soaking myself from my hair to my feet. The water splashed against the rocks that formed the floor of the well house.

I can't stay here. Not two days, not two minutes longer. I set the bucket down carefully. I was nearly naked, except for my shift. I had no food, no water, no shoes. *I'll just go back to Kyros. He wouldn't expect me to stay here, not after this. He wouldn't.* Jaran's aeriko, the "Fair One," flashed suddenly in my mind. *Are you afraid I'll tell your secret? That would be funny. Whatever would your old master say?*

I'm getting out, I thought. *Now. Tonight.* I left the well house and started toward the wall.

"*Lauria.*"

The strangled whisper made me turn around. It was Tamar. She had been sitting in the shadow of the well house; I had no idea how long. "Have you been watching me?" I blurted out.

She ran quickly across the dark yard. "I know what you're thinking," she whispered. "I've wanted to run away, too. But you'll die if you try tonight."

Another gust of wind hit me and I almost fell to my knees. Tamar grasped my arms and steadied me.

"You are soaking wet. You have no shoes, no food, no water, no container for water. You'd never make it to the Alashi. If you go back to your old master, he'll just beat you and send you back here, even if you make it there alive, which you probably won't."

"I can't stay here," I whispered.

"I know," Tamar whispered back. "But you can't try it tonight. Come upstairs. I'll get you a fresh shift, and a blanket to warm you."

"Why were you watching me?" I asked as Tamar began to lead me back upstairs.

"I thought you might need some help finding the

well," Tamar said. "That night when I was ten, I wanted nothing more afterward than to take a bath. Boradai wouldn't let me. I screamed, and she beat me and told me to shut up. It was a waste of water. I was planning to tell you not to bother asking, just to slip in and wash if you wanted to. Boradai is asleep."

"Was it Sophos who did it to you?" I asked, on the stairs.

"Oh no." Her shoulder flicked in the hint of a shrug. "He gave me to a friend of his. Your old master, actually. Kyros."

My stomach rebelled again, but this time there was nothing left. Tamar let me lean on her, and then we went in and I collapsed onto a pillow.

It was very dark; Tamar crossed the room to dig through one of the cabinets, and returned with a clean shift and a large shawl. I dropped the rags of my old shift onto the floor, dressed in the fresh one, and wrapped up in the shawl. After a while, I stopped shaking quite so hard. Despite the bucket of water, my hair still reeked of perfume.

"I hate this smell," I whispered.

"You'll get used to it," Tamar said.

The cloying smell hit the back of my throat and I almost retched again. "You're not used to it," I whispered.

"I'm not like you," Tamar said. "Meruert is used to it. Aislan is more than used to it. You'll get used to it in time."

"It's making me sick."

"It's probably not the perfume. The drug Sophos had us give you makes some women sick. You'll feel better in the morning."

I doubted that, but fell silent. Tamar sat beside me

for a few more minutes, then slipped off to her own corner and left me alone again.

No one will lay a hand on you. Sophos's lie rang in my ears as I stared into the darkness.

I thought about how I would tell Kyros when I returned. *Sophos broke his word. He did not treat me with respect, like a free woman. He laid hands on me, and worse.* Kyros's face would grow dark with rage, as it had when I returned to tell him about the military commander who had attempted to poison me. Sophos might not report to Kyros, but there were laws against rape, and Kyros could see that they were enforced. He would send soldiers to fetch Sophos, or perhaps a djinn. *What do you have to say for yourself, Sophos?* Perhaps he *would* let me castrate him. And I'd be the one to tie him, in the desert, to be torn apart by vultures while still alive . . . I wouldn't cry, telling Kyros, of course. I would maintain a steady reserve, the calm of a soldier the day after a battle. *I wish I'd killed him. I wish I'd grabbed his knife when it was within reach. I should have killed him, the bastard, the betrayer.*

I could hear someone moving around in the dark harem, and I pulled the shawl tighter around myself, thinking, unwillingly, of Alibek. *Don't take me back there. Don't give me back to Kyros. Have you ever visited a harem, Lauria? Because of my sister, he took me to rape.* And Tamar's voice, steady in the darkness—*He gave me to a friend of his. Your old master, actually. Kyros.*

In the whirl of anger and betrayal, I dozed, finally, for an hour or two toward morning. *Not tomorrow night, but the night after,* I thought, grimly, when I woke to see daylight. *The night after. The sooner I'm out of here, the sooner I can get to the Alashi, accomplish my mission, and report back to Kyros to have Sophos executed. I can trust Kyros. I can trust Kyros.*

I had stopped shaking by the night I was to leave, and the ache between my thighs had subsided. Sophos hadn't sent for me again. The night I was leaving, Boradai came up to say that Tamar should attend on Sophos in his chambers, but her courses had come and so she was excused. Jaran was sent down instead. The rest of us were told we could go to sleep early. I picked at my dinner, though I knew I'd need my strength; I had had little appetite since my night with Sophos, and I'd have been nervous before my escape in any case. No matter how orchestrated it was, something could still go wrong. A slave caught escaping would be flogged, or worse, and I had little doubt that Sophos would apologetically tell me that he *had* to punish me, to avoid suspicion.

I stretched out after dinner and waited as the harem fell asleep around me, curled up in my shawl while I waited. I passed time trying to think about how I would rid myself of the smell of perfume, once I was out. I wouldn't be able to afford to waste water to wash myself. Maybe, I thought, if I rubbed a great deal of sand into my hair, that would get rid of the smell . . .

Finally I was sure that everyone was asleep. I stood up; Tamar lay on the floor near me, and for a moment I almost wanted to bring her with me. It would certainly piss off Sophos if I did—but there would be water for only one person, and Tamar had no shoes for the walk across the desert hills. And I was pretty sure that if I brought Tamar, there would be complications in the mission I hadn't planned on. Still, she looked cold in the night air, and I covered her gently with the shawl. I tiptoed to the door and looked around; everyone was still. I eased the door open—Sophos must have had the hinges oiled; it was perfectly silent—and slipped down the stairs.

The courtyard was empty, as Sophos had promised. And there—a cache of supplies. Sophos had brought along my own boots, from Kyros's house; I slipped them back on my feet. The other clothes could wait until later. I shouldered the backpack and walked briskly toward the gate.

"*Hsst.* Lauria."

My stomach turned over and I whirled. In the dim moonlight, I could see a slight figure dressed in white; she clutched the shawl I'd left with her around her shoulders. *Tamar.* "You're running away," she whispered. "You've got supplies and everything. *You're running away.*"

"You've got a problem with that?" I glanced around with alarm; if Tamar had seem me leaving, what if someone else had?

"A *problem*? Are you *crazy*?" Tamar had caught up with me, and she grabbed my arm. "Take me with you."

I can't. But I fell silent, looking at her, and said nothing.

Her hands clenched like claws and her face went livid. "If you try to leave me here, *I'll give the alarm.* I swear it! Take me along or I'll mess up your escape. *You're not leaving me here.* Do you think I'm stupid? You have *supplies.* You *must* have bribed the guards.

Anyway, I don't care. You've got a sure way out and *I'm coming with you.*"

I told myself that I had to bring her because she'd spoil my escape. But the truth was—*we'll have to find water anyway, and I know Tamar would walk a hundred miles on broken glass if it would take her away from Sophos.* The truth was, I didn't want to leave her behind.

"Come on," I whispered. "But once we're clear of the city, I'm going to make you help carry the supplies." I hoped to hell there would be enough in the pack to see us both safely to the Alashi.

Helladia was much smaller than Elpisia, but Sophos lived in the center of town, a long way from the wall. Tamar padded silently behind me, and I thought about her bare feet, wondering if there was *anywhere* that we could steal her some shoes before we left Helladia. I kept hoping we might spot a pair of muddy boots, left out to dry and then forgotten, but of course we saw nothing nearly so useful. At this late hour, the streets were dark and quiet, and nothing, not so much as a broken pail, seemed to have been left out on the street. *It's her problem, not mine. Forget about Tamar's feet, worry about your own task.*

There was a sudden noise, and Tamar shrank into the shadows beside me. I realized as I pressed my back against the stone wall that we'd heard the huff of a horse; the building we were passing was a stable. I gave Tamar a reassuring nod, and stepped back out into the street.

"How long, do you think, until we're missed?" I whispered.

Tamar shrugged. "Boradai usually checks on the harem at some point during the night."

I hoped she wouldn't do that tonight. I bit my lip. Sophos might find some excuse to keep them from searching for me, but would he refrain from searching for Tamar? "We'll have to move quickly once we're over the wall," I said, and we picked up our pace.

We reached the wall quick enough and after a short walk along the edge, I found the spot that Sophos had mentioned. As with the Elpisia wall, there was a crumbled spot, and several handholds. I climbed up quickly and lowered my bag gently to the ground. "Come on," I whispered to Tamar.

Tamar had clearly not spent her childhood clambering over rocks in the desert plains outside of Helladia as I had in Elpisia. Still, she scrambled awkwardly to the top without my help, and dropped down gracefully enough to the ground below. "Do you want me to carry something now?" she asked.

"Not yet," I said, glancing up quickly to orient myself. "Come on. It's too dark to search on horseback, even if Boradai finds us gone. When it gets close to dawn, we'll find somewhere to hide, but let's try to get as far from here as we can."

"Wait," Tamar said, grabbing my arm as I turned toward the desert. "You are going to *check* your pack, right? Make sure the guard gave you what he promised?"

I swung the pack off my shoulders and opened it quickly. Despite my comments to Kyros about how I'd take water but no food, Sophos had packed me *seven* waterskins, not eight, along with food—bread, cheese, apples. *Apples*. Well, at least they would give us a bit of water as well as strength. I gritted my teeth.

We'd need to find water soon; for two people, this wasn't even a two-day supply. Sturdy clothing was in there, too; rather than carry it, I yanked off my shift and pulled on the shirt and trousers. Then I realized what was missing, and rooted through for a frantic moment. *He didn't give me a knife.* My anger rose up in a hot choking cloud. I forced it back down. The guard who I'd supposedly bribed wouldn't have been foolish enough to promise me a knife. Tamar couldn't see my anger.

"It's what was promised," I said, and tied the pack shut again. I started to swing it onto my back, then paused and looked at Tamar's bare feet. "You're going to cut your feet to ribbons if we don't at least wrap them in something."

"I won't hold you back," she said.

If I had a knife, I could cut some of the wool from my trousers—or, better, leather from the tops of my boots. *No knife. I hope Kyros boils you in cooking grease.* I tugged experimentally at the cloth, but it was well woven and was not going to rip, at least not without a knife to get it started. Well, at least the shift would tear easily. I ripped it into strips and wrapped Tamar's feet in them.

"This won't last long," she said.

"It'll be better than nothing. I'll think about it." I swung the pack onto my back. "Try to keep up."

Tamar did keep up, to my surprise. We spent several hours walking and occasionally climbing before we slowed to look for a hiding place. The hills around us had turned from gray to gold in the sunrise; we found a hollow in a hill, screened by some bushes. Not quite a cave, but as close as I thought we'd find.

"I think this is the best we're likely to find," I said. "They'd have to be right on top of us to find it."

"We should keep going," Tamar said.

"Then they'll definitely find us." *If they're looking.* "They have horses; it will be broad day in another half hour. They'd spot us walking like a hawk spots a hare."

"What about Sophos's djinn?"

"Djinn aren't actually all that good at finding people who are trying to hide. Or, or so I've heard, at least."

Tamar shrugged and sat down, squeezing herself into the back of the hollow. I set the pack down and sat beside her.

"Can I have some water?" she asked in a small voice.

I pulled out the waterskin. "Two swallows," I said, and passed it to her. She drank, then I drank.

"That won't be enough to get us to the Alashi, will it?" she said.

"It wouldn't have been enough even if you hadn't come with me. There's water on the plains—somewhere. We'll find it." I took out one of the apples and gave it to Tamar, then ate one myself. That would get us through the day with less water, and apples were heavy—not something I wanted to carry far.

"Let me see your feet," I said, when I'd licked the last traces of sticky sweetness from my fingers.

Tamar stretched out her legs, her face rigid. Despite the wrappings, she had cut her heel and it had bled. I swore softly.

"I won't hold you back," Tamar said again.

"Not unless this festers and you fall into a coma from fever," I said, biting back *You fool* before the words spilled out. "Besides, your blood will make an easy trail for anyone to follow."

"You can just leave me."

I rolled my eyes. I'd have to use some of the precious water to wash out the cut, but then what? Wrap her feet again in the linen? I poked my head tentatively out of our hollow and spotted a few plants with thick, tough leaves. I crawled out, ripped some of them up, and brought them back. Pouring water into my hand a drop at a time, I cleaned out Tamar's wound as well as I could, bandaged the injury with the cleanest fragment of shift, then tied the tough leaves to her feet like sandals. She watched me work in silence.

"I don't know what we're going to do about your feet," I said, sitting back on my heels. "You really ought to have shoes, or at least sandals."

"Well, feel free to go knock on Sophos's door and ask for them," she said. "I'll wait here."

I shook my head. "Try to get some sleep."

Tamar pulled the shawl over her shoulders and closed her eyes, leaning her head against the packed dirt. I closed my eyes, but I was too keyed up to sleep, and I think Tamar was as well. *If we're found,* I thought, *maybe we can try to bribe the guard who finds us the way Alibek tried to bribe me. And then grab his knife and stab him in the back.* That would solve all kinds of problems, if it worked. We'd have his boots, his knife, and his clothes. He'd probably even have a *horse.* Tamar was small, so we could ride double on a horse, though there was the problem of water for the horse, and food . . . The guard would have extra water, too, and probably some food. And a sword! I found myself almost *hoping* we'd be found, though of course there was no guarantee that the guard would be tempted by the bribe. It would be foolish in the extreme for him to take us up on that sort of offer. Still, I found myself straining my ears through the afternoon with a mixture of fear and anticipation.

Tamar stirred at dusk. I gave her a little more water and drank a little more myself.

"Are we going to walk through the night?" she asked.

"It's cooler," I said. "And the moon is almost full."

Before the last of the daylight vanished, I went for a quick walk, alert for the sound of hoofbeats, looking for something, *anything,* with some sort of edge, or even just a point. An animal's tooth. A sharp rock. Anything. After hunting for a while, I found a rock that had cracked in half, leaving a sharp edge, and a weathered stick that with a few minutes of effort I could sharpen to a point. I slipped off my trousers and managed to drive the pointed stick through the thick black cloth. Then I held the edge on the ground against the cloth with one foot, and yanked the cloth with my hands; the cloth gave at the weak point, and I was able to tear a strip loose. I did the same with the other leg of the trousers, then put them back on.

"They'll still wear out," Tamar said, as I bound the doubled-over wool to the soles of her feet with more of the linen.

"Not as fast," I said. "If you see something else we can use, while we're walking, let me know."

When the shoes were ready, it was quite dark. I stepped out of our hole and stretched, looking around. A quick movement in the corner of my vision turned out to be a fluttering hawk. I looked up at the stars: there was Alexander on his throne, and there was Bucephalis, with the faint star in his tail that marked the north. We were headed mostly north and a bit west; I set the star a little to my right.

"I can carry something," Tamar said.

Two of the waterskins had straps to let you sling them over your shoulder, so I gave those to her to carry, and shouldered the pack again.

"How did you learn to navigate?" Tamar asked.

"From one of the other stable hands," I said.

"Were your parents stable hands, too?"

"My parents are both dead."

"Oh." Tamar glanced at me. "I thought Kyros was probably your father."

"I heard Meruert say that."

"Well, you're clearly part Greek. And that explains why he never raped you. Some men are squeamish about it when it's their own daughter."

I should have claimed him as my father, I thought; it would have explained a great deal. Too late now. "Kyros bought me when I was a child, along with a whole lot of other slaves, from an officer who was being transferred back to Penelopeia."

"Were your parents already dead?"

"Yeah. Why are you so curious about this?"

"My mother died a year after I was sold to Sophos. I couldn't be with her."

Ah. I nodded. "There was an epidemic of dysentery the year my parents died. I'm not sure why I lived, and they didn't. Kyros bought me pretty soon after that."

"How old were you?"

"Eight."

Tamar glanced at me, and I thought that she was

probably trying to guess what I looked like as an eight-year-old. Why Kyros would have left me alone.

"The stables are pretty dirty," I said, trying to offer an answer to the question that hung in the air. "I think all Kyros ever saw when he looked at me was the dirt. Now . . ." I shifted my pack, which was digging into my shoulders. "Tell me about *your* family." Anything to get her to quit asking about mine.

"We were all owned by Androcles—he's a friend of Sophos, and lives in Helladia. My father got sold to someone in Elpisia before I was old enough to remember him. I lived with my mother until I was ten, and then Sophos saw me and took a fancy to me. I never saw my mother again. It was the Fair One who told me that she'd died."

I swallowed. "What was your mother like?"

Tamar was quiet for a moment, thinking over the question as she trudged along behind me. "Some slaves just give up, at some point. You could throw the gates open and say, 'Look, out there—four days of walking and you'll be with the Alashi, no one is watching, let's go,' and they wouldn't move. My mother was like that. Even when she knew Androcles was going to sell me away from her, I don't think it ever crossed her mind to run away with me. She gave me a hug and a kiss and said, 'Be a good girl, and maybe your new master will let you visit sometime.' "

"Would it have done any good to run?"

"Probably not. I was young. Slow."

"Maybe she figured that if you tried to run, he'd *never* let you visit."

"I'm sure that's what she figured."

I wondered where Tamar had gotten her spirit, if her own mother had been such a compliant servant.

"What do you know about the Alashi?" Tamar asked a few minutes later.

I thought of all the horrible stories. "I've heard that they'll take in any slave who reaches them," I said. "But I've also heard that they sacrifice humans to Prometheus."

"Oh yeah. 'Burning them alive on a fire.' I don't believe it. The Fair One talks about the Alashi sometimes, and she says that's a lie."

"What about the other stories?"

"What else have you heard?"

"That they make newcomers prove their worth with a spider bite."

"Ugh! I'd never heard that story." Tamar shuddered. "That can't be true."

"And I heard they eat horses."

"I think by the time we get there, we'll eat horse if it's offered to us."

My stomach growled. "Yeah," I said. "You're probably right."

"I heard that their most committed warriors are mutilated," Tamar said. "The men are castrated, the women have their breasts cut off. I don't believe it. Too many would die from that; it's not something you'd do to your best warriors! I don't believe the spider-bite story, either. Too many people would die."

I had to agree that they were unlikely to risk their best soldiers, but I wasn't so sure that these scruples would apply to strangers asking to join them. "What else has the Fair One said about them?"

"Mostly stuff that doesn't make a lot of sense. But she's always made them sound better than Sophos, at least."

"That wouldn't take a lot." The words slipped out before I thought them over.

Tamar laughed a little. "You know there are plenty who are a lot worse, don't you?"

"I know," I said, and we fell silent. The pause stretched into a silence that lasted for several hours.

The spring rains hadn't completely ended yet, and in daylight the steppe beyond Helladia had been a muddy green. By moonlight, the ground around us was gray and silver, and the light wasn't always strong enough for us to see whether we were stepping on firm ground or loose gravel. I slipped and fell badly twice, once scraping my knees and my hands; Tamar fell more than that. The plant life was scrubby and often thorny, clinging to the dry soil with roots that went deep. Some of those roots would be full of water, but the plants I'd recognized so far were poisonous to humans.

Despite my best efforts, we were already running low on water by the time we found shelter for the day. I thought it was best to keep walking at night and stay put during the day; even once we were beyond the range of searchers, saving our exertion for the cold of the night would allow us to conserve water. Even so, drinking only sips of water when we were very thirsty, we were running out. I wondered if we should both eat our fill of the meager food supplies immediately and lighten our load. I couldn't stomach the idea of bread and cheese without a few sips of water to wash it down; it would be a shame if the food went to waste because our water was gone. Of course, if we didn't find more water soon, we'd probably die before we reached the Alashi. I knew I wasn't thinking entirely coherently, and after meditating on it for entirely too long, I tore off a slightly more generous portion of bread and cheese for both of us, then tucked the rest away for later.

"We need to find water tomorrow, don't we?" Tamar said.

"Yes."

"Do you know anything about finding water out here?"

"Follow the birds." That was the first lesson I'd learned: watch for birds at dusk and at dawn as they fly to the water holes.

"I don't see any birds," Tamar said.

"Me, either. I've been watching for them since we set out."

"What else?"

"Bugs. Animals. Anything alive has to have water, so if you see a crawling thing, watch to see where it goes. Water flows downhill—if we're going to find it, it'll be someplace low."

"The rainy season wasn't that long ago. We'll find some."

"I hope you're right."

We dozed through the day. I thought once or twice that I heard hoofbeats, but I stayed where I was and they faded away a short time later.

At dusk, I crept out of our shelter to watch for birds. Tamar followed me. "There," she said, and pointed; I saw a sudden blur, and then it was gone.

"Did you see where it went?" I asked.

"I didn't see where it landed. Can't we just head where it was going?"

"I guess we'll have to."

We both drank some water; we had barely a cup of water left. It occurred to me that even if we found the water hole, we'd need to find *another* one in another day or two. I pushed that thought out of my mind; at least if we found a water hole now, we could drink our fill. *Drink our fill:* the thought obsessed me as we walked. I could hear the slosh of our meager remaining water in the pack on my back, and it took all my self-control not to stop and simply drain it all on the spot.

"There!" Tamar hissed. I thought she meant she'd seen the water, but she was pointing at another bird. It skimmed over the dry brush and then dipped down. We followed, and minutes later the sound of our approach sent a cloud of screeching birds into the air.

The water hole was a stagnant, scum-covered pond, but the water was fresh and not brackish. We covered the mouth of the bottle with a layer of the cleanest remaining part of my shift to strain out the weeds and as much of the dirt as we could. We filled one of the water bottles, drained it, filled it again, drained it again. It was quite dark by the time our thirst was slaked.

Once I was no longer thirsty, I realized how hungry I was. Shivering in the night wind, I broke off small hunks of cheese and bread for Tamar and myself. We ate silently, washing them down with more slightly gritty water. Tamar huddled in her shawl, trying to stay warm.

Though we would run out of food soon, it was tempting to stay put for the rest of the night, and through the next day. Surely we were beyond Sophos's searchers by now. And at least camped by the pond, we wouldn't run out of water. "How are your feet?" I asked Tamar.

She stretched them out so I could see. The makeshift

sandals were wearing thin, but there didn't seem to be any new blood. I considered unwrapping the bandages to take a look, but something in me cringed at the idea of washing her injuries again with this filthy, scum-laden water.

"Do you want to rest here for a while?" I asked.

"What do you mean, a while?" Her teeth were chattering.

"Tonight and tomorrow."

"No," Tamar said immediately.

"I think Sophos will have stopped looking . . ."

"I don't want to risk it."

I shrugged and stood up to fill the rest of our waterskins. We refilled all of them, drank still more water, and then topped them off again. The birds were still circling furiously overhead; I glanced up apologetically. "You'll have it back soon," I said aloud.

Tamar stood up, wincing, and resolutely picked up her two waterskins. I lifted the others, though my shoulders now felt bruised where the pack rested. "Let's go," Tamar said, and fell into step behind me as I turned us northwest again.

As we searched for shelter at dawn, Tamar caught her breath and pointed. "Look!"

I turned, expecting—hoping for—water, but instead I saw a narrow plume of smoke, curling toward the sky.

"It's the Alashi! It must be!" Tamar said, her eyes searching my face.

I shook my head. "We're too close to the Greeks. It can't be the Alashi yet. Come on, we need to find a good place to hide today."

"If it's not the Alashi, who is it?"

"Bandits, maybe."

"But—"

"The Greeks call the Alashi bandits, but there are real bandits as well. Most are former soldiers who mutinied and fled into the desert." I thought of the outpost of Arachne worshippers who had tried to kill me to keep me from learning their secret. "These are real bandits, not Alashi. I know what I'm talking about."

"How can you be sure without at least looking at them?" Tamar mumbled, falling into step behind me as I turned away from the smoke and picked up our pace.

"I told you, we're too close to the Greeks. Speak softly. Someone might be out hunting, and there's no sense in attracting attention."

We found a cave this time—a very small cave, but it would give us shelter and conceal us thoroughly. I squeezed in first, and Tamar slid in next to me. I split the last of the bread with Tamar and broke off a small piece of the cheese. Then I passed her a waterskin. "Two swallows," I said. She drank her water in two big gulps, then reluctantly put the stopper back in.

"There has to be water near here," she said.

"Yeah, but the bandits are probably camped right by it," I said.

"I'm *thirsty*."

"I'm thirsty, too."

"I want to drink more of our water *now*. I'm carrying my share, why do you get to be the one who decides when I drink?"

"You— Fine." There were six waterskins still full;

I handed three of them to her. "Ration your own water, then. But don't come crying to me if you run out."

Glaring at me, she unstoppered the waterskin and took another two gulps, then put the waterskin down. I ignored her as well as I could, drank as little of my own water as I could stand, and put it away. "We should trade off watches," I said. "In case we're found."

Tamar nodded. "I'll go first," she said. "You go to sleep."

"Wake me at around noon," I said, and laid my head down on my pack to sleep.

When I woke, it was well past noon. I sat up, rubbing my neck, which was stiff and sore from the way I'd slept. It was late afternoon, I realized, not long until dusk. Tamar was nowhere to be seen. But I was not alone in the hollow.

There was a shimmer in the doorway, like hovering raindrops, or a wisp of fog in the sun. "Kyros sent me," the aeriko said.

I squinted at the aeriko as it shifted in the air. "Kyros? Why now? We left Sophos's days ago."

"Kyros said to wait until you were alone."

I nodded, recognizing the sense of that. "What is the message?"

The aeriko shifted again, and its voice fell an octave, in a rough approximation of Kyros's voice. "Lauria, Sophos told me that one of his slave girls escaped the same night you left. I've told him that if you brought her with you, you had a good reason. However, this could cause you to run short on water. I've sent this aeriko to help you find water. I don't care how miffed Sophos is about the loss of his slave; my concern is for *you,* and for *your* mission."

Listening to Kyros's words, I felt as if I'd been wrapped in a soft cloak and handed a cup of chilled juice to drink. *I can trust Kyros,* I thought again, and smiled to myself.

"I've asked Sophos to quit searching; it's not worth the risk to your mission. This aeriko will return to me as soon as you've made contact with the Alashi. Good luck."

The aeriko fell silent.

I can send word to Kyros about what Sophos did, I thought. *Right now!* Relief washed over me; Kyros would take care of things. But first, water. Water and Tamar; where *was* she?

"Where is Tamar?" I asked. "Did you see her leave?"

"The slave girl slipped out shortly after you fell asleep."

"Why hasn't she come back?"

"Possibly the bandits have detained her."

"Bandits—oh, hell!" I started to crawl out of hiding, then sat back on my heels and looked at the aeriko again. There was no point in risking reconnaissance when I had an aeriko to serve as my eyes. "Tell me what Tamar did after I fell asleep."

"She sat beside you for a while. Then she crawled out of your cave and went to one of the hills overlooking the bandit camp."

"Was she at least trying to stay hidden?" I asked. The aeriko bobbed in the air silently. I sighed and rephrased. "Did she walk up to the camp, or did she stay close to the ground?"

"She crawled to the crest of the hill and lay there."

"What happened next?"

"She lay still and watched; then she stood up and walked down into their camp."

She went in voluntarily? Surely she wasn't so stupid as to think these were the Alashi? That can't be it; Tamar may be a pain in the ass, but she's not stupid. "And then?" I asked.

"The bandits seized hold of her. She said that she'd come to join them—"

"Tell me *exactly* what she said."

The aeriko's voice went a little high, in a credible imitation of Tamar, but far breathier and more girlish than I'd ever heard her speak. "She said, 'I wondered how long it would take for you to find me, boys! Aren't you going to welcome me?' The bandits all spoke at once, and one stepped forward to take her arm. And the girl said, 'I escaped from a Greek man's harem; I can satisfy all of you, but not all at once. Surely *you* must be the bandit king I've heard about; wouldn't you like to enjoy my company first?' He took her to his tent. I came back here."

"How long ago was this?"

"The sun was near the horizon, but still bright in the sky."

I bit my lip and let my head fall back against the hard dirt wall. *What in Zeus's black pit was she thinking? What an idiot. Why would she voluntarily put herself in their power?* As my initial fury ebbed, I thought I could guess what she'd been about. Tamar hadn't believed me; she'd wanted to take a close look at the bandits herself, fearing that if we continued into the desert we'd die of thirst before we found the Alashi. She'd crept out while on watch. Once she reached a vantage spot, she'd taken a good look and realized quickly that I was absolutely right; these were Greek deserters, outlaws, not people we could trust. As the camp roused for the day, she'd probably realized that if she moved, she was more likely to be seen, so she lay where she was, hoping for the best, planning to creep back to the cave at dusk. But then she was seen—that's why she'd said, *I wondered how long it would take for you to see me.* Once she was seen, there was no point in running; they'd have caught her. So she played the role she'd learned in the harem, buying time and perhaps more lenient treatment so that she could try to escape later.

Now what?

Kyros would tell me to leave her here and continue my mission. But my stomach turned at the thought of leaving Tamar in the hands of bandits. Leaving her with Sophos would have been one thing, but here . . . Besides, she was a determined and resourceful person. She probably *would* escape eventually, and if she joined the Alashi after I reached them, she'd tell them that I'd abandoned her. I couldn't imagine that the Alashi would look fondly on someone who would abandon a friend so callously. No, I had to fetch her out. The success of my mission might depend on it.

The sun was setting. "Go back to the camp," I said to the aeriko. "Go into the tent of their leader and check on Tamar. If she's in no immediate danger, come back and tell me what you saw. Both in the tent and outside it."

"And if she *is* in danger?"

I licked my lips, trying to decide how to phrase my orders for the aeriko. I wanted Tamar back alive and able to travel, but I didn't want her to know an aeriko was helping us, not if I could avoid it. "If she is in danger of injury or death, then move her here. Go now and obey my instructions."

There was a shimmer in the air and the aeriko whisked itself off. I waited in the gathering darkness for what seemed like a very long time, then the aeriko returned.

"Within the tent, the man sleeps with the girl at his side. She is bound, hand and foot. Her eyes are open and she breathes, but she lies still."

"And outside the tent?"

"Some sleep, some are awake."

"Are they talking?"

"Yes."

"What conversation did you hear?"

A pause, then the aeriko began to repeat the snatches of conversation it had overheard, run together like unsorted coins tossed into a bag: "Worse, I think last night's—so then the butcher says to the blacksmith—snake in his boot—damn bloody bastard ought to—already?—You! Over—already took care of—it's not a bloody flux, at least—check it—she said she had—at least the water's—latrine duty—"

"Enough," I said. If the bandits were grumbling about their leader's refusal to share, I would never find it out by listening to their mumbling through the aeriko. At the very least, it sounded like he'd kept her to himself, and that was a relief. It would be much more difficult to remove Tamar from the middle of a crowd.

It was quite dark now. I slipped carefully out of the cave, gathered up the water and stored it in the pack, and set out for the camp. "Circle overhead, and come let me know right away, *quietly,* if anyone's coming,"

I whispered to the aeriko. "I'll have more instructions for you once I can see the camp."

The easiest solution, of course, was simply to have the aeriko pick up both Tamar and myself and take us somewhere safe. In a few terrifying minutes, we could be left a short walk from an Alashi encampment. But then there would be the matter of explaining all this to Tamar later. An escaped slave had no plausible business with a bound aeriko, and rogue aerika were not known for being helpful to humans. Quite the opposite, in fact. If possible, I wanted to accomplish her rescue myself.

I'll need something to cut her free, I thought. Sophos hadn't put a knife into my bag; I would have the aeriko fetch me one. For that matter, maybe it could find a pair of boots for Tamar, and sturdier clothes for her to wear. I eased myself down to peer over the crest of the hill to the encampment below. As I'd suspected they were camped by a water hole. I thought of the nearly empty bottles in my pack, and pushed the thought away.

"Aeriko," I whispered, and saw a shimmer in the air. "First, do not let anyone see you and don't attract attention. Second, I need a knife. Take one from someone who's asleep. If you can, bring me some boots as well, any clothing no one's wearing, and— some waterskins, full, if you find them."

Again, a long pause. I could see the flicker of firelight in the valley, and I could see men moving around. Occasionally, I heard a raucous laugh and the low murmur of conversation, though I could make out no words. A gust of wind brought the smell of horse manure.

The knife hit the ground beside me with a *thunk*. It

was followed a moment later by two pairs of boots and a shower of loose clothing. Then two waterskins fell, full, and I realized my mistake as they hit the ground with a splat. Both burst open and spilled their precious water on the ground. I grabbed one and was able to gulp a little before it ran away; the other was a loss. I bit my tongue and refused to curse out loud; I had always suspected that bound aeriko were pleased to no end when they could follow the letter of your instructions while completely ignoring your intention. I sorted through the clothing quickly: the smaller pair of boots was in better shape, and there was a decent shirt and pair of trousers in the pile of clothes. I stuffed it all into my bag as well as I could, and picked up the knife. "What's going on in the camp? Speak softly."

"Some are awake, some are asleep."

"How many are down there?"

"Twenty-seven."

"How many are awake?"

"Twenty-three."

I wondered how many of those were drunk. With luck, most of them. "Is the man with Tamar still asleep?"

No."

Damn. "What's he doing?"

"He is talking to the girl."

I decided that I didn't really care what they were talking about. "Which tent is his?"

"The largest."

"Right. I want you to free the horses, then scare them so that they run away. Then come and check on me and Tamar. If we're in serious danger, pick us up and move us to safety, and I'll worry about explanations later."

I moved toward the camp. I couldn't see the aeriko, but I quickly picked out the tent of their leader and moved toward it, keeping to the shadows. From the edge of the camp, I could hear the high-pitched scream of a frightened horse; closer, I heard one of the bandits curse foully, and they ran toward the horses. The bandit leader appeared at the opening of his tent, tying the drawstring of his trousers and looking around wildly. When he took off to see what was going on, I slit the side of the tent with my knife and stepped inside.

Tamar was inside; she was naked, her hands bound behind her, her face a wide-eyed, utterly impassive mask. I had imagined her crying, but her distant, stony calm was far more disturbing than tears. "We have to hurry," I said, and cut her free. "Can you run?"

She nodded, her eyes not quite looking at anything. I couldn't bear to leave her naked, so I snatched the blanket off the bandit leader's bed and wrapped her in it; she followed me out the back of the tent and we ran out into the night.

The camp was in chaos around us. The horses were galloping through it, screaming in true equine panic and trampling everything in their path—men, tents, food stores. One tent caught on a horse and was dragged through their campfire, scattering smol-dering fuel in its wake. With a lurch, I hoped it wouldn't be dry enough for a grass fire to catch; while it would be an admirable distraction, it would have the distinct drawback of probably annihilating us along with the bandits. Some of the bandits set to work frantically stamping out the glowing coals; the others I saw were trying desperately to catch or calm their horses or else to get out of their way.

I thought for a moment that we'd be able to slip away easily. Then I felt a sharp pain against the back of my head; my vision exploded into stars, and I realized a moment later I'd collapsed to my knees. Tamar was trying to drag me up by my arm, saying, "We have to hurry, we have to hurry," in a monotone. My ears were still ringing, and I realized that I'd been clipped on the back of the head by a tent pole that was being dragged by a panicked, tangled horse.

I managed to stagger to my feet, only to realize that the bandit leader had returned: still shirtless, he held a long, curved sword, and he stood between us and the open desert. He looked from Tamar to me, and laughed out loud.

"Aeriko!" I shouted. *This is where you just grab both of us and I explain later to Tamar that the djinn miraculously answered our prayers, or something.* Tamar was so dazed, I wasn't certain she'd even notice. But I saw no shimmer in the air; we weren't going anywhere. Of course, it was also possible that Kyros had called the aeriko back to him . . .

"Drop the knife you're holding," the bandit said to me in Greek. "Kneel on the ground and put your hands on your head."

Not a chance, pig-face. I could hear hoofbeats, and I realized that the tangled horse was running back around, still trying to free itself from the mess of tent and poles. I dropped my knife and started to raise my hands, then grabbed Tamar and pulled her down. The pole went over our heads and cracked against the bandit's. He roared in pain and fell to his knees as I had, grasping his head. He tried to struggle to his feet but collapsed with a groan. His sword fell from his hand.

Another grunt, and for an instant, the knife was within my reach; but this is a friend of Kyros, this can't be happening, and then—

This time, I won't miss my chance. I grabbed the sword and brought it down on the bandit leader's unguarded neck. It didn't cleanly cut off his head but severed his spine where it met his skull; his blood spilled out in a red flood and he toppled forward, dead, as I realized that I'd killed an unarmed, half-conscious man. I had never killed anyone before; I had rarely killed animals. I recoiled from the blood and nearly threw down the sword, but some practical voice in my mind made me wipe it off on his clothes and hold on to it, just in case we ran into more trouble. "Come on," I said to Tamar, and she grabbed my free hand as we fled into the desert night.

We ran, in our fear, probably a great deal farther than we had to. Their leader was dead, their horses stampeding, their camp in disarray—if anyone noticed us leaving, he lacked the presence of mind to pursue us. I was the one who stumbled, finally, and flung myself to the ground to rest. Tamar crouched beside me in the dry grass like a hunted animal, still clutching the bandit's blanket around her body. I laid down the sword and took out a waterskin. "Have a drink," I said, passing it to Tamar and taking out another one to drink myself.

She took a gulp and I saw a glint of tears in the moonlight. With effort, she lowered the waterskin from her lips. "I'm sorry," she said. "I took one of my waterskins with me. The bandits took it away." She thrust the stopper back in. "That was my water ration. You shouldn't have to go short."

"Drink your fill, Tamar." I sighed. "We're in this

together, and I don't imagine you've had much to drink since you left our hiding place this morning."

She shook her head, and now her tears spilled silently down her cheeks. She unstopped the water-skin and gulped water for a long moment.

"Sadly, I wasn't able to pick up a spare waterskin in the bandit camp, but I did find a few other things you might find useful," I said, and flipped open my pack. "A shirt—" I tossed it to Tamar, who caught it in mute surprise, "a pair of trousers, and—" I pulled out the boots and held them up, silently.

"Oh," she whispered. "Oh, Lauria."

Tamar put the clothes on immediately, shivering in the freezing night. The pants were too loose, and the shirt was very long on her. "Let's cut off some of the shirt and use it for a belt," I suggested, and then real-ized that I'd never picked my knife back up after the bandit told me to drop it. I did, however, still have the bandit's sword, so after I scrubbed off the dried blood as well as I could with the steppe grass, that's what we used. The boots were a little too big; we cut off the bottoms of the trousers and stuffed cloth into the toes to make them fit. Tamar looked very small in her oversized clothes.

When we were done, I stared at the sword; there was still a stain where the blood had splashed across it and dried. I shivered. His shade could come after me, I thought with uneasiness. He had done *me* no harm and I struck him down while he was helpless.

Tamar looked at the stain as well, then at me. "You saved my life," she said.

"You would have had the opportunity to run, sooner or later."

She shook her head and gently pressed my sword-hand to the ground. "No," she said. "I played for time and tried to distract them from looking for anyone else, but no. I would have died there. If you're thinking that you shouldn't have killed him the way you did—"

"I was thinking that he could come seeking just revenge," I said. "He hadn't hurt me and I didn't *have* to do it. I was striking—I struck at—" *Sophos*. Not the bandit leader.

Her hand closed over mine. "*I* had the right to kill him."

"But I held the sword."

"Become my blood sister. Then you'll have avenged the dishonor of your sister." I looked sharply at Tamar and she dropped her eyes. "If you *want* to," she said. "I mean, you don't have to. I just thought—well, I'm sorry."

I considered the possibility for a long moment. I had no sisters. No brothers, either. Blood sisterhood was one of the rites recognized by all three religions of the Danibeki. The members of the Sisterhood of Weavers were rumored to take oaths using knives that still bore stains from the blood of Penelope; the followers of Prometheus and Arachne used their own knives or swords, but they swore blood sisterhood in much the same way. And of course the worshippers of the aerika took sibling oaths, sometimes—though it was rare among slaves. There were obligations that you had to blood kin, and it was bad enough that sometimes you couldn't keep those obligations to the blood kin you started out with.

Kyros wouldn't want me to do it . . .

But I wanted to.

And Kyros had called his aeriko away just as I'd

needed it; I'd had to fight our way out. *It's my right to do this if I want to.* "We need to get all the blood off the sword first," I said. "I don't want any of his blood mingling with ours."

We had to use up a little of our water, wetting the edge of my tunic and cleaning off the sword. Then I cut the palm of my right hand and she cut hers, and we clasped hands, palm to palm. We actually both knew the words to the ritual, so we spoke together. "Water to water and blood to blood. Like rivers join, our blood is joined; sky to rain to river to sea, and you are my sister forevermore."

After sharing blood, we were supposed to give each other more mundane gifts, and we each rifled through our meager possessions, trying to come up with something. "I should've waited to give you the boots," I said. "Those would've made a great gift."

"They *were* a great gift."

I could have given her a waterskin but I didn't feel like they were mine to give or withhold anymore. So I plucked some of the star-shaped yellow flowers that had bloomed in the spring rains, threaded them together stem-through-stem, and made a flower necklace for Tamar, as I'd done for myself when I was a child. Tamar had never seen one of these before, but she brightened at the idea; she made a wreath of red-flowered vines for my hair. I breathed in the scent; it was light and dewey, nothing like the perfume I could still smell faintly when I thought about it.

Blood magic is real magic, as real as what the Sisterhood of Weavers does when they summon and bind aerika, or so I'd always been told. I'd expected something to happen: to see lights, or feel faint, at least, or maybe to have a sudden feeling of extra fondness for Tamar. But all that happened was my hand hurt, and I felt worried that the cut might fester. And I felt the same way toward Tamar that I had before: a little protective and a little irritated. *At least now I struck out in defense of my sister. The bandit can't come drive me mad for killing him unjustly.* That thought offered me some relief.

Even with the gifts, it was a short ritual. After everything that had happened that night, I felt like it must be nearly dawn, but a glance at the moon confirmed that it was still before midnight. "We should keep walking," I said. I tied the sword to the back of my pack, and we set out northeast again.

"So did you cut the horses loose as a distraction?" Tamar asked.

"That was the idea. How did you persuade them not to look for anyone else?"

"I don't think it ever occurred to them that I wasn't alone." She swallowed hard. "When I realized I'd been seen, I pretended I'd come to join them on purpose. I knew I'd have to spread for them, but I figured if I acted like I wanted it—you know, like Aislan—they might be satisfied with that and not try to hurt me. I guess it sort of worked." I glanced at her and she shrugged, her eyes sliding down to the ground. "I think the bandit leader was one of the men that likes to hurt girls. He'd have been the same with Aislan." Tamar's face was white, but she wasn't crying. "It's odd," she said, after a little while. "When I pretended I liked the idea of spreading for the bandits, I figured it couldn't be any worse than being taken by Sophos. But then—well, I decided I was wrong."

I found myself thinking about that night with Sophos as we walked, turning it over and over in my mind as I might a coin. I hadn't had the chance to send word with the aeriko about what had happened, and that rankled; I wanted to be able to imagine Kyros confronting him, and instead I knew that right now Sophos was comfortably at home. Probably in the company of one of the women or boys from the harem, in fact. At least he was probably disgruntled about the loss of Tamar. When dawn neared and we found a place to hide for the day, I felt sick and tired, and I slept fitfully, wrenching myself to half awareness each time my dreams threatened to tip me into Sophos's bed. When I woke, my hand was resting on the bandit's sword, still tied to my pack.

Six waterskins. *Not enough, not enough,* I thought, trudging through the dry grass, blinking in the sunlight. I had told Tamar to wait in the shade we'd found; I would check just the area nearest us to see if I could find some water. I hoped, of course, that with Tamar away, the aeriko would return. "Aeriko," I whispered. "If you're nearby, show yourself to me." I thought I saw a shimmer in the air, but I realized when I turned my gaze fully on it that I was just dazzled by the sunlight. A sudden rush of wind hissed over the grass, but there was no other answer.

Well.

I made a quick circuit around the area I'd told Tamar I'd search. Finding nothing, I returned to our little hollow, shaking my head. "We'd better drink less water," I said.

We slept through the day as much as we could; my stomach ached from hunger, but my throat was too raw from thirst to eat anything, even if we'd had enough food to fill our stomachs. We had a little cheese left, still, but I wouldn't be able to swallow it without water, and we hadn't the water to spare. *If we find water,* I thought, *we can drink our fill, eat the rest of the cheese, and fill our waterskins.* I tried to push the thought out of my mind, but water obsessed me: the cool embrace of water on my skin, the ripple of water in a fountain, the sound of water splashing against pavement, the roar of the Arys River at the height of the spring flood . . .

I slept, finally, and dreamed, of course, of water. The Jaxartes—the Syr Darya—had been unbound from its spell-chains, and came roaring down from the high valley. The wall of water traveled faster than a grass fire, crashing down like an avalanche of rock, sweeping away everything in its path. I could hear screams. I watched the water rushing down from some high place and looked down to find a broken spell-chain in my own hands. *This must belong to Kyros,* I thought, trying to understand what I was seeing. *I must have been trying to return it to him.* But the spell-chain was broken, and no use to anyone; I flung it out, to be carried away by the flood, and thought, *The river returns. Tamar, at least, will be pleased.*

I woke from my dream of the river, and for a moment, my thirst almost seemed lessened; then it returned with full force. Night was falling. I woke Tamar, who stared blearily up at me and muttered, "Are we near the river? I thought I heard water, for a moment." I shook my head; it wasn't worth the effort of speaking.

We had one full waterskin left. Tamar and I held up the others to our lips, draining out any drops we could find, then swallowed a little from the remaining waterskin—first Tamar, then me. "Let's go," I whispered, and we set out again.

We saw no birds that evening to lead us to water. No small animals, no snakes, not even crawling insects. We heard the hum of cicadas a few times, rising out of the night like the sound of a dombra, but we saw nothing and found no water.

The morning dawned gray and with a hint of moisture in the air. "Do you think it might rain?" Tamar asked, her voice nearly a whisper. In hope, we spread out our clothing, ready to catch any drop, but the fog burned off without so much as dampening the cloth; we dressed ourselves again and curled up for our daily sleep.

We woke to the sound of thunder. "It *is* going to rain," Tamar hissed, and quickly, we stripped off our clothing. I set my boots upright; my shirt and pants I spread out on the ground. I tried to dig a depression to catch water in, but my fingernails scratched uselessly against the sun-baked earth. I wished I'd found myself a stout stick and dug that morning, but it was too late now. The sky darkened more, and then opened; rain poured down. We tried to catch water in our hands, and sucked the drops off our own skin; when my shirt seemed drenched, I wrung it out into one of the empty waterskins, then unfolded it again to catch more rain. But it was already stopping. We wrung out our clothes and emptied our boots. I even sucked on my hair to get at the moisture there, though my hair tasted bitter, and still smelled faintly of Sophos's perfume. We managed to partly fill two of our waterskins.

"The water will run downhill, and might pool

there," I said. "Come on." I pulled on my damp clothes, thinking bitterly of the moisture I hadn't been able to get out. Tamar dressed as well, and we put on our boots before we set out downhill.

The ground here was thirsty, and most of the rain had sunk in quickly. But there were boulders at the bottom of the hill and rain had pooled in every crevasse; we used the fabric of my shirt to harvest the water; it seemed less foul than the things we'd taken from the bandit camp. We hunted for more boulders, and found a single large puddle which we managed to drain into our waterskins. The sun was back out and drying the grass, but before all the water had been burned back into the air, we plucked handfuls of grass and squeezed the last precious drops into our waterskins.

We filled three, all told. It was still day, so we rewarded ourselves with a drink, and retired back to our hollow to wait until evening. At least the damp clothes kept me a little cooler in the heat of the day, though I still thought grudgingly of the lost moisture we couldn't wring out.

Night came, and we set out again. *We have to be getting close,* I told myself. How did any slaves ever make it this far? Had I really been a slave escaping, I would have only the waterskins I'd managed to steal, only the clothes and boots I'd been clothed in by my master. I might have run, like Alibek, with only one waterskin, barefoot in sheer linen. Maybe no slaves had *ever* actually made it to the Alashi. But no; Alibek said that his sister had run there, and that when Kyros took him as a harem slave, he sent an aeriko to his sister to tell him what he'd done. Though maybe he just told Alibek he'd done that . . . but if Alibek's sister was dead, it was hard to believe Kyros wouldn't have told him *that,* instead. I shook myself. I didn't need to be thinking about Alibek right now.

At dawn, I saw a plume of smoke rising in the sky. Tamar saw it, too, and turned to me with trepidation. "It might be the Alashi this time," I said. "It might."

We approached cautiously, uncertain, but the first plume was joined by a second, and then a third; only the Alashi would have such a large encampment. "So what do we do now?" Tamar asked.

"I guess we just walk in."

"What do we *say*?"

"I don't know."

"What if they don't want us?"

I shook my head; I had no answer for her. I couldn't very well take her back with me to Kyros.

We were still a long way from the edge of the encampment when a slim woman with three silver hoops in one ear rose up suddenly from the grass, like a bird flushed from cover. "Stop!" she said. "Who are you? What do you want here?"

Tamar fell back a step, so I cleared my throat and spoke. "We are escaped slaves, Danibeki. We've heard that you take in escaped slaves who reach you."

"And if it turns out that we don't?"

Tamar spoke up now. "Then I'll die in the desert, because I will *never* return to my master."

That garnered a smile of stiff approval. The woman was older than I'd initially thought—her face was lined and her hair was streaked with silver. "Welcome to the Alashi," the woman said. "What you've heard is right; we take in any with the wit and courage to free themselves. Follow me to the encampment; we'll have water and food for you there." She spun on her heel and we started toward the camp. I couldn't help but notice, though, that while there was a warm welcome in her words, there was no welcome in her eyes. We were intruders, not recruits.

Tamar saw that, too, and stiffened. She glanced at me, but I looked away, afraid that she'd sense what I was thinking: *Oh well. As long as they don't throw us into a fire or let poisonous spiders feast on us, the only other thing that matters is that they don't suspect what I really am.*

CHAPTER FOUR

The Alashi were rising for the day as we entered the camp: men and women, soldiers and camel herders, children barely old enough to walk and women with long white hair that hung in slender braids to their waists. The tents were black and brown and dirty gray on the outside; each was round and solidly built. They seemed to form a chaotic, featureless jumble, but our guide led us unhesitatingly through the encampment toward, I realized eventually, the center.

"It's so much . . . bigger . . . than I'd pictured," Tamar said faintly.

Our guide glanced over her shoulder. "The Alashi meet now for our spring gathering," she said. "The gathering ends tomorrow; we'll be splitting out into smaller groups for the summer." She looked me over, taking in the sword tied to my pack, then turned back to Tamar. "She'll probably be sent out with one of the fighting sisterhoods, but you might be placed with one of the subclans, since you're so young." Tamar bristled visibly at that; our guide shrugged and continued on.

Plumes of smoke rose from the center of a few of the tents; there seemed to be a hole at the top of each one, but most of the fires had been lit outside, probably to keep the interiors as cool as possible. The Alashi kept a wide variety of herd animals, including goats, sheep, chickens, horses, and camels. I had seen camels only rarely back in Elpisia, but the humps were unmistakable. A dog trotted past; the Alashi kept dogs to herd their animals. A woman came out of her tent as I passed it, and before the door fell back, I caught a glimpse of a brick-red rug and a yellow-gold tapestry. The vivid colors of the inside room were completely hidden by the muddy exterior.

I recognized the dank scent of livestock manure, but other scents of the camp were foreign to me. I smelled earthy spices and greasy meat, sweet rice and burned porridge, the sharp smell of soap and the dusty one of straw. I had, to my relief, long since stopped noticing the stink of the perfume Tamar had doused me in before my encounter with Sophos, but I found myself wondering now if our guide could smell it. And if she could, what she thought of me.

Two children dodged between us, then ducked under a clothesline full of damp laundry that had been hung between two of the circular tents. The older lady who'd hung the laundry shouted after them, then muttered something like "little savages" under her breath. I heard a shriek from one of the children and then they came pelting back the other way, scattering chickens as they ran. They looked to be about nine years old. The game came to an abrupt end when the mother of one of the children came out, grabbed her daughter by the scruff of the neck, and dragged her off. I stifled a smile, thinking of my own mother's attempts to force me to sit inside and learn embroidery and arithmetic instead of playing tag in the streets.

I smelled incense, and heard someone strumming a dombra; Tamar turned to look and pursed her lips when she realized it was a shrine to the Alashi gods, Prometheus and Arachne. The shrine was a stone altar and a lone tree by the narrow stream of water that ran through the camp. Fire burned in a small dip in the center of the altar; when I looked up, I could see a colony of large spiders busily weaving in the branches.

"Greek gods," Tamar muttered. If our guide heard her, she gave no sign.

A cairn of rocks stood by the doorway of one large tent. Behind it was a tall wooden post with a crossbar that stuck out like a bent arm; a strand of small brass bells hung from a ribbon tied to the bar. Our guide cleared her throat and brushed the bells to announce her presence. "Come in," someone called from inside, and we did.

It took a moment for my eyes to adjust to the darkness. There were no windows in the tent; some light came in from the doorway and the hole in the roof, and the rest came from an oil lamp. Despite my glimpse of the brick-red rug, I had expected the inside of the tents to be black and plain, like the outside— or, perhaps, clean and stark, like the designs favored by Kyros and the other Greeks. Instead, the interior of the tent was lavishly decorated with a riot of color and patterns. Felt rugs of red, blue, and brilliant yellow carpeted the ground. The felt was locked into patterns: vines and swirls and the crisscross of a woven basket. The walls were hung with cloth of woven interlocking diamonds and triangles, with glittering bits of metal and glass sewn into the center of each shape. I had always pictured life among the Alashi as marginal at best. That even their leaders would be able to equip themselves with such rich decoration was a revelation to me. *Perhaps they, alone among their people, live in luxury,* I thought.

Sitting cross-legged on an embroidered cushion on a low platform against the opposite wall of the tent was a very old woman. Her back was perfectly straight, and I found myself straightening my own tired shoulders in nervous response. Her hair hung in long white braids, interwoven with strands of silk cord and colored stones; she wore a gold necklace looped three times around her neck, with a medallion at the end. "Janiya," she said to our guide. "Good morning."

"I'm sorry to disturb you so early, Eldress," Janiya said.

"You never disturb me for trivial reasons. What do you have for me?"

"These two." Janiya gestured, and Tamar and I edged forward. "I met them as they were trying to enter the camp. They say they were slaves of the Greeks and found their way to us across the desert."

The eldress raised her eyebrows and glanced at us. "Quite lucky, you finding your way here. We're all gathered in one spot right now; if you'd missed us, you could have walked a long way before any of us found you."

"We saw the smoke from your fires, Eldress," I

said, as Tamar spoke at the same time: "We were lucky."

The eldress smiled, the lines in her face deepening with mild amusement. "You can get back to your sisters if you want, Janiya. I'll take care of the new arrivals."

"Thank you, Eldress." Janiya bowed to her and went out; her face showed clear relief to have us off her hands.

"Sit with me," the eldress said, gesturing to cushions at her feet. I pulled up a cushion and sat down; Tamar sat beside me. I eased my backpack off and set it on the ground beside me, hoping that I wasn't violating some odd piece of nomadic etiquette.

"What are your names?" Her voice was gentle. "Tell me how you came here."

"My name is Lauria," I said.

"Mine is Tamar."

We hesitated, and the old woman prompted, "And your story?"

Though I'd rehearsed this mentally, I hesitated now, and Tamar spoke before I did. "We were the concubines of Sophos, commander of the Helladia garrison. Sophos bought me when I was ten; Lauria he bought just a few weeks ago from a friend in Elpisia. Lauria was a stable hand before she came to Sophos's harem; I was a kitchen maid." She swallowed, considered what to say next, then went on. "Lauria was very new, and she caught the eye of one of the guards. She was able to bribe him and he agreed to leave the gate unguarded for a night, and to leave a pack of food and supplies where she could find it. She checked to make sure that the way was clear, then woke me and asked if I'd like to come along. We couldn't *all* run—not if we were to have any hope of actually escaping—but Lauria knew how much I hated Sophos, how much I hated—everything. So she woke me, and I told her that I'd escape with her or die trying." Her voice shook a little. "We got out that night, hid in the desert, walked by night to avoid the heat, and drank water as we found it. We've been walking for about a week. I've lost track of the days." She lifted her chin. "Is that all you wanted to know?"

Tamar's version of events had startled me—but, I concluded after a moment's reflection, with her lie she protected both of us. The Alashi didn't have to know that I would have left Tamar behind if she hadn't woken up; they also didn't have to know that she was foolish enough to let herself be captured by bandits, or what she did to avoid being killed on the spot. Of course, there was the little matter of the sword strapped to my pack . . .

The eldress glanced from Tamar's face to mine with a faint look of amusement. "The younger speaks for the elder?"

I cleared my throat. "Tamar knows that I don't like talking about the harem."

Tamar nodded.

"Generous guard, to give you two pairs of boots. And a sword."

Tamar's lips twitched and she held out her battered feet in their too-large boots. "We stole all these."

"I see." The eldress looked from Tamar's face to mine; she still looked amused, not angry, though I was quite certain she knew that Tamar had lied—or at least left a great deal out. She clasped her hands in her lap. "So," she said. "You wish to become Alashi."

"Yes," I said, as Tamar said, "Of course."

" 'Of course,' you say. 'Why else would we have come here?' you think to yourselves. But perhaps we will not be quite what you expected. You were not raised among us; you don't know our ways. You have, in short, been taught to be slaves. It falls to us to teach you to be *people*." Tamar bristled slightly at that, and the eldress laughed at her, a little unkindly. "Oh yes, my dear. It may take some time. How old are you now?"

I suspected that Tamar was considering adding some years to her total, to make sure she wasn't sent to live with children, but after a moment she said, "Fourteen."

"Fourteen! That's not so bad. You've only had fourteen years to learn to obey, to be helpless, to be passive."

"Would we be here if we were helpless?" Tamar said.

"Probably not." To the side of the platform where the eldress sat rested a small wooden box, carved with a constellation of stars and polished to a velvet sheen. The eldress leaned over to open it; from inside, she drew out two leather thongs and two beads of a deep, watery blue. She strung a bead on each thong and tied them off with her gnarled fingers.

"There will be lessons, my new soldier sisters. And then there will be tests. Some are merely physical: you will be taught to ride a horse, shoot a bow, pack and put up a yurt, survive on the steppe. Others are mental: you will have the opportunity to prove that you have unlearned how to be a slave. As you pass each test, you will be gifted with a blue bead. When you have passed all the tests, you will be accepted as

Alashi." She handed each of us a necklace. "Put them on."

"How many tests are there?" I asked, pulling my matted hair out of the way as I put the necklace on. The lone blue bead rested against my breastbone.

"When you have earned them all, we will tell you."

Great. A rigged game. I kept my face neutral, but suspected that the eldress guessed my thoughts. She smiled slightly and then tapped the blue bead with her withered finger. "The first test was to prove that you cared enough about your freedom to *take* it. You proved that by running away from your master and finding us." She sat back with a nod.

"So what do we do now?" Tamar asked, still afraid that she'd be sent to live with the children.

"We split up in the summer, into subclans and soldier brotherhoods and sisterhoods. Lauria will go to live with the soldier sisters," the eldress said.

"I want to go with Lauria," Tamar said.

"Ordinarily we would not assign two newcomers to the same band."

"Do you divide sisters?" Tamar asked. "Because we are sisters by blood."

The eldress sat back; for the first time, she had the faint smile of one who'd been ever-so-slightly bested. "No," she said. "We do not separate sisters—especially not sisters by blood. Well. It was Janiya who found you; I will send you to serve with Janiya. She'll be pleased, no doubt." The acid tone in her voice made it clear she knew Janiya would be anything but. "I'll have someone take you to her. There will be a feast tonight, to welcome the two of you, and to celebrate the end of the spring gathering." The eldress struck a small brass bell, and a young man quickly presented himself to escort us to Janiya's encampment. "Oh," she called as we reached the door to the tent. "The Greeks tell their slaves all sorts of stories about us, so perhaps you'd like to know, you won't *be* the feast tonight. We don't eat human flesh, and Prometheus and Arachne don't ask for sacrifices, let alone the lives of young men and women. We offer our courage and our strength to the gods, not the flesh of former captives. We're not fools enough to keep poisonous spiders as pets, either, and we don't throw away the lives of new recruits on meaningless 'tests' of spider bites or walking through flames."

Although Tamar had insisted that the stories of human sacrifice were lies, I saw a slight exhalation of relief at the eldress's words. *Of course, she could be lying, to put us off our guard,* I thought. But she hadn't taken away my sword, and that was a good sign.

"The only people we kill in cold blood," the eldress added as we turned away, "are bandits, rapists, spies, and traitors."

Tamar smiled at that and gave an approving nod. It took every drop of self-control I possessed to do the same. *Bandits, rapists, spies, and traitors. Well. I'm two out of four. I wonder how they'll execute me if they figure it out?*

Tamar twiddled the bead with her fingers as we walked across the valley. The Alashi were up for the day now; people were carrying buckets of water from a well or stream I hadn't seen, hanging laundry, visiting with friends, mending clothes and boots. A pack of children tore past us; I overheard one of them shout, "Kill the Greeks! Mount up your horses!" They pantomimed leaping onto horseback, waving sticks in the air like swords and spears. I bit my lip, and Tamar smiled a little to herself.

When we reached Janiya's encampment, our male guide bid us an abrupt, embarrassed good-bye; I realized that somewhere we had crossed a border into female territory. The eldress had used the term *sisters,* and everyone in the camp was a woman. Tamar seemed to be one of the youngest; Janiya, the woman who'd met us earlier, was probably the oldest at around forty. Tamar glanced at me; I looked around for Janiya, spotted her, and approached.

She looked us over with clear dismay. "Did the eldress send you to me? *Both* of you?" We nodded. "Well. Put your packs down inside. The sisterhood is just now gathering, so I'll introduce you to everyone later."

We stepped into the round tent Janiya had pointed to. Like the eldress's, the inside was very different from the dull exterior. The walls were hung with the same glittering tapestries; the floor was covered with overlapping wool rugs, and ringed with pillows. Blankets were stacked in a basket near the door. No fire burned in the center of the tent, but a brightly polished copper kettle caught the sunshine that streamed down through the smoke hole. We set our packs down near the door and stepped back outside; the air was cooler inside than out, but the thick wool walls kept out the breeze as well as the heat. We settled ourselves in the shade outside. Tamar lay down, her head on her arm; I stayed awake to observe Janiya and her sisters-in-arms.

More women trickled in, in ones and twos, throughout the morning. Many clearly hadn't seen each other in a while and greeted each other with clear warmth and excitement. Janiya was more formal with the women, clasping arms instead of hugging them. People glanced at Tamar and me with evident curiosity, and I saw Janiya murmur explanations to a few of them. I twisted my blue bead on its thong, wondering if Kyros's aeriko was watching me right now. If it had been around, it certainly hadn't been very useful. I had assumed I would feel more certain of my footing once I reached the Alashi, but if anything, I felt more out of place and nervous than I had in Sophos's harem.

With effort, I recollected myself. *The first step is the same as it's always been,* I told myself. *Observe.* Unlike an aeriko, I could be trusted to analyze and draw conclusions based on what I saw, and to properly report those conclusions. Anyone who dealt with aerika knew they simply withheld anything we didn't specifically ask for.

So. The women here were meeting again for the first time in a while. The eldress had said that the Alashi split into small bands for the dry summer season, both subclans—*families,* I thought I would probably call those—and soldier sisterhoods and brotherhoods. Presumably Janiya commanded a soldier sisterhood. It made sense, I thought, to keep the young men and women separate if they were supposed to concentrate on their military skills. The Sisterhood of the Weavers maintained a small, independent army of swordswomen; they were kept strictly separate from men. I'd encountered a few of these swordswomen on my errand to the Sisterhood. I'd been tempted, at the time, to ask if they were recruiting, but had ended up returning to Kyros, as I always did.

I wondered how the Alashi spent their winters—

surely not in one big camp like this one. I'd have to ask later.

All the women seemed to own weapons, though they were something of a mixed collection. Some owned short, broad swords that looked like they'd been stolen from a Penelopeian armory; others owned curved swords like mine. Others had daggers or spears. Nearly everyone had a bow and a quiver of arrows. The weapons were as immaculately kept as any military commander could ask for—the blades clean and sharp, the leather scabbards well oiled. Greek commanders often owned swords that were as much jewelry as weapons, with gems set into the handle or at the base of the blade, but Janiya's sword seemed as plain and functional as everyone else's.

All the women wore loose linen trousers with a tunic over them, and an embroidered vest over that. I saw bits and pieces of armor stashed around camp—leather vests, padded helmets, gauntlets—but apparently they put it on only if they were expecting trouble.

A few of the soldier sisters had sat near me in the shade of the yurt and I could overhear their conversation a bit. Two of the women were a year or two younger than me: Erdene and Saken. I caught their names after a few minutes of listening. The third, Ruan, was a bit older. Erdene and Saken seemed very close; they suffered Ruan's presence, I decided after listening for a few minutes, mostly out of respect for her seniority rather than fondness for her personally.

"I can't believe you're back," Saken said to Erdene with a laugh. "I heard at the beginning of gathering that you spent all winter . . ."

"I can't believe I'm back, either," Erdene said. "I swear on Arachne's web, Arai and I did it *every night.*" She sighed deeply. "But I bled just last week. I'm definitely not pregnant."

Saken shook her head with a fond smile. "You'll just have to try again next winter."

Erdene brightened a little at the prospect. "But for now, I'll have to cut off my *hair.*" She raked her fingers through black curls that barely reached her shoulders, and let out her breath in an audible wistful sigh. "It's almost long enough to braid properly."

"I've got the scissors right here," Ruan said, holding up a set of shears.

"Thanks, but no thanks, Ruan, I think I'll wait until sundown at least," Erdene said.

Ruan set the scissors down a little stiffly, and Saken took pity on her. "Give them to Erdene; she can cut my hair now," she said.

Erdene took the scissors and trimmed Saken's hair, cutting it into a neat black cap. "Are you ready to lose your locks, Ruan?" Saken asked when she was done. Ruan nodded, and Saken trimmed her hair as Erdene had trimmed hers.

I touched my own matted hair, which undoubtedly reeked of sweat and long-curdled perfume, and was tempted to go ask for the scissors immediately. But there was clearly a way that these things were done, and I didn't want to slip out of step, unknowing, if I didn't have to.

As the sun rose in the sky, Ruan built the fire up a bit, then brought a pot out from the yurt; a short while later I smelled the familiar, earthy smell of lentils and rice. Saken wandered by at around midday and asked, "Is it almost ready? I'm famished." Inhaling the smell of cooking lentils, my nervousness had been almost replaced by ravenous hunger. When was the last time I'd eaten? Just the previous day, I realized after a few moments, but it had been only a fragment of food. There was still a little bit of cheese in our bag, I'd hoarded our food so carefully, and for a moment I was almost tempted to go get it. *No*, I thought. I'll wait and eat with everyone else.

Tamar roused as Ruan and Saken carried a pot out of the yurt. "Are we eating?" she asked, her voice still a little hazy from sleep. I stood up; Tamar clung to my arm, and we turned toward the pot of rice and lentils like the starving vagabonds we were.

Erdene had brought out earthenware bowls; they were golden-red and decorated with pictures of horses. Ruan filled a bowl for Erdene, and a bowl for Saken; others from the camp lined up quickly and got their food. When everyone else had been served, Tamar and I stepped forward.

Ruan looked us up and down with a sneer. "Ah yes. New arrivals to share our food; how lucky we are, to get two at once." She dropped the ladle back into the pot. "Until the welcome banquet tonight, you are not in Janiya's sword sisterhood. See to your own food."

Tamar fell back a step, her face going red, then white. But she was too proud to beg, and I was too desperate to avoid attracting suspicion. "We have food in our bag," I whispered to her, thinking faintly of the tiny morsels of cheese that remained. "We can eat that."

Tamar shook her head, her lips tight. "Wait here," she said, and limped quickly into the yurt. She returned a moment later with the cheese, and unfolded the rag it was wrapped in. "You must be very poor, to have nothing to share with a hungry stranger," she said to Ruan. "Here. We share our surplus with you." And she set the cheese down on the ground, and stalked away.

Saken laughed out loud. "I'd yield now if I were you, Ruan." When Ruan neither picked up the cheese nor the ladle, Saken rolled her eyes, picked up the cheese and two bowls, and filled them herself. "Welcome to both of you, and I accept your invitation to share food. My name is Saken." She handed a bowl to Tamar, and a bowl to me. "Sit beside me, new sisters, and eat." She added, in a low, kind voice, "You can tell me your names when you've filled your stomachs."

I devoured the bowl and she refilled it, offering me a waterskin when I slowed down. I quenched my thirst, then ate some more of the lentils and rice. For the first time since leaving Sophos's house, I was neither thirsty nor hungry. Saken, I noticed when I finally stopped to look up, had eaten the cheese.

"My name is Lauria," I said after scraping the last of the lentils from the bowl. "This is Tamar."

"You have a Greek name," she observed.

"I have a Greek father."

"The man you escaped from?"

"No. I was sold, not long ago."

"We don't talk about that here," Ruan muttered, glaring balefully at Saken.

"It doesn't give them much to talk about if they can't mention their old lives," Saken said.

"What's your point?"

"It doesn't matter," Tamar said. "We don't wish to talk about it."

Saken picked up the scissors from where they were lying on the ground. "During the summer, when we're serving as sword sisters, we all wear our hair short, for convenience."

"And safety," added a short woman with a cleft chin.

"My sister Erdene was planning to wait until sunset, but if you'd like to trim your hair now, you are welcome to."

Tamar's eyes flashed, and she snatched up the scissors, took her hair in one hand, and slashed it off in a single tangled mass. It fell to the ground, nearly as long as her arm. "Sophos never let us cut our hair," she murmured, forgetting Ruan's rule already.

Saken laughed, showing crooked teeth and a dimple. "Actually, it's customary to cut each *other's* hair; I probably should have mentioned that. Maybe Lauria can even it out for you, and then you can cut hers."

Flushing scarlet to her ears, Tamar put the scissors down; I trimmed her hair to match Ruan's and Saken's, and then Tamar took the scissors and cut mine. My neck felt suddenly cool even in the hot sun. "No loss," I said, looking down at the hair around me. "It was tangled past redemption, I think."

We gathered up our shorn hair and, on Saken's instructions, tossed it into a growing pile left by the others. Heaped together like drying grain, the shades of hair were in stark contrast. Thanks to my Greek ancestry, my own hair wasn't the pure black of Saken's—it was a dark nut brown, though so coated with dust it was hard to really see the color. Tamar's hair, when clean, was almost red. Saken's hair was as black as a raven's feathers and almost straight, but Ruan's had a little curl to it. *I'm not the only Alashi to have a Greek father,* I thought, and wondered which of the other sword sisters here had themselves been born as slaves—or who had a mother or a father who'd once crossed the steppe like Tamar and I had.

Saken escorted us back to the yurt, with Erdene tagging along, and had us empty out our bags. Then she inspected our clothes. My boots passed muster, but Tamar's boots made her bite her lip and shake her head disapprovingly. "You'll need a pair that actually fit. I'll take these back to my subclan and see if maybe someone's outgrown a pair recently and could trade with you."

"What do we do about our clothes?" I asked.

"The Unegendai will give you linen and you can make new clothes."

"The . . . Who?"

"Our sponsor subclan. They take care of material needs that we can't meet for ourselves. We herd a few animals, of course, but the subclan provides most of our food, our clothing, and so on. Every subclan supports one of the brotherhoods or sisterhoods."

I nodded, pretending that I understood, while wondering what to do next: did I find the subclan and ask? Did Saken ask for me? Would thread be provided as well, and needles? The clothes were in a different style from the Greek clothes I'd worn in Kyros's household; I wasn't even sure how to cut the cloth for clothes of this style. I was afraid that if I asked too many questions, I'd appear foolish. Like someone who couldn't even begin to simply watch and imitate.

"I'll ask for cloth when I'm looking for a pair of boots for Tamar. You can wear those things for now," Saken said, answering at least one of my questions and reassuring me that I didn't have to ask. "Sit down, Tamar, and let me get the measure of your feet."

Tamar sat and pressed the sole of her foot against the boot that Saken held up; Saken marked where her toes reached with a piece of chalk. "You should show her your feet, Tamar," I said softly, and at Saken's quizzical look Tamar unwrapped her feet. I rose to my own knees to take a look.

The cuts, to my relief, had not festered, but they hadn't healed well, either. Saken looked them over and quickly sent for a woman named Maydan, who apparently was known for a bit of knowledge and a gentle touch. "This one probably should have been stitched when it happened," Maydan said, tracing the largest cut with her forefinger. "Too late now, and it looks to be healing as well as can be expected. I'll wash your foot and bandage you up again, and tell Janiya to go easy on you for a few days, until it heals properly."

"Thank you," Tamar said stiffly. I knew that her instinct was to insist that she could wash her own damn foot, but Saken's kindness had disarmed her a bit and she was able to show a modicum of graciousness. Maydan sponged off the injuries and wrapped Tamar's foot again, this time in clean new linen.

Saken returned before sunset with a different pair of boots and some clothes ready-made. "Hand-me-downs," she said happily, waving the bundle at us. "Come on back into the yurt and you can try everything on."

Saken's family had been perfectly happy to exchange an outgrown pair of boots for a pair that would actually fit her fast-growing younger brother, and had sent the two of us some outgrown clothing besides. Saken outfitted each of us with a pair of dark brown wool pants, a leather belt, a dun-colored linen tunic, and a white linen head scarf that shielded our bare necks from the sun. The only thing we lacked was an embroidered vest of thick black wool, like the one Saken wore. "You'll make your own vests later," she said. "We make new ones each year anyway. For now at least you've got some clothes, and they fit you just fine."

They did fit us; Saken clearly had an excellent eye. Tamar buttoned her tunic and buckled her leather belt with an almost exaggerated care; I thought of the flimsy shifts we'd worn in the harem and wondered what she'd had to wear as a kitchen maid. *I probably wouldn't have had a belt as a stable hand, either,* I thought, and fingered the leather strap. Tamar was far too fascinated by her own new clothes to notice my own reaction to mine, but Saken might.

The sun was going down; Ruan had built up the campfire a bit and the rest of the sisterhood had gathered. At Saken's invitation, Tamar and I sat down beside her and Erdene; a few minutes later, we belatedly leapt to our feet, imitating everyone else. Janiya had arrived.

Janiya smiled broadly around the circle, basking for a moment in the affection of her troops. "It's been a good winter," she said, and there was a ripple of amusement through the sisterhood. "But it's going to be an even *better* summer." A shriek of approval. "We have two new sisters, Tamar and Lauria." She waved in our direction, and everyone turned to look, though I'd have sworn anyone curious had taken a good hard look at us during the long afternoon. "To welcome them, and to celebrate our new season together, we feast tonight! But don't stuff yourself sick; we break camp at dawn tomorrow and head out onto the steppe." Janiya sat down, dished herself some of the food, and everyone else immediately dug in.

The "feast," such as it was, featured mostly goat meat; it wasn't a terribly young goat, and the meat was greasy and gamey. I hadn't been fussy when I ate that afternoon, I was so hungry, but now that I was no longer on the brink of starvation I noticed how strange the spices were, not at all like the Greek spices I was used to. The rice and lentils were mixed with a strange sauce; there were vegetables in the mix, but small pieces. I was hungry enough that I dug in with a will anyway, but I knew that within a few weeks I would be very tired of the taste of Alashi food.

"Where do you get the rice and lentils?" I asked Saken. "You don't grow them, do you?"

She laughed. "No, we don't grow them. We trade for them with the people north of the steppe; just because the Greeks think we're dangerous outlaws doesn't mean the rest of the world feels that way."

"What do you—" I paused. "What do *we* trade for them?"

"Horses, mostly. Our horses are the best anywhere, everyone knows that. We also keep our eyes open for karenite, that's a pretty stone you can find on the steppe—we carve it into shapes and make it into jewelry. There's a constant demand for it."

"And the weapons? Where do they come from?"

"Some of them come from raids on the Greeks, others we trade for, others we make. That's an awfully nice sword you've got; you're lucky."

Saken scraped her plate clean, sucking every drop of juice and gravy from her fingers, and I imitated her. We scrubbed our plates with sand when we were done, and wiped them clean, stacking them in the yurt, where they would be packed in the morning. Saken came by to give each of us a small clay cup of something; expecting water or wine, I took a ready swallow and nearly gagged. It was something thick and sour; forcing down what was in my mouth, I smelled it cautiously. "It's kumiss," Saken said. "Fermented mare's milk." She was enthusiastic and I tried to force a smile and nod while sneaking a look at Tamar, to see how she was reacting to it. Tamar's expression was far more openly shocked than mine; then she set her jaw and drained the cup.

I took a deep breath and steeled myself to do the same, but then changed my mind, afraid that I *would* gag and vomit up my dinner. Instead, I took another sip. Another. It was alcoholic; I tried to tell myself that it was merely bad wine, but the worst piss water I'd ever drunk at least didn't have the throat-clogging sticky *thickness* of this stuff. I forced down another sip, wanting to discreetly dump it out but fearing that someone would see me—for all I knew, it might constitute sacrilege of some kind to throw it away. I looked down in the cup; one final gulp would do it. I steeled myself, downed it, and shuddered.

"You finished that fast!" observed a woman sitting near us. "Would you like some more?"

"No! Thank you." I saw the look of mirth on her face after I'd answered and realized that she knew perfectly well what I thought of the stuff, and was teasing me. I managed a ghost of a smile in return.

The fire was burning down; Erdene tossed on more of the dried animal manure the Alashi used as fuel. A gust of wind made it flicker, then flare higher momentarily; I saw that Ruan was watching me and smirking. I scowled and turned away from her. Erdene fetched a big kettle and placed it in the flames to heat.

One of the other women had slipped away from camp a few minutes ago; now she was back, carrying a sack. "I've got the wool," she said, with a broad smile. "It's time."

Ruan went into the yurt and returned with a large straw mat; one of the other women helped her unroll it into a rectangle the size of a very large rug. Then she held up the scissors. "Anyone left?" she said.

Erdene stepped forward, sighing dolefully, and Ruan gave the scissors to Saken. With a flourish, Saken snipped off Erdene's black curls, and tossed them into the pile with the rest of the hair. "That's all of us," Erdene said.

Erdene and Saken held open a large sack; Maydan, the woman who'd tended Tamar's feet, gathered up the shorn hair and dumped it into the sack. When every scrap had been retrieved, the sack was closed and shaken vigorously, then emptied out onto the reed mat. The women carefully distributed the hair so that it was evenly scattered over the mat; there was enough that at least a scattering of hair could reach from end to end. Even with it all mixed together, I thought I saw a handful of reddish hair that had come from Tamar. Then they took out big handfuls of black wool from the other sack, and spread it out over the mat, fluffy, thick, and even.

"The water's ready," Erdene said.

Janiya had stood back for this entire operation; now she took her place at one end of the mat and gestured; the sisterhood formed a circle around it, clasping hands. I counted, for the first time: with Tamar and me, there were twenty-one women in the sisterhood. "We are sisters, bound through our duty," Janiya said. "We are sisters, bound in shared water. We are sisters, bound through the mingling of our bodies." She paused, and Saken and Erdene picked up the kettle and poured steaming water down over the wool, hair, and mat, soaking every inch.

"Bound in Arachne's tightest web; wrapped in Arachne's purest cloth," Janiya said. "Bind us together, bind us together, make us one."

We broke the circle and stepped back; three of the other women rolled up the mat, the wet wool and hair bound inside. They each pinned the mat under one knee to press it tightly together. When it was done, they tied it shut. The ritual complete, Saken happily brought out the jug of kumiss again, but thankfully didn't try to force any of it on me.

"What was that about?" Tamar whispered. I shrugged. Saken couldn't have overheard, but she came over when she was done filling cups to explain.

"We'll drag that along behind our horses tomorrow," she said. "The wool and our hair will lock together and become black felt—we call it sister-cloth. We'll cut up the felt and use it to make vests." She smiled and lifted the jug. "More kumiss?"

"No thank you," I said.

Her face fell slightly and she said, "You've been through a lot. If you want to go lie down, I can show you where you'll sleep."

"I'd appreciate that," I said, so Saken showed me to a spot in one of the yurts. Apparently I was supposed to just lie down on the rugs on the floor; she gave me one of the pillows—it had a quilted appliqué of a sun and a spider—and a blanket, which was relatively unadorned, only having alternating stripes of yellow and white.

"Good night," she said kindly.

Tamar lay down beside me. "You can stay out by the fire if you want," I said as she curled up in the blanket Saken had given her. "You don't have to go to bed early just because I am."

"Thanks," Tamar said. "Saken is nice, but I'd rather not be out there all on my own."

The blanket smelled rather strongly of sheep. I had expected to lie awake worrying—about my mission, about the tests to come, about Ruan, about Janiya— but I had underestimated how truly exhausted I was. The rugs were less comfortable than my soft bed back at Kyros's house, but they were a great deal more comfortable than the ground had been while we were traveling. I fell asleep almost immediately.

*L*auria!"

Waking with Tamar's face before me, for one moment of dizzying terror I thought I was back in Sophos's harem. But I smelled wood smoke and curried goat and wool felt, and a moment later the memory of our trip caught up with me. "What?" I whispered. "What's wrong?"

"You were moaning in your sleep, whimpering. I thought you were having a nightmare."

I lay back down. "I think I was," I said. "Thank you for waking me."

"*Shut up,*" another voice hissed out of the dark; I wasn't sure whose. "Bad enough when blossoms *snore.*"

I fell silent and put my head back down, but now I

couldn't sleep. After a while, I got up—I was sleeping close to the door—and tiptoed out. The stars were fading, but it wasn't yet dawn. *I suppose it's not surprising that I can't fall back to sleep. Just yesterday, this would still have been prime walking time.* I wrapped my blanket around my shoulders and sat down, wondering if there was something useful I could do, since I was up. Probably, but I had no idea what. I could fetch water if I knew where the bucket was. And how to get to that stream I saw yesterday. And how to get back here from the stream. I sighed. I felt very lost, and very *foreign*. Even for Tamar, I suspected, this didn't exactly feel like coming home.

I heard a rustle behind me. "Hey," Tamar whispered. "I couldn't sleep."

"If we're going to sit around and talk we should probably go a little farther from the yurt," I whispered, thinking of the vicious hiss inside. She nodded, and we strolled over to the banked coals of last night's fire. The rolled-up reed mat still lay on the ground nearby.

"What do you think so far?" Tamar asked.

"I'd rather hear what you think," I said.

She took a deep breath and let it out in a whoosh. "The Alashi are everything I ever dreamed they were," she said. "Everything I ever dreamed of becoming." She studied the ground and half smiled. "I kind of wish I were one of them already and didn't have to go through their tests." She pulled the blue bead out from under her shirt and studied it in the dim light. "And Ruan's a jerk."

"I think there are jerks everywhere."

"Yeah." Tamar sighed again. "It's just—well. I'm sure you're right."

They sky was lightening from black to charcoal gray; there was enough light now for me to clearly make out the shapes of the camp around me. Somewhere far away, I heard the single low tone of a horn made from a sheep's horn. Then another; then another. Beyond the camp, we could hear the vast rustle of thousands of Alashi stirring. Dawn approached; the camp was awaking.

I turned back to the yurt. Ruan stood in the doorway. From her face, I thought she'd been there for some time; she'd probably heard us talking about her. Tamar saw as well, and I saw her go rigid. "Be easy," I whispered in her ear. "She already hated us." Tamar smiled, then laughed. She straightened her skinny shoulders and waved brightly at Ruan. "Good morning!" she called. Ruan narrowed her eyes and stomped away. For the first time since we had arrived at the Alashi camp, I felt my stomach unknot slightly.

CHAPTER FIVE

"Lauria! Tamar!" Janiya rode up, leading two horses behind her. "You'll both need horses for the ride out. These two mares are gentle and predictable—suitable mounts for inexperienced riders. Have either of you ridden a horse before?"

Tamar shook her head. I nodded: "I used to work in the stables."

"Among the Alashi, you'll still find that you'll need a gentle mount at first." She dismounted. "Tamar, you'll ride Kesh. Lauria, you'll ride Kara. Take the reins and follow me; we're going to need to step outside of camp to learn the basics."

Tamar took the reins in her hand, looking like she expected the horse to try to take a bite out of her. I was glad I didn't have to feign that sort of nervousness. I took the reins with more confidence; our horses plodded calmly behind us until we were beyond the tents and out on the open hills.

The Alashi saddle was different from the Greek style. It came up high in front and in back, and was made with much more padding. The stirrups were better made and better attached, though they were so far off the ground I wondered how anyone actually got her foot up into one.

"The basics of riding a horse really aren't that difficult," Janiya said. "Always approach from the horse's left side. To get on, hold the saddle, put your foot in the stirrup, step up, and swing your leg over." She demonstrated. I followed her lead, then watched Tamar. Tamar could barely reach the stirrup with her foot, but she grabbed the saddle, swung herself up, and landed, exhilarated, on the horse's back. Janiya nodded slightly, unsmiling. "There you go. To get off, you just reverse the process. Tuck your foot into the stirrup, grab the saddle, swing your leg back over, and lower yourself to the ground." I dismounted; Tamar hesitantly followed along again, sliding gracefully to her feet beside the horse.

"To tell your horse to move forward, nudge her a little with your knees. And sit back when you want her to slow down or stop, or pull her the reins—*gently*. You don't have to intimidate your horse; these are horses we give to children to ride. They want to take you where you want to go—just tell them, gently, where that is and they'll do it." She looked gravely from my face to Tamar's; satisfied with whatever she found there, she went on. "To guide her in a direction, for now, you can turn her head gently with the reins. To go to the right, tug to the right; left, tug to the left. When you fall off—and you will, sooner or later—try to land on your side and roll. Now mount again, and we'll practice."

Contrary to Janiya's apparent fears, Tamar had a gentle, almost cautious touch with her horse. We rode our horses at a walk out to a large boulder and then back, several times. The saddle was more comfortable to sit in than the Greek saddle, but had a strange, foreign feel; comfortable or not, it wasn't what I was used to. *Just as well.* It would make it easier for me to look uncomfortable, and less likely that I'd find myself executed with the bandits and rapists . . .

When Janiya was satisfied that we were comfortable with walking, she had us encourage our horses to a faster pace. Back again, Janiya was reasonably pleased. "You can dismount now," she said. "Lead your horses back to the camp; you'll fetch water for them, then we'll all pack to leave." Tamar watched me stroke Kara's neck and carefully mimicked me. That brought a reluctant smile to Janiya's lips. "We'll have some treats for the horses before we go. You can each feed your horse an apple, so that Kesh and Kara will know that you're their friends."

When we returned from the stream with buckets of water, Saken bustled over to give us instructions on what to do to help get the sisterhood ready to leave. She put Tamar to work counting waterskins and checking each for leaks; she had me shovel scoops of lentils from a huge heap into smaller sacks of oiled linen, then loosely sew each sack shut when I was done. Five of the other women joined Saken in dismantling the yurts. They came apart in pieces. First the contents were moved out and packed up: every rug, hanging, trunk, and spindle. Then the huge pieces of black wool that formed the roof and the walls were taken down and rolled up. This exposed the skeleton of the yurt, a series of panels of crisscrossed wood, lashed together. The thongs and ropes that bound them together were painstakingly untied, and the panels that formed the framework were stacked and tied together. Finally, the ashes from the hearth at the center (though I hadn't seen a fire burning inside since I arrived) were carefully swept away.

While all this was going on, most of the other women had left the camp. I found out where they'd gone when they returned with an entire herd of animals. There were at least two horses for each woman—each woman had a primary mount, like Kara and Kesh, but there were plenty to spare. The herd also included camels, goats, and sheep; finally, there were three dogs that tore excitedly around our camp before trotting obediently to Janiya, to help keep the sheep and goats from wandering off.

Though Tamar and I tried to help, and Saken tried to let us, we were more of a hindrance than anything else for the next step: everything in the camp, from swords to lentils, jewelry to rugs, yurt frame to leftover dried animal dung, was loaded onto the animals. The horses bore some of it; the camels bore the rest. Every animal was loaded with a precise, balanced load, tied so that it wouldn't bounce and bruise them, or rub badly and leave a sore. Even Kesh and Kara were loaded with waterskins and some of the food. To the back of one horse's saddle, Janiya tied two ropes that hung slack; those went to the rolled-up reed mats that crushed black wool together with our shorn hair. "These will drag along behind," Saken explained. "Bouncing over the ground helps to compress the fibers."

We were ready before most of the other Alashi. Our camp was a tiny, bare hole in the still-roiling sea of yurts, animals, and people. I expected to ride out at that point, but there seemed to be one last task; everyone still stood by her horse, holding the reins and waiting. And then—a short blast from a horn. The eldress approached, sitting gracefully on a huge black horse. "Janiya," she said gravely, and Janiya placed her hand flat over her heart and bowed.

"All has been made ready," Janiya said.

"Until the rivers return," the eldress said.

"May it be soon."

"For now, take this with my trust and blessings." The eldress presented Janiya with a horn; it was small and curved, made from a polished sheep's horn, not much bigger than my hand. Metal had been fitted around it, and a chain to that, and Janiya hung it carefully around her neck.

"You'll take the Ash River grazing grounds for the summer. We will see you at the fall gathering."

Janiya saluted again, then lifted the horn to her lips and blew.

"Move out!" she ordered. We mounted our horses, and I rode out onto the open steppe with Janiya's sisterhood.

The mood, riding out, was festive. Saken and three others urged their horses to a gallop, racing across the plain ahead of the herd animals and the rest of us; Saken's friend Erdene took a turn riding the horse dragging the felt, and chatted with Tamar and me. "What are the Ash River grazing grounds?" Tamar asked.

"The Ash River is a little creek that runs through that part of the steppe; it's fed by a spring and runs even in the summer. We call it the Ash River because the stones on the bottom are gray, like ashes. They're excellent grazing grounds. I think the eldress is being nice to us because we have two new recruits." She said it kindly, but Tamar flushed a little anyway. "The Alashi all split up during the summer; there's nowhere with enough water and grass to take care of *all* of us and *all* our animals for very long. The unmarried men and women split off into sword brotherhoods and sword sisterhoods." Erdene sighed, a little bitterly. "The subclans . . . well, some of them stay nearby. Others travel north to trade for lentils and rice, things we can't grow ourselves."

"Erdene!" It was Saken, circling back, another woman beside her, and with a quick smile, Erdene switched back to her own horse and urged it forward to join Saken, while the new woman mounted the horse that was dragging the felt.

Riding in the back with Tamar, I observed the other women as carefully as I could. There was Ruan, who seemed so intent on intimidating us; everyone, I decided, was cordial to her, but she had no special friend. Of course, Janiya had no special friends, either. The commander rode near the middle of the group, yet alone. Erdene and Saken were clearly best friends; Maydan, the healer, rode beside the woman who'd offered me more kumiss—Jolay, I remembered her name was, and she had a musical laugh that carried over the steppe better than Janiya's horn.

Toward the end of the morning, Jolay took a turn with the felt. Maydan dropped back to ride beside her. "Have you met Maydan?" Jolay asked us.

"They've met *me* but I don't think they've met *you*," Maydan said. "I patched up Tamar's feet when they arrived."

"They met me," Jolay said with mock indignation. "Alone of all the sisters, I personally made *certain* that they had sufficient kumiss during the celebration last night."

Maydan giggled. "I'm sure they *deeply* appreciated it." She gave me a sidelong smile that made it clear that she, like Jolay, was aware that newcomers to the Alashi weren't always fond of the stuff.

"Yeah, well, I think I deserve some credit for my hospitality."

"They say the Greeks have servants that do nothing but pour wine—maybe we'll make you the kumiss-pourer for the sisterhood."

"*You* get out of real work because of *your* talents; I don't know why I should have to pick up manure when I'm so talented at pouring kumiss," Jolay said.

We stopped to rest at midday. "You two are doing well," Janiya said, as Tamar and I slid to the ground. Tamar moved gingerly; her legs were already aching, I knew, and raw from the saddle. Since I was used to riding, I felt a bit better than she did—but even for me, it had been close to a month now since I'd bid good-bye to Zhade, and the saddle was not shaped quite like a Greek saddle. My body held aches I hadn't felt in a long time. I stretched my muscles, wishing I'd done so before mounting the horse to begin with, then sat down with the others and took a share of lunch: mare's-milk cheese, thin flat bread that had been cooked that morning, and dried apples. The cheese was sour but not too bad—better by far than the vile milk drink Jolay had offered me more of. I had a bad feeling that I'd be drinking kumiss again, and probably soon.

Maydan wandered back over as we were finishing our cheese. "How are your legs doing?" she asked. "Any soreness?"

"I'm fine," Tamar said.

"Me, too," I said. I had some aches, but not that bad.

Maydan laughed. "Janiya was right," she said. "She thought you were both the 'I'm fine, leave me alone' type. Drop your pants; I'm taking a look at your legs myself."

Tamar's face went red to her ears—Ruan was staring at us both with an amused smile—but I was too panicked to feel shame. Would Maydan be able to read my past in my skin? The look on Maydan's face made it clear that I was not going to be able to get out of this; setting my teeth, I untied the drawstring of my pants and let Maydan check me for saddle sores. To my intense relief, her touch was light and her examination very brief. "No blisters," she said. "You're not so bad. Here's a salve, spread it on each night if you think you need it." She slapped a small clay pot into my hand. It reeked of unwashed wool. Tamar's saddle sores rated a sigh, a scolding for having lied about her condition, and a larger pot of salve with stricter instructions to use it. Tamar withdrew with the pot to a more private spot and returned a few minutes later, still walking gingerly.

"What fragile little apple blossoms you are," Ruan said. "Needing *salve* from a healer just to ride a horse."

I ignored her and stalked back to my horse, putting the pot into one of the open saddlebags near the back. "Oh, you must think you're going to *need* it, too," Ruan called after me. "You're keeping it right where you can get at it . . . ."

"That's right," I said. "I might need the pot to throw at your head."

I thought there was a ripple of amusement, but for the most part the sisterhood seemed to be ignoring both Ruan's taunts and my response. Ruan stepped closer to me, her eyes narrowing. "Maybe you don't know how we settle our differences here, blossom, so I'll fill you in. When we fight, we *fight*. Unarmed combat: fists and feet. Till someone gives up. And anytime you want to challenge me, *slave girl,* just let me know." She turned on one heel and strode away.

Despite myself, I was shaken. I didn't actually really fear that Ruan could hurt me; Sophos had been able to rape me because he was armed, I was drugged, and I wasn't suspicious until it was too late. The knife that had been within my grasp flashed briefly through my mind; I pushed it away. I could hold my own in a fair fight. But it could compromise my identity. Though undoubtedly slaves fought among themselves occasionally, I had picked fights with most of the boys in my neighborhood. I doubted that your average six-year-old slave girl had scrapped with the other slave children quite so often.

I glanced at Tamar; she was white-faced and white-lipped. Definitely not someone who thought back to fistfights with neighbor boys with mild nostalgia. In Tamar's experience, a raised fist meant a beating. A slave who fought with another slave would likely be punished; a slave who raised her hand to her master might well be killed. I finished tucking the salve away and squatted down next to Tamar. "She doesn't own us," I whispered. "If she tries to hurt you, just hurt her back."

Tamar shook her head, not saying anything.

"Don't worry if you don't know how to fight. They'll teach us soon enough." *And if they don't, I'll teach you how to make a fist and swing when the other person isn't looking. Before I do—whatever it is that Kyros has me do. You deserve better than to be a target for bullies like Ruan.*

We rode through the afternoon and into the twilight; the light was fading and we were still riding. I had begun to wonder if we were simply going to ride through the night when someone crested a low rise and called, "There it is!" There were glad exclamations around us, and we all urged our tired horses faster.

"It" turned out to be a small cairn of stones marking a well. Janiya unpacked a bucket with a long rope tied to its handle and then coiled neatly inside the bucket. Over the well, she quickly fitted together a small frame so that the rope could be drawn over a bar instead of pulled straight up. Finally, she drove a metal stake with a loop at one end straight into the ground, and tied the loose end of the rope to the stake. She lowered the bucket down into the well; we heard a faint splash as it hit the water. "Right," she said to me and Tamar. "Start drawing water."

It was one of the few tasks that we couldn't screw up. Another bucket appeared moments later, and we took turns, one of us drawing up the new bucket of water and draining it into the second bucket, and the other carrying the second bucket to wherever water seemed to be needed now: to the animal trough, first, for the horses, goats, sheep, and camels; then, when all the animals had drunk their fill, to a second trough, where the women refilled their waterskins. Finally, a large metal kettle was set out, and we filled that. It took a long time, and by the end, our arms and backs were as sore as our legs.

While we drew water, the other women set up the camp: the framework for the yurt was lashed together, the wool and canvas was bound to it, the roof drawn over the top. Dried animal dung was unpacked and lit; some of the water we'd drawn was mixed with rice and lentils and set over the fire. The horses and camels were all unloaded, the horses' saddles removed, and the horses rubbed down and groomed as well as fed and watered—Kara and Kesh as well. The sisters worked together efficiently; I wondered whose job drawing water *would* have been, since I saw no one standing idle.

When the troughs were full and seemed to be staying full, dinner was ready. Ruan served the stew; she made no comment as she dished up lentils and rice for me or Tamar, but she made no eye contact, either. I was already growing tired of Alashi spices, and had little appetite for the food, though I finished my bowl.

"Is it all right if I have a little more?" Tamar asked.

Ruan held out her hand in response; Tamar handed her the bowl and Ruan filled it again. I thought of the meager portions at Sophos's—foreign spices or not, for Tamar it was a treat just to be able to fill her stomach.

To my relief, the kumiss didn't come out; everyone just got out the blankets and went to sleep. Tamar and I slept in the same yurt we'd slept in the previous night; in addition to us and Ruan, five other women slept inside: Saken, Erdene, Maydan, Jolay, and a woman I didn't know yet. The stranger unrolled her blanket close to mine; she had raven-black hair and dark eyes, and smelled faintly of incense. No one really had the energy for conversation, but she flashed me a brief smile as she laid out her bed. "I'm Zhanna," she said. "It's nice to have you with us."

"Thank you," I said. A moment too late, I heard the slight bitter edge in my voice.

Zhanna sat back on her heels, running her fingers through her cropped hair to work a little of the sand out. "No, I mean it," she said. "I love getting new people. I've served with the sisterhood for eight summers now, and it's nice to spend a little time with someone I don't already know."

Across the tent, I heard a contemptuous grunt from Ruan. Zhanna shrugged and shook her head, and then lay down to sleep. I lay down as well; despite my aching legs, back, and arms, and despite the snores coming from somewhere far too close to my head, I fell almost instantly into a dreamless sleep.

We woke at dawn, and Janiya set Tamar and me to work drawing water again. I clenched my teeth and said nothing as we drew up bucket after bucket. Fortunately it didn't take as much water to satisfy the animals after a cool, quiet night, and by the time the yurt was down and packed, we were done as well. Saken led our horses over to where we were, saddled and ready. "We'll teach you to saddle them up and everything else once we get to the Ash River grazing ground," she said. "How are your legs?"

"Fine," I said. I realized only after I'd spit the word out how defensive I sounded. Tamar just nodded.

Saken laughed. "There's no shame in being sore! We're all soft after the winter, and you're not the only ones here with a jar of salve. I had Maydan make me up one last night, too."

But we *were* the only ones who had had to drop

our trousers to let Maydan inspect us. Saken probably guessed what I was thinking because she laughed again and poked my arm playfully. "Next time just admit when you're sore. She only pulls rank if she thinks she can't trust you to be sensible instead of stoic. Don't act so *Greek,* refusing bandages when you're bleeding from every limb."

I laughed a little at that, and Saken gave me a pat on the shoulder and went to get her own horse.

The steppe we were on got a bit more moisture than the hills around Elpisia—the spring rains were heavier and lasted longer. The low hills flattened out as we rode today, and became almost a plain, covered in rippling grasses high enough to brush the soles of my boots as I rode. The green grasses were everywhere, but we also rode through patches of scarlet poppies, vivid yellow and purple flowers that spilled from vines that climbed anything they could find, and something that smelled vividly of honey. We reached the Ash River in early afternoon—it cut through the green fields like a narrow silver chain. Spindly trees stood in knee-high water; the spring rains, I thought, had swollen the stream a bit.

I urged my horse a little to fall in step beside Saken. "What's it like in high summer?" I asked.

"An ice-cold trickle. It's spring-fed and sticks around all year."

I nodded, thinking in relief that at least I wouldn't be hauling buckets up from the bottom of the well. No doubt there would be some other just-as-unpleasant task. Someone this morning had gathered up all the animal dung and put it in sacks to bring along and dry out; perhaps that would be my next job. I sighed and tried to cheer myself up with the thought that my *real* job was working for Kyros. But that made me feel guilty that I'd done little real observation. I spent the rest of the afternoon trying to observe the sisterhood, but my legs hurt so badly that mostly I just focused on staying on my horse.

We followed the stream for several days, finally reaching our camp early one afternoon. It was by a bend in the stream, and like the well, was marked with a cairn. The cairn seemed a bit redundant to me, as three good-sized tamarisk trees grew right by it. We dismounted and led our horses to the stream for a drink; the camels and other livestock had a drink as well, then set to work grazing. One of the camels tried to nibble at the leaves of the tree and was firmly warned off by Erdene.

"Let's show you how to unpack your horses," Saken said.

"Lauria used to work in a stable," Tamar said.

Saken glanced at me with a flash of interest, then shrugged. "Lauria, why don't you show Tamar what to do, then?"

A knot of panic twisted in my stomach. To perform as a stable hand, with an observer? I wished that Tamar had kept her mouth shut. "I worked in a Greek stable, not an Alashi one," I said. "I don't know if we did things the same way you do them here . . ."

"I'll let you know if you do something wrong," Saken said, and stepped back to watch. Under her supervision, I helped Tamar to unload, unsaddle, and rub down the packhorses and remounts. Ordinarily I would have found the task pleasant, even soothing— certainly preferable to hauling water. But now my stomach churned and I had to breathe deeply and remind myself that I had groomed my own horse thousands of times since going to work for Kyros, and the stable hands groomed the horses the same way. Of course, I was unfamiliar with the Alashi saddle and other equipment, and Saken stepped in to help us. Other than that, she seemed to see nothing wrong with my approach. Tamar, though, seemed to sense my nervousness; she glanced at me a few times, a worried look on her face, as if she knew she'd done something wrong by pointing out that I'd worked with horses before.

"Do we have to move again tomorrow?" Tamar asked Saken.

"Oh no. We'll be here for a couple of weeks. When the animals have all the grass that's easy to walk to, then we'll move on down the river a bit."

Tamar nodded and turned back to the horse she was grooming with evident relief.

"Hey!" The vicious tone had to be Ruan, and sure enough, it was Ruan who ripped the curry comb out of Tamar's hands. "That is *my* horse."

"It's a remount," Saken said defensively.

"I rode her today, she's mine to groom."

"You have your task, she has hers," Saken said. "*I* told her to groom this horse, Ruan sweetie, so if you've got a complaint, take it up with me."

Ruan elbowed Tamar aside and gave Saken a glare. "I take care of my own mounts, Saken. I don't need some blossom to do it."

Saken rolled her eyes. "Yeah, Ruan, fine. And when they make dinner, you can make your own soup that night, too, so you don't have to eat something that came from a blossom's hands. But what will you do when they're learning to set up the yurt? Sleep outside until we move?"

"I. Want to. Groom. *My own horse.* Is that so hard to understand?" Ruan threw the curry comb to the ground, slipped a sweet to the horse, and stomped off; the horse trailed after her, happy enough to spend more time with her. *Better the horse than us.*

Saken shrugged. "Well, the next horse was ridden by Gulim for part of the day. She'll just be glad you're learning horse care today and not cooking, since horse care really *is* supposed to be one of the first tasks a recruit learns. I think she was annoyed yesterday that you were put to work drawing water."

"I'd have been glad to let Gulim do it," I said.

"Oh, of course. Janiya stuck you with it because we reached the well so late, there really wasn't time to let you learn a new task. And you had to do *something*. Drawing the water didn't require a lesson."

"It was fine," Tamar said, raising her chin. "I was just glad we could do something useful."

As I'd expected, the kumiss came out again after dinner, and while I could have refused it, I knew that to fit in I needed to drink with everyone else. From the look on Tamar's face as she held out her cup for Erdene to fill, she'd had the same realization. I took a deep breath, then a gulp of the kumiss. I told myself that it wasn't quite as horrible when you knew what to expect. "Yogurt," Tamar muttered. "Think of it as really thin yogurt."

I had never much liked yogurt, either. I swirled the cup, stared in it with distaste, then took another gulp. "It's like thick vinegar."

"I'd rather think of it as thin yogurt," Tamar said,

and forced down a sip. "Did you ever get to drink wine, at Kyros's?"

I wondered what the hell the right answer was to *that* question. "On festival days," I improvised. "We each got a little. Also, there was an older slave who would get drunk sometimes. I have no idea where he got the wine, though."

"When we went *downstairs* at Sophos's, the men would often offer us wine." She sighed and leaned back on her elbow, staring into the kumiss. "I suppose you never did the lineup, did you? You were gone too fast for that."

"What lineup?"

"You know, when all the concubines went downstairs after dinner."

Someone—Jolay; I dredged up her name after a moment—had brought out a dombra, Erdene had a flute, and Maydan and a woman whose name I hadn't learned yet had drums. Maydan sat cross-legged on the far side of the fire and began to tap her drum: *dum duppa duppa dum dum. Dum duppa duppa dum dum.* The other woman slapped her drum with a ringing crash and Erdene and Jolay joined in. Other women began to get up to dance. Saken went first, circling her hips and then swirling herself into a spin, while the other women hung back for a moment to watch. Tamar watched with them, a little bleakly. "When Sophos had guests, after dinner, we'd all go downstairs, and usually first we'd dance. We danced together; you saw us practicing. How long we'd dance—well, Boradai would make the call, depending on how much the men seemed to be enjoying the spectacle, how drunk they were, how late it was, and so on. When we were done, if Sophos had a particularly honored guest that night, we'd line up so he could choose the one he wanted. Once that guest had chosen, the other men there—Sophos, other guests— would stand up and choose a girl for the night, or a boy. They didn't always take you back to their room. Sometimes they'd have you sit with them at dinner and drink some wine. So every now and then I'd have wine. I didn't much like it."

I remembered the cloying taste of the drugged wine Tamar had given me that one night, and shuddered. I wanted to rinse my mouth suddenly, but had no water handy, and I knew that the taste of kumiss would truly make me gag. I set my cup down.

"Girls are always given a little wine before their first time. It's supposed to make it a little easier for them. The drugs, too."

I really didn't want to think about this, but I didn't want to get up and dance, either. "Talk to me about something else, Tamar," I said. "Please?"

She was silent for a little while, then said, "I miss Jaran."

"The shaman," I said. "Right?"

"Yes. He was apprenticing me. I had learned most of the rituals; there were a few left, but he thought that on the night of the summer solstice, we could invite one of the djinn through the Bright Gates to visit me."

"Maybe there's a shaman here . . ."

"They all worship Prometheus."

"There must be a shaman. Who would banish rogue djinni? Even the worshippers of Athena have to go to a shaman for that."

"I wonder if the women in the Sisterhood of Weavers ever get possessed by djinn? Do you suppose they just spit it out into one of their necklaces and bind it up on the spot?"

I shrugged, for once not dissembling. I had no idea. The Sisterhood didn't exactly chat with messengers about the technical details of summoning and binding aerika.

Saken sat down beside us, breathless, and refilled our cups with kumiss. "Are you having fun? You're not dancing!"

"I don't much like dancing," Tamar said.

"And I'm terrible at it. I'd rather watch you," I said.

"Oh . . . well. Just so long as you aren't homesick and miserable."

"Never!" Tamar said.

Saken poured herself some kumiss, too, and gulped half of it down on the spot. "Well, I'm going to go dance some more—catch you later!" She got back up, now a little unsteady on her feet, and stumbled back into the circle. Ruan was dancing now, I saw, to raucous approval. She was an excellent dancer. Far better than me, or even Tamar. I felt a twinge of disappointment at seeing her skill. I forced down a little more of the kumiss.

The evening wore on. It was clearly the big first-night-back-with-the-sisters party, now that we'd reached the grazing grounds, and I knew I couldn't go to bed. Though privately I had to admit that Saken's question had struck home. I *was* homesick, and I *was* miserable. Not that I wanted to be back with Sophos; the thought made me shudder and reach, despite the taste, for another gulp of the kumiss. No, I wanted to be back with Kyros. Doing tasks I knew I could accomplish; riding Zhade, not Kara. Sleeping in my bed in my own quiet room. Eating Greek food, wearing Greek clothes, worshipping a Greek goddess who hadn't run away from Olympus to become goddess of a bunch of troublesome nomads. Not having to constantly watch my tongue lest I say *aerika* instead of *djinni*. I missed the privacy. I missed the *respect. Accomplish your task, then; the sooner you're done, the sooner you'll be back there. And the sooner you'll be able to have Sophos staked out in the desert for the vultures as well.* What was my task? Well, to earn those damn beads, I supposed. I touched the single cerulean bead that rested under my collar, and thought, *Staying here, miserable at the party, is my task right now. I might as well make the best of it.* But I still didn't get up to dance.

Very late, I found myself sitting, half in a stupor, with an even more drunk Tamar, Erdene, and Gulim—Gulim, the one who wanted us to do tasks in the *right* order, who also, as it turned out, was the one who played the drums along with Maydan. Gulim flopped down on her back and pressed her hands to her head. "I think I had too much kumiss."

"I know you had too much kumiss," Erdene said, and giggled uncontrollably.

"You're the *recruit,*" Gulim said, blinking at me. "And you're the *other* recruit." She didn't quite manage to focus on Tamar. "I should probably ask you if you have any questions. About—this." She waved her hand and closed her eyes again.

I had a hundred questions, of course. Were there shamans here, and if not, how did they get rid of rogue djinni? How many of these women were lovers? How many beads did I need to earn? What the hell *were* the tests and was Gulim drunk enough to be persuaded to explain to me what I had to do to pass them? I was drunk enough to think it was a good idea to ask them, but by the time I had decided that the test question was by far the most important and I should go ahead and ask that one first, Gulim had either fallen asleep or passed out.

I woke with the sun in my eyes and a raging headache. Someone had thrown a blanket over me where I'd dropped; Gulim still lay beside me, snoring. Tamar was rubbing her eyes, one hand pressed to the side of her head. Janiya stared down at both of us, her eyes bloodshot but looking wide-awake. "It's time for your first test," she said. "Get up and get ready. You're going to go out, on foot, and bring back a piece of karenite."

We stumbled out from under our blankets. "Move!" Janiya said.

"I don't even know what karenite looks like," Tamar said.

Janiya held out a stone, turning it back and forth in her hand so that it caught the light. It was plain gray until you saw it at the right angle; then it abruptly flashed blue, green, and red. I blinked at it, trying to remember where I'd seen it before. "That's karenite. It's found on the ground, out on the steppe—you don't have to dig for it." She pointed out toward the open plain. "It's important to the Alashi; we trade it for things we can't make for ourselves. Any other questions?"

My head hurt, my mouth tasted foul, and I was ashamed of my utter confusion and befuddlement. "Can we keep that with us so that we know what we're looking for?"

Janiya flipped me the stone. She waited, staring at

us impatiently, until Tamar and I both turned and headed out of the camp, heading in the direction that Janiya had pointed.

It was weirdly discouraging, to be back out, wandering around on foot. At least Tamar was wearing boots that fit her now—but we had no water. I hoped it wouldn't take long to find a piece of karenite. We walked along, our eyes on the ground, as the sun rose in the sky. Waving gold-green grasses were waist-high, making it hard to spot much of anything. I could hear a bird singing somewhere nearby, and farther off, another bird answering. A breeze lifted the corner of my head scarf, briefly; the grass rustled around me like water rippling around a dipped cup. A drop of sweat trickled down into my eyes; I blotted at it with the corner of my scarf.

"There's a rockfall," Tamar said, pointing. "Maybe we'll find a piece in there somewhere."

Part of an eroded low hill had broken away, rocks and dirt and long-dried bits of wood sliding into a heap. It seemed like a better bet than just striding along through the steppe, particularly since the sun was growing higher and we had no water. Tamar and I sat down and began to sort through the rocks.

"I wish we had some water," Tamar said. I nodded silently. "And karenite. Why wouldn't Janiya give us more of a clue of how to find it?"

"Maybe the point of the test is to see if we can reason out how best to look for it."

"Well, then, I hope we find some in here. This was certainly the most *reasonable* spot we've found to look."

An hour passed. We found plain gray stones, chunks of crumbling sandstone, even a stone that held the outline of a snail's shell, which I set aside as an interesting curiosity to bring back to the camp, even if it wasn't what we were looking for. But no karenite. I swallowed, thinking longingly of my waterskin. *Just one sip,* I thought. *One swallow.* If only we could find karenite and go back to the camp . . .

"Hey!" Tamar pulled out a chunk of something that glittered a little in the sun. "I think I might have found some!"

I compared it to my stone. "Yes, that's it. Let's get the hell back to camp."

It was past noon when we arrived, hungry and thirsty. Janiya stood near the border, waiting for us. Tamar offered her the piece we'd found; Janiya made no move to take it. Her face was dark, her voice brimming with audible disgust. "You walked *right* out of the camp. You didn't bring food. You didn't bring *water* and you didn't just follow the stream. You didn't bring a weapon to defend yourself. You walked out there with the clothes on your back and the boots on your feet, and *nothing else.*"

"That's what you—" I said.

"*No.* I sent you on an errand. I never told you not to bring *water.*"

"But you—" Tamar started.

"But I didn't tell you *to* bring it, either. And you're so helpless, so dependent, that you need *orders* to bring water with you into the desert?" We both fell silent. Tamar was flushing angrily and biting her lip. Janiya went on: "You are acting like *slaves.* A slave doesn't have to *think;* a slave just has to obey. A slave doesn't have to protect herself; a slave can rely on her master for *protection.* A slave doesn't have to ask questions, see to supplies, *take initiative.* Questions are to be feared, supplies are provided by someone else, and initiative is *dangerous*."

"But we found the karenite you sent us for," Tamar said.

"This was not a test to see whether you could find karenite," Janiya said. "It was a test of whether you could act like free women. Whether you could use the common sense that you *must* have in you somewhere if you reached the Alashi alive—to fetch yourself water, or at least *ask* for water, or at least ask for *advice* on whether you should take anything with you rather than stumbling blindly out onto the steppe. *That* was the test. And you *failed*."

"We failed the minute we walked out of the camp," I said.

"No, you could have turned back while you were still in sight. But you didn't. You completed your errand. So you failed."

Tamar's hand stole to the thong around her neck, with its single blue bead. Janiya gave her a cold look and stalked away.

CHAPTER SIX

I t wasn't a fair test."

"No."

Tamar and I sat at the edge of camp, picking at our bowls of lentils and rice. I ate another lentil and put my bowl down, feeling that even one more mouthful of the Alashi spices would send me over the edge, yet I was still hungry.

"She told us to bring back karenite and we *found* a piece of karenite." Tamar thumped the lump of rock that still rested at her side. "We did what she asked. We *should* have passed the test. Anyway, so what if we didn't bring water? We came back alive, we didn't need to be rescued or anything."

I nodded silently. I had to admit—to myself—that the test *had* been fair. They wanted us to demonstrate that we could take care of ourselves, plan by ourselves, think for ourselves. They couldn't very well tell us at the outset, "Show me that you can act responsibly." Then we'd know just what to do to pass the test. No, this was the way to do it. What galled me was that I had fallen for it, running out into the desert with no water. *What an idiot. I* was never a slave. I was quite capable of taking care of myself— thinking for myself. Why had I fallen for such a stupid trick? I gritted my teeth and lifted a little more of the lentils and rice, swallowing the mouthful fast without chewing much. *I could handle eating dirt. Dirt would just be bland. This is—this is—* I gagged and put my bowl down.

"At least we know, now," I said, when I washed the mouthful down with water. "The tests are going to be *tricks*. We need to be suspicious of instructions, particularly from Janiya, particularly when we're already off-balance. Don't forget that she woke us up early; we were confused and sleepy, not at our best." *That's why I failed. Tired, hungover, cold, disoriented.*

"Yeah," Tamar said bleakly. *Her* bowl was empty, at least, though she wasn't going over to ask for a second helping. "I thought we could trust Janiya, at least."

I forced down another mouthful. "Well, now we know."

"Yeah," Tamar said again.

No one came over to talk to us this evening— Saken didn't come over to comfort us, but sat by the fire with Erdene, laughing about something. Ruan avoided us, too, fortunately; I didn't think I could bear her taunts after the day we'd had. I forced down the rest of my bowl, a little at a time, so as not to waste food. Then I scrubbed it out, stacked it with the others, and went into the yurt to sleep.

I had vivid nightmares that night. I was out in the rippling grasses on a moonless night, deep in Alashi territory, but I wore only a ripped gauze shift, and I knew Sophos was nearby. I ran as fast as I could, desperate to get away, but I knew he was gaining on me, though I couldn't see him. I had only one hope; only one person could protect me, the one person I could trust. *"Kyros,"* I screamed at the black night sky. *"Kyros. Kyros. Kyros."*

Someone was shaking my shoulders, and I struggled to consciousness, expecting Tamar but hearing Maydan's voice in the darkness, instead. "You were *screaming*. If you keep disturbing everyone's sleep, we may have to arrange for you to sleep somewhere else."

"I'm sorry." I was acutely aware, in the darkness, of the harsh breath of the other women; I had clearly woken the whole tent. I wondered why Tamar hadn't woken me up this time.

"Who is Kyros?"

"Kyros was my old owner. I dreamed—" I swallowed hard. "I was dreaming that I was here, and Kyros was coming. I tried to scream a warning. I guess I succeeded a little better than I thought in my dream."

Maydan's hands relaxed a little. "You're safe from him here. Someone always stands watch at night; perhaps in a few nights it'll be your turn. Go back to sleep." The last instruction was pitched for everyone, and around me I could hear people settling back down in their blankets.

Tamar slipped in beside me before I'd fallen back asleep. "I went out to pee," she whispered. "I'm sorry."

"Not your fault."

"It's only just after midnight."

I nodded, though Tamar couldn't very well see the

gesture in the darkness. I expected to be up the rest of
the night, but sank into dreamless sleep a short while
later.

"Relax," said Jolay. "Trust your horse." She wasn't
making jokes today; horseback riding was serious
business.

Tamar smiled stiffly. I wondered how much unease
I should feign. I might have ridden occasionally as a
stable hand, maybe, but I wouldn't have developed
the sort of skill I had from tearing across the desert on
Zhade. On the other hand, I wasn't sure how much
unease I *could* feign. I was a decent rider—not as
skilled as some of the Alashi, but I had spent a lot of
time on horseback and I didn't think I could convince
anyone that I hadn't. At any rate, I relaxed into the
saddle, keeping my back straight. The Alashi saddle
felt familiar now, rather than foreign. I wondered if
Kyros would let me bring one back and try it with
Zhade.

"Sit up straight," Jolay said to Tamar. Tamar
straightened her back, tensing up even more. "No, sit
up straight *and* relax. Lauria's got it—look at Lauria."

I bit my lip. *I should have tried to look more nervous.* Tamar glared at me but examined my back and
hips and tried to adjust. Jolay rode up alongside her
and prodded her back; Tamar flinched away instinctively, and Jolay drew back, shrugging. "I guess that's
as well as we're going to do today."

"Are we done, then?" Tamar asked, already shifting her weight to dismount.

"You wish!" Jolay shot Tamar a look of genuine

amusement. "Relax, blossom. We've got *hours*." Tamar winced and Jolay smiled even more broadly. "Next lesson: the reins. Use a *light* touch. Kesh and Kara will take good care of you, and all they need is a nudge to tell them where you want to go. If you're riding another horse and they don't want to obey, you need to work out that problem on the ground, not by hauling on their mouth. For now, we're going to practice communicating with the horse. You're both going to ride out to that tree over there." She pointed to a dead tree some distance away. "But not straight out and straight back. I want you to veer back and forth on your way, left and then right, left and then right." She traced a snaking pattern with her hand. "Use the *lightest* touch you *possibly* can to guide your horse. I want you to experiment, you understand? If you can, don't use the reins at all. When you shift your weight, your horses can read that and follow your lead, and ultimately that's what you're going for. In battle, we guide our horses without reins, to leave our hands free for our bows, and eventually you'll need to be able to do that, too. Right now, you can ride at any speed you like, fast or slow; the point of the exercise is to work on communication."

I had always used a little firmer hand with Zhade than she was suggesting, and I wondered now if that had been absolutely necessary. It was how Kyros's stable master had taught me to ride. *Never trust a horse,* he'd said. *They're bigger than you and they're faster than you. You need to teach them who's the master, and* never *let them forget it.* Now, riding my Alashi mare, I leaned into my saddle and was pleasantly surprised to discover just how right Jolay was. Kara pricked up her ears as I leaned left and leaned right, and veered as directed, even if I left the reins completely slack. A gentle shift of the reins was enough to make her turn quite sharply, if that's what I wanted. I had started out at a walk, but I picked up the pace, and wondered if I could communicate *fast* and *slower* the same way, just shifting my weight around. I discovered that it took a little more urging to convince Kara to canter, but relaxing back in my saddle was quickly taken as permission to slow down again, even if I didn't touch the reins.

I met Tamar out by the tree; we glanced back at Jolay, who sat on her own horse, watching us. Bored, probably. Oh well.

"What do you think?" I asked Tamar.

She bit her lip. "Am I as hopeless as she says?"

"You're doing fine," I said. "You've never ridden a horse before. I have. Though the Alashi ride very differently from the Greeks." *I'll have to take Zhade out once I'm back, and see if I can ride her like this, or if the Alashi training is just different. I wonder if I can share some of this with Kyros's stable master?* "Aren't you enjoying it at all?"

"I don't like being up so *high*," Tamar muttered.

"Just remember, on a horse you're taller than Sophos," I said. "You're taller, faster, and stronger than any human on two legs."

Tamar brightened a little at that. We set out back toward Jolay and arrived a few minutes later.

"Good!" she exclaimed as soon as we were in earshot. "You're doing well, a lot better than I expected, if you want to know the truth. You can dismount now, we're going to do some ground work."

The ground work turned out to be learning how to fall. I had a bad feeling that I was going to be required to fall off Kara—or at least jump off—at some point in the future, but for now she simply had us practice falling down from standing. "Land on your side and roll," she said. "Tuck if you can, you're less likely to get kicked or stepped on." Tamar blanched at the thought, but obediently practiced falling down, tucking into a ball and rolling as she did.

When we felt thoroughly bruised and sore, we led our horses back into camp and took them over to the stream to allow them to drink. We took off the saddles and bridles, groomed our horses, hobbled them—though that hardly seemed necessary; Kesh and Kara were such placid animals—then cleaned their tack and put them away. The tack was stored in a smaller wool tent that was pitched next to the yurt. That was used, as far as I could tell, entirely for storage of things that shouldn't get wet—riding gear, food stores, wooden chests I hadn't actually seen opened. There had been no rain since we rode out with the sisterhood, but Alashi weather was unpredictable, as Tamar and I had experienced on our walk. And it was still spring.

When we were done, Jolay found some bread and cheese for lunch, and told Tamar and me to go relax for a bit. We sat down with our food. Some of the other women were nearby, eating their own lunch or mending clothes; others were off somewhere.

"Lauria," Janiya said. I looked up. "Go get me some tea."

I stood up and headed toward the storage tent. I hadn't made myself tea but I'd seen other women help themselves to it, so I knew where it was kept. The tea was stored in a white canvas sack; I put a scoop of tea in one of the small teapots, then found one of the heavy mugs that the Alashi drank tea from. Water was kept simmering on the campfire; I dipped some out with the ladle, poured it over the tea, let it brew for a few minutes, and then brought it to Janiya and set it down beside her silently. I was moving away when she spoke again. "Lauria."

"Yes?" I turned back. She was visibly fuming, and I glanced back at the tea, panicky. Had I let it steep for too long? Not long enough? Was there another bag of tea, something special and reserved for Janiya, that I should have taken it from? "What's wrong?"

"Did I say *please*?"

I stared at her, mute with total confusion.

"Is there something wrong with my legs, that I can't go get my own tea?" She stood up and dashed the tea to the ground with a splash. "You are my *sister*, not my slave. Why did you get me tea, Lauria? *Why*?"

"Because you asked—"

"Asked, hell. I ordered. I have the right to give you orders when we're fighting, or when it's something for the good of the sisterhood, but I do not have the right to *order* a sister to wait on my whims. Have you ever seen anyone *else* wait on me?" I shook my head. "That's right, you haven't. Erdene!" Erdene glanced over from her seat by the campfire. "Get me some tea."

"Piss off," Erdene said cheerfully. "Get your own damn tea, Janiya."

"There," Janiya said, and settled herself back down. "Maybe *next* time this comes up, you'll earn yourself a bead."

My blood went cold. "I failed *another* test?"

"You failed another test," Janiya agreed. "And here is what you need to learn: you are a sister here, not a slave. Erdene!" she called again. "Would you be a dear, since you're by the fire, and get me some tea, please?"

"I'd be glad to," Erdene said, and vanished into the yurt.

"There. You see? *That* is how a sister expects to be asked for tea."

"I see." My teeth were clenched. Janiya nodded, dismissing me.

I was too angry to go sit back down with Tamar, so I stalked back over to where the horses were gathered and began to groom Kara again. She looked a little surprised, but quickly relaxed under the attention. Red-brown hairs scattered in the sunlight. Beyond the edge of the camp, I could see some of the other women out riding; one was still dragging the rolled-up mass of wool and hair. Others raced their horses, practicing what I realized after a few minutes were battle maneuvers. I had heard that the Alashi shot arros from horseback, and now I could see some of the sisters practicing. Balancing neatly in their stirrups, they shot at a target set up on the ground. It was hard to believe that anyone could hit anything while riding a galloping horse, but a good number of the arrows they shot slammed into the target of stuffed goatskin. I leaned my head against Kara, watching them.

"Impressed, blossom?"

Ruan. I clenched my teeth and forced the words *get the hell out of my face* back down my throat. "Of course I'm impressed," I said instead.

"You'll have to be able to do that by the end of the summer if you want to join us."

"Then I'm sure I'll be able to," I said. "I can't imagine that the eldress would set me, or Tamar, an impossible task."

"I'll be teaching you archery," Ruan said, and with a smile that looked like she'd rather bite me, she turned and walked back to the fire.

*W*arm up first, blossoms. You'll be sorry if you don't."

She gave us no more guidance than that. I led Tamar in a series of stretches—arms, back, wrists. Ruan tossed each of us an unstrung bow. "There's your target," she said, and pointed: a bright yellow cloth was stretched over a stuffed goatskin, some distance away. I had only the most rudimentary archery skills, and knew I would never be able to hit it at this distance. "Watch carefully," she said. She strung her own bow, and slipped a carved stone ring over her thumb. She plucked an arrow from the quiver and rested it in the crook of her thumb and forefinger; then she tucked her thumb around the bowstring, drew, and released the arrow. We heard the *thwock* a moment later as the arrow hit the target.

"Tamar, you use the red-and-white fletched arrows; Lauria, you use the red-and-black. That way, if either of you actually *hits* the target, we'll know which of you it was." She nodded once. "Well. Let's see you try, then. What are you waiting for?"

More of a lesson than that might be nice. I braced my bow against my leg and bent it until I could loop the string over the free end. It slipped out of my hands a few times before I managed to do it. Tamar, with her skinny arms, couldn't bend the bow enough to string it. Ruan watched us both through half-lidded eyes, offering no suggestions. After a few minutes, I bent the bow for her and she slipped the loop over the free end.

"Do you have one of those rings for each of us?" I asked Ruan.

A look of irritation flickered across Ruan's face, and I quailed a little, instinctively, after all the scorn of the last few days. But I realized as she contemptuously tossed each of us a leather thumb ring that she had been hoping to see us fail, and was disappointed that I'd had the wit to ask for equipment she hadn't given me. I looped the leather around my thumb, plucked a red-and-black-feathered arrow out of the bag, looked in the direction of the target, drew, and released.

The rebounding bowstring snapped against my elbow like a whip and I yelled out loud in pain. I managed to keep from dropping the bow, and set it down carefully to rub my arm. Ruan was convulsed in laughter. "Tuck your elbow, blossom," she said when she had breath for it. "You're a sister, not a brother." She held out her own bow again, showing me. I picked up my own bow and held out my still-stinging arm. When my arm was perfectly straight, the underside of my elbow bulged out a little; that's where I'd been struck with the bowstring. I rotated my elbow slightly; I could keep my arm straight and avoid being smacked by the bowstring, though it was a little harder to hold the bow this way. Ruan, no doubt, had known I would probably do this.

It was just as well, I reflected, tucking my thumb around the string and drawing the bow again. Even the most basic archery skills were not likely to be found in a former slave. If I *hadn't* made this mistake, she might have started to wonder. I could still resent the fact that she hadn't warned me. The welt on my arm still burned and would smart for a while yet.

Tamar had watched and learned from my mistake, but was making plenty of her own. Her first arrow went straight into the ground, just a short walk away. Her second got only a little farther. I decided I wasn't really in much of a position to encourage, let alone coach, and loosed my second arrow, firing high. Too high: it sailed right over the target and landed somewhere in the field beyond. It would be a lot of fun *finding* all these arrows again. Maybe I should be firing short, like Tamar . . .

Tamar got her next arrow higher, though it was far to the left of the target. My arm grew tired quickly and when I tried to pause with drawn bow to aim, it started to shake. I almost forgot and let my elbow turn in again, but tucked it just in time. That arrow went almost straight into the ground.

I plucked out an arrow without looking closely and felt something coil around my hand. I looked down, had the briefest impression of a flicking tongue and a smooth body and shrieked like a child, shaking my hand furiously. The snake tumbled into the grass and glided off. I turned furiously to see that Ruan was convulsed with laughter again.

"Was that to teach me to look carefully before I reach into the quiver?" I said. "I've heard that the Alashi poison their arrow tips. Do they also bring along whole snakes to fling at their enemies?"

"Oh, that was just for my own amusement, blossom," she said, wiping tears of laughter from her eyes when she could finally get breath. "To think that you'd get so upset over a little grass snake!"

"Oh yes, when it coiled around my wrist, I'm sure

I should simply have *known* that it was a grass snake and not venomous," I shouted. "After all, *you* knew, so why wouldn't I?"

Ruan just said, "Eek! A snake!" in a high-pitched voice that was apparently supposed to be a mockery of me. I turned away, shaking with anger. Snakes didn't really frighten me—not really—but they weren't exactly something I liked to cuddle. I grabbed another arrow and shot at the target. The arrow went even wider than before.

"Eek! Eek, I say!" Ruan said again, throwing up her hands in mimicry of ladylike panic. Tamar was watching her, her lips tight. She plucked out an arrow, tucked it into her hand, drew it back, and released—and a moment later, Ruan's exclamations died as we heard the *thwock* of the arrow hitting the target. Tamar drew out another arrow: *thwock*. *Thwock*. *Thwock*.

I watched, openmouthed.

"Have you done this before, blossom?" Ruan asked.

Tamar gave her a contemptuous look and didn't answer. After a moment, Ruan shrugged. "Beginner's luck," she said.

I finished firing my arrows, and Ruan sent us both to gather them up again.

*W*e unrolled the felt that evening, but apparently it still wasn't completely done: the women heated up more pots of boiling water to soak the wool and hair, then rolled it back up, even more tightly. Once it was secured, Jolay stepped forward with some strips of black cloth. Murmuring something in a low voice, she tied the strips together, then tied the knotted strand around the wrapped felt. Then she turned toward the sisterhood. "Glory to Prometheus, Brother of Freedom! Glory to Arachne, Sister of Freedom!"

"Glory to Arachne and Prometheus," most of the women responded. I glanced at Tamar; she was mumbling along with everyone else, reluctantly.

"Sister Arachne, breaker of chains, bless and shelter our sisterhood. Brother Prometheus, bringer of fire, bless and shelter our sisterhood."

"Prometheus and Arachne, bless and protect us!" Around us, the women clasped hands, enthusiastically. Out came a small sack, which Jolay shook out to empty. There was a cascade of little scraps of black cloth; the other women scrambled forward, snatching up scraps. Then they scattered around, laughing, tying strips around the wrists of their closest friends. Saken had grabbed a good-sized handful of strips, and had tied one around Erdene's wrist. Now she came over to tie strips around my wrist and Tamar's wrist as well.

"What is this?" I asked.

"Scraps from last year's sister-cloth. It's good luck to get a strip from a friend."

A little reluctant to brave the melee, I went up and scrounged a scrap to offer to Tamar. Out of the corner of my eye, I saw Ruan approach Saken, and exchange strips of cloth with her. I tied the scrap I'd found around Tamar's skinny wrist, but the piece she'd found was too short go to go around mine. Mimicking the other sisters we saw with this dilemma, we tucked it into my belt. The last of the scraps blew away in the night wind.

While everyone had been busy exchanging strips of

black cloth, Zhanna had stepped forward. She carried a drum, a bowl of water, and a bundle of feathers. "We bless our cloth with river water. As they flowed once, they will flow again." She poured the water in the bowl over the straw mats, then beat the drum, chanting a low, monotonous song. Though I'd heard most of the Alashi worshipped Prometheus and Arachne, they maintained a respectful silence. After a time, I could see the sparkle in the air that I recognized as a djinn; it passed briefly into Zhanna, and she stopped chanting, hugging herself tightly and sweeping her eyes over the assembly. I was afraid that the djinn would speak to me, as the Fair One had, but this one seemed much less social. Zhanna's hands went up in blessing, and with another sparkle, the djinn was gone.

The kumiss came out again; I accepted the smallest cup I thought I could get away with. "I thought all the Alashi worshipped Prometheus and Arachne," I said to Saken when she poured my kumiss.

"Well, most of us do. But of course there have to be shamans to keep the djinni from making trouble . . ."

"Zhanna is a shaman?"

"Oh yes. There are just a few of the sisters who primarily worship the djinni—Zhanna is one, there are a couple of others. I suppose both of you are djinn-worshippers." She glanced at Tamar, who stared down at her kumiss. I wondered if she was ashamed of her slave religion, or if she was simply bracing herself to down the kumiss.

"I was raised worshipping Arachne," I said, since I'd told that story to Tamar. "I was told that the djinni weren't gods, but slaves like us."

Saken glanced again at Tamar and bit her lip.

"Well, some of them are certainly slaves, but others are *out there,* and sometimes they make trouble . . ." Saken shrugged and stood up to go get more kumiss. I accidentally put my hand in my cup and decided I didn't need to refill.

"That answers your question, doesn't it?" I said to Tamar. "There *are* shamans here. There are some who worship the djinni. As long as you want to keep worshipping them."

"I wonder if it will mark me," Tamar said, raising her eyes to mine. "You know. As a—*blossom.*"

"Zhanna's not a 'blossom,' " I said. "If she was ever a slave, I haven't heard anyone talk about it." Thinking it over, I thought that Saken and Erdene had never been slaves; I was quite sure Ruan had been, once, and Maydan. I wasn't sure about Jolay and Zhanna, and I couldn't have said why I was so certain of Ruan and Maydan. Ruan's cruelty, and her clear lack of a close friend, made me think that she hadn't been born here. Maydan, though, it was just a hunch. I shook my head; *Lauria the escaped slave would not know this.* "Follow your heart, Tamar. I don't think anyone honestly cares. Except for maybe Ruan, and who cares what the hell she thinks?"

Tamar smiled at that and glanced at my cup. "Oh dear," she said in a slightly mocking tone. "You've spilled your kumiss, haven't you? I'd better go get you some more . . ."

"Don't you dare," I said.

She gulped hers down and shuddered. "Ah. Well. Having done my duty, I'd better sneak off to bed before someone refills my cup."

A shadow fell over us, and we looked up to see Janiya.

"Do you two know how to cook?" she asked. Without waiting for us to answer, she said, "It doesn't really matter. Saken will explain the basics to you. You two will cook dinner for the sisterhood tomorrow evening. You'll need to start at around noon, I expect, since you haven't done it before. Good night."

This chest holds sacks of rice." We stood in the supply tent; Saken pointed to a big wooden chest with a hinged lid. "This chest holds sacks of lentils." She opened the lid briefly so that we could peer in and look. "Spices are in here." Another chest, this one smaller, and when she opened it, we saw smaller sacks of tightly woven linen. "Flour's in here." Another big wood box. "Game has been scarce, so probably no meat tonight. Here." She set a big iron pot at our feet. When I looked in, I could see lines etched inside from years of use. "Rice up to this line, then water to here. Bring it to a boil and cover it with the lid. It'll be done when all the water's absorbed. That doesn't take long, but it takes a long time to come to a boil, so leave plenty of time." She set out another pot. "This one's for the lentils: lentils to this line, water to here, two handfuls of spices, and start it cooking when you start the rice."

"This doesn't sound like it'll take all that long," I said. "Why did Janiya tell us to start at noon?"

"She'd also like you to make bread." Saken took a big pottery bowl, scooped in flour, and added a little water, stirring until she got a stiff dough. "It's going to take you awhile to make as much bread as we'll eat. Scoop out a ball, roll it, pat it flat and thin, and then cook it over a flat griddle. You want it cooked but still soft. You can snack on your mistakes; it'll take you awhile to get the hang of it, don't worry about that." She demonstrated quickly, patting out a little round circle and baking it briefly on the griddle. "There. Fill these three baskets. When bread's available, everyone always eats a *lot* of it. Have fun! Oh, and come get me if you have any questions."

It was a long, long afternoon. We sat close to the hot fire in the hot, dry sun, patting out little balls of dough and stacking the cooked pieces on a plate. The first couple came out much too brown, and we snacked on them, as Saken had suggested; the crunchy brown bread crackled in my mouth, and I ached to cook up the whole batch just like that and eat it *all,* just for a little variety. "Do you suppose they'll toss us out into the desert if we don't add the spices?" I asked Tamar. "I am so very tired of the spices the Alashi cook with . . ."

Tamar laughed. "I know. I'm tempted, too. Maybe I'll burn another piece of bread . . ." I burned one instead, and we shared it.

We finished the bread and moved it into the supply tent to wait for dinner. I fetched down one of the pots Saken had pointed at earlier, and Tamar scooped rice out of the sack into the pot. She returned the scoop to the chest, and gasped.

"What is it?" I moved over quickly, half expecting a mouse or some vermin in the food.

"Shh!" Tamar glanced toward the door of the supply tent to make sure no one was in there with us. Then she pulled back one of the sacks to reveal what she'd seen. *Honey.* A single glass jar of dark amber liquid, sealed tight with beeswax and oiled linen.

"This isn't where the honey is stored," Tamar whispered. "The honey is kept in the yurt; I've seen it. If anyone knew about this honey, it wouldn't be here." She extracted it delicately, closed the chest, and set the jar of honey on top. "We could share it between us."

Desire for the honey rose up like tears, and I caught my breath; my mouth watered. Without a word, I grabbed the plate of bread and took the top piece, ripping it in half. Tamar's eyes glinted, and she had started to peel loose the wax seal when something occurred to me. "*Wait,*" I hissed.

Tamar froze and looked at me. "What's wrong?"

"What if this is a test?"

She pulled her hand back slowly. "A test like being sent out for the karenite?"

"Yeah, exactly." I put down the bread and looked in the chest with the rice, as if it might hold a clue to whether we were being tempted deliberately. "When we were slaves, if something like this came our way, we grabbed it. Because we were stealing from our owner—someone who was already stealing our freedom from us." Tamar nodded. "But here—here, if we take the honey for ourselves, we're stealing from our sisters. Maybe Janiya planted it where she knew we'd find it, to see what we would do."

Tamar's eyes went wide. "I think you're right." Her face fell and she glared at the honey. "But I *want* some."

"Let's offer it up with the meal. Share it with everyone. We'll get some, then."

Tamar nodded. We set the honey aside and filled the rice pot at the stream, setting it on the fire to simmer. My suspicions were more or less confirmed when I saw Janiya watching us carefully from her spot in the shade. I grudgingly stirred spices into the lentils, despite being tempted to forget. We sat down to wait in the shade for dinner to be done.

"Maybe we should ask Janiya before we bring out the honey," I said.

"No," Tamar muttered. "She could just say *no*. It's bad enough that we have to share it."

When the sisterhood gathered for dinner, we brought out the plates of bread, and then—with a smile and a flourish—the jar of honey. "We found it in the rice!" Tamar said. "Just wedged in between two sacks."

"We figured it must have been put there by accident," I said. "Since it wasn't set aside for anything and it wasn't being saved for anything, we thought we could all eat it tonight."

There was a great deal of enthusiasm for that plan. Tamar and I managed to grab generous dollops of honey before it was all gone, and when all the loose honey had been eaten, we finished out the jar with our fingers. We probably should have made more bread; as it was, all the bread got eaten with the honey, rather than with the rice and lentils. Well, if this was all some sort of test, it wasn't surprising that Saken had had us make bread. It had been *intended* to be eaten with the honey, assuming we were honest and passed the test.

The meal done, we took the pots down to the river to scrub them out. Janiya approached a few minutes later, a big smile on her face. "You passed," she said, and tossed each of us a blue bead.

"What was the test?" Tamar asked. She feigned ignorance well.

"Whether you would share the honey, or eat it yourselves. When slaves steal, they are stealing only from their master. When a member of the sisterhood steals, she steals from her family. You showed that you understand this." Janiya nodded to each of us, and headed back to the main camp.

We threaded the beads on our thong and retied them: two beads now. They clicked against each other on the string. I wondered how many more we had to earn. I slipped the thong back over my head, and continued to scrub out the pot.

"I don't deserve this," Tamar said.

I glanced at her; her face was hard and sad. "Why do you say that?"

"I would have eaten the honey without a second thought. The only reason I didn't was because you convinced me it was a test. That was the *only* reason."

"Then I don't deserve it, either, because the only reason I didn't eat the honey was that it *occurred* to me that it was a test."

Tamar was silent for a while. I could hear the scrape of sand against the inside of the pot. She dumped water inside, swirled it around, dumped it out, and checked the inside for food particles with her hand. She took another handful of sand and scrubbed some more. "I think we should tell Janiya," she said. "When we're done cleaning up. Confess to her. It's not fair."

"Don't be ridiculous," I hissed. "What if she takes back our beads?"

"You said yourself you didn't deserve yours, either."

I dunked my pot in the stream with a bit more vigor than was probably necessary, swirled the water, and dumped it out. Rinsed it again; it was clean.

"Fine," I said, finally. "You want to, we'll go together and you can tell her."

Tamar was silent. When she had finished scrubbing her pot, we dried them out and carried them back to hang them up in the supply tent for tomorrow. Then we went to find Janiya. She was near the fire, listening to one of the other sisters singing a long, complicated ballad. "We have something to tell you," Tamar said.

"Yes?" Janiya looked both of us over; she wasn't smiling now.

"We guessed," Tamar said rapidly. "That the honey was a test. We knew. That's the main reason we didn't eat it. Do you want your beads back?"

Janiya's lips quirked up, and for the first time I noticed that she had not one, but two dimples, one in each cheek. She grinned and then finally laughed out loud, just a little chuckle, not a mean one.

"I'm glad you came to me," she said when she had mostly regained control of her features. "The fact that you came to me to say this proves that you deserve the recognition for honesty. In fact, it demonstrates other things I like to see, too—like a trust that as the leader of this sisterhood, I am sensible and fair, and not as capriciously cruel as a Greek master of slaves." My heart leapt, and sure enough, out of her pocket came two more blue beads. She handed one to each of us, and then patted Tamar on the shoulder. "Quit worrying, new sisters, and go to bed. You've had a very long day."

I dreamed that night of running. Again, I was surrounded by waving grass on the dark plain, and I knew that Sophos was following me. *Kyros,* I thought, but the part of me that knew I was dreaming knew that I couldn't scream, because I would wake up the sisters . . . I bit down on my fear, and kept running, though my legs slowed as if they were tangled in a net, and my chest felt as if it would burst from fear. *I can never run fast enough to escape. I can never run far enough to escape. I can't call for help. There's nowhere left that's safe . . .*

I reached out, desperately, toward the blackness above me, and with a twist of strength that came from some mysterious place within, I ripped a hole in the night sky, thinking, *There, I can hide there . . .*

But beyond, there was a flash of light, and then a sudden rush of wind that lifted me up and blew me back to awareness. I woke with a gasp, but knew that at least this time I hadn't screamed. My ears were very cold, as if the rush of wind had been something real. My heart was pounding.

I ran my fingers over my three beads as I lay in the dark, trying to calm myself, and thought about that strange wind. At least tonight I didn't have to remove myself from the tent to placate my irritable tentmates, but it still took me a long time to fall back to sleep. As I hovered on the edge of sleep, I thought I heard a voice whisper, *"Gate,"* and then darkness swallowed me again.

CHAPTER SEVEN

Saken fetched me from grooming the horses to tell me that the felt was done. I must have looked at her blankly because she laughed and said, "Come *on,* you need to be there." I put down the brush and curry comb and followed her back to the main part of camp.

The felt was still bound with the straps that had been used the last time it was unrolled and rerolled, though the more delicate strips of cloth that had been tied by Jolay had worn away or snapped off as the rolled-up felt bounced and tossed over the ground behind someone's horse. Now Janiya unbound the straps and kicked out the reed mats so that the felt unrolled completely. Saken, Ruan, Jolay, and Zhanna each took a corner and peeled it carefully back from the mat. It stayed together, a solid black mass.

Janiya stepped up behind the felt and took careful hold of it. "Bound with our hair; bound with our flocks. Bound with our horses, bound with our water. Bound with our labor, bound with our rest." She took a deep breath, and yanked back on the felt with all her strength, trying to tear it. The felt stayed whole. "Bound like our sisterhood—may it never be rent!"

Even I could recognize a cue for wild cheering when I heard one. One by one, the sisters stepped forward and took a turn trying to tear the felt. When it was my turn, I didn't try that hard—if it *could* be torn, I really didn't want to be the one who did it. Then Saken strode forward with the same scissors we'd used to cut everyone's hair, along with three pieces of leather that she used as a guide for where to cut. Within a few minutes, the felt was in pieces; everyone else began to gather them up. Tamar and I hung back, and after a moment Saken came over with three pieces for each of us.

"What do I do with these?" I asked.

"You sew them into a vest," she said. "Everyone in the sisterhood wears a black vest made of the felt. We sew our vests, and then we decorate them. I'll show you my vests from other summers, if you want some ideas."

Tamar and I sat down with her; she had a spool of black thread and a needle. "Do you know how to sew?" she asked. We both nodded. "This shouldn't be too hard for you, then." She put her own three pieces together: the biggest piece formed the back, and the other two formed the left side and right side. The texture of the felt allowed her to sew her vest without hemming the fabric; she sewed neatly, the seam turned inward, holding the two pieces together as she worked. "Do you see how they go together?"

We nodded again. There were a limited number of needles, so we had to wait our turn. When Erdene finished, she gave Tamar her needle and a rod of tightly wound thread. Tamar cut a piece of thread and threaded her needle, and Erdene helped her orient her pieces to put them together properly.

As I started working on mine, Saken laid hers aside for a moment, then went into the yurt and came out with a small bundle. "Here are my vests from previous years," she said, laying them out. She had five vests in all: the four from previous years were each richly decorated with thread. The first one was the most elaborate: a horse galloped past a yurt, and two rivers cascaded from top to bottom. Smaller pictures were scattered around the rest of the vest: a shovel, a bouquet of poppies, a tiny snow-capped mountain, a sleeping cat. Saken tapped the vest and said, "Your first year in the sisterhood, you're supposed to make a design that tells the story of your life until then. I made this when I was fifteen."

"It's beautiful," I said. I'd spent enough time with a needle, under my mother's eye, to appreciate the time and skill required. Tamar nodded, and silently stroked the threads in the horse's neck.

Saken tapped the second vest. "So the next year, since I didn't have to sew pictures, I didn't." The second vest had no pictures on it at all, but designs that marched up and down the back: lines, broken lines, dotted lines, zigzags, triangles, squares, interlocking circles, interlocking swirls. The third and fourth vests had pictures of vines and flowers, and were much simpler than the first two.

"So are we supposed to make designs that show our lives—as slaves?" Tamar asked.

"Yes," Saken said. "You can use symbols, though; you don't have to be able to embroider pictures of people. Like, that shovel on mine?" She tapped it.

"That's actually a symbol for my mother, because she used to take me out hunting for karenite, and those are the times I most enjoyed her company."

Great, I thought. *More lies to invent.* Well, it wasn't hard to think of images that I could incorporate easily enough: horses, since I was supposed to have been a stable hand. Some symbol of Kyros, since he was supposedly my old owner. Images from the harem. I shivered a little and stroked the black felt. I wondered how I could represent Sophos. Or Tamar, for that matter.

Everyone seemed to have immediately set to work embroidering; I turned my half-finished vest around ~~and around in~~ my hands, thinking. It would be easiest to start with a horse, except that I wasn't certain I could embroider a nice-looking horse. Even the most complicated pictures on Saken's vests were done perfectly, and I didn't want to have to wear a vest with an ugly, badly done horse embroidered on it all summer long.

A wine cup.

I bit my lip, trying to push the image from my mind, but it intruded again: the wine cup, pressed to my lips by Tamar. The drugged wine, blurring my senses, unsteadying me, making me . . .

Saken had brought over some colored thread to work with. Once I was done stitching the vest together, I cut a white strand, threaded my needle, and started to sew again.

Shhhh. Shhhh."

Kyros. I opened my mouth but no sound came out; I looked around frantically, but we sat alone by the banked coals of the campfire. It was night; the yurt stood behind me, dark and quiet. "What are you *doing* here?"

"I'm here to see you, of course." Kyros settled down beside me. "How are things going?"

"Well, thank you for sending the djinn to help me find water." I paused, then frantically corrected myself. "The *aeriko,* I mean."

"Yes." Kyros stared into space for a moment. "Have you been successful?"

"It's taking some time to be accepted as Alashi. Also—" I swallowed hard. "Things didn't go as planned at Sophos's."

"The other slave?"

"Well, her. Yes. But—" I bit my lip, finding the words sticking in my throat. "Sophos broke his word. He acted dishonorably. He—he used me, as he would a concubine. I want him punished."

Kyros's face darkened. "I am sorry to hear that," he said softly. "Sophos was always a useful tool, for me. But he will pay the price, oh yes, for *you*—you are far more useful."

I studied his face, feeling uneasy.

"Honey cake?" he said, and held out a small tray. I reached for a cake, then drew back my hand; the honey cakes were a writhing mass of snakes. *Harmless snakes,* I thought, but snakes, not cakes—

"Or perhaps some wine?"

"No!" I shouted, swinging my hand wildly to knock the wine cup from his hand. "Stay away from me, no!"

"Shh, shh, shh—"

"*Leave me alone!*"

"Lauria!"

Tamar had grabbed my shoulders; I wrenched away from her in the dark, my heart pounding. Around me, I could hear the harsh breath of rudely wakened women; without a word, I picked up my mat and blankets and moved outside, lying down by the fire, where I'd dreamed of seeing Kyros. Tamar settled down beside me a few minutes later.

"You don't have to come out here," I said. "*You're* not the one who just woke everyone up."

"No," she said.

Shivering a little in the cold night wind, I looked up at the stars, thinking about the dream. In retrospect, of course, it should have been obvious from the beginning that I was dreaming; what would I have been doing simply sitting out by the fire, alone? Still, I found myself weirdly relieved that Tamar was with me now, as if her presence would keep Kyros from materializing. *He* could *have a djinn bring him here,* I thought. *But there would be no sense to it. It could horribly compromise my cover, not to mention risking his life.* It occurred to me as I drifted on the edge of sleep that I shouldn't feel *relief* that Tamar's presence would keep Kyros away, but disappointment. *It's because I know how dangerous his presence would be to our plans,* I reassured myself.

I heard a footstep and sat bolt upright; it was only Zhanna, coming out of the yurt, wrapped in her own blanket. "Are you two warm enough?" she asked.

"I'm fine," Tamar muttered from under her blanket, which she'd pulled over her head.

"You can come back in the yurt, you know. No one's annoyed with you except Ruan."

"It's nice of you to say so," I said.

"No, really." Zhanna sat down beside me,

wrapped in her own blanket. "I mean, so sometimes you have nightmares. Ruan snores like a geriatric dog, especially when she's been drinking. I've been told that I snore, too, though not quite as loudly. Saken scratches in her sleep. Erdene *whistles*."

"You're making that up," Tamar muttered.

"No, really. Not every night, but she does it. *And* she talks in her sleep. Once Jolay led her through a whole bizarre conversation—'The lentils, they're coming.' 'Oh? And are they bringing the rice?' 'Oh, Prometheus, the rice! It's dressed in its finery . . .'—while the rest of us listened. And laughed. Eventually Erdene woke up, though she didn't remember a word she'd said."

"I'll sleep out here tonight," I said.

"Suit yourself." Zhanna dropped her blanket on me. "Stay warm. I'm going back in the yurt."

I spread out the extra blanket over both me and Tamar, who curled up warm at my side. After a few minutes, I stopped shivering and went back to sleep.

I woke again, with a start, what felt like bare moments later. From the edge of camp, I heard a sharply indrawn breath, and a woman's voice shout, *"Raiders!"*

I scrambled to my feet, throwing my blanket aside, and ran back into the yurt, where I'd left the sword I'd taken from the bandit camp. I was nearly knocked down by Saken, running out, but I got in and found my sword and ran back out with everyone else. Tamar had snatched up the only thing handy, a rock, to defend herself. "Here," Ruan shouted, and thrust a bow and a quiver of arrows into her hands. "See if you can hit bandits as well as you can hit a stuffed goatskin." Tamar threaded the ring over her thumb and strung the bow, still stumbling a little from confusion and tiredness.

I drew my sword, having no real idea how to make myself useful. Then horses swept in.

The raiders were Greek bandits, deserter soldiers, like the bandits Tamar and I had run into on our trip to the Alashi. All were mounted, and they were here to steal livestock and possibly women—though surely they knew that any Alashi would be more trouble as a slave than she'd be worth. I slashed at a passing horse, realizing quickly the disadvantage of my position on the ground. The Alashi usually fought mounted; so did the bandits. I should have bolted for the horses instead of my sword; I'd have been more likely to survive the battle that way. At least on the ground I could watch Tamar's back; Tamar, a novice rider, wouldn't have gone for her horse even if it had occurred to her.

Planting her feet firmly where she was, she shot two arrows high over everyone's head (at least she didn't shoot one of the sisters by accident; that, I thought, would be unlikely to earn either of us a bead), then found her stride and hit a bandit square in the gut. He bellowed in pain and galloped out of the camp, clutching at himself. That diverted his friend's attention to the archer on the ground, and he turned toward us: Tamar, panicked, sent one arrow too high, and then I shoved her aside, out of the way of the charging horse, taking a swing at the rider as they passed. He was far out of reach. She shot again, just missing him. He turned his horse and looked at the two of us, pausing for just a heartbeat as if he was deciding which one of us to kill. Then one of the sisters saw us—Saken, I realized after a blurred moment—

and charged in, a spear raised. The bandit wheeled his horse and fled the camp.

"Get to your horses," Saken was shouting, but beyond the perimeter, we heard a loud whistle. That seemed to be the signal for the bandits to retreat; they withdrew from the camp and galloped off.

"Count yourselves," Janiya shouted.

There was a tense moment or two, then the sisters were all accounted for. Several had injuries, and Jolay's was severe: a bad cut across the shoulder. But no one was bleeding black blood, the sign of a poisoned wound, and Jolay's wound was probably not life-threatening. Then we counted the herds, and found that they'd taken most of the camels and a half-dozen horses. There were goats and sheep missing as well, but the dogs quickly rounded them up; they'd just strayed in the confusion.

"At least all the horses were spares," Saken murmured.

"Maydan, tend to Jolay," Janiya said. "Everyone who isn't injured, check your weapons and horses and mount up; we're going after them."

"Not the blossoms," Ruan said instantly. "They can stay here."

I wouldn't have argued this, but Tamar's chin went up. "We drew blood. I shot a bandit with an arrow, and Lauria got one with her sword."

"I got his horse," I muttered.

Janiya glanced from Tamar to Ruan to me, a faint smile on her lips. "I think they've proved they can be useful, Ruan." She jerked her head toward our horses, and we went to mount.

Janiya pulled up alongside Tamar and me as we

settled onto our horses. "How are you two at riding these days?"

"I can stay on," I said, not really wanting to declare myself proficient. Tamar said nothing, tight-lipped.

Janiya sighed. "You can stay here if you want," she said. "Usually we wouldn't take you into battle until you were confident riders, at least. I know you're a confident rider, Lauria, and not too bad with that sword you got from the bandits. Tamar is a natural with the bow. You'll both be useful enough if you come, but you'll be safer here."

"Anyone would be safer here," Tamar said.

Janiya's lips quirked. "No one else is in quite so much danger of falling off her horse."

Tamar's hands tightened on her bow. Janiya shrugged, looked us over quickly, and urged her horse to a quick walk, then to a canter. We fell in with everyone else, our horses running smoothly across the steppe in the direction the bandits had gone.

The moon was nearly full, so there was enough light to see by, barely. I glanced at Tamar, riding beside me; she sat up straight like we'd been taught, and her jaw was clenched. Her fist was still wrapped around the bow, though she'd hung the quiver on her saddle like the other sisters. I caught her eye and gave her a questioning look. She nodded firmly and forced a sick-looking smile to her lips.

Janiya signaled a stop, and Gulim dismounted to look for the trail. She found it, we remounted, and followed again. And so it went for a while, until we reached a long-dead streambed. The loose, shifting gravel made for uncertain footing for a horse, but would leave a much less obvious trail. Gulim checked one way, then the other, and was uncertain. "They could have gone either way."

"They probably followed the streambed for a while and then headed south," Ruan said.

"Maybe. Or maybe they're just beyond that next rise . . ."

"We could split up."

"No," Janiya said. "Not worth the risk." She gently turned her horse to face the rest of us. "Zhanna? Can you summon a djinn?"

"This isn't exactly ideal . . ."

"I know. But please try."

Zhanna closed her eyes and stretched her hands up to the sky. She had no drum with her today, no flute, nothing to lull her into the trance state that made her receptive to the djinni. The women waited silently; Kara shifted from foot to foot, then dipped her head to begin to graze. Nearby I heard another horse blow out its breath in a loud snort, and Kara raised her head to snuffle in response.

I was beginning to think that the call for djinn was futile, when there was a sparkle of light and Zhanna lowered her hands and sat with an odd rigidity. "What do you want?" she said. Her voice was harsh and brittle.

"We want to know where the bandits went," Janiya said.

"North."

We had been headed west.

"Directly north from here?"

"Northwest."

"Thank you."

A shimmer in the air, and Zhanna slumped in her saddle. She shook herself and rubbed the side of her head. "That was a bound djinn," she commented. "I wonder what it was doing out here? And why it decided to visit us?"

I shivered, suddenly alert, wondering where the djinn was. I had no doubt that the djinn was Kyros's, and it was hovering around us because it was observing me. No doubt Kyros was keeping a close watch on me, and I anxiously reviewed the events of the last few days, wondering if Kyros would approve. *I have been doing the best I can. If my thoughts have not always been on my assignment, well, the aerika can't read thoughts.*

Around me, the women were urging their horses forward again, and Kara and I fell in with them. A hiss of excitement ran through the group as someone spotted the bandits up ahead. Our horses sped up to a gallop; the bandits wheeled around to face us, and a few moments later we collided like a rock striking a rock.

I drew my sword, the sword I'd taken from the leader of the bandits who'd captured Tamar. *And here are more scum like them,* I thought, and felt a sudden dizzy joy that *this* time I was on horseback, holding a sword, facing down these men. Tamar and I had fled those bandits as fast as we could; here, we were the ones attacking.

I had trained a little with a sword in Kyros's service: basic techniques, mostly. I had never learned to fight from horseback. Working for Kyros, I was armed mostly to protect myself from desperate attacks from unarmed slaves I had been sent to recapture. On the rare occasions that I was sent somewhere that I was actually in danger from bandits, Kyros made sure I had either an escort or a spell-chain for protection. Or both. Of course, his aeriko was watching me even here . . .

One of the bandits charged toward me out of the darkness; I deflected his sword with my own just in time, and my pleasure at the fight was replaced with sudden cold fear. I could get hurt, I could get killed, and there was nothing Kyros could do to protect me. Certainly I couldn't imagine that his aeriko was instructed to save me from danger, since that would make me utterly useless in my assigned task. My mouth was dry, my hands were steady but freezing cold, and I swung my sword back at the bandit. He deflected my blow easily and swung for me again. I threw the blow aside, realizing that I was facing a *much* better swordsman than myself, and it wouldn't be long before he landed a blow.

But he cried out in sudden pain and clapped a hand to the arrow in his sword arm. As his arm drooped, I slashed at him with my sword again, wounding him badly. His horse wheeled and he was quickly obscured by the darkness. I gasped for breath and realized that the sisters were withdrawing; the fight was over already. I wondered if we had our horses back, and our camels, and turned Kara to follow everyone else. My sword was bloody, still in my hand; I had nowhere to clean it and cringed at the thought of putting it back in its sheath covered in blood, so I simply held it until we paused a short time later to be counted.

Everyone was there. A few women were wounded, but none severely. I found a piece of cloth to wipe my sword and then slipped it back into its sheath. We'd retaken some horses and camels—in the dim light, I thought we might have taken horses and camels that were originally theirs, not ours. Served them right.

Zhanna gestured suddenly for quiet, and listened for a moment, her nostrils flaring in the night wind. "They're coming after us," she said.

"Right," Janiya said. "Back to camp. We don't want them coming on the wounded without us there to protect them."

But our horses were growing tired, and halfway back to camp, the bandits caught up with us. This time, I felt as exhausted as the horses; my head pounded as I drew my sword. I told myself that surely the bandits were as tired as we were, but I was desperately conscious of the aches in my arms, of the way that each beat of my pounding heart echoed through my head and made it ache even more. For a fleeting moment, I wondered if this was yet another odd dream, and I was actually back at camp, still sleeping beside Tamar.

They swept in against us. I swung my sword wildly, afraid to close with any individual bandit, afraid to attract attention. I wanted to turn Kara and run away, and I felt a brief flash of clear jealousy for Tamar's skill with archery: she could keep her distance from the fray. Then one of the bandits turned toward me and all I could think of was the desperate need to keep his sword from my flesh. The world narrowed: I saw his sword, I saw my sword, I saw the bandit's dark eyes glittering in the darkness.

Then suddenly I felt a coldness against my side, and then a surge of pain. I'd been cut, maybe stabbed. I had no idea how badly, but in my weakness surely he would finish me off. To die out here, surrounded by strangers, in someone else's cause! My throat tightened in fury and frustration, and I defended myself against a last swing. *Maybe I can kill him, even if he does kill me.* He knocked my sword aside—and behind him, one of the sisters rode up, kicked him off his horse, and then brought her sword down, cutting a huge red gash into his unguarded neck.

It was Zhanna. "Come on," she said, and seized Kara's reins, kicking her own horse to a fast canter. "We're moving again."

The bandits, too, were pulling back; the man Zhanna had killed was not their only loss. *Now* the pain from my wound flooded through me like scalding water; I bit back a scream and whimpered instead. I clung to my horse; Zhanna turned as we ran, took my sword, wiped it on a cloth kept on a hook on her saddle, and put it away. "Just hang on," she said. "We'll get you back to camp and Maydan."

I still had no idea how serious the wound was, and clung to the idea that surely it was minor or Zhanna would have called for a halt to at least bind it up temporarily. Either that, or it was so serious that there was no reason to bother, but I didn't feel like I was dying. I just felt like I might like to.

Finally, ahead we saw the yurts and the embers of the fire; Zhanna let go of Kara's reins and sprinted ahead, shouting, "Maydan! Maydan!"

Kara came to a stop in camp and I slid awkwardly off her back. My shirt and trousers were soaked with my blood. I wondered if it had run down all the way to my boots; I couldn't tell in the dim light. Tamar joined me, white-faced but apparently unhurt, and grabbed my arm, helping me to sit down. Maydan took a knife and cut a larger hole in my shirt, pressing her fingers carefully against the wound. "It's not too bad," she said. When I cringed away from her touch, she added, "I think you might have gotten some broken ribs from the blow, but the cut is very shallow. Prometheus was watching over you."

"Or he doesn't want her company yet," Jolay said.

"I won't need to stitch it, just bandage it tightly. You'll be able to ride and fight again in a week or two."

"We may have to ride sooner than that," Janiya said.

"Well, she'll do as she has to," Maydan said. She checked the other injuries, then went to get her bandages.

"Do you think the bandits will come for us *again*?" Tamar said. "Their losses were far heavier . . ."

"I know. But that was true after our first attack, yet they came after us."

"Could they have been that desperate for horses?" That was Zhanna now, not Tamar.

"Perhaps . . ." Janiya walked around our booty, looking over the horses and camels we'd taken from the bandits. "Unload the camels. Let's see what's in their packs."

Maydan returned with bandages and water. She sponged the cut clean, then wrapped my ribs tightly with yards of clean linen, pinning it in place when she was done. It eased the pain slightly, and I had to admit, now that I knew how minor the injury really was, that some of my pain had really been from fear. Maydan wanted to help me into the yurt, but it was almost dawn now, and I was too keyed up to be able to sleep anytime soon. She fetched me a blanket instead, and I settled down where I could watch the sisters unloading the camels.

The contents of the camels' packs were mostly unremarkable. There were some sacks of beans and rice, which were added to our own food stores, and bolts of cloth, some very nice, which would come in handy for replacing my shredded, blood-soaked clothing. One bolt of cloth elicited gasps, and as I saw it catch the light I recognized what it was—silk. The bandits must have robbed traders shortly before robbing us. We found some good-sized waterskins, some empty and some full. Then a small, tightly closed metal box came down; it required a key, but it didn't take long to force it open. And inside was the prize—glittering, gem-set jewelry. The wealth of the bandits, most likely. The women sorted through the jewelry admiringly, holding up some of the flashier pieces. Not flashy enough to be eye-catching, one glittering necklace was tossed aside after a quick glance. But it caught *my* eye. *A spell-chain.* I wondered if any of the women here would know what it was. That, that surely was what the bandits were so desperate to retrieve.

If they know it's here, and they know what it is, why did they keep it locked in a box, rather than around someone's neck, where it could be used? I thought immediately of the garrison Kyros had sent me to, years ago, where the second-in-command had taken over. They'd locked their spell-chain in a box as well, and then put it under guard. For a moment I wondered if these were the same men, but I doubted it. I thought this spell-chain had probably been stolen.

The soldiers at the garrison had feared madness. There were other reasons to be wary of a spell-chain as well; binding-spells could grow unstable after the death of the sorceress who performed the initial binding. If an aeriko was going to break free from the spell, it would happen when the spell-chain was used, and keeping it locked in a box when it wasn't in use would do no good. But those with a small amount of knowledge and a large amount of superstition might well keep it locked away anyway.

Now, would the sisters know what they'd taken? I wondered if I could make my way over and pocket the chain without anyone noticing. Of course, if it were found on me, even if they didn't recognize what it was, they might want to know why I was stealing common property; I thought briefly of the honey. But still, it was tempting . . .

Janiya stopped by to look over the loot we'd robbed from the robbers. I saw her pick up the spell-chain and curl her fist around it—*she* knew what it was, I thought with a pang of disappointment. She glanced around, her eyes sweeping over me, and I quickly looked away.

The sun was up now, and the excitement and tension was finally beginning to ebb, leaving exhaustion behind, and giving me the opportunity to start to fret. Not that I was terribly expert with a sword, but surely anyone paying attention last night would have noticed that I'd used one before. Slaves were *never* permitted to touch weapons; had anyone been watching me closely enough to notice? Certainly Zhanna saw me get wounded, she rode in so quickly; and Tamar must have seen me during the first attack, since she was shooting at my attackers. Would they become suspicious? Who else might have seen?

Worse . . . It was strange for there to be a "worse," but now there was. What if the bandits came after us again? We had the spell-chain; they would want it back. Of course, Janiya could use the aeriko to her own advantage, but they might gamble that we wouldn't recognize the chain and attack anyway. And using the spell-chain carried its own risks. Aerika obeyed their orders because they had to, but they would twist those orders anytime they could. Janiya would not be experienced at spell-chain tactics. It wasn't as if you could just order the aeriko to kill your enemies; you had to come up with something else for them to do. Even ordering them to *move* your enemies, to some remote spot, was risky; sometimes people were killed accidentally on trips like that, particularly since the aeriko were not terribly inclined to be careful.

The cloth, supplies, and jewelry from the camels had been packed away again, and Zhanna came over to sit by me. I tensed, wondering if she was going to ask me about my skill with a sword, but instead she offered me a waterskin and then stroked my hair gently. "I'm sorry you were hurt last night. It wasn't fair, sending you into battle."

"I was glad to be able to do something useful," I said, since that was what Tamar might have said. Well, no. Tamar would have bitten her head off for suggesting that she might have wanted to stay behind.

"Were you ever a shaman-trainee?" Zhanna asked.

"No," I said. "Tamar was, though." I handed the waterskin back to her.

"Huh." Zhanna picked meditatively at her thumbnail. "Did your shaman try to tap you, at least?"

"Why do you ask?"

"The djinn seem . . . interested in you."

My scalp prickled as I remembered the Fair One's taunting. "Eh. I wouldn't know. At Kyros's, I worked in the stables; I saw the shaman seldom, if at all. I met the shaman in Sophos's harem, but I was there only briefly . . ."

"Would you like me to train you?"

"No," I said. "You should ask Tamar. *She* would."

Zhanna nodded. "I could train both of you, I suppose."

"I'll think about it."

She was silent for a few moments, her hands in her lap. "Are you and Tamar summer friends?"

"What?"

"Summer friends." She looked at me with wide-eyed frankness, and the baffled look on my face must have told her that I had not the faintest idea what she was talking about. "Well, you know. During the summers, when we're with the sisterhood, some of the women have summer friends. Maydan and Jolay, for instance."

"You mean they're lovers."

"Right. Summer friends." She took a swig of water herself. "Of course, some women just aren't interested in that sort of thing. Erdene is one of those—poor Saken! And then there are women who have all-year friends. But most of them end up like Janiya."

"What do you mean?"

"Commanders of sisterhoods. And then they see their all-year friends only in winter."

"Wouldn't those be winter friends, then?"

"You'd think that would be the way it worked, wouldn't you?" Zhanna winked at me. She brushed a strand of hair from my forehead, and laid her hand gently across my face. "I'll talk to Tamar about shaman training, too. We can discuss it later."

"Tamar and I aren't lovers, but we're blood sisters," I said.

"Ohhh," Zhanna said. "I'd wondered why the eldress sent you to us together! Usually new people are split up."

Janiya strode over, a slightly grim look on her face. I braced myself, thinking that she would surely be here to confront me about my ability with the sword. But she squatted down beside me, looking a little ashamed.

"I shouldn't have let you come along tonight," she said. "Ruan was right to question it, and even after Tamar protested, I should have ordered you to stay here. You could both have been killed—especially you, in the thick of the fight with a sword you barely knew how to use." I felt a wave of relief at her words, followed by a rush of shame. Was I *that* unskilled with my weapon? "But I did, and luckily you both came through with no permanent damage."

I nodded.

Janiya tucked a blue bead into my hand. "You proved your courage in that first fight, little sister," she said. "I'm not sure what you proved by coming with us into the second fight—courage or foolishness, or perhaps that you felt yourselves to be sisters. But I think you earned a second bead then." She placed a second bead beside the first on my palm. "Both you and Tamar." She patted my shoulder. "Rest and let your body mend itself. You're to take it easy as much as possible until Maydan says you're recovered."

As I lay around camp with Jolay, I worked on embroidering my black felt vest. The picture of the wineglass was quickly completed: shaky, but I supposed that was almost appropriate. I needed an image for my life at Kyros's—other than a horse, because I still wasn't ready to try to make a picture of a horse. I could embroider a shovel, I supposed, for the manure

I had supposedly shoveled in the barn, but some mischief in me made me think that it would be nice to do the vest using *real* images, images that truly represented my past but could still be explained to the Alashi. Kyros wasn't my owner, but he *was* my boss. What image could I use to represent him?

Honey cakes, I thought, picturing myself in Kyros's office. *I never went in there without being offered tea and a honey cake.* But that didn't really capture Kyros; an image of a honey cake implied a glutton, and Kyros was never a glutton. Particularly since I couldn't very well say to the Alashi that he always offered me honey cakes when I returned from a mission . . .

I summoned up an image of Kyros in my mind's eye. Though he was technically a military commander, he had the softness of a man who spent little time in the saddle and even less doing real work, but I'd seen him training with his sword, and he could move as fast as a diving hawk when he wanted. *A hawk.* That wasn't a bad image for Kyros; the hawk circled high above the desert, waiting to spot its prey, and that was often how I thought of Kyros. But in truth, Kyros wasn't a hawk; he was more like a hawk's master, sitting in the cool of a cave and waiting for the hawks to return with offerings of rabbits, squirrels, and sparrows. *You've returned with my little straying bird already.*

His spell-chains—he wore one around his neck, the other looped around his left wrist, so that no one could possibly miss the fact that he had two of them. On rare occasions he'd loaned one to me; I remembered the feel of the cool stones against my neck. I could embroider a picture of a spell-chain; I could use that to outline the back of the vest. And that way, if

Janiya saw me looking at the spell-chain she picked up, she'd understand why. *Perfect*, I thought, and reached for the thread.

"Lauria." Janiya's voice broke into my reverie. "I need a cup of water."

I set down my vest and stood up, with some effort, and picked up the waterskin. As I put my hand on it, it occurred to me that Janiya was testing me again. I threw the waterskin to the ground and sat down with a thump.

Janiya laughed. "Better," she said. "But you still fail."

Tamar sighed as I sat back down. She seemed to have the morning off from practicing archery or horseback riding or whatever they'd been drilling her on while I was recovering, and she'd settled down beside me. She was still embroidering her first image—a rosebud, ripped in half, with feathers scattered across the bottom of the vest. "I don't know why she didn't tell me to get her water that time," Tamar muttered. "I was all set to ask her what was wrong with her legs that she couldn't get it herself."

I shrugged, though it disturbed me a little that someone who'd actually been a *slave* would have no trouble seeing through the demand to the test underneath. "It'll be your turn next time. Probably."

Tamar laughed a little.

"You should talk to Zhanna, you know," I said. "She really *is* a shaman. Maybe she'll finish your training, if you ask."

Tamar gave me a long, mournful stare. "I think she likes you better," she said, and went back to her embroidery.

CHAPTER EIGHT

My wounds were still painful when Janiya announced that it was time to move, and to move quickly.

I looked her over carefully as I rose to join the others in packing our bags, and I thought I saw the glitter of the spell-chain peeking from the edge of her fist. *She's been using the aeriko to watch the bandits,* I thought. She'd wanted to give me and Jolay time to heal up before we moved, if possible, but now the bandits were presumably moving toward us again.

Well, I wasn't really looking forward to moving, let alone moving quickly, but I could if I had to. Around me, women began to pack bags and take apart the yurt; others went to gather in the flocks, which had been kept close by since the raid. I gathered up my own belongings—vest, blankets, sword— and strapped them to Kara's saddle. Tamar joined me a few minutes later, pink-cheeked and breathless; she'd been out riding. She greeted me breathlessly and ran to help pack the yurt.

I returned to camp to offer to help with the yurt, but Maydan firmly told me to sit down somewhere and rest until it was time to leave. I withdrew to the edge of the river to sit in the shade of a tree, watching the activity back in the camp.

There was a shimmer in the air in front of me. "You are seldom alone," the aeriko said.

It sounded almost like a complaint, and I suppressed a laugh, mindful of the fact that someone might glance in my direction and see me talking to the air. "Do you have a message for me?" I asked.

"Kyros sends the following words." The shimmer shifted slightly and I heard Kyros's intonation in its voice. "Greetings, Lauria, and I will try to keep this short. You are my most trusted aide and you have my complete confidence—however, I have been very worried about your safety, which is why I sent the aeriko to keep watch over you. Please give the aeriko a brief update, to set my mind at rest."

The ache in my ribs subsided as I listened to Kyros's words, and I felt the calm reassurance of his words wrap around me. I hadn't even realized that my stomach was churning until I felt it settle. "Things are going well," I said softly. "Well, mostly. We're— *I'm*—working to be accepted as one of the Alashi. It hasn't been easy but I've passed some of the tests." I fingered the bandage on my side. "We were attacked a few nights ago, and I was wounded in the fight. I'm recovering now." Should I mention Janiya's spell-chain? I hesitated—no, surely he knew that the Alashi had many resources, one more could hardly matter to him. *But I could tell him about Sophos.* "There's something you should know about what happened when I was with Sophos," I said. I paused for a moment to collect my thoughts, but suddenly my breath was ragged and my mouth was dry. The aeriko shimmered silently in the air, waiting. "I—" No, that wasn't how to begin. "He—"

Back at camp, I could see Tamar conferring with Maydan, and Maydan pointing toward me. "Someone's coming," I said. My voice was unsteady, stumbling. *I wish I could talk with Kyros about this face-to-face, not through an aeriko.* "You'd better go, someone's coming."

The shimmer vanished. I glanced toward the camp again, hoping that nobody had seen anything, and saw that Tamar was not coming toward me after all. I could have finished my report. I rubbed my forehead with my hand, hoping that anyone who saw me would think my headache was from the glare of the sun. At least this way, I could mull over how to tell my story, instead of thrashing around for words while facing an aeriko.

I hugged Kyros's reassurances around myself like a blanket as I made my way back toward camp. Everything was loaded up; women were mounting horses and moving out. Someone had saddled Kara for me, and I mounted with a little bit of difficulty and joined the rest of the group. As I started to ride out, I suddenly remembered something I'd seen, but not entirely *noticed,* down by the river. A cooking pot—the big iron pot we cooked rice in. Someone had been scrubbing it, probably, and left it behind. Well, I'd ride down to the river and grab it and catch up; even injured I thought I could probably manage that.

It was right where I remembered seeing it—tipped over and full of water and sand. I started to lift it and had to stop; the strain on my ribs was too painful, and it felt like my entire back seized up in protest from the effort. I swore, in Greek; I had pictured myself simply scooping it up and tying it to the back of my saddle. I hadn't remembered it being this heavy, but then, when Tamar and I had cooked the meal, I hadn't had a broken rib. I kicked it over to dump out the water and sand, let it drain for a moment, then tried again. I thought I could probably lift it, but whether I could get it, and myself, up on my horse— well, that was another question entirely.

"What the hell are you doing?"

It was Tamar. Relief washed over me. "I saw this pot when I was down by the river and I realized someone had forgotten it. I thought . . . I thought I'd . . ."

"Why didn't you *tell* someone instead of taking off by yourself? Oh, don't worry about it. I'll get it." Tamar efficiently loaded the pot onto her own horse and helped me mount back up. "Come on, we'll have to hurry to catch up."

We encountered Maydan on the way; she had doubled back to look for us. I was keeping up, but with a tight jaw and clenched fists, and Maydan sent Tamar on ahead while riding with me. "We can stop and rest if you need to, I know where everyone else is going."

"What if the bandits . . ."

"They're moving but they're not within striking distance of us yet." Despite her confident words, Maydan glanced over her shoulder to scan the horizon. I wondered if she knew about Janiya's spell-chain. What would Zhanna and the other djinn worshippers think of Janiya making use of a bound djinn?

For that matter, I wasn't entirely certain I trusted Janiya's information. Janiya couldn't possibly have a lot of experience getting useful information out of bound aerika. It could have told her that the bandits were *close* just for the fun of seeing us scurry around like mice in a hawk's shadow; after all, without a precise definition, *close* could mean "closer than Penelopeia." By the same token, if the bandits were too far away to see, it could have told her they were *far*. Did Janiya know just how precisely she had to phrase her questions, in order to trust the answers?

I knew how to get information out of aerika. Throughout the ride, I mulled over whether I could offer to help, and if so, on what pretext. I could plausibly claim to have recognized the spell-chain, but I could think of no excuse for a former slave to have much experience at questioning aerika. Perhaps if I'd been a longtime trusted servant at Kyros's I would have occasionally overheard him giving instructions to an aeriko, but as a stable girl . . . no. There was nothing I could say; it was too risky.

Regardless of whether Janiya's aeriko was providing her with reliable information, Maydan and I were not attacked by the bandits before we joined the rest of the sisterhood at dusk. We had fallen so far behind during the day that camp was entirely set up by the time we reached it. The other women had built the yurts, lit a fire, and started dinner. I let Maydan remove Kara's saddle but insisted on grooming her myself; it wasn't as if it was *that* strenuous a chore. I had underestimated how utterly exhausted I was, and when I was half done, she took the brush from me and I didn't protest.

I slumped to the ground beside Tamar, hating my weakness, hating myself for having been so careless as to get injured. Tamar handed me a bowl of lentils and rice, which I ate without even really tasting them. I washed them down with water, refused the skin of kumiss, and went to get my blanket; all I wanted was sleep.

Janiya stopped me as I was returning to the yurt. "Tamar says that you went to get the cook pot, that you noticed it had been forgotten."

"Yeah," I said, wondering what I'd done wrong now.

"Why didn't you tell someone else to go get it?"

I shrugged. "Everyone else was busy. I thought it would only take a minute; I hadn't realized how hard it would be to lift the pot."

Tamar saw Janiya talking to me and joined me; her nervousness was palpable. She glanced anxiously at me, and shot Janiya a hostile look. "We didn't get that far behind," Tamar said.

"You went after Lauria," Janiya said to her. "Why?"

"What was I supposed to do? Tell someone else to go look for her? I was the one who noticed she was missing. I didn't think it would take long to find her, and if she'd fallen behind because of her injury, I could ride after the rest of the sisterhood and tell them to slow down."

"But she hadn't fallen behind because of her injury."

"Not then, no," Tamar said, her voice impatient. "She was struggling with the pot, so I loaded it up and we went. What did we do wrong *now*?"

"Nothing," Janiya said. She slapped a blue bead into my hand, then one into Tamar's. "For showing initiative. The initiative you failed to show that first day, when I sent you out looking for karenite. You acted as sisters and free women, not as slaves."

"For getting a *pot*?" I blurted out.

"It's no simpler than getting water for *yourself* before heading out for a walk in the desert," Janiya said. She gave us each a cordial nod and walked away.

Tamar was grinning; I shook my head, hovering between elation and disgust. I would *never* figure these women out. *Ever.* My mission was doomed, then, unless I happened to pass the tests by luck, which seemed unlikely. I threaded my new bead on the leather thong, then strode into the yurt, threw down my blankets, and went to sleep.

I woke early, before the sun was up, and had to get up to relieve myself. The sky was just beginning to lighten; I stepped out of camp to squat in the long grass, and became aware after a moment or two that an aeriko was watching me.

I quickly finished my business, uncomfortable with the audience. I hadn't yet decided how to tell Kyros what had happened—I hadn't expected him to send the aeriko back so soon. "What now?" I whispered. It said nothing, hovering in the air. "Did Kyros want more information?"

"Who is Kyros?"

I realized that the aeriko was unbound—or perhaps this was Janiya's aeriko. I bit back a Greek curse and said, "Did Janiya send you?"

"No one sent me."

Well, that was something. "What do you want with me?"

Silence and the shimmer. Then: "You are followed by one of my kind."

That would no doubt be Kyros's aeriko. "I see," I said.

"An enslaved djinn. A slaver wishes to spy on you."

"Why are you telling me this?" Was it trying to be *helpful*? Or to find out if I knew who'd sent the spy?

Silence again. Then the shimmer vanished like a faint star behind a cloud, and I knew I was alone.

I wasn't going to be able to sleep after that sort of conversation, but I was still hurting too much to go start on any useful work. After shivering on the edge of camp for a short time, wondering what to do with myself, I went and sat by the embers of the fire.

Ruan was the first of the sisters to get up in the morning. "Oh," she said as she stepped out of the yurt. "So that's where you went."

"Did you miss me?" I asked, unable to keep the sarcasm out of my voice.

"Oh yeah," she said. "It's such a disappointment when I don't get woken up in the middle of the night." She wandered over closer to the fire and tossed on some fresh fuel. "You must think you're quite the newly polished sword, little blossom— wounded in your first fight, everyone hovering over you like a clutch of hens with a limping chick."

"I'm sure everyone's wounded sooner or later," I said. "You, for instance, clearly had your face re-arranged at least once."

"You certainly have a high opinion of your wit."

I squinted. "Maybe twice."

"Do you want to see the wound I took defending the sisterhood, little blossom?" Ruan pulled up her tunic to show a long, ragged scar along her side. It had clearly been a much deeper wound than I'd taken—in fact, it was amazing that she'd survived it. She let me take a long, incredulous look, then dropped her tunic and walked away without another word.

The sisters spent the morning settling into the camp

they'd set up so hastily the night before—unpacking food, sorting out things that had been jumbled together when they had to load up in a hurry, exploring the area. "We'd have had to move soon anyway," Saken said. "The grass near our old camp was nearly grazed out."

I helped where I could, but found myself mostly shooed away to rest in the shade along with Jolay. She didn't seem nearly as frustrated by her injury as I felt by mine; in fact, she almost seemed to be making the most of it, sending her friends running to get her water when she was thirsty so she didn't have to budge from the shade. I felt restless and bored, and sick to death of embroidery. I cut a fresh thread and grudgingly poked the needle through the black felt, thinking back to the endless hours I'd spent under my mother's eye as a child. I'd hated embroidery then, too.

In early afternoon, there was a shout from someone at the edge of camp; she could see a cloud of dust in the distance. The news flew through the camp like a swarm of gnats, and even Jolay got to her feet to gather at the edge of camp to see what was going on. "They tracked us," Ruan muttered furiously, then glanced over at me as if it were somehow my fault.

Janiya bit her lip and shook her head; I saw her hand go to something tucked under her shirt. She'd been keeping an eye on the bandits, and was confident this wasn't them—but what if the bandits had split up and the aeriko had chosen to interpret the other group as the "bandits" he'd been asked to watch for? I itched to take Janiya aside and ask to use the spell-chain myself.

Then Janiya pulled her empty hand back and said, "Right. We have to assume it's them. Jolay and Lauria, take your weapons and hide yourselves away from camp—I don't want you fighting unless it's your only chance of survival. Tamar, you can go with them to help protect them if they're found. Everyone else, get your weapons and horses; we're riding out to meet them."

Tamar bit her lip, then fetched her bow—the one she'd practiced with seemed to be *her* bow now—and her thumb-ring and arrows. Jolay had a bow and a long knife, and I took my sword and grabbed a water-skin for good measure. It was daytime, and there was no guarantee we'd be hiding anywhere near water.

Jolay took the lead. Tamar and I followed her along the river and then away from it, heading over a low rise. After a few minutes of walking she found a spot shaded by a little bit of overhanging rock; long grass grew around it, and once we settled down on the ground we were invisible to anyone who didn't stumble across us.

"How will the sisters find us?" I asked.

"Well, eventually I'm sure they'll stumble across our starved and withered bodies . . ." Jolay said. "Oh, don't look so stricken, Tamar! I was joking. Janiya will blow the horn when it's safe to return, three long blasts."

We settled in. Jolay was out of breath and cradling her injured arm. I passed her the waterskin and she gave me a wry smile and a nod of approval. "Very good, blossom," she intoned. "You remembered to bring *water* without being told. Beads all around!" I couldn't help snickering at that.

I strained to hear the sounds of battle—shouts, the clash of metal, anything. I heard the wind moving through the grass, and a moment later, the piercing whistle of a bird nearby. Below that, I could hear the hum of insects. If there was a battle going on, it was too far away to hear. Jolay took a drink of water, then leaned back against the rock and closed her eyes. Tamar sat with her bow in her hand and an arrow out, even twitchier than I was.

"Do you just hate this?" I asked Jolay after a few minutes.

"Hate this weather?" She opened her eyes and turned her head to look at me. "No, I think it's rather fine."

"Not the weather." I rolled my eyes. "Being wounded. Not being able to fight. Not knowing what's going *on*."

She rolled her eyes back at me. "Of course I do. Why would you feel the need to ask?" She shrugged with her good shoulder. "But hating it won't heal my arm any faster." She closed her eyes again. "Relax," she said. "It will all be over soon."

I strained again to listen, but could hear only the wind, the birds, and Jolay's even, regular breathing. Tamar tapped the ground with the point of her arrow; after a few minutes, Jolay opened her eyes and saw her and said, "Don't do that. You'll dull it." Tamar bit her lip and stopped.

I wished I'd at least brought along my vest and a needle, or *something* to do. Anything. Jolay still looked relaxed enough to nap. I couldn't hear anything. Tamar set the arrow down and switched to ripping up the long dry grass from the ground, then shredding it. I wanted to pace, but that would pretty well destroy the whole point of hiding. Also, my ribs hurt more when I was walking.

Finally we heard three long blasts on Janiya's horn.

Tamar put her arrow back in the quiver and picked up my waterskin, and Jolay led us back to camp.

The first thing we saw as we approached were the camels—lots of them, and with short, sparse hair instead of the luxurious silky coats our own camels had. Then we saw a dozen newcomers standing by the camels—*men,* I realized after a minute. "Merchants," Jolay exclaimed in relief and pleasure. "That's who was raising the dust. Not the bandits after all." Her eyes glinted. "And *men.* Oh my, this should be interesting."

"Don't you have a summer friend?" Tamar asked.

"Yes, Maydan and I keep each other good company. But Ruan . . . Erdene . . . well! It's like getting a sack of sweet oranges out of season." She lowered her eyes in false demureness, then glanced up to see if she'd made Tamar smile. She had.

Janiya motioned us over. Two of the newcomers were clearly the owners of the caravan; they were well dressed and conversing with Janiya. "This is Amin, and this is Gerhard," Janiya said. "They're silk merchants."

Amin and Gerhard turned to us and bowed. Though they were dressed identically, in loose robes that covered them from their heads to their feet, they couldn't have looked more different. Amin was very dark-skinned, much darker than any Greek or Danibeki I'd ever seen; Gerhard had the palest skin I'd ever seen, so ivory he almost looked ill, and yellow hair. His eyes were pale blue, like the morning sky. Amin's eyes were a rich dark brown and very large, and his hair was tightly curled like sheep's wool. I realized I was staring, and averted my eyes as I muttered a greeting.

"You and your men are welcome to join us for dinner," Janiya said to them, glancing at me with a hint of exasperation. I wondered if she worried that I was going to grab one of these men as a bed partner for the night, a desire-crazed girl with no "summer friend" to keep her company. I couldn't think of any way to reassure her that wouldn't have sounded even more foolish, so I started to edge away instead. "When you make your camp," she continued, "please set your tents a little removed from ours."

"As you wish, gracious lady," Gerhard said in accented Danibeki, and bowed again. "We would be honored to join you at your meal."

"We may have some goods to trade with you," Janiya added. "More than just karenite."

Gerhard raised an eyebrow at this; Amin gave her a brilliant smile. "We would be delighted to discuss it after we've seen to our camels. May we draw water from your stream?"

"Of course." Janiya nodded her permission and the two men led their camels down to the river.

The tangible fear was gone, replaced by a festive mood. The sisters hadn't even put their weapons away, but had gathered by the door of the yurt to discuss the newcomers in low voices. "Did you see Gerhard's *eyes*?" Erdene was asking.

"I liked Amin's eyes better," Ruan said, for once laughing with everyone else.

"You can have Amin, I'll take Gerhard," Erdene said.

"Oh, but wouldn't Arai be jealous?"

"At this point, I don't think he'd complain, so long as Gerhard got me pregnant," Erdene said, and sighed. "Do you think Janiya would be *furious*?"

"Probably," Ruan said.

"Of course she would," Saken said. "The question is, are Gerhard's beautiful eyes worth it?"

"*Almost,*" Erdene said with a dreamy sigh.

Jolay opened her mouth, then shut it and slipped her arm around Maydan's waist. Maydan glanced back at her with an amused smile and said, "I'm so pleased for you that you have the opportunity for some *company*." Ruan shot her a sour look, and Maydan beamed back at her.

When the men returned from watering their camels and setting up small tents for themselves and their men, Janiya brought out the bolt of silk we'd taken from the bandits. It was dark red, and caught the afternoon sun like a cut gem. I heard a faint sigh from Saken, near my side, and I thought she probably wanted to rub the fabric just to feel its sheen. Amin and Gerhard were good traders. Though this had to be an unexpected find, their faces showed only the same polite interest they had shown before. Amin took the bolt and unrolled it partway, to examine the fabric more closely. "This is really quite lovely. How did you come upon it?"

"We were raided a week or so ago. The bandits found the encounter less than profitable." Janiya let herself smirk.

Gerhard laughed out loud and bowed yet again. "I salute you, lady, and your warriors. We encountered bandits some weeks back, but fortunately our men were able to drive them off."

"If the bandits you met came off the worse for your encounter, you've done us a good turn," Amin said. "So we'll give you a very good price for your silk . . ." At that point, of course, the bargaining began in earnest. I listened with some interest; I thought it a fair enough deal by the end. After the deal was concluded, Gerhard magnanimously threw in a sack of oranges for the sisterhood to share.

There was meat with dinner; Janiya decided to have a goat slaughtered, and stewed in the pot with the beans. The meat was greasy but at least it offered some variety; I chewed each piece for a long time. There was bread, too, and even honey in a heavy clay jar. "This is the finest meal I've tasted since leaving Axum," Amin said. "Your hospitality to us strangers is most gracious, and we humbly thank you. All of you." I noticed that he drank as little of the inevitable kumiss as he possibly could while still being polite.

"Let us offer you something," Gerhard said after taking his own tiny, polite swallow of the curd-laden kumiss. He retreated to his own camp for a minute, then returned with a clay jug. I saw him glance at Amin, who grinned and nodded assent. "Fine Greek wine."

"Lovely!" Saken exclaimed, and held out her cup as Gerhard poured.

"Aren't you men heading west?" Ruan asked with some amusement. "Who are you going to sell the Greek wine to?"

"No one," Gerhard said in a conspiratorial whisper. "We drink it ourselves. And share it with our hosts. Who else would like a cup?"

There was an instant clamor; kumiss might be what everyone was used to, but exotic Greek intoxicants were certainly not to be refused. I gladly let Gerhard fill my cup, and brought it to my lips.

"Let me get you some wine," Tamar said. The wine had a strange taste, as if it had started to sour. I

pushed the cup away, wanting to be sober for my meeting with Sophos, but Tamar pushed it back to my lips.

I jerked back, my hand shaking; the smell of the wine had summoned the harem so vividly for a moment I almost thought I was back there. I felt sick to my stomach; I forced myself to take a sip anyway, and shuddered. Tamar had not taken any wine at all, I noticed. I played with my cup, looking at the other women; Ruan took only a small amount, but everyone else happily let Gerhard fill their cups. From the looks on their faces, not everyone liked the taste once they tried it.

I tried again to take a sip and could barely choke it down. Saken seemed to be enjoying her wine, so when she'd finished, I poured my wine into her cup. Ruan was watching me, a faint smirk on her face, but for once she said nothing.

"So we heard strange rumors when we passed through Meleinaia," Gerhard said. "The Penelopeians are planning an offensive in the fall, to wipe out the Alashi once and for all."

"They're always planning to wipe us out once and for all," Janiya said. "Did you hear any *new* rumors?"

"Well, they're bringing troops north," Gerhard said.

"It won't be good for trade, if they win," Amin said. "The Alashi keep the bandits in check along our route across this desert, mostly. The Penelopeians won't have any reason to care. Especially as they have their own profitable trade, using djinn caravans."

"How can you possibly compete with that?" I asked. "They can transport far more with djinn than you can with camels."

"Lucky for us, the Penelopeians are greedy," Gerhard said with an amiable laugh. "They *could* undercut us but they don't bother. *We* aren't enough of a threat to their empire to be worth stomping out."

Saken shook her head. "Neither are we—you'd think. I don't know why they care that we're up here."

"We're their one failure," Ruan said. "They said they'd punish the Danibeki by flooding our lands and enslaving our people, but some of us escaped. And keep escaping."

"Well, it doesn't matter how many troops they bring up," Maydan said sturdily. "We can always retreat into the desert and let the *sun* kill the Greeks."

There was a round of laughter, and everyone added the tidbits they knew about how stupid the Greeks could be: they couldn't find water if it was right in front of their nose, they couldn't navigate on the featureless plain, they rode oxen and called them horses, and so on. I stared into the fire, thinking about how wrong these claims really were. I'd learned how to find water from Nikon, Kyros's kinsman and my good friend. I'd made it to the Alashi alive, even with an unexpected companion. The Greeks had spell-chains and bound aerika; they could have the aerika find water for them. For that matter, they could have an aerika water-caravan, doing nothing but refilling jugs of water from somewhere to the south and bringing them up to the army. Kyros knew how to navigate by the stars, he didn't need landmarks any more than I did, and while the Alashi horses might be better for long rides through the desert, Zhade—a sudden lonely longing for my *own* horse rose up in my throat and choked me, for a moment—Zhade was certainly no *ox*.

I fingered the almost-completed spell-chain on the back of my black vest. *Those Greeks you're laughing at could wipe you out,* I thought. *They* are *planning something, or Kyros wouldn't have sent me here.* And then another chilling thought: *They will wipe you out, and I will help them do it.* I stroked the embroidered stitches, picturing, against my will, Greek soldiers riding through the camp; the women here fought well, but if they were outnumbered, *betrayed* . . . It was easy to feel a small spark of pleasure imagining something bad happening to Ruan, but I had no malice toward Jolay, Maydan, Saken, Erdene. Not even toward Janiya. *And certainly not Tamar.*

And why had the Sisterhood of Weavers decided suddenly this year that it was time to wipe out the Alashi? *The Arch-Magia has reason to believe that the bandits are planning a larger offensive against us.* So the sorceress had said. But I'd seen no evidence of that. For that matter, Kyros's djinn hadn't even asked me about these rumors, only whether I was trusted yet. *It's the Greeks who are planning an offensive, with me as the poison on their own arrow-tip, ready to betray from inside.* But why now? And why bother? As Kyros had noted, it was the Greek bandits that caused most of the trouble anymore.

The Greeks must want something that's in Alashi territory. But what? I'd seen little but steppe and sky in the months I'd been here. *Wiping out the Alashi is a lot of trouble to go to just for some dried-out grass and weathered rocks.* No, wait. *Rocks.* I closed my fist over some of the loose pebbles on the ground, and remembered the iron mine I'd passed with Sophos. There were mines in the hills on the edge of Greek territory, where people dug deep into the ground to bring out iron, lead, gold, and other things of use or value. No doubt there was more of everything under the ground I was sitting on right now. Perhaps that was what the Greeks wanted.

Still. Even for gold, it seemed like a great deal of trouble to go to.

Despite the fire, I was growing cold, and I could see another wineskin coming out. I excused myself and retreated to the yurt to sleep. I would have to think about this more later.

*Y*ou are my most trusted servant, and you have never disappointed me, Lauria."

I was in Kyros's office, munching on a honey cake. It was early winter; there was a fire on the hearth. One of the logs snapped suddenly, sending a shower of sparks up the chimney. The light caught on a faceted bead of the spell-chain wrapped around Kyros's wrist.

"Is my mission complete?" I asked, wondering why I couldn't remember how it ended. Oh yes: attack, blood, victory for the Greeks. It all seemed very distant.

"You did perfectly. *Brilliantly*." Kyros had an apple on his desk, as red as a spring flower. He cut it into slices, passing me a succulent wedge. "You have never let me down—but you truly surpassed yourself this time."

"I'm glad," I said. And I was, though it was a strange, distant pleasure.

"Name your reward, Lauria."

My reward? "Sophos's head on a stake," I said instantly.

"I had him executed months ago, as soon as I heard. Besides, that's justice, not a reward. I want to offer you more than that."

Then, of course. "Tamar," I said. "She was one of Sophos's slaves, and she escaped when I did. She's become a good friend of mine. I'd like her to be freed, to come live with me. Perhaps we could find a place in town . . ."

"A house and a . . ." Kyros almost said *slave,* I realized. "Tamar," he finished. "Of course, those are easy things to arrange. I'll have the young lady sent to you this afternoon."

The room seemed oddly dark, despite the fire, and I saw another glint from Kyros's spell-chain. "Wait," I said, and grabbed his wrist for a closer look. One bead shifted in color as I looked at it: gray to green to blue. "That's karenite," I said. "The soul-stone of the spell-chain is made from karenite."

Kyros pulled his arm back from me, looking confused. "I understand now," I said, as the dream faded into the darkness of the yurt. "Now I know what it is you're looking for."

I woke, freezing cold. I'd lost my blanket somehow in my sleep, and I was close enough to the door of the yurt that the night wind was blowing across my head. I retrieved my blanket and noticed that the yurt seemed strangely empty. Tamar was where she belonged, but Ruan was missing, and Erdene. I suppressed a snicker, thinking about the merchants and their pretty eyes. They must have slipped off to the merchants' camp. I wondered where summer friends found the time and privacy to enjoy each other's company . . . Well, people tend to find a way when they're determined.

I tucked my blanket in around me and thought about the dream. Karenite was scattered across the steppe; after that original errand I'd spotted it and picked up pieces several times. But I'd never seen it lying on the ground near Elpisia. *If it's the foundation of the Sisterhood's power, then of course they want more of it. Need more of it.* I was quite certain, mulling over what I'd pieced together, that I was right about this.

It was strange, knowing something this important when Kyros hadn't told me. As I slipped back down into sleep, I thought about the other part of the dream. *I can trust Kyros,* I thought. *And whatever else comes, I will keep Tamar safe.*

CHAPTER NINE

"Close your eyes," Zhanna said. "Find a comfortable position to sit in. Now watch your breath: in, then out. In, then out."

I pulled my legs up beside me, thinking that I'd be more comfortable in a chair, and wondering where the nearest chair was—probably no closer than one of the Greek garrisons on the very edge of their territory. I sat up as straight as I could, since before I'd closed my eyes I'd seen Tamar carefully arranging herself with a perfectly straight back. I tried to pay attention to my breathing, as Zhanna had suggested: *in, out. In, out.*

It didn't take me long to get bored.

Also, my butt began to tingle, and pretty soon after that, it went to sleep entirely. So did my left leg. I considered changing position but I hadn't heard Tamar shift, so I felt like I probably wasn't supposed to. If I were *really* paying attention to my breath, if I were doing this right, I probably wouldn't even be noticing how uncomfortable I was. I shifted discreetly. My ribs

ached, though the wound was mostly healed. *In, ou*
I told myself sternly.

I was *not* cut out to be a shaman.

Tamar, on the other hand—I could hear *her* breath
when I listened for it. Perfectly even, and as far as
could tell, she hadn't moved a muscle. Beyond Tama
I could hear a bird singing, and insects humming
Even Zhanna wasn't moving, rot her. I *had* to move
finally, so I rearranged my legs and tried again to ge
comfortable. Now my numb left leg began to com
back to life; it felt like it was being stabbed by severa
hundred tiny needles. I leaned forward, suppressing
groan, and flexed my foot inside my boot. *Breathe.*
wondered if Tamar had actually entered the open, re
ceptive state that I suspected was supposed to be ou
goal here. *Probably.*

Time passed. I watched the play of sun an
shadow inside my eyelids, and tried to shift positio
often enough that my limbs didn't fall asleep and m
knees didn't ache. I clenched my hands into fists an
rubbed my thumbs against my fingers. An inse
landed on my shoulder and I twitched it off. I wo
dered if Zhanna was going to make us sit here lik
this all afternoon.

Then I heard something new: a snort. No, a snore
Then, closer, a giggle. I opened my eyes and saw tha
Tamar had fallen asleep; Zhanna was laughing a
Tamar, and at me.

"Wake up, sleepyhead," she said, prodding Tama
Tamar's eyes flew open and darted back and forth be
tween me and Zhanna.

"I didn't—" Tamar said.

"I can't believe you got *comfortable* enough to fa
asleep," I muttered.

"I was more like Lauria," Zhanna said cheerfully. "Twitching around like a headless chicken. I figured it was worth a try. There are people who can enter the shamanic trance just by meditating. I can do it, very occasionally. It's the easiest way, if it's a path that's open to you. Clearly it's not going to work for either of you, so let's talk about what might work."

"Jaran dances," Tamar said. "The shaman back at . . . where Lauria and I used to live. He had me drum for him."

Zhanna nodded. "That's one way to do it. Drumming itself is another way. What moves you? What makes your soul to another place?"

Riding my horse, I thought, thinking of Zhade.

"Not dancing," Tamar said.

"All right, not dancing. Drumming?"

"I don't know."

"What about you, Lauria?"

"Riding," I said, because I hadn't come up with anything else.

"Well, that's not a very practical way to enter a state where you can invite the djinn. But if physical things work well for you, maybe *you* can try dancing."

I shrugged.

"We'll bring a drum along next time," Zhanna said.

"You're teaching us how to talk to the djinn," Tamar said. "What if the djinn decide on their own to talk to us?"

"Well, that happens sometimes, of course," Zhanna said. "Sometimes djinni possess people who didn't invite them. Has that ever happened to either of you?"

We shook our heads.

"Djinni who possess the unwilling are sometimes very angry; more often, they're just trying to cause

trouble. They seem to find it amusing. According t
our stories, djinn-possession used to be very rare. It'
become much more common as the enslavement o
djinni has become more common."

"It seems to happen a lot less here than it did bac
in Helladia," Tamar said.

"The djinn know that we aren't their enemies,
Zhanna said. "It *does* happen here sometimes, bu
you're right, less often. At any rate, the djinn can pos
sess the unwilling, as well as shamans; if this happen
to you, you probably won't be able to do much abou
it. Do you know of any other ways that the djin
might speak to you?"

"Dreams," Tamar said.

"That's right. It is *my* belief—" Zhanna lowere
her voice a little, though no one else was aroun
"—well, there are those who say that Athena spoke t
Alexander in dreams, before he conquered Olympu
and took Zeus's throne. I think that when people thin
their dreams were sent by Athena, or by Alexander–
or for that matter by Arachne or Prometheus—the
are actually hearing the djinn."

I thought about the vivid nightmares I'd had abou
Sophos. If those were from the djinn, what were th
djinn trying to tell me? *Don't trust Sophos?* I bit bac
a snicker. I didn't need the djinn to tell me that.

"Do you believe in Arachne and Prometheus?
Tamar asked Zhanna.

Zhanna shrugged and I could see that she was tryin
to think of a diplomatic response. "I don't know. I'v
never seen either one. I pray with the rest of the sister
hood as a sign of respect for my sisters; if Arachne an
Prometheus don't exist, I've wasted nothing but tim
If they do exist, I'm sure they're bright enough to kno

that my devotion isn't exactly heartfelt, but I doubt they worry too much about me and the other shamans. Now, back to the djinn; there is one other way that the djinn might choose to speak to you, and that is simply to *speak* to you. It's rare, but they can do it if they choose to."

"Why wouldn't they just talk to us instead of sending dreams?" Tamar asked.

"Dreams are the closest most people ever get to the Silent Lands. When you're asleep, sometimes the djinn can talk to you from their own side of the web."

"How do you know if a dream was sent by the djinn?" I asked.

"Well . . . you can't, always. But djinn-sent dreams are particularly vivid. I suppose your nightmares are, too," she added with a sympathetic smile. "Those are probably *not* sent by the djinn, although they might be. When there's a lot weighing on our hearts, our hearts can keep our nights pretty busy without any help." She glanced at Tamar. "Since you're blood sisters, you know, someday you might be able to learn to communicate with *each other* using dreams. They'd be kind of like djinn-dreams, very vivid. Shamans can do that when they share blood with someone."

"Is it just shamans who can use that sort of magic?" I asked, thinking about some of the other sorts of magic I'd heard about.

"Well—mostly. I've heard stories about mothers and children . . ."

I laughed a little. "I thought a few times growing up that my mother could hear my thoughts."

"It's rare, but *some* people can do that with their blood kin, along with sending dreams. Some can even control thoughts, at least up to a point, but that's pretty complicated magic. It's not something I know how to do. It's not something I've ever *wanted* to do." Her face was bleak for a second, and then she laughed and added, "If you'd met any of my blood kin, you'd understand why! Anyway—" She stood up and brushed herself off. "We should be getting back. It's going to be time for dinner soon."

On the way back to camp, Tamar asked her, "What will happen to us if we don't pass all the tests?" She held out her leather thong with its blue beads. "I feel like we fail half the tests no matter what we do."

"You'll pass them all," Zhanna said.

"But what if we don't?"

"You will."

"You're not answering my question."

Zhanna glanced at me and saw that I was watching her closely, waiting for the answer as eagerly as Tamar. She sighed. Finally she said, "There *are* sometimes people who escape from slavery but aren't able to unlearn how to be a slave. They're offered a choice. Either we can sell them back into slavery—north, not back to the Greeks. Or they can kill themselves."

"Oh." Tamar's voice was almost inaudible.

"But don't *worry*. You *will* pass all the tests. You get a lot of chances, haven't you noticed that yet?"

"Have you ever seen this happen to someone?" I asked.

"I really can't answer that question," Zhanna said. It was quite obvious that the answer was yes.

"What did she choose?"

"She chose suicide," Zhanna said quietly. "Now stop asking me about this. I don't think I'm supposed to tell you things that are just going to worry you."

"So whose slave are *you*?" Tamar asked. "Who tells you what you're allowed to tell us?"

"I wouldn't be beaten and cast out to die in the desert, if that's what you're thinking." Zhanna looked at Tamar, her eyebrow quirked. "Or bound and thrown onto a fire as a sacrifice for Prometheus, or even used to test arrow-poison, no matter what the Greeks say about us. But I understand the reasons for some of these customs. I'm not supposed to tell you things that will worry you because there is really no cause to worry. You *will* pass the tests."

In the late-afternoon sun, I finished stitching Kyros's spell-chain on my vest, cut the thread, and slipped the vest on. Tamar had finished her torn flower and started on something else, but she wasn't working on it; she rolled the needle back and forth between her thumb and forefinger, and stared into space. Thinking about the blossom Zhanna had talked about, no doubt; that was certainly what was on my mind.

"Lauria!" Janiya called, her voice sharp. "Come here a minute."

I jumped guiltily to my feet, wondering what chore I'd neglected or task I'd forgotten. Then I saw the look on Janiya's face and slumped back down, biting my lip.

Beside me, Tamar leapt to her feet. "What is *wrong* with you?" she demanded shrilly—speaking to Janiya, not to me. "Can't you tell that she is *trying* to fit in here? Trying to be a *good* sister when she answers you swiftly or does what you ask her to do?"

Janiya folded her arms silently, a look of amusement on her face.

"You aren't being fair. *You aren't playing fair.* You change the rules on both of us every time it suits you.

I bet the first time she ignores you or tells you to go stuff yourself, you're going to tell her that she failed *again* because this time you were testing whether she responded promptly to the leader of the sisters. And *we* are supposed to *trust* you? Maybe if we could rely on you to treat us like sisters, we'd have an easier time acting the way you expect us to act!"

"Well, little one," Janiya said softly, when Tamar paused for breath. "*You* certainly have learned that I'm not your master." She drew out a bead and tossed it to Tamar. "Maybe you can help Lauria learn that same lesson sometime soon." She glanced at me. "Lauria, please step into the yurt with me, if you don't mind."

I stood up again and followed her reluctantly, feeling like a small child that was about to get yelled at. But instead of ripping into me she stepped behind me and traced the outline of the spell-chain I'd embroidered, with her finger. "Do you know what that is?"

"It's a spell-chain for binding aer—djinn." I cleared my throat. "My old master, Kyros, is a military officer. He owns two of them; he wears them looped around his neck and his wrist, to show off his power."

"Did you ever see him use one?"

"Maybe a few times," I whispered.

Janiya slipped her finger under her collar and pulled the spell-chain she'd taken from the bandits over her head. "See this?" she said. "We got it from the bandits."

"Have you used it?" I asked.

"Yes. But I'm not sure if I'm doing something wrong. The djinn is belligerent; it never does what I ask him to do."

"They follow orders *exactly*," I said. "If they *can* subvert their instructions or misinterpret what you said, they will. They are not willing servants. Not like Zhanna's friends, who come at whim rather than will, but come freely, and usually wish to be helpful."

"But Zhanna was visited by a *bound* djinn once recently."

"It hadn't been bound by *her*."

"Ah." Janiya rubbed the knuckle of her thumb against her forehead. "Well. Can you . . ." She paused, wet her lips, and considered how to phrase this, as if she were giving orders to a bound djinn. "Perhaps you can help me phrase the instructions, if you've seen someone do it?"

"Maybe."

"Right now I want to know what the Greeks are up to. We heard those rumors from the merchants, and I want to know how true they are."

"That's going to be hard," I said. "You could . . ." *You could send it to Elpisia to watch Kyros.* "I'll need to think about it."

"I'd appreciate hearing any thoughts you come up with." She nodded dismissal, and I went back out to have dinner.

I mulled over her request as I ate my lentils and rice. I could dodge her request entirely by coming up with a vague request for the aeriko that would never work. I had told Janiya that I'd seen a spell-chain used a few times; that wasn't really all that much experience. On the other hand, Janiya wasn't stupid, and she knew that I wasn't stupid, either. She had no reason to think I'd been anything other than a slave—but she knew I was a bright slave, someone who would have followed directions as necessary but would have found ways to subvert their intention when I could. Just like a djinn, in fact. That, along with the spell-chain embroidered

on my vest, was almost certainly why she'd asked me
to think about this.

So. I had to give her an answer—something that
plausibly seemed like it ought to work, but wouldn't
give her *too* much useful information. I could *not* sug-
gest sending the djinn to watch Kyros; he might talk
about *me* and the djinn might repeat the conversation.
But there was a garrison in Elpisia; we could send the
djinn there, to count soldiers. In fact, we could have
him count soldiers all over—would Janiya know what
a normal complement of soldiers was? I wasn't sure. If
the Greeks were planning something, though, they'd
need to be bringing up more men. And probably plac-
ing them, not only at Elpisia, but just beyond Alashi
territory to the east and west, if they could.

Tamar had added her new bead to her leather
thong, and gave me an abashed smile when she saw
me looking. I shrugged. At least it looked like Tamar
wouldn't be offered the choice between suicide and
slavery. And if I was—well, I hoped I'd know in time
to run away and head back to Kyros.

In the light of the setting sun, Maydan examined
my wound and removed the bandages. "You should
probably take it easy for a bit longer," she said. "No
riding unless it's necessary, because your ribs are going to hurt for a bit longer. But it doesn't need a bandage anymore." I took a deep, experimental breath;
the stabbing pain in my side was really just a dull
ache now. I smiled gamely at Maydan; she told me to
tell her if it took a turn for the worse and left me to
my own devices.

I had to relieve myself before bed. This campsite
was set up a bit differently from the last one; there
was a screen of a rubby bushes a bit beyond the edge

of the camp, and that's what had been designated as the latrine, since it offered a little privacy. As I was preparing to do my business, I saw a shimmer in the air: Kyros's aeriko.

"Report," the aeriko said.

That's all you have to say to me? I thought with some irritation. "What does Kyros want to know?"

The shimmer bobbed slightly. "Report," it said again.

I felt a slow burn of anger. "Here's my report," I said, gripping the edge of my vest. The words came easier now. "Despite your promises, and his promises, Sophos raped me. He threw me down, and held a knife to my throat, and said that if I didn't submit to him, he'd murder me and tell you that I got lost in the desert. He claimed that it was 'necessary' to convince the other slaves that I was really what I claimed to be." With the tip of my thumb, I traced the edge of the embroidered spell-chain as it curved around the front of the vest. "The next time you send your djinn, I think I'd like to hear what you're going to do about this. Other than that—there's no change in my status since the last time."

There was a shimmer and the aeriko vanished.

As I squatted to relieve myself, a horrible thought struck me. *All it said was "Report."* What if this wasn't Kyros's djinn, but Janiya's? What if she suspected that *something* was going on with me, and sent her djinn to try to trick me into betraying myself? *She has no reason to suspect,* I told myself, but how could I be so sure? *If she had any doubts at all, it would be easy enough to send the djinn. Oh, Kyros, have I betrayed myself?*

I was alone right now, but carrying nothing—not a waterskin, not my sword, nothing but my clothes.

My only hope was that this *wasn't* a trick from Janiya, because I certainly couldn't run. I crept slowly back to camp, scanning them from a distance to see if they might be watching for me—waiting, on Janiya's orders, to seize me as I returned.

"Lauria," said Tamar as I walked past. "Maydan says you're healed up well enough to work on your archery again."

"Probably," I said. "Are you going to teach me?"

Tamar made a face. "I think we're still both going to be supervised by Ruan. I've been practicing shooting from horseback—Gulim's been working on that with me. But tomorrow we're both supposed to meet for target practice."

"That will probably be Ruan," I said. My heart was pounding so loudly, I was surprised Tamar couldn't hear it.

"Lauria!" I looked up to see Janiya waiting in the doorway of the yurt. "Can you come here for a moment, please?"

I felt a surge of fear in the base of my throat, but managed a friendly smile to Tamar before I strode into Janiya's tent. *If she thought I was a traitor, she'd have had me seized already. She doesn't suspect. It wasn't her aeriko.*

"Have you had time to think at all about what instructions to give the djinn?" she asked.

I nodded. "Maybe you could send it to count the Greek soldiers in each of the garrisons on the edge of our territory? If you did that several times, over the course of a month or two you'd know if the Greeks were moving soldiers in. They'd need more soldiers to attack us. Wouldn't they?"

Janiya nodded. "That's not a bad idea. I wish I could get more specific information . . ."

"They're really not very good for that sort of thing," I said, the words spilling out in my relief that she didn't seem to know about my conversation with the djinn outside of camp. "If you have them spy on someone for their conversation, they can do that, but they'll repeat it *all*. If the Greeks sent a djinn here, to watch us, the djinn might hear this conversation, but it would repeat the conversation I just had with Tamar about archery as well. And everything else it heard. All jumbled together. Or, or, or—so I've heard." I faltered as my sense finally caught up with my tongue.

"You listened well," Janiya said. "I wonder if your old master realized half the things you were picking up? It's too bad I can't just send *you*." Her smile was guileless and teasing, and I hoped the darkness of the yurt hid my sick smile and my white face. I excused myself and went back out to the fire, thinking that even the vile kumiss would be welcome at this point to soothe my nerves.

I was embroidering a horse on my vest; I was doing it in the middle of the night, by moonlight, but it looked absolutely perfect, not a stitch out of place.

I looked up, and saw Kyros coming toward me. "What do you want?" I asked as he sat down at my side.

"Nice," he said, pointing to the horse. "Did you do that?"

"Yeah, I did that," I said, irritated. "Did you get my message about Sophos?"

"Yes, of course I did."

"And?"

"And I'll deal with him. You can trust me."

"Deal with him?"

"Yes, deal with him. That's what you expect, right? That's what you want?"

I bit my lip, clutching the vest in my fists.

"I can count on you, Lauria, I know I can always count on you . . ." But Kyros's voice was lost in a swirl of sparks as the needle I'd been using to embroider went deep into my palm.

I woke with a gasp in the darkness of the yurt. I listened carefully, but heard none of the telltale rustling that I'd have heard if I'd woken everyone else up. My palm still burned, and I rubbed it with my thumb. The pain ebbed away, and I stroked the edge of my vest, which I'd worn to sleep in that night. I smiled a little, closed my eyes, and went back to sleep.

I went with Tamar after breakfast to set up the target. I stretched my stiff muscles, thinking resentfully of the weeks of inactivity and how much weaker I was now than before the fight with the bandits. My ribs still ached, and I knew it was going to hurt to draw the bow. I stretched my side again and then fingered the sore spot.

Ruan strode up to us. "Right," she said, and tossed me a bow and a thumb-ring. "String it."

I strung the bow, and then gave it an experimental tug. It was much too heavy—it required more strength to bend it than I had, particularly with the injured ribs. "I need a lighter bow," I said.

"You need a *lighter* bow?" Ruan asked with pointed incredulousness. "That's a *very* light bow, blossom."

"I know. But my ribs still hurt. Surely you have even lighter bows for children learning to shoot."

"There are no children in a warrior camp."

"Well." I unstrung the bow and handed it back to her. "If I can't shoot, I can't shoot. And I can't shoot with this."

"I think maybe you should try a little harder."

"I think maybe I should talk to Maydan; she's the one who told me to take it easy."

"Oh, so now you're going to run to Maydan to whine about how I'm mistreating you?"

"No. But since Maydan knows my injuries better than you do, she can tell me whether I can actually draw this bow without making my injuries worse."

"Fine," Ruan said, and waved back toward the camp. "Go ask Maydan, then. You—" she turned to Tamar. "You can certainly draw your *own bow*. I think I'd like to see how far you can get from the target and still hit it."

I walked slowly back to camp, feeling ridiculous and a little ashamed, like the tale-bearing child Ruan had pretty much accused me of being. Maydan was sitting in the shade of the yurt, grinding up some dried herbs with a mortar and pestle. She looked up when she saw me coming. "Do you need something, Lauria?" she asked.

"I guess I just wanted your opinion as a healer," I said, and held out the bow. "I'm supposed to practice target shooting today, but it hurts to draw this bow. Should I just, you know, pull through the pain?"

"Well, how much pain?" Maydan bent the bow and released it without even stringing it. "Oh, this is much too heavy to use while you're injured, you're right. I'll find you a lighter one." She strode brusquely into the supply yurt and came out with a slender bow. "This is the lightest one we've got. See what you think."

I strung the bow and drew for a moment. "Oh. That's not nearly as bad."

"Use that one, then." She sat down and went back to crushing herbs.

When I returned to where I'd left Ruan and Tamar, I heard their raised voices before I reached them; the argument abruptly ended before I came close enough to hear what they were saying, and I returned just in time to see Tamar picking up the last of her scattered arrows from the ground. "She *pushed* me," she said through clenched teeth.

"You need to learn to shoot despite distractions."

"I shot a man in battle. And I'd like to see *you* shoot arrows while someone shoved *you* off your feet."

"Take your spot," Ruan said to me, and pointed. She handed me a quiver of arrows.

I remembered to tuck my elbow under this time. The arrows went far astray, and they didn't even all go astray in the same direction. I thought one almost nicked the target as it passed, but that was as close as I came. I collected the arrows when I was done and silently took my place beside Tamar.

"Show your friend how it's done, blossom," Ruan said to Tamar.

Tamar shot her arrows. Ruan didn't push her this time, and they thudded solidly into the target. She silently collected them and took her place by me again.

I took my turn. This time one of my arrows hit the target, but none of the others did.

Tamar's turn again. Ruan edged toward her. Tamar glanced at her, then resolutely shot at the target. A hit. She nocked another arrow and drew the bow back. This time, Ruan shouted, almost in her ear, "Look! What's that?" Despite knowing that Ruan was just trying to distract Tamar, I glanced to the side. Tamar didn't even look up; the arrow hit the target, dead center, and she got off another shot before Ruan slammed her body against hers, knocking her off-balance and her next shot wild.

"Get the hell off of me!" Tamar snarled, rounding on Ruan.

"This is how training works," Ruan said. "Got a problem with that, blossom?"

"What *exactly* am I supposed to be learning from this? I suppose you can hit a target when someone slams into you?"

"I'm not exactly as *gifted* as you are. It's hardly a challenge for you to just stand here and shoot, is it?"

"Then *maybe* I should go work on shooting from horseback some more," Tamar said.

"Oh, poor blossom. You don't *like* your training?"

Tamar clenched her teeth, turned back to the target, and actually managed to get two arrows off before Ruan shoved her again.

"Speed," I said.

"What?" Tamar whirled to face me, still off-balance from Ruan's push and ready to spit venom—at *either* of us.

"She's trying to teach you to shoot arrows quickly," I said. "In a battle, you'd need to seize your opportunities to shoot as many as you could, as fast as you could. If you stood, drew, aimed, and thought about it, there wouldn't actually be time to make your shot."

"Very good," Ruan said, though her voice dripped

a distinct lack of sincerity. Tamar's eyes widened, and she turned back to the target and took a shot. Ruan lunged toward her, and she ran a few steps, turned, and shot again. When she'd loosed all the arrows in her quiver, she gathered them up, and then returned, panting for breath.

"I wondered how long it would take you to realize you were allowed to dodge," Ruan said. "If the other blossom hadn't figured it out, how long do you think it would have taken you, little slave?"

The blood drained from Tamar's face. "What did you call me?" she said hoarsely.

"You heard me." Ruan turned away to pick up her own bow.

"Put your bow down," Tamar whispered.

Ruan turned back, a slow smile spreading across her face. "Are you challenging me to a *fight,* little girl? Little *harem* girl?"

"Ignore her, Tamar," I whispered. "She's itching to hurt you."

Tamar's lips were pinched and her face was the color of dry sand. I glanced from her to Ruan's smile and felt my stomach churn. *Until the other yields,* Ruan had said. Tamar couldn't fight—she could *shoot* better than anyone I'd ever seen, but it didn't even occur to her to dodge Ruan's body-blows until I suggested it. But she was stubborn. She was even better at being stubborn than she was at firing a bow. *Ruan's going to break her arm,* I thought, *because short of that, Tamar won't ever yield.*

"I'll give you one chance to apologize," Tamar whispered.

Ruan just smiled at her, waiting.

"*I* challenge you," I said, my voice cutting across Tamar's. "Your words insulted *both* of us."

"But—" Tamar turned to me, her eyes wide.

Ruan just shrugged. "One blossom is the same as any other, as far as I'm concerned. I could snap either of you like dry straw."

I handed Tamar my bow and quiver—the more she was holding, the less she was likely to try to jump into the fight herself. *I'll put up a little bit of a fight, then yield. I came home with enough black eyes growing up* . . . Ruan set down her own bow and smiled at me.

"Anytime you're ready," I said.

She began to move in a slow circle around me. "Slaves make me *sick,*" she said.

"We're not slaves," I said, turning slowly to keep my eyes on her.

"Oh, that's right—you 'took your freedom.' But it certainly took you *long* enough."

I heard a hiss of breath from Tamar.

"You slaves *outnumber* your Greek masters. If you just one day decided to snatch the weapons out of their hands, you could kill them all. Free yourselves and solve a lot of problems for the Alashi."

She used to be a slave, whispered the rational—the Greek—part of my mind, but the rest of me was too angry to listen. "It must seem awfully simple to you," I said. "I suppose in your world, all the slaves in every household would simply *rebel* on exactly the same day. No planning necessary. No discussion, no risk of betrayal . . ."

"How long do you have to be a slave before you've had enough?"

"Fourteen years, if you're Tamar," I said.

"Ah yes, but she escaped with *you*. I heard the story. If it hadn't been for *you*, how long would it have taken?"

"How long would it take *you* to gather the courage to flee barefoot through unknown desert with no food and no water?" I asked. "If you don't have the supplies you need to get across, you're almost guaranteed to die."

"I'd die of thirst a thousand times before I spread my legs for any Greek," Ruan spat. "It doesn't get much worse than *that*."

I heard Tamar suck in her breath, and that was when Ruan charged me, aiming her first punch for my injured side. I'd planned to let her take me down easily, but in that moment, I was so utterly furious all I wanted was to see Ruan bleed. I dodged the blow, caught her wrist, and jerked her off-balance, kneeing her in the stomach as she passed. She stumbled and almost caught herself, but I slammed into her once more and knocked her again off-balance, then punched her in the face. She stumbled back, clasping her bleeding nose.

Speed, some part of my mind whispered to me. *Don't give her time to recover.* She took a swing at me, but it was easy to dodge; she was seriously off-balance now. I caught her arm and twisted as I stepped behind her; she yelled out in pain and kicked at me, trying to get away. One kick connected and I let go, but followed with a hard kick toward her knee. I knocked her legs out from her and she hit the ground hard.

I jumped onto her chest and slapped her as hard as I could across the face. "That was for your insult to Tamar," I hissed. I slapped her again. "*That* was for your insult to me." Again. "And *that* was for your insult to my *mother*."

"I yield," Ruan croaked.

I climbed off her.

Only then did I realize how many of the sisters had gathered at the edge of our target-practice field to watch. One of them was Janiya, and I felt sinking horror in my stomach. Whether this was the normal way to settle differences—as Ruan had told us, I belatedly remembered—or not, I had a hard time believing that it was exactly approved of. No army actually approved of fighting in the ranks.

Janiya jerked her head, and Maydan went over to examine Ruan. I thought I saw the twitch of a smile on her lips, quickly concealed, as she gave Ruan a rag to press to her bleeding nose and helped her to her feet. "I think you'll live," she said, clearly trying to sound sympathetic.

Janiya looked from me to Tamar. "How did this start, exactly?"

"She called me a slave," Tamar said, lifting her chin.

"Ah. Then why weren't you the one who gave Ruan a bloody nose?"

"I *tried*," Tamar said, sounding petulant. "But Lauria—"

"The insult was to both of us," I said.

"I'm sure it was," Janiya said. "Well." She looked from me, to Tamar, and back to me. "I can't approve of fighting in the ranks, no matter how grave the insult. I'm sending you both out on shit-pickup duty tonight, to gather up the fresh animal droppings and spread them out to dry for fuel. You can consider that your punishment."

"Yes, ma'am," Tamar whispered.

"On the other hand, it's nice to see you two standing up for yourselves, finally." She handed each of us a blue bead.

"I can't think of a more deserving person to get a bloody nose," Zhanna muttered, and she wasn't concealing her approving smile at all. I glanced at her, and then back to Janiya. Janiya was looking at me with a cool, appraising look, and I felt my fear return. *No slave fights like that.* Well. I hoped I could come up with a good story before she asked me about it. Right now, the elation of having had Ruan yield to me with no more immediate consequence than manure pickup—well, that made it awfully hard to regret the fight.

CHAPTER TEN

Janiya called me into the yurt when the aeriko returned from counting Greek soldiers. I sat down with her and listened as the aeriko rattled off cities and numbers. The number for Elpisia was significantly higher than it had been when I'd left a few months earlier; they *were* moving soldiers in, not that this should have really been a surprise to me.

Janiya listened to the numbers, then reluctantly fetched paper, ink, and a pen, and laboriously wrote them down as the aeriko recited them again.

"This was a good idea," she said to me. "Thank you for suggesting it. I'll send him back in a few days to count again."

I hesitated before leaving the yurt. "And in the meantime?" I asked.

"What do you mean?"

"What are you going to do with the djinn in the meantime?"

Janiya set down her paper. "What are you suggesting?"

"You can send it out on other errands, you know. You could have it fetch supplies from somewhere else, if there's anything we're running out of. You could even have it take *you* to wherever the eldress is, if you think she ought to know about the rumors, and then have it bring you back."

Janiya stroked the spell-chain absently for a moment, then said, "I have to admit, Lauria, I have mixed feelings about using the djinn at all." I thought she was going to say that she feared the dangers it posed, but instead she said, "It's a slave; we don't . . . usually . . . keep slaves. It's not the Alashi way."

"It's not really like keeping a *human* slave." I said.

"Oh, I know. A human slave would pose far less temptation." She stroked the spell-chain again. "I guess right now I don't feel like we can risk freeing him; we too desperately need information on what the Greeks are doing, not to mention where the bandits are." She sighed. "Anyway, I kind of wonder if I should let him, well, *rest* for a few days. What do bound djinni do when they're not out on errands?"

"I have no idea." I looked for a moment at the necklace, glittering at Janiya's neck. "I guess you could summon it—him—and ask, couldn't you?"

"I could. I suppose I could." Her eyes were distant. "Anyway, thank you, Lauria. If you have any other suggestions regarding the djinn, please let me know."

As I stepped back out of the yurt I found myself thinking about Janiya's question. What *did* bound djinni do when they weren't following orders to work on some task? Did they sleep? Perhaps they wandered around and possessed irritating slaves like Aislan. Perhaps they visited their friends and families, if djinni had friends and families.

I hadn't thought about Aislan in a while. I wondered if she was still the smug, self-congratulating little ass-kisser she'd been during my short tenure in the harem. Probably.

Saken summoned me after the midday meal for a lesson in swordsmanship. "You seem to have a knack for it," she said. "Like Tamar with the bow. But you'll be more effective with some practice." She'd brought two wood practice swords for us to work with, to avoid the risk of getting cut, and she showed me some techniques with both of us on the ground, then fetched our horses so that we could practice on horseback.

We spent the afternoon at it—either sparring or with Saken stopping to show me some move and leading me slowly through the technique. Nearby, I could see two of the other sisters practicing their own swordplay; beyond them, Tamar was working on shooting from her horse. It was a hot day, the sort of day when it would have been tempting to lie in the shade of the yurt and count dragonflies, but it was good to use my muscles again, to ride Kara and work until I was breathless and thirsty.

After taking care of our horses, we splashed in the creek to cool down and went to have dinner. As we were finishing the meal, Janiya stepped out of the yurt with a secretive smile and said, "You can thank Lauria for giving me the idea for this." She handed Erdene a sack. "There should be one for everyone."

Erdene looked in and shrieked. "*Apples!* Fresh apples. And they're *huge*."

I'd seen apples like this once before; they'd been brought down to Elpisia as a curiosity. They grew somewhere up north. Smooth-skinned and red, they were the size of a baby's head; you had to use both hands to hold just one. True to Janiya's word, there was one for each of us. I marveled that the djinn would bring back such nice apples on an errand like this— clearly Janiya had thought to specify *ripe* apples, but such big ones certainly hadn't been expected. I wondered what shortcut the djinn had used—maybe these were already picked and sitting in someone's cart and the djinn stole them. Certainly there was nothing wrong with the flavor. It had been months since I'd had a fresh apple. This one was tart and perfect, so full of juice I could have drunk it out of a cup. I ate it down to the very seeds, which I carefully buried by the creek.

Janiya called for everyone's attention after we were done. "We're going raiding," she said simply. "We'll break camp tomorrow."

There was a loud cheer, and someone got out the kumiss to pass around. "Who are we raiding?" asked Zhanna when she appeared at my side.

"The Greeks, of course," she said. "We try to get in at least one raid every summer. We'll ride down to the edge of their territory, hit one of their outposts, make as much trouble as we can, and then head back out to the steppe before they've pulled their boots on."

"Are you sure that's a good idea?" I asked, glancing at Janiya. "I mean, if they're planning something . . ."

"All the better to hit them before they hit us," Janiya said.

"Will we bring their slaves back with us?" Tamar asked.

"If they can't free themselves, why would we free them?" Ruan asked. Her voice was sullen.

Tamar looked at Zhanna, who shrugged uncomfortably. "Remember what I told you?" she said in an undertone. "It doesn't come up that often because we don't free slaves."

Tamar's face was bleak with horror. "But—" she said. "There are slaves at Sophos's who may never have the opportunity to run. It's not that easy! It's not like you can just walk out the door one day, you need to get waterskins and shoes . . . they'll never have the opportunity, but they *would* be able to overcome their past. They would make great sisters. Or brothers." I knew she was thinking of Jaran. "Maybe some of them wouldn't, but the others deserve a chance. Don't they?" Her voice wavered, with the first real uncertainty I'd heard from her in a long, long time.

The other sisters were passing around the kumiss; only Zhanna was really listening to Tamar. She patted Tamar's shoulder. "Maybe someday you'll be the leader of a sisterhood; you'll be the one making the decisions."

After Zhanna had stepped away, I leaned over to Tamar and whispered, "Just grab a slave and throw her across your saddle as you ride away. What are they going to do, send her back?"

I woke in the night having to pee, but I knew that as soon as I stepped out beyond the edge of camp I could be approached by Kyros's djinn. I spent awhile tossing and turning in the dark, wondering if I had to pee bad enough to make it worth it. I finally decided that I wasn't going to get back to sleep until I went and relieved myself, and slipped carefully out of the yurt. As soon as I was alone, I saw the shimmer in the air. I suppressed a groan and asked, "Who sent you?"

"Kyros sent me."

"What do you want?"

"Kyros asks if you have anything to report."

I ought to tell Kyros about the planned attack, thought. I don't know the details yet, but certainly could report in again as I get closer. This is precisely the sort of thing I'm supposed to tell him—he'll want to know if there's anyone who could compromise my false identity, because it would be easy to focus attacks on them during the raid. For that matter, he could warn the soldiers to avoid shooting at me. He could capture and interrogate the entire unit, sending me back to the Alashi as the lone survivor of a raid gone-wrong . . . "I asked Kyros a question last time you came," I said. "Do you remember the question, djinn?"

It occurred to me that Kyros might have sent his other djinn this time, but the shimmer shifted in the air and I thought I saw its *color* change slightly, from silvery to faint pink. "I do remember," it said, and I felt the prickle of my hair lifting, because this was not the sort of answer I usually got from djinni. "You said *The next time you come, I think I'd like to hear what Kyros is going to do about this.*" It paused, then added, helpfully, "I delivered your message to Kyros."

"Did he send a response?"

"He sent no response."

There was an undertone, I thought, of malicious pleasure in the djinn's words. "Fine," I said. "I have nothing new to report to him."

The djinn vanished instantly—*before I could change my mind*, I thought, with a wave of frustration. Of course this one was unusually helpful, I realized a moment later; it no doubt knew I had things to report, but it could subvert its orders by taking care that I had no reason to report them. Well. *I deserve a response,* I thought, clenching my teeth. *I have a right to know what Kyros is going to do about Sophos.*

As I started back to the camp, I saw movement; Zhanna, I realized a moment later, coming toward me.

"I heard voices," she said sleepily. "*Your* voice. Who were you talking to?"

My blood ran cold. "Myself," I said. "I was out here muttering to myself."

Zhanna shrugged, not looking at all alarmed, and my heartbeat slowed down to something close to normal. I went back to my bed, but I didn't sleep well, or dream, for the rest of the night.

I was woken from my doze by Erdene, who was stumbling rather frantically out of the tent. As I rolled over, I heard the sound of her retching, and sat up. So did some of the other women. "Do *you* feel ill?" I heard someone ask. "We didn't eat meat last night . . ."

"She didn't drink any kumiss," someone else said.

Saken went out after her, to help her down to the stream to wash her face and drink some water. She ate breakfast with everyone else, but a few hours later, she was sick again.

"I know what's wrong with her," Tamar whispered to me as we scrubbed the pot and bowls after breakfast. "Remember how everyone was talking when the merchants came through? She's *pregnant.* Meruert got sick right away, just like that."

Sure enough, Janiya took Erdene into the yurt to talk to her alone, and came out looking utterly exasperated. "We're going to have to wait on the raid," she said. "We'll have to escort Erdene up to the summer grazing pastures for her clan, first."

"What *is* Arai going to say?" Jolay asked softly.

"I think Erdene's right," Gulim said. "If she's carrying a child, he'll be so happy about it, he wouldn't care if it was born with two heads. He can claim the baby if he wants . . . it's happened before. Do you suppose Rishad will let him out of the brotherhood for the rest of the summer, to be with Erdene?"

"If Arai claims the baby, won't he have to? Even if he doesn't, Rishad isn't heartless. And it's not like Amin and Gerhard and their caravan will be coming back this way anytime soon . . ."

We broke camp that morning and started heading east. Saken looked sad at the prospect of Erdene's departure, and I remembered Zhanna's comment, *poor Saken,* when she had told me about women who didn't take summer friends. If Jolay had gotten pregnant, I wondered if Maydan would have gone with her back to their clan? Except Jolay wouldn't have gotten pregnant; I remembered her slipping her arm around her friend, a little smugly. Well. I could ask Zhanna about it later, if I remembered.

Jolay had Tamar and me practice our riding skills as we traveled; she made us gallop and have our horses jump over rocks and other obstacles. Tamar fell off twice and I wondered if I should try to fake a fall, but I was afraid I'd rebreak a rib. Besides, they already knew I was a competent rider. And a competent swordswoman. If anyone was suspicious, falling off my horse wasn't going to make her any less so. Tamar climbed back on her horse after each fall with a grim look, but no complaints. Maydan looked her over when we made camp that evening and pronounced her bruised but without serious injury.

Erdene looked miserable. She ate some dinner, then ran to throw up. Saken brewed her some tea with honey; that, at least, stayed down, and she ate a little bit of plain rice that stayed down. There were tears in her eyes as she went into the yurt to sleep.

We took the next day slower, because of Erdene— or rather, everyone else took the next day slower. Saken made Tamar and me, and our poor horses, work just as hard as we had the day before. At least today Tamar managed to stay on her horse. Her bow and a quiver of arrows were slung from her saddle; I saw her caress the edge of the bow with her fingers at one point, but of course practicing her shooting was not practical while we were moving camp.

When we neared the summer camp of Erdene's clan, Janiya sent Saken on ahead to tell them we were coming. Most of the camp turned out to greet us. I could see some children, waist-high to their elders, and a man with snow-white hair and a stout stick to lean on, and thought how quickly I'd grown to think of *young, short-haired, and female* as the way the whole world looked. Gerhard and Amin and their men had been *so* foreign that their appearance had barely disrupted that.

Erdene shrieked as we rode up, and tumbled off her horse into the arms of a woman who must have been her mother; she looked like Erdene would look in twenty years or so, with gray hair and lines in her cheeks. Then she turned away from her mother and threw up, to her own distress and the amused disgust of the watching children. Her mother immediately began to fuss over her, leading her away to the cool interior of one of the yurts—no doubt she'd feed her sips of honeyed tea and rice mixed with milk and whatever else Erdene could keep down. I saw Janiya sigh with obvious relief: the problem of Erdene's health, at least, was out of *her* hands.

"Welcome, sword sisters," said the man with the white hair. The elder of the clan, no doubt. "You will join us for dinner, of course, and spend the night with us."

"We are honored by your hospitality," Janiya said.

We began to dismount our horses, and then froze in place as Janiya's glare swept over all of us. "*No one else* had better need to leave before the summer is over," she hissed. "Am I understood?"

She was. Amply.

Not that it mattered all that much; the young unmarried men, like the young unmarried women, were gone for the summer; the boys in the camp were *boys*, too young to interest anyone except Tamar (who was clearly not interested); and while there were young married men with a wandering eye, their wives were keeping a close watch on them tonight. The welcoming feast was lively; everyone wanted to hear how our summer was going, what adventures we'd had, how Tamar and I were settling in, and of course, how Erdene had managed to get herself pregnant. I ate roasted goat stewed with raisins and listened as Saken and Jolay proudly described my and Tamar's progress in riding, shooting, and fighting; Tamar would have to give a demonstration of her shooting prowess the next morning, as everyone wanted to see whether she really was as gifted as was claimed. The visit from the merchants was described in detail, complete with loving descriptions of the Greek wine they'd passed around, and the exotic looks of the two men, one dark and one pale.

As the evening wore on and the kumiss was passed around, I caught Tamar's eye and saw that she looked as tired and worn as I felt. There was something about being in a large crowd of people who were catching up with beloved relatives and old friends that made me feel like much more of an outsider. We made some quiet, polite noises and withdrew to the sisterhood's yurt. Ruan was already there, snoring. "And she complains about your nightmares," Tamar muttered, snuggling down under a blanket. "She should hear herself."

That made me start worrying that I would have a nightmare that night, and I lay awake for a while, listening to the sound of conversation from the campfire. It wasn't close enough that I could make out more than voices, and that was just as well. If they were talking about me, I didn't really want to know what they had to say when I wasn't there. At least they'd been kind enough in our presence, talking about my skill with the horse and the sword, Tamar's skill with a bow, and both of our courage in battle.

I dropped off, finally, and dreamed of my mother.

I *knew* I was dreaming, this time; I stood in the room and knew that I could see my mother, but she couldn't see me. My mother wore white linen, and when she looked up, her face was much younger than the face I knew, and when she shifted suddenly at the noise outside her door, I realized that this was the harem she'd been in before she was freed.

The door swung open, and my mother swiftly stood up. "Good morning, Kyros," she said.

Kyros, like my mother, looked many years younger. "What do you think of your new quarters?" he asked.

"I am . . ." she hesitated, and a smile rose to her lips but not her eyes, "unaccustomed to the luxury of such privacy."

He swung her suddenly into his arms, and she

melted in his embrace, then pulled away slightly. "Your wife."

"I've told her to stay away from this *entire* wing."

"You don't know how much she frightens me."

"She's harmless. She'll obey me, at least."

"Didn't you tell me once that she apprenticed with the Sisterhood of Weavers?"

"Yes, but they sent her away because she had no talent. Don't worry!"

My mother raised her chin stubbornly and Kyros sighed.

"You know how I love to spend time with you," my mother said, melting into his arms again briefly and stroking the stubble on his chin. "I just wish I weren't always so afraid."

"I'll think on this," Kyros promised, and drew her close to him again.

The room tilted suddenly, like a leaf in a flooded river, allowing me to see that while she pressed her body to his and stood on tiptoe to nibble his ear, she had a satisfied, faintly calculating look on her face.

I woke with everyone else at dawn and thought about the dream as I helped to take down the yurt and pack up the horses and camels. My mother *had* been a harem slave, and at some point, somehow had talked her way into freedom—she was still the mistress of her old owner, but the more I thought about it, the more *I'm so frightened of your wife* seemed like a plausible line for a harem "favorite" to use to gain her own freedom. I could imagine it working for Aislan, at least; Tamar, well, if she'd tried it on Sophos, I imagined that he'd just consider her fear an extra bonus. Why *Kyros* had appeared in the dream, well, that was just strange. Perhaps because I preferred to imagine my mother with a kind owner, rather than a brutal owner like Sophos, and Kyros was the Greek man I knew the best.

Just pebbles spilling from my weighted heart, I thought, but I had to admit that it seemed distinctly like an djinn-sent dream, the way Zhanna had described them. *Vivid. And not a nightmare.* Were the djinn trying to tell me that Kyros was my mother's old owner, the one who had freed her? *Does it even matter?* I shrugged off the dream and tried to focus on the coming raid.

Janiya apparently struck an agreement with the eldress to leave the bulk of our flocks behind with the clan during our raid; we'd bring the horses and enough camels to carry our yurt and other necessary gear, but leave behind the sheep, goats, and dogs. Some careful sorting and repacking was done—most of our extra food would also stay behind until we came back. Then the clan, including Erdene, turned out to say good-bye. Saken gave her a tight hug and a kiss on the cheek, and she was clearly upset as we rode away. Ruan kept trying to offer words of comfort, though it was fairly clear that Saken didn't want her company. Around midmorning, Zhanna picked a fight with Ruan; I was pretty sure she was mostly trying to distract her. All conversation had to be conducted at a yell, during the periods when we were letting our horses walk, which made the fight embarrassingly public. At least neither ended up with a bloody nose.

Everyone was in a surly mood by the time we stopped for the evening. We put up the yurt and took care of the animals and had dinner, Ruan and Zhanna still periodically muttering insults at each other. Saken hardly even seemed to be aware of it; big tears dripped into her bowl as she ate. Though Ruan was clearly in a foul, vicious mood, none of her usual arrows were aimed in my direction, or Tamar's—nor did she "accidentally" spill our food, step on our hands, or engage in any of the other harassment she'd found so amusing only a few weeks ago. Despite everything, I had to hide a smile when I realized this. *Take that, you petty bully,* I thought as I finished the last of my food.

There was no drumming, dancing, or drinking that night; Janiya went to bed early, probably hoping that the evil mood would evaporate with the night dew, and everyone else followed.

*I*n the darkness, I heard someone come into my room. "Who's there?" I muttered sleepily.

Light gleamed suddenly from a lantern, blinding me momentarily; I blinked and saw that it was Kyros. "This is important," Kyros said. "I have a gift for you."

"Now?" I asked, trying to remember how I'd gotten back to my own room, my own bed. *I was in the desert . . .*

"Here." Kyros held out a glittering spell-chain, then swiftly pulled it back as I reached for it. "I need to know that I can count on you."

"You always know that you can count on me," I said. "That's what you've always said."

"I need for you to say it," Kyros said. "*Kyros, you can count on me. I am your most trustworthy servant.*"

"Kyros, you can . . ." I glanced at the spell-chain; glittering in the light, it reminded me of something. "That one's not yours," I said.

"It will be *yours*." He held it out to me again. "Say it." I blinked in the light. *"Say it."*

I opened my mouth to repeat the words, but what spilled out was different: *"Tell me what you did about Sophos."*

There was a howl of frustration and the dream dissolved into the familiar darkness of the yurt. At least I hadn't woken up screaming; after the rising tension of the afternoon, I had half expected to. That really would have improved everyone's mood for the next day.

It occurred to me that if I wanted to know what Kyros had done about Sophos—if anything—I could simply step out of the yurt and slip out of camp. He'd almost certainly sent the djinn back to try to speak to me again.

I bit my lip, stroking the edge of the embroidery on my vest. *Right, Kyros,* I thought. *I'll make you a deal. If you've actually done something with the information about what Sophos did to me, I'll tell you about the raid we're planning. If you haven't, then you can whistle to the wind for the information. You'll hear about the raid when you get the report on it.* I pushed my blanket aside and slipped out.

As I'd expected, I saw the shimmer of the djinn as soon as I was out of the camp. A cold wind was blowing. "Kyros sends this message," the djinn said without preamble. "Lauria, you must trust me on the question of Sophos. To bring a charge of rape, you need to return from your mission and give testimony for the Sisterhood of Weavers to consider. They will take it *very* seriously, I'm sure, but right now, you have to trust me. Have I ever failed in your trust in the past? The aeriko tells me that your band is moving; where are you going? I need your report. I know I can count on you."

Anger churned in my stomach. "Tell him that I have an answer to his question 'Have I ever failed in your trust in the past': *You handed me over to Sophos.* And you might add, *I don't want to wait for Penelopeian justice. You have a sword, you have a horse, I want you to deal with him* now."

"My orders are to wait for your full report," the djinn said.

I almost said that this *was* my full report, but felt a flash of caution. There was no need to make it clear to Kyros that I was withholding information on purpose. "As I've told Kyros repeatedly, I'm not trusted yet. I don't *know* where we're going." Which was true, as far as it went. "That's my report."

The djinn shimmered in the air for another moment or two, then winked out. The flush of my anger had faded and left me shivering; I hurried back toward the warmth of the yurt.

I ran into Zhanna on the way. "Is someone else out here?" she asked. "I heard you talking again . . ."

"Muttering to myself again," I said.

She gave me a penetrating look. "Lauria, are you trying to talk to the djinn?"

I decided to give her a noncommittal shrug. She smiled and squeezed my arm. "We can work some more on your training once we're back from the raid—it's hard when we're riding all day."

"It's all right," I said, since she sounded apologetic.

"And in the meantime—well, feel free to try to talk to the djinn however you want. Every now and then you'll see one, if you're watching. If you talk to them, sometimes they'll talk back."

I gave her a hesitant nod. To my surprise, she kissed me on the cheek. "Go get some sleep," she whispered.

It felt as if I'd just fallen asleep when Tamar shook me awake. Around me, the camp was getting up. I stood up groggily and packed with everyone else.

"Is the raid going to be today?" I asked Saken. "Or soon?"

She shook her head. "We'll ride today for about half the day and make a camp. That camp will be about an hour out from the Greek outpost. We'll make camp, spend the night, and strike tomorrow at dawn."

At least Saken, and everyone else, was in a better mood that day. No arguments broke out; we made camp in early afternoon by a well marked with a cairn of rocks. We took turns drawing water up for the horses and camels. People were tense, but it was tension over the planned raid rather than over conflicts with each other.

Janiya called us together as soon as the camp was set. "We're going to raid the garrison guarding a mine," she said. "It's in the southern hills, so they won't be able to see us until we're pretty close." She glanced at Zhanna, who jumped up and went into one of the yurts for a moment; she returned with a wood box that was bound shut with leather straps. Zhanna unlaced the straps and set the open box at Janiya's feet. Very carefully, almost as if she were handling a living creature that might turn around and bite her, Janiya removed a small metal vial with a cork in the top.

"When we go to battle against the sorcerers who

bound our rivers, we bring the gifts and weapons of
Prometheus and Arachne. As a sign of Prometheus,
we bring fire. As a sign of Arachne, we bring venom."
She passed the vial to Ruan, who slipped a belt
through a metal ring at the top and buckled it carefully to her waist. Tamar watched, her eyes wide and
eager. I realized that my hands were shaking. Would
they expect me to do this? To use poison against the
Greeks? I remembered how much the prospect had
terrified me before I set out on this mission. I hadn't
even warned Kyros that we were coming—my trea-
son compounded.

Janiya passed out vials to each of the other sisters,
then stopped. "Tamar and Lauria, you're recruits, not
full Alashi yet. You will have to go into battle with
clean arrows."

Tamar's face fell. Zhanna gave her an apologetic
look. "We'll give you some of the fire arrows if you
want," she said. "But no venom until you're truly
Alashi."

Tamar rubbed one of her beads between two fingers, still crestfallen. I knew my relief showed on my
face, and when Zhanna looked at me I gave her a little shrug and said, "Given my aim, it would be pretty
foolish to hand me venom and turn me loose." No
doubt, that was the real reason for the prohibition.
"You probably shouldn't give me any fire arrows,
either."

Janiya's lips quirked. "It's a wise warrior who
knows her own limitations, Lauria. No, you're right.
You've wielded your sword well in our service, but
raids are fought with arrows more often than steel.
We'll surprise the Greeks, and most will be on foot;
they'll outnumber us, but we'll be much, much faster.

Stay well back and keep moving. They are terrified of Arachne and her venom; it won't take long for them to lose their nerve and run. That's when we'll close in. Round up as much of their livestock as you can, take any weapons you can carry from their armory, and burn anything that will catch fire. Listen for my horn; I'll blow one long blast when it's time to retreat."

Everyone was listening, the vials of poison glinting at their belts. Janiya went on, her voice calm and quiet.

"This is our sacred opportunity to take back some of what the Penelopeian thieves have taken from us. Prometheus and Arachne do not ask for sacrifices: there is nothing that humans have that true gods want or need. Instead, they ask us to show our faith and loyalty by striking at the gods who enslaved them, at the men who enslaved us, or our mothers, or their mothers. Revenge is what we offer on their altar. We feed Arachne's hunger when we use her venom in her service. Prometheus stole fire for us; stealing from his enemies is our offering to him."

I tried to summon the eager look that I had no doubt was still on Tamar's face, but I found myself suddenly picturing Nikon, dying from a poisoned Alashi arrow. *The Alashi aren't interested in a fair fight. They don't want to be honorable. All they care about is killing as many Greeks as they can.*

And I threw away my opportunity to at least warn them that we're coming.

Though the poison was reserved in a secret store, and the arrows were dipped one at a time just before being loosed against the Greeks, we had to prepare fire arrows before the battle. Again, Zhanna provided the preparation itself, and we coated arrows with the sticky resin, propping them up carefully against a rock to dry.

"Why didn't we use the poison during the bandit raid?" Tamar asked Saken as we worked.

"Venom is reserved for use against people who are not only our enemies, but enemies of our gods," Saken said. "Most of the bandits actually worship Prometheus and Arachne, just as we do. And they certainly don't serve the sorceresses. In their own way, they're sort of Alashi."

"But they *attacked* us," Tamar said.

"Well, yes. But you know, in the past, the Alashi clans haven't always gotten along. There have been fights, raids—but it would be unspeakable to use venom against other Alashi."

The Greeks would say it's unspeakable to use that weapon against anyone, I thought bleakly, staring at the fire as I dipped another arrow.

Maydan gathered everyone a little while later, and everyone except Tamar and me drew tokens out of a closed bag. Gulim drew the black token, and everyone gave her an apologetic pat on the shoulder. She would have to miss the raid and take the camels up to a well some distance from the garrison; we'd meet her there later. Tamar and I were excluded from this because we couldn't be expected to find the well on our own.

The fire arrows were made and dried; they were divided into quivers. Next we made torches. Jolay would carry a torch in each hand to allow others to light their fire arrows. "Why don't we put the venom on the arrows now, too?" Tamar asked as we set the torches to dry. "Doesn't it take time to dip them in battle?"

"It takes a little time, but this way we're less likely

to bite ourselves with our own venom," Saken said. "Besides, it's more potent when it's still wet."

When all the preparations were made, we went to bed; no kumiss tonight. I listened as the women around me fell asleep; I could hear Ruan's snore. Tamar lay awake for a long time, but eventually I heard her breathing become deep and even.

Even if the Greeks don't use poison, they use spies, I thought. *I'm the poison on their arrow, ready to betray from inside. They have spell-chains, they have mines full of slaves to get them iron, they have conscript soldiers from all over the Empire. It's not as if the Greeks are really interested in a fair fight, either.*

But poison. I thought again of Nikon. *And they don't know we're coming. They don't know.* Even if Kyros hadn't done anything about Sophos, that wasn't the fault of the Greeks at the garrison. Most were probably conscripts like the guards at the Elpisia gates.

Maybe the djinn is outside. It's not too late to warn them. After everyone had fallen asleep, I slipped quietly out of the yurt and went beyond the edge of the camp to see if Kyros's djinn approached me. I waited there for hours, hugging myself in the cold night air and hoping that no one would notice my absence, but saw no sparkle in the air. Kyros had not sent his djinn tonight. I had missed my chance to warn the garrison.

We rose the next morning when it was still dark, and broke camp; Gulim wished us all good hunting, and headed north as we headed south. As the sky lightened to twilight gray, we urged our horses to a run. The sun broke across the horizon as the Greek garrison came into sight.

I had half hoped that we'd raid the garrison guarding the mine I'd visited with Sophos, so that at least the soldiers I'd be attacking would be defending the interests of someone I hated, but this wasn't it. The garrison was completely unprepared for us. I could see the soldiers running out, hastily buckling on armor. Some were stumbling as they pulled on their boots.

Jolay's torches were blazing, and out of the corner of my eye I saw Tamar light one of her arrows and loose it, a keen look on her face. I plucked one of my own arrows out of the quiver and managed to steady myself in the stirrups enough to get one arrow off. It went completely wild. At least I was unlikely to wet my own weapons with Greek blood, even if I wasn't deliberately aiming high. I could feel my heart pounding in my chest, in excitement or fear. I wondered if the djinn was watching me now, and what it would tell Kyros about this raid.

The soldiers formed a ragged, panicked line in front of the garrison. Their bows lacked the range of ours and most of their shots fell short. I watched as they were cut down, one after the other. I saw the buildings around them go up in flames. *Just run,* I wanted to scream. *We have poison—if you stand and fight, you'll die.* Nikon had stayed and fought, and had died seeping black poisoned blood from his wounds. *I should have warned them. Should have warned them.*

A few of the Greeks had managed to get on horses and were riding out to meet us; I drew my own sword and miserably urged Kara up to meet one of them. *I have to do this. If I don't, I'll fail at my mission, too.* Besides, at that moment I longed for the simple focus of face-to-face fighting. The soldier had a sword; Kara dodged us both aside as he approached, and I swung my sword at the soldier's back as he passed. I missed him and nearly fell off Kara. He wheeled his horse around, I raised my sword, and ours eyes met.

"Lauria?" he choked out.

It was Thales, the soldier who used to guard the Elpisian gate. He pulled his sword back abruptly. "Just run away," I hissed at him. "They won't follow you, just run!"

He looked from me to the other Alashi. "What are you doing with them? Do you need help?"

"No. Now get going!"

Zhanna was looking my way. *I need to make it look like we're fighting.* I gave Thales a shove and knocked him off his horse. He went sprawling, and his sword was briefly knocked from his hand. "Run," I said again. "Thales, run away!"

He stood up and picked up his sword. "Kyros told me to remember your face. I can't just leave you here!"

"I don't need your help. I'm ordering you to run!"

But Thales, the fool, made a grab for my horse's reins. Kara whipped her head away from him and pranced away a few steps. A moment later I saw a quick blur and heard the thunk of an arrow striking its target. Thales screamed and looked down at the wound in his thigh. *Oh. Oh no.*

"Come on!" It was Zhanna, breathless, at my side. She took Kara's reins. "They're running, it's time to move in!"

Thales was moaning. *I can't help him anyway. There's nothing I can do for him, nothing.* I followed Zhanna in toward the burning buildings.

"Was that arrow poisoned?" I asked Zhanna.

"Which arrow?" I pointed back toward Thales.

"Of course not! He was much too close to you for that. Don't worry, Lauria, we don't hold the lives of our sisters that cheap." She reached out briefly and squeezed my arm.

The sisters were darting in and out of the buildings, piling armloads of loot into sacks to carry off. Zhanna had me hold her horse while she dismounted to snatch up a clay jar. Then we heard Janiya's horn; Zhanna tossed her torch into the building and jumped back onto her horse, and we wheeled back toward the steppe.

A handful of soldiers followed us on horseback, but they broke off the pursuit as soon as it was clear that we weren't coming back for a second pass. We stopped to catch our breath, check for wounded, and see what the looters had found.

And that was when everyone noticed that Tamar had taken my whispered advice. I hadn't actually *seen* any slaves in the garrison part of the mining camp, but Tamar apparently had spotted one, thrown him across the saddle, and galloped after everyone else. The slave was taller than Tamar, filthy from working in the mine. For one terrifying moment I thought it was someone I knew—a girl that I'd hunted down for Kyros. But then he turned his head and I saw that it was a young man, and not Alibek or one of the other young men I'd brought back to Kyros. *Safe, for now.*

Everyone looked at him, and he shrank back against Tamar. Janiya looked at Tamar, who lifted her chin and glared back defiantly.

"We don't—" Janiya said.

"Maybe *you* don't, but *I* do," Tamar said.

"What are you going to do with me?" he asked. He spoke with a heavy Greek accent.

"I don't know," Janiya said. "What do you think we should do with you? Send you back?"

"No. Please! Don't send me back there—I'll do anything you ask."

Janiya closed her eyes and shook her head; I felt the suppressed groan that rippled through the circle. "You throw yourself on our mercy as if you expect to be *our* slave. What makes you think we're kinder masters than the Greeks?"

"I don't know," he whispered, averting his eyes.

"We're not sending you back," Janiya said. "We're not sending you anywhere, and you are certainly not our slave." She started to say something else, then broke off. "Tamar, you decided to take him with you; you can arrange for his transportation back to our camp." She turned away.

"She just means that you can ride double with me," Tamar said consolingly, and helped the boy back onto her horse. His cringing fear made it hard to think of him as anything other than a boy, though he might have been as old as sixteen. She flashed me a quick triumphant smile, as if to thank me for my suggestion. I managed a sickly smile back. It was nice to see Janiya thrown so completely off her stride, but I had to admit that there was a logic to the Alashi practice of not freeing slaves. In addition to the limited resources of the Alashi and the need to spread out the arrival of "blossoms," there was the problem of slaves who simply could never learn to live as free men and women. This boy seemed like an awfully good candidate for being offered the choice of killing himself or being sold, like the former slave Zhanna had told us about.

Aside from the unplanned rescue—Tamar was the

only one who saw liberating a slave as a victory—it had been a very successful raid. None of the sisters was injured. We'd taken a few horses, and someone had found the armory and collected an entire basket of Greek helmets, and a dozen sword belts with short Greek swords on them. The jar Zhanna had grabbed turned out to hold honey; someone else had grabbed a jar of wine. Probaby the most valuable find was a sack of pure white salt. We sorted it out and loaded it onto the stolen horses, and headed up to the meeting spot. We glanced back a few times and saw no pursuers, but a hazy column of smoke was still rising; we congratulated ourselves and continued on our way. The freed slave never looked back.

I didn't look back, either, but I thought about the devastation we'd left behind us—about Thales. That wound. Even if it wasn't poisoned, the arrow had gone deep. In the chaos of the raid, he could bleed to death before anyone helped him. Or die from infection, even if the arrow hadn't been poisoned. His blood was on my hands, even if it wasn't on my sword. I stared at the horizon, knowing that I had to try to act cheerful; I couldn't pass off my guilt as nervousness about the raid now that the raid was over.

We reached Gulim as the sun was setting. She'd built a fire and made dinner, but she hadn't put up the yurts—that required several people. Zhanna, Saken, and Jolay set to work putting up the yurts while Tamar and I watered and groomed their horses. It was fully dark by the time we sat down to eat.

"Where's your slave?" I asked as we sat down.

"He's no one's slave," Tamar said, but she started guiltily and looked around. "I don't know where he is. I'd better go look for him . . ."

"Leave him," Zhanna said. "He's free, right? If he doesn't want to come have dinner, who are you to *make* him come eat?"

"I'm not going to make him do anything. I thought I'd *invite* him to come eat," Tamar said. "And he does have a name—Zosimos."

"A Greek name," Ruan said.

"Lots of us have Greek names," Tamar said, glancing at me and quickly looking away. She stood up and went to find Zosimos, returning a few minutes later with the boy trailing behind her. She dished him up some food and sat back down. He took the bowl and vanished back to wherever he'd been lurking; Tamar sighed but didn't go after him this time.

"Maybe you should talk to him yourself," I said. "Explain to him about the Alashi, and how to act like a free person . . ."

"I guess I could try," Tamar said sadly. She set her bowl down. "I wouldn't have been like this. If an Alashi woman had thrown me over her saddle and ridden off with me . . ."

"You wouldn't have been scared?" I asked. "You wouldn't have begged them not to send you back?"

"No, you're right. But . . ." She bit her lip. "I guess I'll talk to him."

When we finished eating, Tamar asked me to come along; I am the other blossom, after all. I shrugged and acquiesced. I found him huddled in the shadow of the yurt, his bowl scraped clean.

"How old are you?" I asked.

"Thirteen," he said.

Even younger than Tamar, then.

"Have you been a mine slave your whole life?"

"I was sold there a year ago, I guess. Last summer." He shuddered. "Are they going to send me back there?"

"No," I said gently. "They're not going to send you anywhere. Tamar grabbed you in order to *free* you."

"Both of us used to be slaves of the Greeks," Tamar said. "Lauria even has a Greek name, like you do. We escaped this spring."

"The Alashi don't usually free people. They welcome slaves to escape, but they don't take steps to help them get out. But they won't send you back or sell you. Unless you'd be happier with a new master than as a free man. It's *your choice*."

"Are all the Alashi women?" Zosimos asked.

Tamar giggled. "How do you think the Alashi make babies? Of course there are Alashi men. And children, and old people. We're one of the fighting sisterhoods. Each summer the childless men and women spend their time training to be warriors, stomping out bandits, and raiding Greek outposts. We're separated by sex because, well, I think it's rather obvious, don't you?"

"We're heading back to a clan camp to pick up most of our livestock," I said. "I expect we'll leave you there. They'll either send you to spend the rest of the summer with a sword brotherhood, or you can just spend the summer with the children. Thirteen is kind of young for a sword brother anyway." And he *seemed* so young. Years younger than Tamar, who apparently had been born fighting.

"Would you like to learn how to fight?" Tamar asked.

He laughed under his breath, in an oddly unguarded moment; the first flash I thought I'd seen of who he really was. "Oh yes," he said a moment later. "I'd *love* to learn how to fight." A moment later the frightened slave boy was back. "Just don't send me back to the mine."

"We're not going to," I said. "No one's going to." Thinking of Ruan, I added, "And if anyone *says* they're going to, they're lying to upset you."

A pained smile flickered across his face, very different from the harsh laugh of a moment before.

"Was the mine very bad?" Tamar asked.

He looked away from her for a moment and his face hardened slightly. "They were about to kill me when your women attacked."

"*Kill* you?" Tamar shook her head. "For *what*?"

"I attacked one of the guards. He was . . ." Zosimos shrugged a little. "They think it's funny to make us dishonor Arachne. One of the guards caught a spider; he doused it in oil and told me to light it on fire. Always before when this happened I just did it, but today . . ." His voice shook. "I kicked him in the nuts and knocked out one of his teeth." He showed us his hand; there was a cut on his knuckle. "I don't know why I did it. If I'd thought about it even for a moment I would have known that it wasn't worth it. Three guards were on me in moments and they hauled me outside. They were going to have the other slaves come watch while they beat me to death, to show them the price of defiance. They'd already gotten out the whip." His voice was ragged. "If you take me back there, they'll kill me."

"*No one* is going to take you back there," Tamar said.

"Please," he whispered. "I'll do anything you ask."

"You're not our *slave,*" Tamar hissed. "You don't *have* to do what we ask. You're free. I *freed* you."

"He freed himself," I said softly, and Tamar lifted her chin in silent acknowledgment.

*J*aniya agreed with me, grumblingly, when we repeated Zosimos's story to her. She called Zosimos into the yurt as well, and when he stopped cringing, which took awhile, she presented him with a single blue bead and a leather thong to string it on. Then she shooed him out and sighed. "It's supposed to be an elder or eldress that hears out the story and accepts the runaway provisionally into the Alashi."

"There's an elder with Erdene's clan, isn't there?" I asked.

"Oh yes. But I'm afraid he'd be too frightened to tell his story there." She rubbed her forehead. "He seems like such a child. I hope they keep him in the clan camp for the summer. There will be plenty of time for the brotherhood next year."

We returned to the clan camp on the day we'd expected, and were greeted enthusiastically. Erdene was still miserable, but her lover had been allowed to join her, even though he wasn't the father. I caught a glimpse of him, briefly; he seemed entirely willing to claim her baby as his own. He also seemed quite worried, given how sick she was.

Janiya made Tamar and me come along to introduce Zosimos to the elder. I wasn't sure what I'd done to deserve that; I wondered if Janiya had guessed that I gave Tamar the idea of simply abducting a slave. *It's not like she wouldn't have thought of it on her own.* The elder looked silently from Janiya to Zosimos to

Tamar to me. I shuffled my feet and nudged Tamar. If we waited until Zosimos spoke up for himself, we'd be standing there all night.

"Zosimos was a slave at the mine where we attacked," Tamar said. "One of the Greek guards wanted him to dishonor Arachne, and he refused. And hit the guard. For that, they were going to *kill* him."

"He knew that," I said. "He chose death over slavery." That was important. Here.

"As they were taking him out to *murder* him, we attacked," Tamar said. "And I saw him and . . . grabbed him." Her voice fell slightly flat at the end. She turned to Zosimos. "*Did* you take the opportunity to come out to us when we attacked?" she asked, a little pleadingly.

Zosimos shook his head.

"You just stayed where the guard left you?"

He nodded.

"Well, it doesn't matter. He *did* take his freedom. It was luck that I grabbed him instead of the Greeks killing him."

The elder looked . . . thoroughly amused, I decided. But he was trying to look surly and disapproving. "Luck indeed," he said. "Lucky that you *happened* to find yourself a slave who deserved the gift you thrust on him." He flicked the blue bead that rested against Zosimos's chest; the boy flinched away like a startled sparrow. "And what if you had chosen someone who *preferred* bondage?"

"There *aren't* any slaves who like being slaves," Tamar said.

"Aislan," I muttered.

"Not even her. If we showed up and offered to take her away, she'd be on the horse so fast, it would make your head spin. Anyway, a slave that preferred bondage would have run away from us. Or taken up arms against us!"

"You're thinking like an Alashi," the elder said. "A good slave obeys orders. A good slave stands where he's left. Like Zosimos did."

"A good slave would have been back in the mine," Tamar said. "He was only where he was because he was about to be punished. *Killed.*"

"What do you have to say for yourself?" the elder asked, turning abruptly to Zosimos.

"Don't send me back there," he whispered.

"And why not? Do you think we need a fearful, cringing, voiceless boy among the Alashi?"

He cringed, of course, and the color drained from his face. His lips worked silently. Tamar opened her mouth, and I pinched her; he was going to have to speak for himself, sooner or later.

"No," he muttered finally. "I don't think you need me."

"Shall we send you back, then? Or sell you to traders who will take you east?"

He shook his head mutely. Finally he opened his mouth and croaked, "You'd have to kill me first."

"Well. Perhaps there's hope for you after all." The elder raised an eyebrow, glanced pointedly at Tamar and me, and shook his head. "You seem very young. How old are you?"

"Thirteen."

"We'll keep you here through the summer, then. You can ride with the big boys next year. Just as well; our brotherhood already has one blossom to train this summer." The elder caught Janiya's eye and jerked his head, dismissing the three of us; we withdrew from the tent and returned to the sisterhood camp.

"Is the brotherhood pretty much like the sisterhood?" I asked Janiya as we walked.

"I guess it depends on what you mean," she said. "The young, unmarried men spend their summers in camps like ours, yes. I imagine a camp of twenty men would be a little different from a camp of twenty women, though." She smiled a little ruefully. "If you're wondering whether the brotherhoods tend to be led by men who prefer their summer friends' company year-round—well, of course. The leader of this brotherhood is a man named Rishad. I like him; we spend a fair amount of time together during the winter. He escaped from the Greeks himself, quite a few years ago now. Like Tamar, he has some reservations about the whole idea that the only people who deserve freedom are the ones who take it for themselves."

"Has he ever freed someone?" I asked.

"No. But he definitely would have approved of Tamar's sense of initiative."

The elder must have arranged accommodations for Zosimos, because he didn't return to our camp to sleep. As we were packing the next morning, though, he came to find Tamar. He had new clothes, worn but clean—hand-me-downs from one of the boys who'd gone off to the sword brotherhood, no doubt. He seemed shy today, but less fearful. "Before you left, I wanted to thank you," he muttered. "Thank you for freeing me."

Tamar beamed and clasped his hand. "You're going to do fine."

As the boy turned away, I brushed his sleeve and

whispered, "You freed yourself. And don't let anyone tell you otherwise."

*A*s we rode out, back to our own grazing grounds, my thoughts turned from the Greeks I'd betrayed to the slaves that I had personally found for Kyros. One was a young woman, barely older than Tamar; I had expected a flood of tears when I caught up with her, but she had held herself as rigid as a soldier and barely made a sound the whole way back to Elpisia. The crier had been one of the men—one of the house servants who had run one day for no reason I could see. He'd been the easiest to find, as he'd walked straight out into the desert. Worse than Alibek with his single waterskin, that man had taken *no* water with him, and had in fact just about collapsed from thirst by the time I caught up with him, but that didn't stop him from unleashing the most unearthly wail I'd ever heard when I walked up to him. *If he'd wanted to die, there are less painful ways to kill yourself,* I thought.

The only one who actually fought me was also one of the men. He'd made himself a makeshift knife with the broken edge of a jar. It was sharp enough to cut my arm when he lunged at me, but not deeply enough to leave a scar. I disarmed him without too much trouble and smashed his "knife" under my heel. He'd crumpled then, and had come back as meek and silent as a frightened rabbit. In an act of spontaneous generosity, I had refrained from telling Kyros about the knife. The cut healed on its own within a few days.

They took their freedom, too. Or tried to. And I took it away from them again.

If I had warned Kyros about the raid, it was unlikely that Tamar would have had the opportunity to free Zosimos. Had I traded Thales's life for Zosimos's freedom? It seemed almost worth it, thinking about Zosimos's story. But then, as bad as I felt about Thales, he wasn't a friend. I might feel differently if it had been Nikon's life that had been traded.

I've betrayed everyone, I thought. *Before I ever came here, I betrayed everything the Alashi stand for when I hunted down Kyros's slaves. And then I betrayed Kyros and the Sisterhood of Weavers when I failed to tell them about the raid.* But the strangest thing of all was that I wasn't sure which I regretted more. Thales had been trying to help me; he hadn't run when I'd told him to run because he'd thought, in his confusion of recognition, that I needed help. But if I could go back and change one thing, I thought I'd go back and tell Kyros that I didn't want to hunt down his slaves.

My thoughts were disturbing, and I tried to push them out of my mind—Thales, Alibek, the crying man, all of them. But I heard the man's wail in my dreams that night. I woke up to Ruan's snarl, and knew that once again the wail had come from me.

CHAPTER ELEVEN

W ho's there?"

I stood up from my spot in the long grass,
expecting to see Zhanna, but no one was there. I sat
back down, dispirited, and gave the drum Zhanna
had given me another halfhearted thump. She'd sent
both me and Tamar out, separately, with drums and
instructions to try to find our way to "openness" to
the djinn. I had spent an absurdly long time tapping
out rhythms, my eyes closed, but I felt no more
"open" than I had the day she had us try to meditate.
I did, however, feel hot; there was no shade where
Zhanna had left me. I took a swig from my half-
empty waterskin and glared at the drum.

Well, if it hadn't been Zhanna in the grass, there was
no one to care if I was actually beating on my drum or
not. I flopped back in the grass, looking up at the blue
sky and the dazzling sunshine. I could hear the steady
hum of insects, and a bird warbling. It wasn't so bad to
simply be idle for a little while; at least I wasn't trying
to shoot a bow while Ruan yelled at me.

"Any djinni here?" I said aloud. "Hello? Anyone want to talk to me?"

I heard what I'd heard before—some sort of rustle—and suddenly I realized that I hadn't heard it with my ears. *Of course not. I was playing the drum.* I sat up, my skin prickling despite the heat. "Is someone here?"

And it was there: shimmering in front of me like a water mirage. "Hello, Shaman's Apprentice," it said.

This is not Kyros's djinn. Or Janiya's. Looking at it, I was certain that it was not a bound djinn; I realized, looking at it, that it was *larger* than the djinni I'd talked with before. Larger, and the shimmer was brighter. *A rogue aeriko,* part of my mind insisted on calling it. I could be *possessed* by this djinn. The idea made me shiver even more.

I'd been approached by a free djinn once before, the one who'd warned me that I was being followed—but it had been gone so fast, I'd barely had time to think about what I was speaking with. I wondered if this was the same djinn, but I had a hard time believing that even a few months ago I could have mistaken this for Kyros's djinn.

Shamans spoke with unbound djinni all the time. But now that I was facing one, I had no idea what I was supposed to say to it. Or ask it. Zhanna hadn't really covered that. "Hello," I said.

The golden shimmer swirled around me; I could almost feel something brush a tendril of my hair. "A little summoner," it murmured. "You long to bind me, to make me your servant."

"No," I said. "Of course I don't want to bind you." *The Alashi don't do that.*

"You think of bindings—but you never see the bindings on yourself."

"What bindings?"

"Look," it said, and it swirled again. And suddenly I saw double: one world of green steppe and blue sky, and one world of strange silver lines and black shadows. I looked at the djinn again, and I saw a face, a woman's face, strange and wild. "Look," it said again, and I looked and saw silver ropes curling around my wrists and ankles. I squinted for a better view, which didn't help at all. I tried to pull the ropes off, but of course I could touch nothing; I shook them, but that didn't work, either.

The djinn laughed; the sound went through my head like a knife, and I closed my eyes and clapped my hands to my ears. When the sound was gone, I found myself lying in the grass again; the world looked like it usually did.

What a strange vision. I didn't think I dared tell Zhanna about it. I picked up the drum and resolutely began to beat it again, but I couldn't stop thinking about the curling silver ropes, and as I pounded on the drum, the words I'd said to the Greek officer during the mine raid echoed in my head. *You're half a slave yourself—a conscript.* I wasn't a conscript, though; Kyros had invited me to come work for him, I hadn't been conscripted for anything. *My loyalty to Kyros is all that binds me,* I thought. *But I chose that. I chose that. Kyros knows he can count on me.*

*I*t was a few days later that I learned how to banish a rogue djinn that had possessed an unwilling victim. This definitely wasn't as much of a problem among the Alashi as it was among the Greeks, but that day a djinn seized hold of, of all people, Maydan. She was grinding up some dried herb with her mortar and pestle, to mix into a salve, when the pestle suddenly tumbled from her fingers and she toppled forward in a faint.

Someone ran to get Zhanna, and she sent someone else to find Tamar while she eased Maydan onto her back. "You're *smiling*," I said, startled. "Are you glad she was possessed?"

"Not exactly *glad*," Zhanna said. "But I'd been half hoping we'd see someone get possessed before the summer was over, just so I could start working with you and Tamar on what to do." She sat up, brushing her hair out of her eyes. "Maydan would understand. If she were training an apprentice—two apprentices—she'd be sorry if I fell off my horse and broke my leg, but at the same time, she'd be a little pleased at the opportunity to teach her apprentices how to set a broken bone."

Tamar arrived, breathless, and the three of us lifted Maydan into the shade of the yurt. "All right," Zhanna said. "To properly do this, you need to have that state of *openness* that we've talked about—you can drum or dance or whatever you're finding works for you."

Tamar nodded, her face serious. I averted my eyes. I'd tried meditating, drumming, and even dancing; nothing made me feel *open*. But Zhanna was looking at me when I looked up, so I nodded, too.

"Don't feel like you've failed if this doesn't work. I'll give each of you a chance to banish the djinn; it's possible that you won't be able to get it to respond to you at all, and if you do, you may draw it out of Maydan only to be possessed yourself. Don't worry about that, though; I have dealt with djinn possession many times and I'll take care of you."

Tamar looked only moderately reassured.

"Go get your vests and put them on."

We'd both had them off to embroider new designs. I was working on a horse; I'd borrowed Saken's old vest to copy the horse she'd embroidered on hers, since it looked so real. Tamar was embroidering a bird clutching a flower in its claw. We both knotted the thread, trimmed off the needle we were using, stuck it in another cloth for safekeeping, and put our vests on.

Meanwhile, Zhanna fetched a carved box from the other side of the yurt and opened it. Inside were ritual items much like the things Jaran had used to banish Aislan's djinn back in the harem: an incense burner, a bundle of feathers knotted together with thread, and a small clay jar. In Sophos's harem, the small jar had held river water, drawn from the Syr Darya when water flowed there during the spring rains; here, to my surprise, it held a mixture of dirt and ash.

On Zhanna's instructions, we each plucked a hair from our heads and placed it in the palm of Maydan's hand. Then Zhanna took the feathers, dipped the tips into the clay pot, and brushed the gray ash onto Maydan's forehead, hands, and heart. "Maydan, daughter of Aiday, daughter of Alina, you are a child of the river, the steppe, and the djinni." Jaran had asked each of us in turn if we claimed her, but that didn't seem to be part of the ritual here. Zhanna set down the feathers and turned to us. "To banish the djinn, you draw it into yourself and then tell it to go away. Put your hand on her forehead and think of yourself drawing the djinn out like you would pull a bucket from a well, or like you'd draw a thorn from your foot. To banish a djinn, we say, 'Return to the Silent Lands, lost one of your kind, and trouble us no more.' "

Jaran had said that, I remembered. Tamar was nodding.

"It's difficult to describe it. Why don't you each give it a try. Who wants to go first?"

"I do," Tamar said, and Zhanna nodded to her.

Tamar stood up and began to dance. She hadn't asked either of us to play a drum for her so it seemed like it would be intrusive to start; she whirled herself in circles until I was dizzy looking at her, then dropped to her knees beside Maydan and placed her small hand on Maydan's forehead. She closed her eyes and clenched her jaw. I watched her curiously, wondering if she felt *open* and what, exactly, this meant to her. Time passed; her nostrils were white from tension. Finally she sat back, looking exhausted.

"I think I can—kind of feel it there," she said. "But I couldn't pull it out."

"That's fine," Zhanna said. "And not surprising. You're doing well to be able to touch it at all. Lauria, you try."

I refused to dance in front of Tamar and Zhanna, especially as I knew it wouldn't help, so I took my drum and beat it for a little while. I was faking, and I knew I was faking, but I didn't know what else to do. After a while, my feet started to go to sleep, and my mind also almost felt a little dazed and numb, like my prickling feet; *maybe that's what she's talking about.* It seemed like it was worth a try. I touched Maydan's forehead and reached in.

And suddenly, I realized that I could *see* the djinn, even though it was inside Maydan: a whirl of golden dust, like sparks flying to the sky from a roaring fire.

I gasped and blurted out the phrase Zhanna had given us: "Return to the Silent Lands, lost one of your kind, and trouble us no more."

"*Gate,*" it hissed, and I wanted to clap my hands to my ears as I had when the other rogue djinn had laughed. I felt it swirl into *my* chest, and for a moment I thought it was going to take me over, as it had Maydan. But it kept moving—*through me like an arrow,* I thought—and a moment later I realized it was gone.

I opened my eyes. Maydan stirred and raised her head with a groan. "What on earth—how did I get in here? Did I take sunstroke?"

"Djinn," Zhanna said. "You should take a nap."

"Ugh, I have so much to do . . ." Maydan muttered, then rolled over and went to sleep.

"You did it," Tamar said, staring at me with open envy. "You made it leave."

"I didn't make it do anything," I said. "It *chose* to leave."

"But it chose to leave for *you.*"

"Sometimes that's all a shaman does," Zhanna said. "We provide a door, and the djinn decides to take it."

It seemed unfair, I had to admit, as I avoided Tamar's resentful eyes. I had barely begun to sweat. And Tamar was clearly understanding the training in a way that I was not. I could dance all day, drum all day, and not feel the way I thought I was supposed to feel. *It was playing with me. With us.* "I bet it left for me just to piss you off," I said to Tamar. "It could feel that you had a grip on it, even if you didn't have the strength to make it go. I could see it was there, but I couldn't grasp it—so it left for me, just to make *you* feel like I was a better shaman."

Humor flickered in her eyes. "You don't have to try to make me feel better, you know, Lauria. But, well, it's nice that you do."

"It said something as it was leaving," I said, trying to keep my voice casual. " '*Gate.*' Do you know why it might have said that?"

"Gate? Back to the Silent Lands, I guess."

Tamar and I stepped back out into the sunshine. I shaded my eyes, blinking, and went over to where Maydan's herbs still lay out on the ground; I figured I would gather them up for her and put them away so that her work wouldn't be scattered by the wind while she slept.

"Lauria!" Janiya's voice broke into my thoughts. "Go fetch some water for the rice."

I stiffened, then took a deep breath and turned to Janiya. "I'm busy," I said. "Get it yourself."

She gave me a faint smile and a little nod. "Better," she said, and turned away.

"Better?" I strode after her, furious. "*Better?* I told you to get it yourself, what the hell more am I supposed to do?"

"You need to mean it." She turned back toward me and raised the edge of one eyebrow. "You had to rehearse that, you had to practice it, you had to *think* about it. It didn't come from *here*." She tapped her chest.

Now I turned away, heading back to Maydan's herbs. Janiya grabbed my arm and jerked me around to face her. "Aren't you even going to *argue* with me? Tell me that it *did* come from your heart?"

"What the hell good would it do? You've already decided how I feel."

"Maybe if you stood up for yourself you'd start to feel like you really are one of us."

"I stood up for myself to Ruan."

"You did. But you still treat me as if I could have you flogged for disobedience. Sometimes I think I could order you to butcher your horse, and you'd do it!"

"You're a *military commander*," I said. "Don't you want to be obeyed?"

"In battle, yes. But most of the time we aren't in battle. I want to know that my women are thinking for themselves. And even *in* battle, this isn't the Greek army! You need to be able to take initiative, to notice a change in conditions and act accordingly, not to stand by your orders like, like, like a *slave* who knows she'll be executed for disobedience."

"I haven't seen anyone else here telling you to get your own water. Or your own tea."

"That's right. Because I don't talk to them the way you let me talk to you. They all know that they're free."

I was never a slave, either, I thought, and clamped down hard on that thought. "Fine," I said, hearing my voice shake, and turned away.

"Lauria . . ." Janiya glanced around; all the sisters were industriously occupying themselves, listening silently. "Come with me for a walk. Please."

I fell into step beside her as we walked a little distance away from the camp.

"You remind me of another former slave who joined us, some years ago," Janiya said. "Though she wouldn't admit it right away, she had not actually been born into slavery."

I stiffened even as I tried not to; I glanced at Janiya, but her eyes were fastened on some distant point on the horizon.

"The Sisterhood of Weavers has their own sword sisterhood as well—women who work as bodyguards for the sorceresses, or who serve in the small standing army that the Sisterhood maintains to guard the seat of their power in Penelopeia. This woman served in that army. But as punishment for some misdeed—she was falsely accused, or so she told me—she was stripped of her rank and sold into slavery. She wound up as a slave here on the edges of Greek territory, ran away, and found the Alashi."

"Good for her," I murmured, since Janiya had paused and seemed to expect a response.

"She quickly put her days as a slave behind her. In some respects, her heart was as free as any woman born to the Alashi. But her days as a sworn servant to the Weavers were harder to leave in the dust. She had taken vows, you see, before their goddess, Athena. Even though she no longer *felt* loyalty to her old masters, those vows bound her to them. There is magic in vows like that, as tangible as the magic of blood sisterhood. It's as real as the bindings on an aeriko—on a djinn, I mean."

I didn't dare look at Janiya now, but I thought she was looking at me. My cheeks were burning.

"Lauria, I don't wish to force my way into your confidence. But remember, we are a people of escaped slaves, ultimately, even if most of us now are born in freedom. We have a ritual to repudiate the vows we now have to leave behind—whether they were forced

on us by our slavery, or we thought at the time that
they were freely chosen. Sometimes our vows *are* our
masters. Will you go through this ritual?"

I thought about the silver bindings the djinn had
shown me. *My loyalty to Kyros is the loyalty he's
earned. Nothing more, nothing less.* But then, what
would be the harm in this? Even if the ritual broke the
magic of the vows, that would just mean I could
choose freely to keep them . . . *And I need to do this
to be accepted, that's very clear. To accomplish my
mission . . . To become one of the Alashi . . .*

"I'll do it," I said.

"Good. Tonight, after moonrise. I'll wake you when
it's time."

Janiya stalked back to camp; I looked at her
straight back and her hunched shoulders and was
quite certain that *she* was the slave she'd just spoken
about.

She shook me awake a few hours after I'd gone to
sleep, and I followed her out of the yurt. It was a cold
night with a stiff breeze and I shivered. Janiya had a
small bundle under her arm, and a lantern, and I followed her out from camp onto the steppe.

Even with the moonlight and the lantern, it was a
dark night and we had to walk slowly. We walked
past the horses and down to the stream, and then up-
stream a short distance to the big tree that grew at the
bend in the stream.

"You need to understand, our gods have been
where we are," Janiya said. "Prometheus gave the gift
of fire to humans, and for that, Zeus—the old king of
Olympus—had him chained to a mountain west of
here, where an eagle came each day and tore out his
liver. Arachne was a mortal woman and a weaver,

and then had the misfortune to fairly beat Athena in a contest of weaving skill; for that, Athena tried to enslave her, and when Arachne chose death over slavery, Athena turned her into a spider.

"And so they lived, for thousands of years. But Arachne heard of the god that had been imprisoned by her own enemies, and slowly she found her way to the mountain where he was chained; she wove a web to trap the eagle, and she forced the eagle to set Prometheus free. Prometheus, in turn, returned Arachne to human form and gave her immortality. And then they headed east, away from Olympus, and became *our* gods, the gods of people who were once the slaves of the Greeks, but have set themselves free."

"I see," I mumbled, thinking about how cold I was. Janiya was also shivering by the time we reached our destination. "I should've brought blankets," she said, and set the lantern down.

I had half expected Janiya to drum or dance or something to summon djinni, but instead she unfolded her bundle and laid out some strips of cloth and a sharp knife. Then she turned her palms up and spoke simply and directly: "Prometheus, hear us."

I wondered if I should repeat her words, but she didn't give me any sort of nudge, so I remained silent.

"You were free, then enslaved, then free again: you, of all the gods, understand. Like you, we were slaves; like you, we are free. Once, we took vows in order to survive; now we ask to be released from those vows." She lowered her hands and looked at me. "Lauria, on your honor as a free woman, answer these questions truthfully. Were your vows taken freely?"

"Yes." My heart began to pound in my ears; some

part of my mind began screaming, *What are you thinking? Lie to her; lie!*

"Did those to whom you swore your loyalty betray it?"

"Yes." I sounded almost relieved. *This is true. Kyros and Sophos did betray my loyalty.*

"The binding is already broken; Lauria asks to be released." She picked up the knife and cut the palm of her hand; she held one of the strips of cloth to her injury and bled onto it, blotting until almost the whole strip of cloth was stained with blood. She wiped the knife and gave it to me. "Cut yourself and put your blood on the strip of cloth."

I'd done something like this once before, when I became Tamar's blood sister. I wondered if this ritual was going to require that I become blood sister to Janiya. This knife wasn't as sharp as the sword Tamar and I had used, and my first attempt to cut myself only scored my hand, drawing no blood. Gritting my teeth, I twisted the knife; this time, I cut more than I really had to, and had no trouble bleeding all over the strip of cloth that Janiya handed me. She wrapped her own hand in a bandage as she watched me, then gave me a bandage to cover my wound when I was done. We laid our blood-soaked cloth strips under the tree.

"Prometheus has never asked for blood sacrifice, but there are other gods who demand it; we'll leave our blood here, so that Prometheus can give it to the gods before whom we made our vows. Now we'll walk through the water: as the two rivers will make all of us free someday, so may the waters tonight make you free."

We stripped naked and plunged into the stream; the water came up to my waist at the deepest part. We crossed to the other side, turned, and crossed back. Now I was *really* cold; the wind felt as it if were going straight to my bones. I dressed as quickly as I could, Janiya bundled up the knife again, and we walked back to camp.

As we reached the edge of the camp, Janiya said, "I had a daughter once, back when I lived with the Greeks."

"I thought you . . ." I turned and blinked at her, trying to phrase what I wanted to say.

"You thought I was one of the women who has winter friends as well as summer friends?" Janiya laughed. "Well, you were right. But back in the Guard of the Sisterhood of Weavers, some of us would endure a man's company, briefly, in order to have children. I wanted a daughter, and I had one. A beautiful young girl. She was six when I was sold into slavery."

"What happened to her?"

"It was I who was accused—not Xanthe. We were separated. She stayed with the Sisterhood; one of my old friends promised to raise her. I never saw her again." Janiya sighed. "She is very close to your age. I've imagined, a few times, that you were her. I would be proud to have a daughter like you."

"Why didn't you go look for her?"

"She was six when I was sold. She would have been twelve when I escaped. They would have told her terrible things about me—that I was a traitor to the Sisterhood, a thief. Better, far better, to let her alone, to live her own life."

Something else occurred to me. "If you worked for the Sisterhood, wouldn't *you* have seen people using spell-chains?"

"Oh." Janiya brushed her hair away from her face.

"Once or twice, yes. I knew what the chain was, I knew how it was used—but it was a rare thing that I heard the careful way that requests were phrased. Also, I think sorceresses are able to control their own summoned djinni better than those who bear spell-chains on sufferance."

I nodded. "My own mother is rather disappointed with how I turned out," I said. "I think she'd have preferred a young woman like Erdene."

Janiya's eyes flickered with humor. "I'm sure that's often how it turns out. Perhaps Xanthe spends her days brushing her hair and mooning over young Greek officers."

I pulled my vest out, before I went to sleep, and put it on; I was still freezing cold. I had no dream, and woke at dawn, feeling surprisingly well rested despite my interrupted night.

A little while after the midday meal, Janiya wandered past and said, "Lauria, go get the manure baskets from the supply yurt and gather up the camel and horse dung."

I was sitting cross-legged, scraping the last of my lunch from my bowl. I glared up at Janiya and said, "Not until I get my goddamn bead."

Janiya laughed, as if she'd been expecting that response, and tossed a small blue bead through the air. It landed in my lap. "There you go," she said. "Now go get the baskets, if you please."

We gathered up the droppings from all our livestock—horses, camels, and goats—in a pair of big baskets, then spread it out along the riverbank to dry. It seemed silly to me to pick it up while it was still wet and smelly, only to dump it on the ground again, but Saken had pointed out that left with the animals, it just got stepped on. I picked my way across the grazing area, thinking that I probably looked as disgusted and squeamish as Erdene usually did when it was her turn to do this task. The other sisters gave me a wide berth, not wanting to feel obligated to pitch in and help me. Even Tamar stayed well away.

"Lauria," a voice said, and I started, dropping a handful of manure. It was a djinn. *Kyros's djinn,* I thought. I couldn't say what made it so distinctive, but I knew it like I'd have known Tamar even if all I could see was her hand. *I'm getting better at this,* I thought.

"Kyros sends the following words: 'Lauria, this is something I wish I could tell you in person, but it is past time that you knew.'" The djinn was good at imitating Kyros's voice and I felt a faint prickle of recognition. "'It was not only because of your talent that you attracted my attention. It was because of your talents that I asked you to join my service, but the reason I was *paying* attention to you is much more simple.'" The djinn paused, then spoke again: "'You are my daughter. I am your father.'"

It should have been a terrible surprise, but I felt only a sad, quiet coldness spreading through my chest.

"'My daughter, I know I can count on you, and you must realize that you can trust me.'" The djinn kept talking but I was listening to the coldness in my heart, not to Kyros's words, and it was saying, *His words are not sincere; he is trying to control me.*

"'Tell me, Lauria, how close you are to winning the trust of the Alashi. That's all I want to know.'"

"Very close," I said.

With that, the djinn winked out, and I was left

breathless with the basket of manure in my hands. After a shaken moment I began to pick up manure again, trying to shrug off my disgust. The contact with Kyros's djinn made me feel as dirty as the goat shit all over my hands. *I don't want to serve him anymore,* I thought. *I don't want to go back there.*

I don't have to go back there.

The thought startled me so much that I stepped right in an apple-shaped pile of horse shit, and I stopped to swear, in Greek, and pick up what was left, hurling it in the basket. *I'd rather be picking up horse shit than tracking down escaping slaves. I could never do that again. I couldn't.* If I looked at Alibek now—Kyros's little straying bird—I would see Tamar. Zhanna. Janiya. Ruan. And I wouldn't wish slavery on any of them. Even Ruan.

I'd rather spend the rest of my life picking up shit than do that again.

Well. I could just tell Kyros he'd have to find other tasks for me. Hunting down slaves was never one of my more frequent duties—I carried messages, more often. Spying on garrisons of Greek soldiers, more or less openly. Kyros could send someone else out to hunt his slaves. Myron, for instance. It wasn't a specialized task—not like spying on the Alashi, which only someone with Danibeki blood could do.

Though I was half Greek, and so was Tamar, and enough of the Alashi had Greek blood that the escaped slaves and the freeborn Alashi were not easily distinguishable, at least not by appearance. A full Greek like Myron could probably claim to be an escaped slave as well, and be taken in, though Myron could never convincingly pose as a slave; he radiated the privilege of the Greek from every pore of his skin.

*But Kyros knew I could do it—he knew I could con-
vince the slaves of Sophos's harem, and more important, the Alashi, that I had been a slave. Why? How
could he know?*

Because he knew that Sophos would rape me.

The answer came to me like an arrow in my heart
and I gasped. The smell of shit filled my nose and
gagged me, and the thought of Kyros's betrayal
gagged me as well. Turning away from the almost-
filled basket of shit, I fell to my knees and threw up
on the ground. Someone saw me vomiting, and a few
minutes later Tamar and Zhanna and Maydan came
running to take the basket away and help me over to
the river to clean up. "You should have told Janiya
that you weren't feeling well," Maydan scolded me.
"No one would have expected you to do shit-pickup
duty while feeling poorly."

I didn't even try to explain; I just let her wash me,
as I had let Tamar wash me when I arrived at
Sophos's harem. I could still smell shit when she was
done, but at least it wasn't harem perfume. It was still
hot, but I shivered in the wind, and went into the yurt
to wrap up in a blanket when we got back to the
camp. I had no appetite for supper and didn't want to
talk to anyone—not even Tamar. I lay awake until I'd
heard everyone else settle down in the yurt, and then
went outside to sleep by the fire. I knew I was going
to have nightmares, and there was no point in waking
everyone else up.

Perhaps, I thought, as I lay looking up at the skies,
I was wrong. Kyros may simply have had faith that I
could make it work somehow. But Sophos knew. *You
may realize later how necessary this was.* It wasn't
lust, it wasn't just the desire to rape someone he had

no right to touch. Sophos knew that the Alashi would see that rape when they looked into my eyes. He knew that it would ensure the success of my mission.

Did Kyros know?

If he didn't know, it was because he closed his eyes and covered his ears instead of looking at what was right in front of his face.

I expected to dream of Sophos, when I finally fell asleep—or Kyros, pleading with me to believe that he had never given Sophos *permission* to rape me. But instead I dreamed of a sorceress, one of the Sisterhood, standing before her loom and speaking to the bound djinn that trembled before her. *Tell them I want this mission to succeed,* she said. *All our spies in the past have been caught. We can't afford another failure: the soul-stone supply is almost depleted. This time, I want it to work. Do whatever you need to do to make it work.* The djinn turned and hesitated for a moment as if I truly stood in that room, and it could see me waiting. *Tool,* it hissed, and the dream faded into silent mist.

CHAPTER TWELVE

I woke from my dream well before dawn. I was stiff from the cold even under my blanket, and as I looked up at the stars, I thought about winter. Penelopeia was a warm city, or so I'd been told, but in Elpisia, the snows came early and deep, and the winds cut through every chink and crack that wasn't stuffed with wool. Kyros sometimes sent me out on winter missions, well wrapped against the winds, but more often I stayed home, gathering with his family and his other trusted servants in his great hall, which was shuttered against the winds and kept warm with a roaring fire, tended by his slaves.

It was hard to imagine that a yurt would really keep anyone warm during a steppe winter, but the Alashi had survived this way for generations. Of course, if I woke everyone up with my nightmares in midwinter, I couldn't just move out of the yurt. I'd have to be certain that I wasn't sharing a tent with Ruan.

I wondered how the sisterhood would scatter with

the end of summer. We had a sponsor clan—would we all go to live with that clan for the winter? Presumably the women born Alashi would live with their parents or their lovers, but where would Tamar and I live? Would we be allowed to stay together or would they want to split us between families? Maybe Zhanna's family would take us both, since we were Zhanna's apprentices.

First, of course, there would be the big fall gathering, like the spring gathering we'd found our way to a few months ago. All the sword sisterhoods and brotherhoods would return, and we'd probably see the eldress again. Tamar might still be fretting, but I'd stopped worrying that we wouldn't be accepted as Alashi. There would probably be some sort of initiation ceremony, for us and for any other blossoms we might not know about. Probably not Zosimos, just yet. I wondered what the ritual would involve. *I hope I don't have to get soaked in cold water again,* I thought, shivering.

"Lauria? What are you doing out here?"

It was Zhanna, stumbling out to relieve herself, probably. "I was thinking I'd have nightmares tonight. I didn't want to wake anyone up."

"You shouldn't be out when it's this cold—especially not when you're sick! Maydan would be furious. Go in the yurt."

Feeling foolish, I picked my way to my usual spot near Tamar. It was very warm inside the yurt, and moist from the communal breath. I lay down, feeling my shivering ease, and thinking, *I guess winter won't be so bad.*

I hesitated on the edge of sleep and thought, *That's it. I've made my decision.* Then I thought, *I haven't told anyone—I could still change my mind, betray the Alashi and go back to Kyros. And then: I'd rather cut out my own heart. I'm staying here.*

A blast from a horn shook me awake in the morning; I scrambled out of the yurt with everyone else to see a strange man waiting by our campfire, a white flag in one hand and a horn in the other. *Greek,* I thought. *But not a soldier—perhaps a bandit.* "I have a message for you *ladies,*" he said, with a mocking bow, and I decided that I was quite certain that he was a bandit.

"We have your leader—the woman with the graying hair." *Janiya.* I looked around for her, and didn't see her. "Oh yes, feel free to look for her in your tents, but don't try to leave camp, any of you. We have someone watching your camp, and he can signal the people holding your 'sister' to cut her throat." I could hear the rising panic around me, and the bandit blew a blast of his horn. "Shut up, all of you! Listen to me. You can have her back. There's just one thing we want—a piece of jewelry you stole from us. A necklace of stones threaded on chain, fairly plain looking. That's all we want. As soon as we have that, we'll let your friend go." He gestured benevolently. "The gems you took from us, the silk, the livestock—*those* you can keep."

They want the spell-chain. I glanced around at the other sisters, not certain anyone but me would even know what he was talking about; their faces were white and set but also confused. I would have expected the spell-chain to be around Janiya's neck, but surely they'd have looked there . . . "We need time to look for what you're demanding," I said, raising my voice to be heard.

"Start looking. And don't leave the camp."

"How do we even know she's still alive?" From the yurt, I heard someone catch her breath, but we had to ask.

"Ask a question. I'll have an answer for you in a moment."

I glanced at the women crowded into the doorway of the yurt, at a loss. Ruan spoke: "Ask her what sort of lapdog Ruan would keep as a pet."

The bandit shouted the question to someone at the edge of the campsite. A few tense minutes passed, and then the answer was shouted back: "A nice meaty one."

Ruan gave a slight shrug. "She's alive."

"We'll look for it," I said to the bandit, and stomped into the yurt where Janiya slept, the other women following me.

"Who the hell was on sentry duty last night?" Ruan demanded, glaring at me venomously.

"Janiya was," Maydan snapped.

"What is it he wants?" Saken wailed.

"It's a spell-chain," I whispered. "You can use it to summon a djinn and order it to do things. Janiya knew what it was; she's been using it since we took it from the bandits. Remember the apples? That's how she got them. Where does Janiya keep valuable items?"

No one was sure. There was a chest opposite the door, kept latched, and we rooted through it quickly; it held money, but not the spell-chain. The other women scattered through the yurt to hunt through other boxes and bags, occasionally bringing a necklace out for me to see, but no luck. On impulse, I checked the spot where Janiya slept—and there, under the blankets, in a little hollow of sand, was the spell-chain. I wasn't certain whether it had slipped off her neck, or if she had placed it there on purpose.

No one was looking at me, and I curled my hand around it, taking a moment to think. If I showed it to everyone else and invited discussion of what to do next, the bandit would hear that *something* had changed inside the tent, and would at least come in to see what was going on; at worst, he might signal the other bandits to kill Janiya. No, I had to think this out for myself.

The bandits seemed to have assumed that we would not know what a spell-chain did, even if Janiya knew. They would not be expecting a rescue. If I summoned the djinn, I could send it to rescue Janiya, and potentially yank her out of harm's way before the bandits could do anything. *Potentially,* that was the key word. If she was being held with a sword literally at her throat, which seemed likely, could the djinn get her out without letting her get hurt? Would it *choose* to, even if it could? Would I be able to phrase my instructions in an explicit enough way without the bandit overhearing? Would Janiya even want me to try this, or would she want me to just hand the spell-chain over?

I thought she'd want me to try. Of course, if she ended up dead, the other sisters would blame me for it.

For a moment, the knife was within my grasp . . .

I said, "I'm going to go search the supply yurt." On my way out, I whispered to Tamar, "Keep everyone searching here, but be ready for a fight." She glanced up, wide-eyed, but gave me a single, emphatic nod.

The supply yurt was empty. I stepped back into the shadows and took out the spell-chain. "Aeriko," I muttered. "Show yourself."

The djinn appeared. "The bandits that used to hold your chain now hold Janiya," I whispered. "You are bound either way; would you rather that we continue to hold your chain, or would you like us to return you to the bandits?"

The djinn glimmered brightly for a moment, so brightly that I was afraid that the bandit would see something strange going on inside the tent. There was a long pause, then it hissed, "You ask *me* to make a choice?"

"Only if you care," I said. "If all human masters are the same to you—well, I won't tell you that you should feel otherwise."

Another moment of intense brightness, and then: "I would stay with you."

I let out a breath I hadn't realized I was holding. "Right then. The bandits are holding Janiya hostage. We need to get her out, and back here, *alive*. I want you to go see what the situation is, and if you can grab her without her getting hurt, bring her back here. If you can't, come back and tell me."

The djinn hesitated for a moment, then said, "Without her getting hurt, or without her getting *killed*?"

The strangeness of having a djinn offer a helpful suggestion made my head spin for a moment. "Superficial injuries *only*."

The djinn winked out. I slipped the chain back into my sleeve, then stepped out of the supply yurt and shrugged apologetically at the bandit, still holding his white flag. I went into the sleeping yurt. Tamar had done her work well: the sisters had picked up their weapons and were waiting inside, tense and ready, though a few were continuing to root through boxes randomly, throwing desperate-sounding words back and forth for the benefit of the listening bandit.

"What's going on?" Ruan hissed.

"Trust me," I whispered back. I stepped back from the door and peered out as discreetly as I could. If the djinn could deliver Janiya, it would probably drop her off at the center of the camp. I retrieved my own sword, and Janiya's, which was jumbled with some of her other possessions along one of the walls of the yurt. I slipped the spell-chain around my neck.

My heart hammered in my ears. Time passed. *How long could this possibly take? Either it could get her or it couldn't. Dammit! Where are they?*

And then, a whirl of light, and Janiya stumbled, alive and unhurt, in the center of camp.

"Now!" I shouted, because just as I'd expected, as soon as they'd lost their hostage, the bandits simply attacked our camp.

I thrust the hilt of Janiya's sword into her right hand and grabbed her left, dragging her toward the horses. She was almost certainly dizzy and disoriented from her trip, but I didn't dare give her time to get her bearings on her own.

Unfortunately, some of the bandits had been posted by our horses while the sisters were all contained in camp, unable to leave, and on the signal that Janiya had escaped, they'd sent in their dogs to scatter the horses. Ruan managed to catch her horse, and so did several other sisters, but Janiya and I saw the horses running and turned back to camp. Janiya didn't have her signaling horn, but she popped two fingers into her mouth and blew a piercing whistle—a long blast and then two short blasts. "Just so everyone knows I'm still alive," she said.

As we ran, I tried to think whether there was anything I could order—ask—the djinn to do for us right now. I couldn't tell it to kill the bandits; that would break the spell and probably result in my death. Having the djinn catch and return the horses would only result in horses that were catatonic with fear rather than merely panicky. Weaponry, though—I grabbed the necklace as we ran and spoke into the air. "See if any of the sisters are without weapons, and provide them with weapons if they're lacking. Make sure Tamar has a bow and arrows."

"Is that—explicit enough?" Janiya asked.

"I think so. I'll explain later."

"You may consider it an *order* that you survive this fight and explain." Janiya gave me a grim smile as we reached the heart of the fight.

Most of the bandits were on horseback. Most of the sisters were not. It made for an ugly situation. I pulled my sword out of its sheath and stood my ground as well as I could, slashing at horses more than riders; I hated to hurt the horses, which couldn't help being ridden by bandits, but the riders were out of reach and getting them off their horses as quickly as possible seemed the best strategy for staying alive.

I found myself in a sea of horses' legs and booted feet, trying to defend myself from blows coming from above. I slashed the flank of a roan horse, and then dodged out of the way as it reared in terror and pain; the rider lost his seat and crashed to the ground. I struck at him before he could get up, and he lay still; I turned, to find a spear leveled at me, and dodged aside desperately, using the flailing horse as cover. *At least it isn't* aiming *for me.* I hadn't injured the horse badly—could I get onto it, calm it? That seemed like a bad idea, but no worse than staying here on the ground. I could reach the stirrup, barely, and the saddle, and I hoisted myself on.

The bandit with the spear jerked back as he found my sword suddenly in his face. I pressed the advantage, and he recovered quickly, realizing that his spear was longer than my sword. I dodged aside but I couldn't get close enough to whack at anything other than the spear itself, and he just whipped it out of the way. Without warning, the shaft of the spear suddenly cracked in half—*the djinn,* I thought, and laughed out loud—and the bandit threw it away in horror, backing away from me as if he thought I'd done it. I took time for a quick look around.

This does not look good. Most of the sisters were fighting from the ground—those still standing. Ruan was still on horseback, and I saw her unhorse one bandit and turn desperately to the bandit beside him. Janiya fought from the ground, dodging both a sword and the hooves of the bandit's horse. I didn't see Zhanna or Maydan. As I turned, though, I saw Saken huddled on the ground, not moving, in a pool of spreading black blood.

"Could you move them?" I asked desperately, speaking to the djinn. "The bandits, I mean? Somewhere else? Somewhere far away?"

A pause, then: "It would be risky. For you. It is difficult to move someone—uncooperative."

This, of course, was why the Sisterhood of Weavers couldn't simply send djinni to the steppe to move all of the Alashi to some distant mountaintop, and why this tactic was used so rarely in battles. Moving people around was a delicate business, and the djinni did not excel at delicate tasks, particularly when they didn't wish to. If a djinn killed a human, even by accident that broke the binding and freed it—killing the sorceress and usually the holder of the spell-chain in the process.

As I looked around, though, I saw Saken, huddled on the ground, her blood spreading out in a black pool. "If I die, it's worth it," I whispered. "Djinn—"

"Wait," it said. "Listen. Free me first, and then I will help you. You won't be at risk then. Free me, and I can take the bandits away from you, far, far away and if some of them die, it will be nothing to you. I can return to the starlit land without passing through your heart." I must have looked uncertain, because it went on, taking on an almost wheedling tone: "I'll have to take them one at a time. If I'm bound, and I drop the first one, that won't do you much good, will it? You'll be dead, and the other bandits will still be here."

Free the djinn. But then it won't have to help me. I wondered if it were an act of cowardice, freeing it this way instead of ordering it to remove the bandits and accepting the risk of death, but I was quite certain that Janiya would approve. "How do I free you?"

"Smash the soul-stone from the spell-chain," it said.

I pulled it out and looked at it. Sure enough, one stone glittered darkly in the sun. *Karenite.* I would need to get off my horse to do this, so I jumped down set the stone on a rock, and smashed it with the hilt of my sword before I could change my mind.

Thank you, the djinn howled into the wind around my ears, and a heartbeat later, the bandits were gone. All of them, in the blink of an eye. *It lied to me when it said it would have to move them one at a time,* I thought, and felt a faint smile rise to my lips. *You don't owe the truth to a slave-holder.* I had clutched the spell-chain in my fist so tightly, I had ground the stones into my palm. I released it slowly, dropping it to the ground, then ran to Saken.

The other sisters were looking around frantically. "Where's Maydan?" I shouted. "The bandits are gone; they're not coming back. Someone find Maydan. Saken's hurt really badly."

"So is Maydan," Ruan said, and my heart sank.

Saken's eyes were closed and her skin was waxy. The wound was in her back, I realized, which was why I could see no injury the way she was lying, only the spreading stain of blood on the ground. I dropped to my knees beside her and whispered, "We should have just given it to them."

The other women gathered around Saken. "Maydan is alive, but unconscious," Zhanna murmured. "I don't think she'd be able to do anything for her anyway." She held one hand to a wound in her shoulder; blood welled up around her fingers.

"Erdene should be here," Ruan murmured, and knelt beside Saken to hold her hand.

If Saken was aware of her best friend's absence and of Ruan's presence, she gave no sign. I heard a faint sob from someone behind me—Tamar. After a few more moments, I realized that Saken was no longer breathing. Ruan bowed her head and lowered Saken's hand gently to the ground.

Out of the corner of my eye, I saw Janiya pick up

the spell-chain, or what was left of it. She touched the smashed stone, and looked at me. "This is what they wanted, yes? And they took me as their hostage."

"I had the djinn rescue you," I said miserably. "I asked it if it preferred to stay with us, or to go back into the power of the bandits, and it said it wanted to stay with us, so I told it to get you out if it could."

"That's why you could give it vague instructions; it was an ally, not merely a slave."

"Yes." I looked down at Saken. "If I'd just given it to them . . ."

"They'd have attacked us anyway," Ruan said.

"You really believe that?"

She shrugged. "I certainly don't trust that they wouldn't have. If I'd found the spell-chain, if I'd known how to work it—well, I don't think that you did the *wrong* thing."

"How did you kill the bandits?" Zhanna asked.

"I don't know if they're dead or not," I said. "The djinn said that if I freed it, it would *move* them. To . . . somewhere else."

We took stock of ourselves: Saken was dead, Maydan had taken a hard blow to the head and was still unconscious, and there were many smaller injuries, broken ribs and bad cuts and one ankle that began to swell badly. Gulim went to soak her injured ankle in the cold water of the river; Jolay sat beside Maydan, holding her limp hand and pressing a cloth soaked in cold water against her head. The rest of us raided Maydan's supplies for bandages to wrap the smaller wounds. "We need to get to a healer," Zhanna muttered as I wrapped her arm. "Both for the rest of us, and for poor Maydan."

Janiya came by as I was dragging water back to

camp for rice—dragging, because although I'd escaped serious injury, I realized as I bent to fill the pot that I'd pulled some muscles rather badly in my back and could hardly lift anything. "Has anyone seen Kara?" I asked, since Janiya had gone to see about rounding up the horses.

"She's made her way back, as have all our other horses. We seem to have kept most of the bandits' horses as well, and their dogs. I'm not sure where their camp is, though, and the rest of their livestock."

"The djinn could've told us," I said apologetically.

She shrugged. "You did the right thing." I saw the glimmer of a blue bead in her hand, though she hesitated.

I glared at her. "Keep the damn thing. I know perfectly well they're useless. That there's no set number of beads we have to earn to win the privilege of joining the Alashi."

Janiya smiled and tucked the bead away. "Yes," she said. "And I think you're ready to be one of us now. Tamar, too, of course—I've thought she was ready for some time. There will be a ceremony, when we rejoin the rest of the Alashi. Which will be soon. We're going to go back to our clan for healing and rest, and we'll be joining the other clans and sword sisterhoods and brotherhoods not long after that."

"So I won't have to choose between killing myself and being sold back into slavery," I said. I tried to speak lightly, but Janiya heard the bitter edge and gave me a quick look.

"You only heard half of that story," she said.

"Oh?"

"Yes. That was Ruan." She paused for a moment to let that sink in. "She chose suicide—*so she passed.*

That, finally, is the only test that really matters. I
you'd rather be dead than a slave, you belong wit!
us."

Ruan and Jolay dug Saken's grave near the stream
where the ground was relatively soft. They dressed he
in her vest, then lay her body on a square of white felt
Jolay held up each of the vests Saken had embroidered
in summers past, then folded it and slipped it unde
her head: the one with the beautiful horse, the on
with the vines and flowers, the one of crisscrossed line
that formed shapes but no pictures. Jolay drew he
dagger, and placed it gently in Saken's right hand
Ruan slipped a thumb-ring over Saken's thumb an
curled her cold hand around a single arrow.

One by one, each of the sisters stepped forward t
tuck something in with Saken's body—a waterskin,
wrist guard, a small piece of carved karenite, a bril
liant blue feather. Janiya slipped the broken spell
chain over Saken's head, whispering something n
one could hear. When it was my turn, I felt briefly at
loss—there was so little I carried that I felt was *mine*
Then I slipped the thong of seven blue beads fron
around my head, and laid it beside Saken. Tamar di
the same.

A skin of kumiss was passed around; I took a swal
low and managed to hide my grimace. Ruan knelt be
side Saken and tipped a little of the kumiss into he
mouth, then tucked the skin in beside her. Ruan an
Jolay wrapped the white felt over and around he
tucking in the ends, and tied it so that it held her bod
and all the gifts from her sisters. Then they lowere
the body into the grave and covered it with dir
Those of us whole enough to carry them brough
rocks and covered the grave with a cairn of stones.

We mounted our horses the next day. Maydan hovered on the edge of consciousness, occasionally opening her eyes but not responding to us in any coherent way. Ruan and Jolay built a bed for her using some of the yurt frame that could be dragged behind a horse. It would be a slow way to travel, but it couldn't be helped. *If we still had the djinn,* I thought, then pushed the thought from my mind. We padded the frame with blankets, then put Maydan on the bed and wrapped her in a blanket, tying her in place so she wouldn't slip off.

With Maydan being pulled behind us, we had to move very slowly. It would take us days to reach the clan at this rate, so two of the sisters were sent on ahead to tell them what had happened and ask for a healer to ride back to meet us. At one point the second day, Janiya fell into step beside me. "What would you have done if one of the other sisters had been taken hostage?" I asked. "If you had been the one to decide what to do with the spell-chain?"

Janiya was silent for a long time. Finally she said, "I would have broken the spell-chain and given it to them. I think the men in camp wouldn't know, looking at it, that it was useless at that point; they would probably have returned the hostage, unless they'd already killed her."

"That's what I should have done," I said.

Janiya shrugged. "If you'd had time to sit and think it over, maybe. I never would have thought to ask the djinn which master it preferred, to gain it as an ally instead of a slave. That wasn't a wrong decision, Lauria. It's just not what I would have done if I had been in the camp, and you had been taken hostage."

It was impossible not to blame myself for Saken's

death. As we plodded slowly across the grasslands, I thought of all the many things I could have done that might have saved her. I could have ordered the djinn to circle the camp, snatching sisters out of danger. I could have ordered it to rip the weapons of the bandits out of their hands and drop them into the river. I could have ordered it to move all of *us* to some remote location—that would have been much safer than having it move the bandits, since we wouldn't have been resisting. It was frightening to be swept up by a djinn, but if I'd had it say, "Don't fear, I am Janiya's djinn" before picking them up, I didn't think anyone would have resisted. I could have had it move us to the very camp we were riding toward now, one by one, in a flash. I could have had it grab the sisters on the ground *first,* the women who were in the most danger. I could have at *least* asked the djinn to spy out the bandits around our camp before it got Janiya, so we'd have known exactly what we were up against. *I should have. If only I'd thought of it at the time . . .*

Tamar fell into step beside me at some point and reached across the space between our horses to take my hand. "I heard what you said to Janiya," she said. "I don't think there's anyone here who thinks you should have just given the spell-chain to the bandits."

"What would you have done?" I asked.

"I'd have given it to them," she said without hesitating. "But it would've been a stupid thing to do. The only thing I was thinking about was getting Janiya back. I didn't think about how they might have people surrounding our camp."

"They might not have attacked us if we'd given it to them. After all, they didn't kill Janiya."

"I think they'd have still attacked us," Tamar said.

"They didn't kill Janiya because they didn't know for sure that we wouldn't send the djinn to check on her well-being before handing over the necklace."

"There's no way to know."

"I suppose not, but that's what I think. Anyway, it doesn't matter. You did what you could to save Janiya, and all of us."

"I did what I could *think* of."

"Well, what the hell else could you do? I'd have given the spell-chain back because I wouldn't have thought to use the djinn."

"Thank you," I said, but I was holding myself rigid and I knew that Tamar could tell that I still felt guilty.

That evening, as we were setting up the yurts and rolling out our blankets, Ruan rolled her blanket out beside mine. "You've got a right to have nightmares, blossom," she said shortly, when I glanced at her. "I'll put a pillow over my head if I have to."

"Don't put yourself out," I said. I sat back on my own blanket. "What would *you* have done?"

"Like I said, I don't know how to work a spell-chain. If I'd known—well, it's tempting to say that I'd have been clever enough to come up with some plan that would've kept Saken alive and Maydan unhurt, but really, I've had two days to think about it, haven't I? You had to come up with a plan standing in the supply yurt hoping that the bandit didn't walk in to check on you."

I didn't say anything. When I glanced up, Ruan's eyes were soft; I'd never seen her look quite like that. She clasped my shoulder gently. "You did the right thing, sister," she said.

I still lay awake for hours that night, thinking of all the ways I could have kept Saken and Maydan safe.

The one thing I felt no regret for was freeing the djinn. The howl of its exuberance when I'd smashed the binding-stone still rang in my ears when I thought of it. And it kept its promise. *It would probably have gotten a bead for that, if it were trying to join the Alashi,* I thought, and smiled.

Saken's death wasn't the first miserable failure of my life, of course. Back when I still worked for Kyros, he had sent me to a garrison, ostensibly to carry a message but really to secretly audit the commander's books. I had warned Kyros that it was unlikely I'd be able to get into the books without the commander noticing. Everyone knows that simple messages *can* be carried by a djinn; when a human messenger arrives, they have an agenda that goes beyond a mere message. Kyros agreed with this and sent Myron with me; he thought the commander would assume the spy was Myron and focus on winning him over with wine and rich food. It had almost worked, but the commander had stepped back into his office for a jar of particularly good wine to share with Myron, just minutes after I'd arrived to sit down and go over the accounts list. I hadn't gotten into trouble, of course; I had a letter from Kyros authorizing me to look at whatever I wanted. I had looked over the books, with the man glaring at me furiously long into the evening. He was *not* lining his pockets with the garrison's money, but he was so shamed and angered at Kyros's suspicions that he deserted a few months later. And he'd been caught deserting, and Kyros had had to execute him. A terrible waste. All because he'd walked in while I was checking up on him. Of course, Kyros hadn't blamed me; it had been his idea, after all.

And that's what it boiled down to, as long as I was following orders from Kyros; what I did was ultimately Kyros's responsibility, not mine. If I spied on an innocent man, if I brought back an escaped slave, I was merely an extension of the hand of Kyros. Like his djinn, except bound only by my vows and my desire to please him, rather than spells. Though it was possible that Kyros *had* used magic on me at some point, using the link of our shared blood to keep me loyal. *Even after he sent me with a man who raped me.*

I have to tell Janiya, I thought as I dismounted at the end of the day to help set up camp. *I can't live a lie for the rest of my life. Janiya has to know. And Tamar—Tamar has to know, too.*

My hands shook as I helped put up the yurt, thinking about it. *The only people we kill in cold blood are bandits, rapists, spies, and traitors.* If I were an Alashi spy among the Greeks and I were caught, the Greeks would show me no mercy. I would be tortured for whatever information I could give them—and when I was wrung utterly dry, executed in some painful and public way. Of course, if an Alashi spy switched sides and came clean, I had no doubt that Kyros, for one, would find uses for him that did not involve his slow dismemberment.

I wondered how the Alashi killed spies: burned alive, like the stories said they did with soldiers who surrendered? Or some other gruesome death? *I don't think they'll kill me,* I thought. *Not when I'm turning myself in.* Of course, they might demand that I return to the Greeks and spy for the Alashi—could I do that? *Yes.* But back among the Greeks, seeing Kyros every day, what if my loyalties shifted again?

Worse, what if the Alashi simply turned me out?

Well, maybe I could become a merchant or something. Because I'd rather die than serve Kyros again. I clung to Janiya's words: *If you'd rather die than be a slave, you belong with us.*

Still, privacy in our little temporary camp was minimal, and I realized that I could hardly imagine facing Janiya right after confessing to her that I'd originally come here to betray them. This trip would be interminable enough without that between us. *I'll wait until we're back with the clan.*

We were camped near the stream but not on it, so I took the animals down to let them drink. I was stroking Kara's neck when I saw a shimmer in the air.

"What do you want?" I said.

"I bring a message from Kyros," the djinn said. "Lauria, I brought charges against Sophos; he is in prison, and will be executed."

I laughed out loud. "I don't believe you," I said. "The Sisterhood would never agree to it. He was their tool, just as I was."

The djinn continued its message without pausing: "I hope you understand how seriously I take his abuse of you. My djinn informs me that you and the Alashi are on the move again. Are you moving in toward the fall gathering, and do you know where that gathering will be held?"

Kyros, you can take a flying leap off the Elpisia lookout tower, I thought, but simply clamped my mouth shut and glared at the djinn.

After a moment, and a shimmering flutter, the djinn said, "If you had no response, Kyros sent the following message: 'Lauria, I realize that you are angry at the Sisterhood right now. Please believe that your rewards will be beyond your wildest dreams.

You will be able to demand Sophos's head on a pike and his testicles as a paperweight, if that's what you'd like. A vast house, slaves to fan your mother on hot summer days and pour tea for her in the winter, a stable of horses—you'll have whatever you like."

I kept my mouth shut. The djinn waited, then said, "If you had no response to *that,* Kyros had another message. 'Realize, too, that you are of no use to me if you give me no information. I have not ordered the djinn to announce your treachery to your bandit queen Janiya, but I could.' "

I should have felt terror at that, but instead I began to laugh. "Djinn, tell me this, just how many messages did Kyros send for me?"

"He sent one more." A hesitant flicker, then the djinn added, *helpfully,* "I think the Sisterhood grows impatient, and Kyros needs to prove your loyalty, whether you still offer it or not. The last message concerns your mother."

Now panic shot through me like an arrow. I felt only the barest sense of betrayal; I'd accepted now that Kyros was no friend of mine. But to threaten my mother—

I need to think of something, I thought, and bit my lip, staring at the djinn. "Wait a moment," I said. "I'm thinking of how best to answer Kyros's question." *I could lie. Or tell the truth, for that matter, that I don't know where we're headed or where the gathering will be. Or I could promise to find out and then confess to Janiya and find out where the Alashi would like Kyros to think the gathering is. Of course, Kyros will have a djinn watching me—I should have thought of that before . . .*

At a loss, on impulse, I put my hand out to touch

the shimmer and spoke the words of banishment "Return to the Silent Lands, lost one of your kind and trouble us no more."

The djinn recoiled briefly from my touch, as if it were staggering away from me, and then it whirled in the air with a strange shriek. *"There is a gate—you are a gate—"* I felt the djinn glowing like a coal against my chest; *it is passing through my heart,* I thought, and tried to step back. *"You have freed me,"* the djinn said, *"and I will thank you with this advice run now."* And then it was gone.

Freed it?

The spell of a spell-chain was broken if the djinn killed someone while acting on the orders of the holder of the chain. I'd known that, of course. And the djinn could be freed if you smashed the binding stone; I'd known that, in a vague way, even before the djinn told me how to free it. And sometimes the spell broke after the death of the sorceress. But this? I had *never* heard of this—that someone could touch a bound djinn, speak the words of banishment, and send it back to wherever djinni came from as if it were unbound. *If it came back here, would it be bound again?* I wondered.

I desperately wanted to talk to Zhanna about this, but then I'd have to explain why I was consorting with a bound djinn that I desperately wanted to get rid of—and I had to talk to Janiya first. So I kept my silence, even as my thoughts whirled, the shriek of the djinn echoing in my ears, the burn of it passing through my heart still trembling in my bones.

Run now. Did the djinn know something I didn't, or was it snatching one last opportunity to mess with a human that it didn't much like? Just because Janiya' djinn had been grateful, and helpful, didn't mean that this djinn would have anything but contempt for me. Even if I *had* freed it . . .

If it was telling the truth, what could it have been talking about? *Kyros,* I thought. He betrayed me once by sending me to Sophos—is he planning some new betrayal? Has he already set it in motion? Maybe he sent another spy here, someone who planned to get rid of me by accusing *me* of being a spy. Except, that didn't make a lot of sense; it would be incredibly risky, since I'd been with the Alashi for a while and would be believed more readily than some new arrival. If Kyros had sent another spy, it would be someone I didn't know, even if he or she had been warned to watch for me.

I have to talk to Janiya, I thought, but as I started to signal Kara to drop back to let me ride beside her, I caught a fragment of conversation, shouted between Zhanna and Jolay, even though they were well away from me. *There is no privacy on horseback.* I bit my lip. *I'll talk to her tonight.*

Dusk fell, and we made our camp, our yurts close together like animals huddling for warmth. As the sun went down, the air grew cold. I approached Janiya; she was chatting with Ruan, who glared up at me as I came over. "Yes?" Janiya said, pleasantly enough.

"I was, was wondering if you had a few minutes. If you could go for a walk with me."

Janiya looked at Ruan, and then at me. Ruan was silently fuming, and I realized that she, too, wanted to unburden herself by sharing some secret, some dark corner of her soul, with Janiya. *She chose suicide, so she passed the test.* "I'm sorry," I said, and my voice was a little shaky. "I didn't mean to interrupt."

"Can we talk tomorrow?" Janiya asked. Her voice was kind.

"Yes, of course," I said, and went quickly into my own yurt. I heard Ruan come in later, much later, but it was so late by then, I didn't dare seek out Janiya and demand that she talk to me instead of collapsing into her own bed.

The healer from the clan came riding back the next day, with the sisters who'd been sent ahead and a few others. He examined Maydan and said gravely that it was impossible to know when, or whether, she would recover. "I have seen people with injuries like this recover completely. And I've seen others wither and die like an uprooted plant." He examined the less serious injuries and rebandaged most of them. Then he told us to leave Maydan with him and the others who'd ridden back; we could ride on ahead, settle into camp with the clan, and recover some of our strength—not to mention our wits. Everyone hated to leave Maydan, but the wisdom in this was clear. Riding at our normal pace, we could be back at the camp within hours. Still, everyone postponed the separation as much as possible, unpacking and repacking supplies for Maydan and for Jolay, who would stay behind with her.

Back in Sophos's harem, Tamar had mentioned that Jaran's djinn could sometimes tell them whether or not a sick person would recover. I nudged Tamar as she strapped a pack to her horse, and asked her about this. "Oh!" she exclaimed. "I hadn't thought of that."

I had expected that she would want to talk to Zhanna, but Zhanna was busy and distracted, so instead we withdrew a little and Tamar sat down and closed her eyes. She opened one eye and muttered, "If I fall asleep, wake me up," and then settled herself and breathed deeply for a few moments.

Her eyes opened again, and I could see a djinn behind them, feral and frightening. "Will Maydan recover?" I asked without preamble.

"You should be more polite," the djinn said. "I am not a chained one." I started to stammer something, but the djinn shrugged me off. "Her soul is still within her body."

"What does that mean, exactly?"

"It means that you may hope for her to recover."

Well. That was better than it could have been. "Thank you."

The djinn inclined Tamar's head slightly, then vanished abruptly, leaving Tamar staring into my eyes. She didn't collapse the way Jaran had, but she accepted my arm getting up. We went to Jolay, who was kneeling by Maydan's still body. "We talked to a djinn about Maydan," Tamar said, awkwardly. "Sometimes they know if the person will recover."

Jolay looked at Tamar, her eyes wide and horrified. "What did the djinn say?"

"She said that Maydan's soul is still within her body," Tamar said. "There's hope for her."

Jolay struggled briefly against tears, then hid her face in her sleeve. "Thank you," she said, her voice muffled. "I'll keep hoping, then."

We pulled out a short time later, and rode the rest of the way back to the camp as quickly as we could. A ragged cheer went up when we saw the smoke from the campfire; another when we saw a flock of their animals grazing under the eye of a watchful young man, who raised his hand to greet us. As had hap pened when we brought Erdene, the clan poured ou of their camp to greet us as we rode up.

We had spent only an evening with them before and I barely recognized anyone; everyone else tum bled off their horses to embrace parents, brothers nieces, and nephews, but I hung back, feeling sud denly intimidated by the crowd of strangers. I saw Er dene, supported by a young man as she stood, pal and thin, to greet us, but no one else I knew.

"Lauria?"

A man's voice: horrified. I scanned the crow again, and saw him: Alibek.

Kyros's slave, the "little bird."

"What's she doing here?" Alibek had turned to on of the other men, his face twisted in fear. "What's sh *doing* here? She's a spy, she must be! She works fo Kyros; she dragged me back to him the first time I es caped! *What's she doing here?"*

Run now. This was what the djinn knew—this wa why the djinn had told me to flee. Alibek was dresse as an Alashi now; I saw the strand of blue beads at hi throat, and a long knife on his belt. He stood, clench ing his fists, and two of the brothers moved in close to his side, as if to defend him if I launched some sor of mad attack. He was dirty and sunburned, just lik me, no longer the soft-handed harem boy I'd hunted I wondered if one of the brothers had teased hir about his soft hands, the way Ruan had tormente Tamar.

For one endless moment, I stared into Alibek' green eyes, taking in his hatred and fury. *I'm not tha person anymore,* I wanted to scream, but why woul he ever believe me?

There was nothing I could say. Nothing I could do, except wish that I had told Janiya *everything* the night I'd made the decision to tell her why I'd originally come to the Alashi, or while riding back, even if everyone had heard every word . . . *They will never believe me now. The best I can hope for is that they'd kill me. Or sell me into slavery . . .*

I wheeled Kara and we bolted back out onto the steppe.

*I*t's over.

I had let Kara slow to a walk; I didn't think anyone was chasing me, at least not yet. I felt lost, bereft. I couldn't return to the Alashi. I *wouldn't* return to Kyros. *It's over. And I'm alone.*

What was I going to *do*?

Well, I could find some overland merchants like the two who'd stopped by the sisterhood camp, and see if I could get hired as a guard. Or perhaps I could make my way to Penelopeia—Janiya had mentioned the guardswomen kept by the Sisterhood of Weavers. Surely they could make use of me. *As Kyros made use of me.* Though the Sisterhood had sold Janiya into slavery as punishment for a crime she hadn't committed. Not people I felt I could trust. *Just as well. I trusted Kyros, and see where that got me . . .*

I found myself thinking of Alibek. *My little straying bird.* As lonely and frightened as I was, I didn't—couldn't—begrudge Alibek his freedom. *He deserves to be one of the Alashi. As much as Tamar, or Ruan, or Janiya, and more than me.* He had taken his freedom, and when it was taken back from him, he took it again. I thought again of that day I'd hunted him down, and the offer he'd made: *Come with me. We'll tell them you were a slave, too.* I couldn't quite wish I'd taken him up on that, though, as I'd never have met Tamar.

Tamar. What if she was tarred by the story Alibek would tell about me? Surely, *surely* he would tell them that he'd never seen her before, and they would piece together the story and realize what had happened. And that Tamar was innocent, deserving of their protection.

Unlike me.

I had returned five slaves in addition to Alibek to Kyros. *And where are they now?* Kyros had sold at least some of them. One was a slave in a mine now; I vaguely remembered hearing where the others had been sold—one to a large farm deep in Penelopeian territory, one to a man somewhere else in Elpisia, another down to someone in Daphnia. I'd heard rumors, each time, and listened with half an ear, wanting to know and yet not wanting to know. *Kyros must have sold Alibek, or he'd have sent a djinn to warn me when Alibek escaped. Unless he'd already decided I had turned against him, and didn't care whether I lived or died. But that's not like him. Even if he knew I'd betrayed him, he'd have some clever idea about twisting my arm, as he tried to do with that last djinn.*

What if they didn't believe that Tamar wasn't also a spy?

She deserves her freedom. They can't cast her out. What if they hurt her? What if they executed her, thinking that she was a spy like me? I felt sick, staring at the horizon. *If anyone deserves that, it's me, not Tamar.*

Before I could change my mind, Kara and I headed back to the clan's camp.

I rode back in with my bow unstrung and my sword tied into its scabbard, to show that I wasn't coming back to threaten them. Not that I *could* threaten them without the Greek army at my back, but I thought the gestures of surrender would make it more likely that I'd be able to say my piece without someone killing me. To my surprise, no one so much as challenged me as I passed the edge of camp, though I knew someone must have been on watch. I dismounted and led Kara toward the center of camp.

Everyone seemed to be gathered there; as I approached, everyone turned to look at me. I could see the sisterhood clustered together on one side of the fire; young men were clustered on the other. The sword brotherhood, no doubt—*Alibek's brothers*. As I approached, many of the men laid hands on their bows or swords, though no one raised his weapon. The sisters kept their hands at their sides, though I could see Janiya's hands gripped into fists.

"Why have you returned?" the elder asked, breaking the silence.

"I came back to tell you not to blame Tamar," I said. My voice was rough in my throat. "She was a slave, like Alibek."

"So you do know each other," the elder said.

"Alibek claims that you work for his former master," Janiya said. "That you hunted him down, the first time he escaped, and brought him back. That if you're here, it could only be as a spy."

I forced myself to meet her gaze; her face was cold

and stony, and her eyes were distant. What could
possibly say that anyone would accept? *If only I coul*
talk to Janiya, just to Janiya . . . I swallowed, an
turned my empty hands up in supplication, or a shrug
"I worked for Kyros when I last saw Alibek. An
Kyros sent me to spy. He sent me first to the house o
his friend Sophos, who—who—" my voice faltere
"—also owned Tamar," I finished, finally. "My escap
was prearranged; Tamar's escape was not."

Tamar stepped forward; she'd been somewhere be
hind the other sisters. "I told you I'd scream if yo
didn't take me with you. Spoil your escape. But tha
wouldn't have mattered, would it? And you took m
with you anyway."

I looked at her, my voice steadying a little as I saw th
warmth in her eyes. "I don't know what would hav
happened. Sophos had already broken his promise."
Tamar nodded slightly, and I knew that she knew wha
I meant. "He might have had me flogged, saying that
was necessary not to compromise my disguise. Or h
might have had you sent to the mines, to keep you from
talking to the other slaves in his household. But anywa
I didn't want to leave you behind."

"And then you rescued me from the bandits."

I nodded.

"Are you still spying on the Alashi?"

"No." I glanced back at Janiya. "I had been drif
ing for a long time—dodging the questions when Ky
ros sent a djinn. Just before the bandits attacked us,
decided that I wasn't ever going back to him.
wanted to stay here."

"*Why didn't you tell me?*" Janiya whispered.

"I was going to," I said. "But then we were a
tacked, and traveling—there was so much else goin

on . . ." *She knows,* I thought, looking into her eyes. *She knows that this is what I wanted to tell her last night.*

"What about your old master's djinn?" one of the brothers asked. "Is it here now?"

"No." I glanced around, looking for Zhanna, and spotted her, finally; she was avoiding my eyes. "It came looking for me a few days ago, and I—banished it."

That got Zhanna's attention. "What do you mean, you banished it?"

"I touched it, and used the words of banishment, like in an exorcism. And it went *through* me. Back to wherever the djinn come from. I can't really explain it; I was actually hoping maybe you could."

Zhanna sat back, looking thoughtful, but didn't say anything else.

"Anyway, Kyros has a second spell-chain. They gave him two, but I doubt he'll want to risk his second djinn when he doesn't know what happened to the first one." I looked around at the brothers, the sisters, the elder, and the other members of the clan. Even Erdene had made her way out, wan and unsmiling. "My loyalty is to you, not to Kyros. I don't expect you to believe that, which is why I ran away. I only came back because I had to make sure that you weren't assuming that Tamar was as guilty as I was."

There was an explosion of conversation. "She has to die," shouted the head of the brotherhood, Rishad. "Not Tamar; Alibek has already said he's never seen her before in his life. But Lauria, the slaver—she's a spy, she's admitted it herself."

"She *was* a spy," snapped Ruan. "*Was,* not is. If she had no loyalty to anyone but her master, why would she come back now?"

"And confess her crimes?" Zhanna added. "She could have denied everything from the start and accused Alibek of being a spy—set us against each other."

"Alibek was flogged and branded by Kyros after Lauria brought him back," Rishad snarled. "A spy wouldn't carry the scars I've seen."

"Lauria was raped by Sophos," Tamar said. "I saw the blood."

"She has to die!" Rishad insisted.

"You have no authority over her!" Ruan shouted. "None. How dare you try to pass judgment on her; it's not even your place!"

"It's for me to decide," Janiya said. She spoke softly, but as she stepped forward, the camp fell silent, waiting. "Not the head of the brotherhood, not the elder, not even the eldress of all the clans. I still hold the sign of authority—" her hand fell to the horn at her belt "—and her fate is for me to decide."

Janiya stepped forward, and her hands were trembling. "I wish you had *told* me," she said softly. "And I believe that you meant to. But you didn't. And so I can't trust what you say now."

"Just promise me that nothing will happen to Tamar."

"Not unless they kill me to get to her," Janiya said, and the corner of her mouth lifted for an instant. Then her face was stony again. "Take off your vest."

I shed the black wool vest I'd embroidered and gave it to Janiya. She dropped it on the ground, then raised her voice, speaking to me, but for the ears of everyone. "You would have been welcomed into the Alashi during the fall gathering, but you are Alashi no longer. You know nothing of consequence and we will *not* kill you, but you can't stay with us. Take your horse and go."

"Her *horse*?" one of the brothers hissed, but Janiya silenced him with a glare.

"Go!" shouted Janiya. "Or we will consider you a bandit, an intruder, and treat you accordingly!"

I mounted Kara, and we fled the camp as quickly as we could.

It wasn't until we were well clear of the encampment that I heard someone shouting to me to wait. I stopped Kara and turned back; it was Tamar.

"Why are you following me?" I asked.

"Because I'm coming with you," she said.

"What? Why? They weren't going to send you away, Janiya promised me . . ."

"No. I chose to leave."

She had left her vest, I realized.

"You're mad," I said.

"I'm your sister," she said, and held up the hand she'd slashed when we'd sworn blood sisterhood to each other.

"That doesn't mean you have to follow me out onto the steppe!"

"I didn't come because I *had* to. I chose to follow you."

I stared at her, perplexed.

"What are you going to do now?" Tamar asked. "Go back to Kyros?"

"I'd rather die."

"So what, then?"

I was silent for a long moment. Then I said, "There were five other slaves, other than Alibek, that I returned to Kyros. None are owned by Kyros now, but as far as I know they're all still slaves. I want to find them. And I want to free them."

"I was hoping you'd have some plan like that," Tamar said. "And that's why I followed you."

I gaped at her. "Like I said—you're mad."

"No, I'm not. You're going to need someone to help you. I bet you don't know where any of the wells are, or the rivers."

"Are you saying that you do?"

"Of course I do. It was something I asked Saken about, to teach me, specifically. And sometimes the djinn talk to me now; they're always helpful when it comes to finding water."

"Where's the nearest water hole, then?"

"About a half mile that way." She pointed. "We can go camp there tonight, if you want."

"Just because you can help me doesn't mean you should throw away your life with the Alashi. You could go back now, tell them that you found me to hear my side of the story, and that I'm a miserable traitor who deserves to die. They'd probably take you back."

Now she was silent for a moment. "It has always annoyed me that the Alashi refuse to free slaves," she said. " 'Take your freedom'—ha! As if it's that simple. As if I could have taken my freedom when I was ten. As if Meruert could take it, pregnant, or with a new-born baby."

"Or Aislan?"

"She acts like she likes to be a slave, but if she could, I think she'd rip Sophos's balls off and feed them to his dogs." Tamar gave me a level glare. "I tell you what, Lauria. You clearly *need* my help, since you didn't even take advantage of your months with the Alashi to find out more about locating water. I'll help you free your old enemies if you'll help me free my old friends."

"And we'll rip off Sophos's balls, and let Aislan feed them to his dogs," I said, beginning to smile for the first time since I'd recognized Alibek.

"I think we may have to draw straws," Tamar said.

"Well," I said. "Did you bring your bow?"

"And food. And water."

"I wish you'd brought a yurt."

"You slept outside half the time anyway."

"Winter's coming."

"Yeah, we'll definitely have to come up with *somewhere* else to sleep pretty soon." Tamar touched the bags on the back of her saddle. "I'm not going to miss Ruan."

"I'll miss Zhanna."

"She liked you better than she liked me."

"Not anymore, I bet."

"You might be surprised."

"Before you left, Zhanna didn't say anything to you about what I said, about banishing the djinn . . ."

"No." She sighed. "And I have no idea how you did that, either. The only thing I know is, I've heard all sorts of strange stories about what people can do with djinni—in stories about the Sisterhood of Weavers. But they keep a lot of what they can do a secret. Maybe when we're done freeing slaves, we can ride to Penelopeia and you can ask someone's advice?"

"Good thought," I said. "Let's go find your water hole."

Tamar turned her horse and I fell into step behind her. *It's over*, I thought, as our horses stretched out to a gallop. And then I thought, *No, it's starting.*

And I'm not alone.

ACKNOWLEDGMENTS

Thanks, first of all, to my agent, Jack Byrne, and to my superb editor, Anne Groell, who rocks.

Many thanks to the members of the Wyrdsmiths, for critique, support, and friendship: Eleanor Arnason, Bill Henry, Doug Hulick, Harry LeBlanc, Kelly McCullough, Lyda Morehouse, and Rosalind Nelson.

It can be amazingly difficult to find answers to questions about Kazakhstan—this is particularly true when you need information about a region that doesn't get many tourists. I am deeply grateful to Kevin Miller Jr., a former Peace Corps volunteer who worked in Kazakhstan and who answered a whole bunch of random questions for me via e-mail. The cultures in this book are only very *loosely* based on real-world cultures, so blame me, not Kevin, for the many things in the novel that don't match up to the real world. My friend Marc Moskowitz answered questions for me about ancient Greek language and culture, but again, this is fantasy, not history, so I changed things when I wanted to. And sometimes I just made them up. Don't blame Marc. Finally, two doctor friends, Jamie Feldman and Lisa Freitag, answered questions about injuries—and, like all my other expert friends, should not be held responsible for my errors.

Thank you to my beta readers: Jason Goodman, Peter Gunn, Michelle Herder, Doug Hulick, Martine

ACKNOWLEDGMENTS

Kalke, John Rowan Littell, Curtis Mitchell, Fillard Rhyne, Bill Scherer, and Karen Swanberg.

Thanks to my parents, for ongoing encouragement, moral support, and remote-site computer backup services.

A very special thank-you to my husband, Ed, for huge amounts of support, understanding, and enthusiasm. And a big hug and kiss to my three-year-old daughter, Molly, just on general principle.

I conceived of a very, very early version of this story while on vacation with my family when I was fifteen or sixteen years old. I scribbled it down in a spiral notebook, and my younger brother, Nathaniel, read it page by page as I finished and nagged me for weeks after I quit working on it. Thank you, Nate, and thank you also to my sister, Abi, for being my very first fans, not merely willing to tolerate listening to my endless stories, but genuinely enthusiastic about hearing them.

ABOUT THE AUTHOR

Naomi Kritzer mostly grew up in Madison, Wisconsin, though her family also spent time living in North Carolina, Indiana, Texas, and England. She moved to Minnesota to attend college; after graduating with a BA in religion, she became a technical writer. She is also the author of two previous novels for Bantam: *Fires of the Faithful* and *Turning the Storm*. She lives in Minneapolis with her family. You can see pictures of her kids (as well as information about her writing, of course) on her website: http://www.naomikritzer.com. She is currently at work on the second book in the Dead Rivers trilogy.

Be sure not to miss the next
exciting installment in

The Dead Rivers Trilogy

The Spirit-Binder's Apprentice

by Naomi Kritzer

Coming soon from
Bantam Spectra Books!

Turn the page for a special excerpt:

The Spirit-Binder's Apprentice
Coming soon!

When the wind was right, I could smell Elpisia from our hiding place down in the track of the old river: greasy smoke and rotting garbage. The Alashi encampments moved frequently and left our—*their*—garbage behind. I'd never noticed the smells of Elpisia when I lived there, but a summer on the steppe had cleared my nose and now I wrinkled my face as the wind shifted and wondered how anyone could stand it.

"Lauria. How dark does it have to be before we move in?" Tamar asked. Her small frame fit compactly into the crevice where she slouched; she chewed on the corner of a ragged fingernail.

"There are a lot of people in Elpisia who could recognize me." *Kyros, for one.* "I should probably wait until it's fully dark. I'll go by myself; you can wait with the horses."

"Aren't you afraid that you'll get caught?"

"If I do, I can probably talk my way out of it, this time. But not if I have you with me. And I've never done anything like this before."

"How are you going to get into the city?"

"There's a spot where the wall is crumbled, or used to be, anyway. I'll climb over there."

The last time I'd scrambled up the side of the Elpisia wall was last spring, when I'd gone in search of Kyros's escaped slave, Alibek. I'd been looking for evidence left by Alibek in his flight. I'd tracked Alibek to his hiding place in the river gorge where Tamar and I were hiding now, and had pulled him out and dragged him back to Kyros. It was only last spring, but it felt like ten years ago.

Well, I wouldn't need to free Alibek: he had freed himself, run away to the Alashi. And when we came face-to-face, he'd told them who I was. *They're having their fall gathering now*, I thought, and wrenched my mind away before I started thinking about what Zhanna and Janiya and the others might be doing. Though I had decided to defect to the Alashi and never return to Kyros, I hadn't confessed my true identity to Janiya before it was too late. I hadn't told her that Kyros was a boss, not a master; that he'd sent djinni up to the steppe to talk to me, though I'd dodged their questions more and more as the summer had worn on. I hadn't told her that I had come to the Alashi as a spy.

I wasn't sure if there was any way to earn the trust of the Alashi again. But at least this way I could make amends to the people I had dragged back to Kyros. Assuming I didn't fail as completely at this task as I had failed at my last.

"What are you going to do if they've fixed the wall since last spring?"

"Find another spot. If there isn't time tonight, I'll go back tomorrow."

I still didn't understand why Tamar had thrown her lot in with me. The Alashi weren't angry with her; she could have stayed with them. But she'd dropped her vest down on top of mine and followed me. Since that first day, I hadn't been inclined to question her too closely. I was too afraid that she'd change her mind and leave.

I didn't like being alone.

"Do you know where to look for—what is her name, anyway? You haven't said."

"Nika," I said. I didn't really want to think about her, but Tamar was waiting silently for me to go on, so after a moment I did. "She was about fourteen when I brought her back. Your age. That was over three years ago. When I caught up with her, I expected her to cry, but she held herself as rigid as carved stone. She didn't say a word the whole way back to Elpisia."

"Is she still with Kyros?"

"No, he sold her to a friend in town. She's still in Elpisia, though, or she was a couple of months ago. I thought she would be a good one to free first, because I don't think Kyros knows what happened with me yet. If I run into someone I know, or screw this up some other way, I can try telling

Kyros I was on my way back to him after Alibek exposed me
I may not be able to pull that off in a few months—if the
other escapes go well." I wondered again why Tamar had
thought coming with me was a good idea. "I know where the
household is, but I don't know how I'm going to find Nika."

"What if she's been sold since last spring?"

"Then I won't find her."

I slipped out of our hiding place and started for Elpisia
at dusk, and it was quite late when I reached the wall. Sure
enough, no one had fixed it since last spring; I found hand
holds easily, and scrambled over the crumbling spot.
hoped Nika would be able to manage the climb. The wall
was guarded by soldiers from the garrison, but I'd been
climbing over the Elpisia wall since childhood; avoiding
the patrols Kyros had set was easy. I had a rock in my boot
so I pulled it off and shook it out, and then pulled up the
hood of my cloak to obscure my face as much as I could.

The streets were dark and quiet this time of night, but
few people were still out. I walked briskly rather than keep
ing to the shadows; acting like I was trying to hide would
only attract attention. Nika's owner lived quite close to
Kyros, not far from the city gate. I took a roundabout route
trying to stay as far from Kyros's house as I could.

It was a cold night. I kept my head down so that the
wind wouldn't blow my hood back, and kept my eyes on
the hard dirt under my feet. Being back in Elpisia like
this—hiding, sneaking through the streets—felt more for
eign to me than my memories of my first days with the
Alashi. But at the same time, I could have found my way
through its streets blindfolded. *It's strange, so strange, t
be back. To be back like* this.

I wondered if my mother was still awake, and if she was
if Kyros was with her. Kyros's djinn had implied, in its las
message, that Kyros might threaten my mother to coerce me
My first instinct, when I decided to return to Elpisia, had bee
to warn her. But then what? I had nowhere to take her and n
way to take care of her. She certainly wouldn't be any safe
with me and Tamar. Far from it. Besides, if she knew anythin
about what I was doing, she would feel obligated to keep it

cret to protect me—and *that* could endanger her if Kyros
elieved that she was somehow in league with me.

No. I couldn't visit my mother.

Just as well, really. If I did visit her, we'd just end up
ghting again.

I turned a corner; there, a stone's throw ahead of me,
vas the household where Nika had been sold. It was built
n the Greek style, like Kyros's house, with a courtyard in
he center. The front door would be guarded at night. Well,
assumed that it was guarded; I couldn't see much evidence
ither way from the street.

The first step was to get inside. The front door, obviously,
vas out of the question. There were a few windows that
pened on to the street, but they were tightly shuttered and
arred from within; besides, the rooms on the other side of
hose windows might have people in them at odd hours. I
ircled the house once, keeping to the shadows now, though
couldn't see anyone watching. The street was quiet.

*Right. The first step is to get inside. You were Kyros's
tost resourceful servant—can't you figure out a way to
o that?*

The windows had a sill; maybe I could climb onto the
oof from there, and then go over that and into the court-
ard. I took off my cloak and mittens and stuffed them into
ny bag; the wind chose that moment to send a gust whip-
ing through the street that left me aching and numb. Before
could change my mind, I climbed onto the windowsill. It
vas awkward and when I shifted I knocked up against the
hutter. Anyone inside would have heard that, and I froze
or a moment, ready to leap off and run for it if I heard
novement inside. But all stayed quiet. If anyone had heard
ne, they must have thought it was the wind.

Now that I was close enough to make a try for the roof, I
ealized that it was a good arm's length out of my reach. If I'd
rought Tamar, I could have boosted her up onto the roof—
ut she didn't have the strength or weight to pull me up after
er, so I'd have needed both Tamar and a rope. *And a lot
tore certainty that we could avoid being seen. Risking my
wn neck is one thing. Risking Tamar's is another matter*

entirely. With freezing fingers, I felt for handholds in the sto[ne]
and mortar of the house. And found one. Maybe I cou[ld]
swing myself up and launch myself onto the roof . . .

I came nowhere near my goal, but managed to make [a]
wonderful crashing sound as I kicked loose a few tiles th[at]
shattered on the street below. I landed on the tiles and ma[n]
aged to bite back a stream of oaths as the shutters bang[ed]
open.

"—a bird or something."

"I just wanted to check."

"Well, you're letting in a lot of cold air, thank you ve[ry]
much."

I held my breath, making myself as small as possible [I]
was right in the open, if they poked their heads out to lo[ok]
for what had made the noise, they'd see me.

"It didn't sound like a bird."

"All right, if you *insist*, I'll send one of the men to s[ee]
what it was."

The shutter closed—but I didn't hear the bar put ba[ck]
into place. The guards would be coming, but it would ta[ke]
a little time—who was in the room?

With the tip of my finger, I eased the window open [a]
crack and peered in. It was the kitchen, and there were tw[o]
women still there, both Danibeki. If I offered to free the[m]
in exchange for their help, would they leap at the opport[u]
nity, or scream to alarm the whole house? Tamar wou[ld]
love to shepherd an entire household's worth of slaves [in]
to the reluctant Alashi, but the practicalities of that we[re]
more than a little daunting to me. Besides, even if Tam[ar]
were right that there were no slaves who liked being slav[es,]
that didn't mean they'd all be willing to flee to the Alas[hi.]
Many believed that the Alashi sacrificed humans [to]
Arachne and Prometheus.

I hesitated too long; if I'd wanted to speak with them, [I'd]
lost my chance. I sprinted around a corner and hid just a f[ew]
moments before I heard the crunch of the guards' boots [in]
the street. "—bunch of jumpy girls," a male voice sai[d.]
"Wanting to hide under the bed from the winter wind."

"Something did knock down a few tiles," another voi[ce]

aid. They had a lantern; I could see the light flickering. "It's not blowing *that* hard."

"Nika's probably right, it was a bird or something."

Nika! Had I looked right at her and not recognized her? Or had she been the one who went for the guards? Probably the latter. So she was probably there, in the kitchen, right now.

Muttering about girls and the cold wind, the guards did a quick search, found a feather that had doubtless been dropped by a bird sometime in the last week, and went back inside. I went back over to the window just in time to hear the bar drop again.

Well, at least now I knew where Nika was. I pressed my ear against the shutter and listened to the conversation. They were up early, not late, baking bread for the morning; the conversation was household gossip, nothing useful or interesting. There were three women working, all slaves. Listening to the chatter and *knowing* that one of them was Nika, I was fairly certain I knew which voice was hers. She had a low, slightly breathy voice that was easy to pick out.

I could just knock on the window . . .

Instead, I put my cloak and mittens back on and waited. *There's no hurry,* I told myself. *I can go back to Tamar, talk about what to do, and try again tomorrow. That's probably the best plan right now, take this slowly.*

Still, it seemed like it would be worth waiting. Maybe the other two women would step out for a few minutes and I'd have the opportunity to talk to Nika. It could happen. So I waited, and waited, and just as I was thinking that I'd have to leave to be well away by dawn, one of the women said she was going to use the privy, and another had to go get something out of the pantry; Nika was alone.

I knocked urgently on the shutter. "Nika. Nika!" I hissed.

The shutter opened so abruptly that it almost knocked me off the windowsill. Nika stared at me, white-faced and startled. "Who are you? What do you want?"

"Do you still want your freedom enough to take it? I have a horse, I'll take you to the Alashi."

"Who *are* you?"

"I'm here to free you, what does it matter who I am?"

There was a long moment of struggle on Nika's fac[e] and then she said, "I can't. Not without Melaina."

"Who?"

"My daughter. I can't leave her here. She doesn't ha[ve] anyone but me."

The other women could return at any moment. I spo[ke] rapidly. "Fine. I'll be back tomorrow night. Figure out [a] way to get yourself and Melaina out this window, and I['ll] take both of you." I jumped down to let her swing the shu[t]ter closed, and ran back for the city wall. I'd stayed t[oo] long; the sun would be up well before I got back to our hi[d]ing place by the river.

Tamar's face fell when she saw me returning alon[e]. "What happened?" she asked.

"She wants to bring her kid. We'll try again tonigh[t]. This time I think I want you to wait by the wall with t[he] horses; it'll be slow going with a young child otherwise."

Morning came, cool and damp. In a few more week[s] thirst would no longer be the worst danger on the stepp[e]; instead we'd need to worry about freezing to death. The[re] was a bit of water in the mud at the bottom of the gorg[e], and we were able to water the horses and drink ourselv[es]. If anyone saw us, they didn't investigate.

I spent the day brooding about Nika and Melaina. S[he] hadn't recognized me, and that was a relief, but a great de[al] could still go wrong. I might be able to talk my own way out [of] trouble, but could I talk Nika's way out? What would Nik[a's] owner do to her if she were caught running away again? Wh[at] if he punished her by separating her from her daughter?

I'll tell them it was necessary to accomplish my missio[n]. That after Alibek identified me, I thought that freeing a sla[ve] and bringing her to the steppe would give me a shot [at] winning back their trust. That I chose Nika because I kne[w] she was in Elpisia, and because I knew she'd run once b[e]fore, so she might be willing to do it again. I didn't conta[ct] Kyros because I was afraid that their Shaman might be kee[p]ing an eye on me through the djinn—they don't have spe[ll] chains but sometimes the djinni will do favors for the Alas[ha] hamans. And I have no idea what happened to the djinn *at Kyros sent to talk to me, the one that never returned.*

Kyros had sent his djinn to try to persuade me, or *threaten* me, into continued service. I had touched the *djinn* and banished it like a Shaman would banish a trou-*blesome* rogue djinn — and though this djinn should have *been* bound to its spell-chain, it had returned somehow to *its* own world. *Gate*, it had hissed. I'd never had the chance *to* talk to Zhanna about this. There were a lot of things I *wished* I could talk about with Zhanna . . .

I wrenched my thoughts back to my task. *If they catch us,* *I'll tell Kyros that he should let me and Nika and Melaina go* *again. He'll want to know what story I'll tell Nika to explain* *all this. I'll say that I'll tell her that I have a confederate in* *town who freed me, and that we killed the guards to get to* *her. I don't think she'll ask too many questions.*

I thought I could convince Kyros that I was telling the *truth*. He liked me. He trusted me. Just as I'd once liked *and* trusted him.

And if he doesn't, I can turn his own weapon on him: *Father, I am your own blood; if you want me to trust you,* *you have to trust me.* I wondered if Melaina was also *Kyros's* child. My half-sister.

Tamar wanted me to talk about the aborted rescue, so I *told* the story. "You should have brought me along," she *said*. "You could have gotten me up on the roof."

"And then what?"

"I could have gone down and talked to Nika."

"You wouldn't have known what she looked like."

"I could have figured it out. You figured out where she *was* by eavesdropping."

"It doesn't matter, this worked."

"You should bring me along tonight."

"Someone needs to wait with the horses."

We napped for a while, though I was too tense to sleep *well*. Once the sun went down, we walked back to Elpisia, *leading* the horses; it was too dark to ride. When we reached *the* wall, I left Tamar with the horses and climbed back over.

Again, the streets were dark and mostly empty. I found a

hidden spot to wait near the window and sat down. I could
hear the voices of the people in the kitchen here, and I w
tempted to move closer, but I stayed where I was. I'd to
Nika what to do; I had to trust her to take care of her part

Then again, if she didn't, how obligated should I feel
free her? If I made a good faith effort and failed, how ma
times did I have to try again? *For Nika, I'll have to t
again. She wants it. If she doesn't manage tonight, it's b
cause something kept her.* But what about the other
What if the man who'd wept so bitterly now balked at t
risk? How many times did honor demand that I return
someone was indecisive?

I'll burn that bridge when I come to it.

The window was opening. I moved over to it just in ti
to see a pair of soldiers rounding the corner. *Damn it to he*
I pushed the window shut again, hoping that Nika would g
the message, and shrank back into the shadows; the soldie
continued past without stopping. My heart beat in my ch
like a smith's hammer. I waited for a few moments to be su
that they weren't coming back. Then I started to knock
the window, but realized that I could hear the murmur
voices again. *And damn again.* Well, at least the soldie
hadn't walked past as I was helping Nika and her daugh
climb out the window. I waited, clenching my teeth a
knotting my hands into fists.

The window opened a crack, then swung wide. "Here
Nika said, and swung a small body out the window. I to
the little girl in my arms. She was surprisingly heavy. Ni
climbed out after her. With a day's warning, she'd a
found a way to have cloaks for both her and the chi
"We'd better run, they'll be back in minutes," she said. S
took Melaina back and swung her up against her should

We ran. *Prometheus and Arachne, keep us from runni
into those soldiers again.* Melaina clung to her mother, n
complaining, and we made it to the wall without incide
I scrambled up first, took Melaina and gave Nika a ha
up; then I jumped down, she lowered Melaina to my arr
and dropped down after me. "There are horses," I sai
and we found our way to Tamar.

"You did it," Tamar hissed, her eyes wide. We helped Nika up onto Tamar's horse, and handed Melaina up to her; we'd lead the horses until it was light enough for the horses to see well.

"We got them out. We still need to get away. The Greeks have horses, too."

"They sent only one person after me when I ran before," Nika said.

"If she comes after us again, we'll kick her ass," I said.

Nika sucked in her breath and looked down at me from her seat on Tamar's horse. She hadn't looked at me closely before: the light had been poor, we'd been in a hurry. Now she *really* looked at me, full in the face, for the first time, and I saw fear in her eyes.

Tamar reached up and clasped her hand. "Trust us," she said. Nika looked down at her, and Tamar's hand tightened on hers. "If that person—the person who came after you before—if she turns up, *we will kick her ass.*"

Nika tightened her arms around Melaina and nodded once. Once the sky lightened to gray, Tamar and I mounted as well; Nika was small enough to ride double with Tamar, and Melaina rode with me. In the daylight I could see that she had dark curls and gray eyes; she was about three, I thought, old enough that Nika had probably been pregnant when she ran. I thought I could see Kyros in Melaina's face. My *half-sister*? I always thought myself an only child. It occurred to me with a jolt that Kyros's wife alone had *eight* children.

We pushed the horses hard; the closest well Tamar knew how to get to was on the Helladia side of the hills. We'd be easy to track, on horses, though if Myron were doing the tracking he would utterly disregard the possibility that the slave could be escaping on horseback. "What did you tell the other slaves?" I asked Nika.

"Nothing. Well, I told them that Melaina had hit her head and needed to be close to me tonight, that's how I brought her with me to the kitchen. I made her a little bed with the cloaks, that's how I made sure we had them. And I made sure to forget something so someone would have to go to the pantry."

"Twice," I said, thinking of the soldiers' untimely arrival.

"I forgot a couple of things, just in case."

"Why didn't you ever climb out that window before?" Tamar asked.

"I knew I'd never get away with a child. And the punishment for running away is severe. I couldn't risk Melaina's safety that way, not with so little chance of success."

Last spring I'd crossed these hills in a wagon, posing as a new slave of Sophos. There was a road that went over the hills, and I briefly considered taking it. We had a substantial head start and no one, even brighter sparks than Myron, would expect that a runaway slave would be on horseback. But my instincts balked at traveling so openly. Besides, the road was cut into the hills with a gentle slope, to allow horses to pull a wagon. Without a wagon, we could simply head straight over for most of the way. Even leading our horses over the steepest spots, it would still be faster. Besides, the road led to Helladia, and I wanted to give Tamar's old home a wide berth.

We reached Tamar's well at dusk; like the other Alashi wells I'd seen, it was marked with a cairn of rocks. We took turns hauling up water for our horses, then for ourselves. The night was cold, and we slept huddled together. Even knowing that Tamar was on watch, I kept rousing, certain that someone was about to catch up with us. I wound up waking up everyone well before dawn so that we could start again as quickly as possible.

"Even if they follow our trail, we're far enough out that it would be too risky for them to come after us," Tamar said. "They're afraid of the bandits and afraid of the Alashi. It's not worth it, not for two slaves." She glanced at Nika and lowered her voice. "Think about it. How stubborn was your old master? How hard would he search?"

Kyros was quite stubborn, but not reckless. "You're right," I said. "A slave who escaped on horseback would've gotten too far too fast to be worth the effort."

"Did he ever use the djinn to search?"

"No. Bound djinni aren't very good at finding people who are making any attempt to hide. If you just tell them to look, they only look in the open. If you tell them to look *everywhere*, they waste their time checking every mouse-sized crevice until you get fed up and call them back to you. No one's ever come up with a way to get a djinn to search in a sensible way."

"But Kyros found *you* with his djinn . . ."

"He had a pretty good idea of where to look. He had the djinn find the Alashi camp, and then wait until it saw me. Now the he doesn't know where to look, it won't be that easy."

"So what will he do?"

I bit my lip. I hadn't really wanted to think about this. "It's a big world," I said. "He'll have to tell the djinn to look *everywhere*. It could take a really long time."

Tamar mulled that over for a few minutes, then asked, "Do you think he'll send a djinn to search, though? Because it probably would find you eventually."

"When I was bringing Alibek back to Kyros, he told me that after his sister escaped, Kyros took Alibek for his harem instead, then sent a djinn up to the steppes to tell Alibek's sister what he did. And that was just out of pique. He'll *never* give up on finding me. Ever."

It was light enough to ride now, so we mounted and moved out. We stopped to rest a few hours later, and Tamar said, "Do you think we met Alibek's sister? I mean, do you think maybe Ruan is Alibek's sister? It would explain some things, don't you think?"

"Yeah, but Ruan didn't act like she recognized Alibek." *Also, she defended me when Alibek said I was a spy.* "It was probably someone else, but who knows. You want to go back and ask?"

"No."

A few more days of riding brought us close to where the Alashi would be having their fall gathering. We moved in close enough to see the smoke from some of their campfires and then stopped, helping Nika and Melaina down from the horses.

"Be sure to tell them that you ran away once, and were caught and brought back against your will," I said. "The Alashi don't rescue slaves; they believe those who truly want freedom will run on their own."

"But I didn't get away," Nika said. "What if they don't accept me?"

"They will," Tamar said. "Anyway, you can't stay with us forever."

"They'll call you a blossom and make you pass tests—oh, don't worry. They'll haze you but they'll accept you. Good luck."

"Wait," Nika said, and took my hand. "I thought I recognized you, that first night. But I was right to trust you. Whoever you used to be, today you are *not* the person I thought you were. When I reach the Alashi, who should I say helped me?"

Saying my own name, my real name, felt like it would be a rejection of her forgiveness. But I wanted Janiya, at least to know who'd done it. "Tell them it was two women, one named Tamar, the other named Xanthe." Xanthe, the name of Janiya's lost daughter. Janiya had told me once that I reminded her of Xanthe. She would know it was me.

"Thank you," Nika said again, took Melaina's hand and turned towards the smoke from the fires.

I was standing in the center of Janiya's camp: the yurts loomed up around me, but I knew they were empty, and I could hear none of the noises from the horses or camels or dogs that I would have usually heard.

"It was you, wasn't it?"

I turned, and saw Zhanna standing in front of one of the yurts.

"It was you, wasn't it?" she asked again. "You sent us Nika."

"It was me," I said, but a gust of wind whipped the words away and I was alone again. "Zhanna? Are you there?"

Out of the corner of my eye, I saw movement, but when I turned, it wasn't Zhanna—it was a man riding toward me on a horse. *Kyros.* I wrenched myself awake with a start and stared up at the starry night sky, listening to Tamar's breath beside me. Zhanna had told me that with practice, shamans could sometimes communicate with each other through dreams—was this a dream like that? Was she trying to talk to me? And if so, what was Kyros doing in my dream? He was no Shaman.

Tamar whimpered in her sleep, but settled when I nudged her slightly. It was almost dawn; I watched as the eastern horizon lightened to gray.

"We need some sort of disguise," Tamar said, startling me. "Some way that we can move around through places like Elpisia without anyone getting suspicious."

"No disguise is going to get us into Sophos's household unrecognized. You lived there for years, and even if I were alone I think *someone* would recognize me."

"Yeah." Tamar sighed. "Maybe we should do one of the others first. You know, for practice. When we go to Sophos's, I want to do it right. I want to get *everyone* out of there, even Boradai if she wants to go."

"All right," I said.

"But now . . ." She sighed. "Maybe we could pretend we were merchants?"

I'd thought about that already. "Merchants have stuff to sell. We could tell them that we'd been merchants but had been raided by bandits and barely got away with our lives. But if we're going to free all the people we want to free, we need to come up with some way to pay for food and shelter. Winter's coming. We have no yurt. We're running out of food."

"Have we got anything at all that we could sell?"

"The horses."

"I don't want to sell them."

"I don't either."

I poked through my packs. They contained what I'd had with me when I'd been banished: some waterskins, some food, a blanket, a knife. My sword, the one I'd stolen from the bandits last spring. Flint and iron. Women in the sword-sisterhoods all carried basic survival materials with them in case they got separated from the group—lucky for me, or I'd have died the first day. Nothing *valuable*, though. Nothing I could sell. And no money.

There was something lumpy at the bottom of one of my

packs, though. I dug out the lumps and examined them in the dawn light. Karenite, two thumbnail-sized pieces of it; they rattled against each other in the palm of my hand. *How did this get here?* I remembered after a few minutes of thought. Janiya had given us a chunk, and then Tamar and I had found another piece when we failed the first test to join the Alashi. We'd found karenite, as instructed, but the real test had been whether we'd have the sense to provision ourselves before going out to look. Janiya had refused to take it when we returned, and in my embarrassment, I'd tossed both pieces into my pack and forgotten about them, until now.

"Can we sell that?" Tamar asked.

"Probably," I said, looking it over. "I don't honestly know how much we'll get for it, though."

"Do the Greeks even, you know, *like* it? It's pretty, but it's not really a gemstone."

I laughed a little and tucked the karenite back into my pack. "That's not what the Greeks use it for. Karenite is used as the binding-stone on a spell-chain; it's needed, I think, as part of the spell." I chewed on my lip. "I think the main reason the Greeks were planning an offensive against the Alashi is that most of the Greek sources of karenite are tapped out."

"There's a lot of it up on the steppe," Tamar said.

"Exactly," I said. "But the Greeks don't go up hunting for it because of the Alashi, and the Alashi don't sell it to the Greeks. That's why I'm not really sure what it's worth." I scratched an itch. "My mother lives upstairs from a gem-cutter, so I know what he'd spend to buy an uncut ruby or sapphire or onyx, and what he'd sell them for after cutting them. But he never touched karenite. I'd never seen it in raw form before coming up to the steppe."

"Could you try selling it to a gem-cutter?"

"It's the sorceresses who want it."

"Do you know where you can find a sorceress?"

"Daphnia," I said.

"Are there slaves you need to free down in Daphnia?"

"Yes. One man was sold to someone down there."

"Well, let's go there next, then."